A
Moment
in
Time

Also by Judith Gould

Sins
The Love-Makers
Dazzle
Never Too Rich
The Texas Years
Forever
Too Damn Rich
Second Love
Till the End of Time
Rhapsody
Time to Say Goodbye

JUDITH GOULD

A Moment in Time

LITTLE, BROWN AND COMPANY

A *Little, Brown* Book

First published in the United States of America by Dutton,
a member of Penguin Putnam Inc., in 2001

First published in Great Britain in 2001
by Little, Brown and Company

Copyright © Judith Gould, Inc., 2001

The moral right of the author has been asserted.

A CIP catalogue record for this book
is available from the British Library.

HARDBACK ISBN: 0 316 85170 1
C-FORMAT ISBN: 0 316 85808 0

Printed and bound in Great Britain
by Omnia Books ltd, Glasgow

Little, Brown and Company (UK)
Brettenham House
Lancaster Place
London WC2E 7EN

www.littlebrown.co.uk

To the memory of the late Marilyn Kimball Austin of Palo Alto, California, a wife, a mother, an animal lover, a reader, an inspiration, besides much more, and a lady in the best sense of the word.

To Dr. Anina la Cour, of the Chathams Small Animal Hospital in North Chatham, New York, a wonder among women, whose devotion to the care of animals is exemplary and who, I believe, truly has a magic touch.

To Marion Bienes of Amsterdam, the Netherlands, whose heroic, courageous, fearless, and untiring hands-on work on behalf of animals should serve as an inspiration for us all.

ACKNOWLEDGMENTS

The author wishes to thank the Bilinskis and everyone else at the Chathams Small Animal Hospital, North Chatham, New York, for their useful information and good cheer, and for their loving care of the late Happy and the very much alive Mina, Billy, and Jeffrey. In particular, I feel a debt of gratitude to Dr. Anina la Cour, who helped Happy go in peace and who has graciously shared bits of her considerable knowledge with me.

Please note that any mistakes regarding veterinary medicine, animal behavior, or animal care are the author's own, and are not the result of information I have been given by any of the above.

The models for all of the animals in this novel are pets of friends and have served as springboards for characters; thankfully, they are all in the best of health.

Beauty and terror are inseparable.
They come from the same place.

—Herbert Muschamp
The New York Times

BOOK ONE

The Beauty

Chapter One

South Chatham, New York

Valerie looked out across the gray stone terrace toward the hills in the distance, watching as the last sliver of the summer's blood-orange sun slipped from view. The clouds were tinged with beautiful violets and pinks, the palest mauve and deepest orange. Valerie smiled to herself. The sunsets from Apple Hill were nearly always spectacular, and tonight's seemed even more so than usual.

She shifted slightly on the weathered teak chaise longue and idly stretched a hand down to Elvis, her Heinz 57 Variety mutt, who lay half asleep at her side on the terrace. His wide white collar set with aurora borealis rhinestones, a gift from Tami, her secretary, gleamed in the fading light. She stroked his jet-black coat, which was still wet from the swimming pool, and his tail swished sideways once, then came to rest again.

"Hey, gorgeous," a man's deep baritone from behind her asked, "what're you thinking about?"

Valerie felt Teddy's hands on her bare shoulders, but her gaze remained on the distant hills. "I'm not thinking about anything," she said. "I've just been watching the sunset. It was so beautiful."

He squeezed her shoulders softly, then leaned down and brushed her cheek with a kiss. "Just like you," he said. "In fact, I arranged it for you." His voice was a croon, full of promise and possibilities for the night that lay ahead.

"I wouldn't doubt that one little bit," Valerie said. And, she reflected, it was true. She sometimes thought that Teddy de Mornay was capable of anything once he set his mind to it. Aside from the fact that he was terribly handsome and had money to burn, he was personable, charming, and extremely popular. There didn't seem to be a man—or woman—for miles around that didn't admire Teddy de Mornay.

She turned to look up at him. "Where've you been?" she asked, noticing that, although he had dried off, he was still in his bathing trunks, his bronzed body tall, its musculature well-defined throughout his lean physique. His blond hair was lighter than usual, sunbleached almost white in places, and his pale blue eyes gleamed against his tan.

"I was in the kitchen," he said, "mixing us some drinks. Hattie's almost done with dinner."

"I guess we'd better get changed, then," Valerie said, reluctant to move from the comfort of the chaise longue.

"Unless you want to eat in your bikini," Teddy replied. He smiled lasciviously, exposing his perfect white teeth.

"I had some food in mind," she said, playfully slapping him on the leg. "Anyway, we'd better put something on. It's already started to get cooler." She sat up on the chaise and looked at him. "And where are those drinks you mixed for us?" she asked.

"In the conservatory," he said, squatting down beside her. He leaned over and kissed her on the tip of her nose. "Ready and waiting."

"Let's get changed," she said. "It'll only take me a couple of minutes to shower off and put something on."

Teddy rose to his feet and extended a hand to her. She took it and let him pull her up, off the chaise. She picked up her rubber thongs and grabbed her towel.

Elvis immediately perked up and slowly got to his feet, then shook his wet fur furiously.

"Race you to the pool house," Valerie said. And before Teddy could answer her, she slipped from his grasp and was off, running across the gray stones of the terrace to the rose-covered pergola that decorated the front of the pool house. Elvis raced along behind her as fast as his old legs would carry him, barking joy-fully.

Teddy padded along behind, watching her graceful barefooted lope appreciatively. *She's like a rare, beautiful gazelle,* he thought with satisfaction. *I couldn't have made a better choice.*

When he reached the pool house, she had already taken one of the bathrooms, its door open wide, her emerald-green bikini tossed carelessly across a sink, her towel on the tile floor. From the shower came her voice. It was almost a yodel actually, for she was bellowing a rendition of "You Ain't Nothin' But a Hound Dog." Elvis, on his haunches, his head lifted to the ceiling, sat outside the shower howling along with her.

Teddy stood still, listening to the raucous cacophony. On the way to the pool house he'd thought about joining her for a little predinner fun, but now he decided against it.

She and Elvis are enjoying themselves too much, he thought, *and besides, I want tonight to be very special for her. One night that she'll never forget.*

He walked to the bathroom at the other end of the pool house. *So I'll hold off till later.*

He pulled off his bathing trunks, feeling foolishly proud of him-self for this uncharacteristic show of restraint.

This isn't like me at all, he thought. *No, siree. Because when Teddy wants it, Teddy really wants it. And when he really wants it, he gets it.*

With that thought, he stepped into the Mexican-tiled shower stall, closed the thick glass door, and twirled the water on, lather-ing up, excited at the prospect of the night ahead.

Valerie poured herself a martini from the silver cocktail shaker that sat perspiring on the marble-topped drinks table in the con-servatory. She tossed four olives in, then a fifth for good measure. It was the gin-soaked olives that she liked best about a martini. Holding the crystal glass up to the light, she admired its sparkling radiance a moment before taking a cautious sip.

"Manna from heaven," she cooed to herself.

She walked over to one of the big, comfortable, down-filled

sofas and sat, enjoying the feel of its crisp white duck against her silk pants and blouse as she sank into its luxurious softness. She set the martini glass down on the coffee table, and stretched her arms above her head, breathing deeply.

She'd had a long, hard week at the veterinary clinic, and the late afternoon swim and the hot sun, followed by a revitalizing shower, had worked their magic: She felt calm, relaxed, even a bit serene. Although she was on call at the clinic this weekend, she didn't anticipate any problems. She'd quickly scanned the patient roster before she'd left the clinic and hadn't noticed any animals that might present her with serious problems.

But you never know, she reminded herself, reaching over and picking up her drink. What she did know, and very well at that, was that you could plan endlessly, trying to anticipate every need, every problem that might arise. Then when you thought you had everything covered, a dire emergency would strike.

Well, I'm not going to think about it tonight, she told herself. *I'm going to relax and enjoy myself.*

"Aha," Teddy exclaimed when he walked into the room. "I see you've been a very naughty girl and started without me."

She looked up and saw that he'd put on spotless, perfectly ironed white linen trousers and an appropriately faded blue knit polo shirt that was the precise color of his eyes. Somehow he always managed to look perfect. Almost too perfect.

"You bet I have," Valerie said. "That cocktail shaker looked so lonely—and so seductive." She smiled up at him. "Besides, I knew you'd take forever in the shower. You always do."

He leaned down and planted a kiss on the top of her head. "You know me too well," he said. Then he made a beeline for the drinks table, where he poured himself a martini and popped in an olive.

Teddy sauntered over to the sofa and sat down, putting an arm around her shoulders and hugging her to him. He brushed her cheek with his lips, lightly and tenderly.

"I'm so glad you could spend the weekend with me," he said. "All weekend. Just the two of us."

"Don't forget Elvis," she said, scowling at him playfully.

"Yeah," he said, "and Elvis." He looked around the room. "And where is the ugly beast?" he asked.

"He's not ugly," she replied. "He might not win any beauty contests, but, well, he's beautiful *inside*."

Teddy kissed her nose again and smiled. "I'm sure he is," he said. "And I'm glad you told me, but where is the internally beautiful beast?"

Before she could answer, he held up a hand to silence her.

"No, wait . . . let me guess," he said, placing a hand on his forehead dramatically. "I'm getting psychic vibrations. Could he be . . . ? He's . . . in the kitchen with Hattie."

Valerie laughed. "Of course he's in the kitchen with Hattie, you fool. He knows where all the good stuff is."

Teddy hugged her shoulders again, leaning over and kissing her neck. "Hmm, you smell so good," he said. "I could eat you up."

Valerie looked at him out of the corner of her eye. "Why don't we have dinner first?" she said.

"Must we?" he countered, licking her neck and ear hungrily. Then he abruptly stopped and sat up, reaching over for his drink.

Hold off, Ted, he told himself. *Remember, you're going to make tonight very special for Val.* He took a long swallow of his martini, finishing it off, and set the glass back down. Then he rubbed his hands together and got to his feet.

"Ready for another?" he asked.

"Not yet, Teddy," Valerie said, surprised that he'd downed his so quickly.

Teddy picked up his empty glass, plucked out the olive, popped it into his mouth, then walked over to the drinks table for a refill.

Valerie eyed him speculatively. *It's not like Teddy to back off,* she thought, slightly puzzled. *I wonder what's gotten into him?*

She nervously ruffled her long strawberry-blond hair with one hand. She'd taken care dressing tonight, even though she'd finished in half the time Teddy had. She'd blow-dried her hair and let it hang loose rather than pulling it back in a ponytail or—her usual for work—a long single braid. Then she'd carefully applied a little makeup—eyeliner, mascara, a touch of blusher and lipstick. Finally, she'd donned a cream silk blouse, matching pants, and expensive leather thong sandals, completing the look with gold knot earrings, a heavy gold link necklace, and a gold link bracelet. All to please him.

If truth be told, she'd much rather have jumped out of the shower and into old jeans and a T-shirt without bothering about her hair and makeup. But Teddy had always hated it when she looked anything less than perfectly groomed and dressed, no matter the occasion. He loved to see her turned out in a ladylike fashion. And she, in turn, hated the disapproving glances he would give her if her attire didn't meet his exacting standards. That furrowed brow, those cocked eyebrows, and those thin, grimly set lips reminded her all too much of the disapproving looks she'd suffered over the years from her mother, Marguerite. For years such looks had diminished her sense of self-worth. When she and Teddy had started dating in college, she had been surprised to see him react to her cavalier attitude toward clothing much as her mother had. She had worked hard to please him, and still did, but lately she'd found herself lapsing in this area and pleasing herself more often.

Teddy looked over at her thoughtfully, swirling his fresh martini in its crystal glass before taking a sip. "You look beautiful tonight," he said after he'd swallowed. "Absolutely beautiful."

Valerie felt all of her doubts and worries vanish as if by magic. "Thanks, Teddy," she said, and she meant it. "And you look as handsome as ever."

Hattie quietly stepped into the conservatory, Elvis at her heels, wagging his tail furiously, watching her every movement with adoring eyes.

"Dinner's ready," she said. "I can serve anytime, Teddy."

"Thanks, Hattie," he replied. "We'll be right in."

Hattie left the room, Elvis prancing along beside her, his tail wagging.

"Hattie's got a serious fan tonight," Valerie said. "I wonder what wonderful goodies she's been giving him."

"Something really special," Teddy said. "Because I came up with the menu."

Valerie looked up at him. "You did?" she exclaimed. "What's the occasion?"

"You," he said, extending his drink toward her. "Me." He took another sip of his martini. "Us."

"You're sweet, Teddy."

"I'm glad you think so," he replied. He walked over, leaned down, and kissed her forehead again. "Ready to go in to dinner?" he asked, looking into her eyes.

She nodded, returning his gaze. He seemed somehow nervous . . . but no, that wasn't precisely the word. *What, then?* she asked herself. *Just a little anxious, I guess. As if . . . as if he's hiding something. But what?*

"I'm starved," she said gaily, dispensing with her concerns. "Swimming always makes me hungry."

"Well, you've come to the right place." He offered her his free hand. "We'll be glad to do something about that."

Valerie took his hand and rose to her feet.

Teddy finished off his martini, set the glass on the coffee table, and together they went to the dining room.

The beeswax candles flickered in their Georgian silver candelabra, casting shadows onto the dining room walls. The elegant robed figures in the antique Chinese murals mysteriously appeared to come to life in the dancing light, as if to bear witness to tonight's special occasion.

Valerie sighed with pleasure, inhaling the heady perfume that wafted through the air from the huge old-fashioned roses. Hattie had stuffed full-blown reds, pinks, yellows, and creamy whites into a turn-of-the-century Tiffany silver bowl placed in the center of the table.

"You look contented," Teddy said from across the table.

Valerie looked over. His eyes glittered in the candlelight, a bit mischievously, she thought, and there was a smile on his lips. "I *am* contented," she said, returning his smile. "Supremely contented. I don't remember the last time I've eaten so much that was so good. And the dessert!" She patted her tummy in an unladylike manner and looked down at the empty Flora Danica dessert plate in front of her. "I don't believe I ate all of it."

"That's one of Hattie's specialties," Teddy said. "*Boca negra.* Killer chocolate cake with white chocolate sauce."

"It's the best chocolate cake I've ever eaten," Valerie said.

"I know," Teddy replied, grinning. "It's the bourbon, I think. It's like the Cartier of chocolate cakes, but I won't let her make it too often. It's so good it could be addictive."

"I'd forgotten what a great cook Hattie is," Valerie said. "And the dining room looks so beautiful. The flowers and candles and everything." She waved a hand and looked around the room. "I don't think we've ever eaten in here, except for a couple of your important client dinners." She paused and looked at him. "The only thing missing is Elvis."

Teddy returned her look. "You're worried about his being out in Hattie's cottage, aren't you?"

"Nooo, Teddy," she replied, shaking her head. "I just hope she doesn't give him too many goodies."

"He'll be fine," Teddy said. "I just wanted us to be alone tonight. Besides, Hattie's crazy about him." He stared into her eyes for a moment. "She's crazy about you."

"I like her, too," Valerie replied. "And I love her cooking." She laughed but stopped abruptly when she saw that Teddy's expression had suddenly turned serious.

"Then you shouldn't be such a stranger around here, Val," he said. "You could have Hattie's cooking anytime."

"Oh, Teddy, you know how busy I am," she replied. "With the clinic and having my own place to look after . . . well, it's all I can do to go anywhere. It's different for you," she went on, "being in the city most of the week, then coming up here to relax or going up to the place in the Adirondacks to hunt and fish. I'm either on call weekends, or I have to catch up on the house and garden and a thousand other things."

Teddy got up and went around to her side of the table, pulling out a chair to sit beside her. She turned to face him, and he took her hands in his. "I could make it a lot easier for you," he said earnestly.

His eyes burned with an intense light that she'd seldom seen in them. It was similar to the terrible gleam they held when he was extremely angry about something. She began to feel slightly uncomfortable. "What . . . what are you driving at, Teddy?" she asked.

"I think you know," he said.

"I . . . I'm not certain," she sputtered.

He released her hands and stood up. She saw that there was a solemn expression on his face as he turned to the mahogany sideboard behind him and plucked something from the huge Imari bowl set in its center.

Valerie gazed at him in silence, her expression curious. Teddy was often quite formal, sometimes even stuffy, but tonight his behavior was practically ceremonial. *What's going on?* she wondered. *Because he is definitely up to something.*

He sat back down, taking one of her hands very gently and reverently. He looked into her eyes, his expression still sober. He cleared his voice. "I . . . I have something for you," he said.

"For me?" she said quietly. She felt that any show of excitement would somehow interfere with the ceremony—or whatever it was—that was taking place.

He nodded and held out his hand.

Valerie looked down at it and saw a small, black, cloth-covered box. Even in the flickering candlelight she could see that impressed into the cloth top was one word: *Bvlgari*. The jeweler who used the Roman *u*. Her breath caught in her throat, and she held it, not daring to breathe. Her mind began to race, whirling around in crazy circles. She couldn't sort out her thoughts and feelings, so overcome was she by his gesture.

"Teddy . . . Teddy . . . ," she finally stammered breathlessly. "I . . . I . . ."

"Shhh," he hushed, squeezing the hand he held. "Just take it, Val," he said. He let go of her long, slender hand and placed the box in it.

Valerie held it cupped there, still at a loss for words. She took a deep breath and looked briefly at Teddy's serious face. Then, hands quivering, she lifted the lid off the box. She was prepared for the gleam of an expensive bauble of some sort, but inside, fitted perfectly, was another box, this one covered in black leather. *Bvlgari* was pressed into the leather as on the cloth box.

She quickly opened the leather box, unable to bear the tension any longer. She gasped when she saw the ring resting in the soft beige suede that lined the interior of the box. It twinkled back at her as if alive, its stunning canary yellow color animated by the candlelight that reflected off it.

"Oh, my . . . God," she stammered. "Oh . . . Teddy, . . . I don't know what . . ." Unbidden, tears sprang into her eyes and, like the ring, they glimmered in the light.

He was watching her intently, his eyes never leaving hers. "You only have to say one word, Val," he said. "One simple little word."

She looked at him, wanting to please him, but she found herself speechless, unable to utter the word that she knew he wanted to hear.

He threw his arms around her, tugging her to him. "Come on, Val," he urged. "Say yes. Just say yes."

Her mind was still in a whirl, and she was not sure how to react.

Teddy pulled back and looked into her eyes. "You can do it," he said, nodding his head. "You don't have to say, 'Yes, Teddy, I'll marry you.' " He laughed and chucked her under the chin with a hand. "All you have to say is yes!"

Valerie felt elated and somehow defeated at the same time. She was thrilled that a man desired her this much, and she found it difficult to believe that the man was somebody as sought-after as Teddy de Mornay. For years she had been genuinely puzzled by his attraction to her. How could she be so lucky? But at the same time, deep down inside, she realized that if she committed herself to him, she would be doing them both a disservice. Some instinct was telling her this was all wrong, despite the fact that she liked Teddy, perhaps even loved him, or once had.

Oh, God, help me, she thought. *What do I do?*

Teddy's eyes searched hers pleadingly, and she saw the earnest, loving expression there, so like a puppy's that her heart was wrenched in two.

Oh, my God. What do I say?

"Say it, Val," he repeated anxiously. "Or just nod. Yeah. That's all you have to do. Just nod!"

And she did.

She felt her head, as if with a will of its own, almost involuntarily begin to nod that yes that he was begging for. A yes that was perhaps a lie, a yes that was a defeat of her spirit.

She looked up at him, her eyes teary. She wanted to tell Teddy that she loved him, but that she wasn't certain that she was "in love" with him. The words, however, could not be summoned up from her tortured soul.

Teddy threw his arms around her again, pulling her to him passionately, kissing her neck, her ears, forehead, eyes, nose, cheeks, mouth. Then he began to lick the tears that had spilled down onto her cheeks.

"I love you, Val," he murmured. "Oh, I love you so much. I want to make you the happiest woman alive. I want to make you *mine*."

Valerie stiffened at these last words, but she remained mute, hoping that her silence would neither offend him nor imply assent to his wishes.

When he drew back again, Teddy smiled at her radiantly. "You've made me the happiest man in the world."

She couldn't help but find his excitement infectious. "I'm . . . I'm glad, Teddy," she said, returning his smile.

"Do you like it?" he asked.

"Like it?" She looked down at the ring. "Teddy, it's the most beautiful ring I've ever seen."

"Put it on," he said. "Let's see what it looks like on."

Valerie took the ring from its nest of softest suede and held it between two fingers. Her hand trembled slightly.

"Here," Teddy said, "let me put it on your finger." He took the ring from her, and Valerie held her hand out straight, trying to keep it from shaking.

Teddy slipped the ring onto her finger, and Valerie moved her hand back and forth, watching the diamond reflect the candlelight. Despite the turmoil that she felt about committing to Teddy, she couldn't help but be mesmerized by the diamond's beauty. *It's truly magnificent,* she thought. *More than I'd ever dreamed of . . . or even wanted, for that matter.*

She moved her hand again, watching the gemstone reflect the light. *Trust Teddy to go for the unusual,* she thought. *He would have to get something extraordinary, something over the top.*

She looked up at him. "I'm practically speechless, Teddy," she said. "It really is the most beautiful ring I've ever seen."

Teddy grinned like a proud little boy. "You don't think it's vulgar?" he asked. Then he laughed.

"It is a little big," she allowed, joining in his laughter.

"If you ask me, only people who can't afford them call them vulgar," Teddy said. He stood up and leaned down, kissing her on the forehead. "Why don't we go back to the conservatory and have coffee and a brandy in there?"

She nodded. "That'd be great."

Teddy took her hand, and Valerie rose to her feet. They walked back to the conservatory, one of Teddy's powerful arms slung around her shoulders.

"I'll go get the coffee," he said. "You get comfortable."

"You spoil me, Teddy."

"I want to," he replied.

She sank back onto the downy luxury of the huge sofa, watching Teddy leave the room. She couldn't help but smile. There was a spring in his step that she recognized immediately. It was almost a cocky strut that said he was immensely pleased with himself.

She looked down at the ring on her finger, becoming entranced again as she watched it sparkle. *My God,* she thought, *this ring must have cost Teddy a fortune. I wonder if he can really afford it.*

The thought made her feel uncomfortable again. He had always kept her in the dark about his mysterious wheeling and dealing. She knew that he'd inherited money and that he had rental income here in the country, but he kept her at a distance about his job in New York City, trading stock and investing money for friends.

When she asked him, Teddy always shrugged off her questions, telling her that she'd only be bored with the details. At the same time, he'd never failed to boast about the enormous profits he had reaped on a particular day or during a particular week.

At first she'd found his secrecy intriguing—just one of the many things she had to learn about him—but lately she'd begun to think that it was vaguely suspicious that he wouldn't be more forthcoming at this point in their relationship.

She sighed. *I really don't want to think about all that right now,* she told herself.

She kicked off her sandals, then walked over to the windows that looked out on the terraces and swimming pool. She could feel the wind coming through the screens. *A storm is coming,* she thought.

Stepping through the French doors, she walked out onto the terrace and looked up at the sky. She stared at the huge, shifting cloud formations that alternately revealed, then concealed the brightness of the full moon. Gazing out toward the pool, she could see that one moment it shimmered with the moonlight and the next it was almost pitch-black.

Music, a soft and sexy jazz tune she couldn't name, drifted out through the French doors behind her. Then Teddy's strong arms encircled her from behind, and she felt his lips brushing her hair, searching out the nape of her neck.

"Hmm," he murmured, "you look so beautiful standing out here in the moonlight."

She felt herself respond to his sensuous touch. It was a kind of giving in that was pleasant, if not yet passionate. Turning in his arms, she faced him with her eyes closed and felt his lips instantly fall upon hers, kissing her with urgency. She put her arms around him and let herself go, responding to his kisses, enjoying his desire for her, taking pleasure in the knowledge that this man wanted her so much.

Teddy pulled her firmly against him, his hands moving slowly up and down her back, down to her beautifully rounded buttocks, one in each hand, massaging her gently, and pressing her against his aroused manhood.

Valerie moaned softly and put her head down on his shoulder, clinging to him.

"You're enjoying yourself," Teddy murmured.

She nodded her head on his shoulder.

"The night's still young," he said quietly. "Why don't we go have our coffee and drinks, then head upstairs? Soon."

Valerie nodded her assent again, but in actuality she was enjoying the feel of his powerful body against her own and didn't really care about anything else to drink. No, she would have preferred to go straight up to the bedroom and crawl under the covers with him, taking more pleasure in his body, in their bodies together.

Teddy drew back and took one of her hands in his, then silently led her back into the conservatory. She saw a big silver tray with china cups and saucers on the coffee table and, alongside them, two crystal balloons of brandy.

They settled down on the sofa, and Teddy handed her a cup of coffee. "I put the cream and sugar in it the way you like it."

"Thanks, Teddy." She smiled and took a sip. The coffee was exactly the way she liked it. Sweet and rich. Much better than she ever made for herself at home. She glanced at him and saw that he was looking at the ring on her finger.

"It's so beautiful," she said. "Isn't it?"

"It really is," he replied. He put his coffee down and slid an arm around her shoulders, looking into her eyes. "When do you think we ought to set the date?" he asked.

Valerie's mind was instantly set awhirl again. *Oh, no! What should I say?*

She looked down into her coffee cup as if it held the answer to his question. She certainly hadn't anticipated this, and she had given it no thought whatsoever. She knew that Teddy eventually wanted to get married and have a family, but she'd always managed to neatly tuck away any considerations of marriage with him—or anybody else, for that matter.

"Oh, Teddy," she said, struggling to keep her voice even, "tonight's been so . . . well, it's already been so much to absorb. Can't we wait to discuss it?" She smiled, and her eyes searched his. "Please?" she added.

"Sure, babe," he said, squeezing her shoulder. He smiled brightly. "We'll wait to talk about it. Anything for you." He kissed her lips. "Just not too long. Okay?"

She nodded in acquiescence. "I promise," she said. "Not too long."

"Good," he replied. He slid his arm from around her shoulders and reached over and picked up a snifter of brandy. "Ready for a nip?"

"Are you trying to ply me with booze?" she joked.

"Who, me?" he asked. "You bet I am."

"Then please do," she said. "I want to be plied. I could use a good stiff drink of that." And she meant it now.

Teddy handed her the brandy. He reached for the other snifter and held it next to hers. "To us," he said.

"To . . . us," she replied, then she took a large sip. She savored the aroma and the taste of the fiery liquid on her tongue before she swallowed. It seemed only moments before she felt a glow spread through her body, warming her and loosening her up, helping cast away the worries that preyed upon her mind.

Teddy, she noticed, had nearly drained his glass in a single swallow. He set it down and turned his attention back to her. He stared into her eyes for a long moment with the hint of a smile on his lips.

"What?" she asked.

"Nothing," he replied, slowly shaking his head. "I just love looking at you when you look like this. So . . . fresh. So radiant. So innocent."

Teddy always says the right things, she thought. *And I always respond to them.*

He took the brandy snifter from her hand and set it on the coffee table, then pulled her to him, his mouth and tongue brushing her ears and neck slowly, sensuously, before finding her mouth and kissing her deeply.

Valerie's body immediately responded to his, and she gave herself over to the erotically charged moment, returning his kiss, her hands stroking his muscular back and shoulders, her tongue dancing a carnal dance with his.

He shifted on the sofa, and she felt his hand on one of her breasts, stroking it ever so gently, then cupping it firmly as his mouth descended to the silk of her blouse and his tongue darted out and began to lick her nipple through the thin silk.

"Hmmm," Valerie moaned. "Ohhhh, Teddy." She moved her hands up and down his back, massaging him, loving the feel of the masculine strength beneath his shirt. She wanted to hurry now, to reach that magic moment when he entered her, engulfing her with his manhood, obliterating the rest of the world with it.

He raised his head and looked up at her. His face was flushed and his breathing was labored. "Ah, Val," he rasped. "This is so good. Let's go upstairs. Okay?"

"Okay," she said, and nodded.

He was off the sofa in a flash, his hand extended toward her. She took it, and they left the conservatory, her head on his shoulder, their arms around each other.

*   *   *

Teddy was on his knees between her widespread legs. When she opened her eyes, Valerie could see, even in the dim candlelight, that his mouth was wet and red from his enjoyment of her most secret place. She could also see his engorged manhood poised to enter her, and she shivered with anticipation.

A sudden clap of thunder so near and loud that it seemed to shake the entire house roared in their ears but didn't distract them from one another. As he plunged into her, she gasped. Her sounds of delight were drowned out by the drumming of the intense rain as it hit the windows and French doors that surrounded the room on three sides. The draperies whipped in the wind, and some of the candles were abruptly blown out by the powerful gusts, but they ignored them, so intent were they on giving one another pleasure.

He rode her and rode her, withdrawing and hesitating before plunging in again and again, each time more ruthless than the last, bringing her to a frenzy of desire and need for him, until she suddenly cried out.

Her body began to spasm as she climaxed beneath him, and Teddy became a man possessed, plunging ever more furiously until he let out a bellow, the cords in his neck standing out, his body convulsing on hers as his seed burst forth, filling her to overflowing.

He collapsed atop her, wrapping her in his arms, quickly peppering kisses on her forehead, cheeks, nose, eyes, and lips, all the while his chest heaving against her breasts as he gasped for breath. Valerie held on to him tightly, absorbed in the moment, unwilling to let it go just yet.

At last they lay on their sides, facing one another, their bodies coated with a sheen of perspiration. He was still inside her, and she enjoyed the feel of him there.

Teddy kissed her tenderly, then drew back slightly, staring into her eyes. "That was so wonderful," he whispered. "So perfect."

Val nodded. "Oh, yes," she said. "It was heaven, Teddy." She breathed a long sigh of contentment, and he pulled her closer to him.

The rain beat a steady tattoo against the windows and doors, and for the first time Teddy looked up and noticed that the wind, still gusting powerfully, had made sails out of the long, silk curtains, blowing them out into the room.

"I guess I ought to get up and close the doors and windows," Teddy said. "But I don't want to move."

She hugged him tightly. "Then don't," she said. "Stay right where you are. You feel wonderful."

He kissed her with renewed passion, running a hand up her back and then on down to her buttocks, where he stroked gently, slowly pulling her against him.

Valerie could feel his cock begin to swell inside her, filling her with its might. A moan escaped her lips, and Teddy began to move his pelvis in a lazy rhythm, enjoying the look of pleasure on her face, relishing the power he had over her. Gently he moved, and slowly, slowly, slowly, until he heard another barely audible moan of pleasure. He rolled them both over then, with his body spread out atop hers, his manhood still in her, teasing her, drawing out the—

Suddenly there was a beep, a terrible shrill-sounding beep like a car alarm.

Valerie jerked upright into a sitting position. When Teddy tried to ease her back down onto the bed, she said firmly, "No, Teddy, that's my pager. I have to—"

His mouth went over hers, determined to keep her quiet, but she shook her head from side to side. "No," she rasped. She struggled to get out from under him. "Let me up, Teddy," she cried. "Let me up, goddamn it! Now!"

Reluctantly he backed off, letting her leap free to pick up her pager. It was obviously the service beeping her to call in. She grabbed her cell phone off the bedside table and snapped it open.

"Dr. Rochelle," she said in a professional voice.

From his position on the tangled bed, Teddy listened to her end of the conversation, looking up at her with a mixture of disappointment and disgust. Becoming increasingly frustrated and angry, he jammed a fist into a pillow, then leapt up off the bed and marched around the room, noisily slamming the French doors and windows shut. When he was finished, he stood, arms akimbo and feet planted wide apart, glaring at her. Then he turned and stomped into the bathroom, slamming that door behind him.

When her conversation with the service was finished, Valerie punched in the telephone number they'd given her. Her call was picked up on the first ring.

"Dr. Rochelle," she said.

"Dr. Rochelle," a man said, "this is Santo Ducci at Stonelair. We have a sick horse out here, and we wondered if you could come take a look."

"I'll be there in about fifteen or twenty minutes."

"Thanks a lot," the man said.

Valerie pressed the end button and quickly placed her cell phone in the big leather and canvas carryall that went everywhere with her. She walked over to the bathroom door. She hesitated a moment before tapping on it.

There was no response, and she knocked a little louder. "Teddy?" she said. "I'm really sorry, but . . . well, you know this comes with the territory." There was still no response, and she knocked again. "Teddy?"

She started to open the door when it suddenly swung open.

He stood there, still naked . . . and so handsome, she thought, a smile on his lips that exposed his perfect white teeth. "Come here," he said, holding his arms out. Before Valerie could move, he stepped forward and hugged her to him.

"I'm the one who's sorry," he whispered. "I . . . I shouldn't have reacted that way, but I wanted this to be a perfect weekend for us." He drew back and looked into her eyes. "Forgive me?" he said in a little boy voice. "Please?"

Valerie couldn't help but smile, even though she found his behavior immature and inconsiderate. She'd become inured to Teddy's little temper tantrums. He was a spoiled rich boy who couldn't tolerate not getting his way.

She planted a quick kiss on his lips. "Forget about it," she said, ruffling his hair with her fingertips. "I'm sorry, too, but I've got to go."

She rushed to the closet, where she grabbed a pair of Levis, a T-shirt, and a white lab coat. Tossing them on a chair, she rifled through a dresser until she found bra, panties, and socks. She began dressing hurriedly as Teddy stood watching her.

"What's up?" he asked. "Somebody's pooch miscarry or something?"

She thought she detected a hint of sarcasm in his voice, but she chose to ignore it. "There's an emergency out at Stonelair," she replied.

"Stonelair?" he said, his eyes widening. "You're not going out there, are you?"

"Yes," she said, grabbing a pair of sneakers from the closet floor.

"Since when did you start working for that creepy drug lord?"

"Since now," she replied, pulling on her socks.

"Je-sus, Val!" he cried, his voice angry. "Isn't that a little stupid? Maybe even a little dangerous, huh?" He stood staring at her, his body rigid, his eyes bright with intensity.

She finished tying her sneakers, then got to her feet, grabbing her carryall and slinging it over her shoulder in one swift movement.

"Look, Teddy," she said in a determined voice, "I don't know anything about the people at Stonelair, and neither do you. I just know that there's a horse out there that's in trouble, and I've got to go take care of it. It's my duty as a veterinarian."

"But-but . . . you don't even know what the hell's going on out there, Val," he sputtered. "I mean, those people could have a drug lab set up or—"

"I don't care what's going on out there," she broke in angrily. "There's a sick horse and I'm going to it. And I'm going now."

As she started for the bedroom door, Teddy rushed to her, throwing his long, muscular arms around her. "Just a quick kiss," he said, all sweetness again.

She turned to him and let him kiss her, then pulled away. "I'm in a hurry, Teddy."

"I know, I know," he said agreeably, nodding. "So go. Go." He slapped her playfully on the butt.

Valerie headed out of the bedroom and down the hallway to the staircase.

"Val?" he called as she reached the top of the stairs.

She quickly glanced back toward the bedroom door, where he stood, his tall, strong body filling the doorway.

"I'll be here waiting for you," he said, one hand shaking his penis at her.

Valerie sputtered helplessly with laughter. "Oh, *you,*" she laughed, then hurried on down the stairs and out into the dark and stormy night.

Chapter Two

Valerie drove like a woman possessed. Forgotten now was the lavish dinner and the bedroom frolic. Even the exquisite canary diamond that still sparkled on her finger went unnoticed in her haste to get to Stonelair. It was after midnight, and the summer storm was lashing the countryside.

Valerie could barely make out the road ahead of her as she raced over the curving country roads. The rain-drenched landscape was a void of total darkness, except when the terrifying streaks of lightning rent the sky, momentarily illuminating the fields and woods and the occasional house and barn in an eerie glow. The accompanying thunder came in such ferocious rolling claps that she involuntarily jumped.

"Jeez," she said aloud, "it sounds like it's coming through the roof." Suddenly she wished that Elvis was with her to keep her company. She reached over and turned on the radio. It was the next best thing, she supposed. It was set on the classical station, and strains of Schubert's piano quintet "The Trout" filled her ears. She laughed nervously, thinking that Schubert's trout would be very happy indeed in this weather.

Virtual rivers, washing off the hills, flowed across the road at points, but the big Jeep negotiated them easily. On she rolled, hunched over the steering wheel, determined to get to Stonelair as soon as possible. She'd never ministered to this particular horse before, but from what she'd heard over the cellular, it didn't sound good. And she never knew when she might be too late.

She slowed down when her headlights picked out the stone walls that surrounded the old estate. She seldom drove on this remote stretch of road, but she remembered that somewhere along here were the big iron gates. *Why would I remember that?* she wondered. *Maybe it's because these gates have always looked so forbidding. Like they really meant "Stay Out."*

"Oops!" she said aloud. "There it is." She'd just passed them on her right.

She shoved her foot on the brake, skidding slightly, then had to back up a few feet, thankful that there wasn't any traffic on the road. She swung the Jeep onto the blacktop drive that led up to the huge stone piers with their black gates. They'd told her that there would be a column with a push-button speaker in the middle of the drive, and now she saw it. She pulled over next to it, rolled down her window, and pressed the speaker button. The sleeve of her lab coat was instantly drenched, and rain lashed into the car, splattering her face and hair as well.

A man's voice asked who it was. *Who the devil are they expecting after midnight?* she thought. "Dr. Rochelle," she replied, raising her voice to be heard above the rain.

"When you come to the Y in the road," the disembodied voice said, "take the one to the left. It leads to the stables."

Then the speaker went dead, and the gates slowly began to swing open. At the same time, she saw that video cameras were mounted on the stone piers. They appeared to focus their eyes upon her like alien monsters in a sci-fi movie.

What the hell is all this security about? she wondered. Most of the horse owners hereabouts didn't have any security at all, and the handful who owned extremely valuable animals usually had nothing more than an alarm system in the stables. But then, she reminded herself, she didn't know these people. She did know that they'd paid a fortune for the vast, somewhat rundown estate, and she had heard rumors that they'd spent another fortune sprucing it up. Stonelair, a white elephant with huge taxes and impossibly large spaces to heat, had sat vacant for years until these people had come along from out of nowhere.

Ah, the follies of the extremely rich, she thought as she sped down the narrow blacktop lane toward the house. *And the paranoia!*

The road was lined on both sides with enormous evergreens—spruce, pine, and hemlock—with rhododendrons tucked in front of them next to the road. On ahead a hundred feet, she spotted the Y in the road, and when she came to it, she veered to the left as the voice had instructed her. The road apparently circled around the mansion and toward the back of the estate.

In another minute she came to a large parking area. On her left she could make out what was definitely a stone stable block. She slammed on her brakes and killed the engine. Grabbing her carryall, she jumped out of the car and hurried around to the rear. Opening the door, she took out her heavy medical bag.

She turned to dash toward the stable.

"Oh, my God!" she gasped.

A giant stood poised in her path. He had appeared from out of nowhere, without a sound, at least none that she could detect over the driving rain and wind.

"Sorry," she said, quickly recovering her composure. "I didn't hear you." She surmised that he must be a benign giant, because he held an umbrella aloft and was opening another one for her. She took it from him, glad for the shelter from the rain.

"Dr. Rochelle?" he asked.

"Yes," she replied, nodding her head.

"Santo Ducci," the man said. He didn't extend a hand to shake. "This way," he said with a slight nod of his head. Without another word he began walking toward the stable.

Valerie quickly fell in step beside him, taking sidelong glances at her decidedly odd escort. His head was completely shaved, and he had a black mustache and small goatee. In his ear was a large gold ring.

Mr. Clean, she couldn't help thinking. As they moved, his body was a study in rippling musculature. Tree trunk arms and legs to match, six-pack abs, a chest from here to yon. *Jeez, a human HumVee.* But then, she decided, she must make a rather odd picture herself: hair practically plastered to her head, wet jeans, T-shirt, and lab coat, and shoes that were already nearly soaked through.

They quickly reached the stable, and he opened a door and held it for her. Valerie stepped into a truly luxurious office. Mahogany-paneled walls, an old Tabriz rug on the floor, handsome old leather-upholstered couches and chairs, a huge mahogany table that served as a desk, and, the only giveaways that she was in the twenty-first century: a computer, printer, fax machine, and filing cabinets.

She closed her umbrella and put it in the old iron stand by the doorway. "Which way do we go?" she asked, in a hurry to get to the sick horse.

"Over this way," he answered. He led her through a door into a tack room. Its walls were covered with riding accessories: saddles, bridles, reins, breastplates and collars, jawbands, browbands, nosebands, halters, leads, and on and on, all of it, Valerie noticed, leather and brass alike, gleaming from the polish of meticulous care. From the tack room he led her through another door and out into the stable proper. Valerie calculated that there must be at least thirty stalls in the immaculately kept space, but her attention immediately switched to the air of anxiety, of instinctual nervousness, that she sensed about the stable tonight.

The storm, she thought. *The lightning and thunder have them on edge.*

Then she heard it, above the sounds of the storm and the restlessness of the other horses: the sound of an animal in acute distress. *That only increases the nervousness of the rest of them,* she thought.

Without waiting for Ducci, she quickened her pace, heading in the direction of the sound. When she reached the stall, she looked in through the barred opening in the stall door and saw the magnificent Arabian stallion, to all appearances of excellent bloodlines, lying on its side though tethered to the stall. In its pain it might do harm to itself, so they'd tied it down. She could see that the horse had been rolling in agony and was sheathed in sweat.

She set down her carryall and medical bag and started to open the door to the stall, but the giant grabbed her arm from behind.

"Wait!" he said with alarm. "You're liable to get hurt. He's an extremely high-strung animal and could be dangerous like this. Hadn't you better try to sedate him or something first?"

Valerie turned to him. "He's tethered, and I know something about what I'm doing. Just back off a little bit," she said calmly. "Let me be alone with him for a few minutes."

"I don't know . . . ," Ducci said.

"I do," Valerie replied emphatically. "I don't mean to be rude, but I know what I'm doing. If you could just wait over there"—she indicated a bench near the door to the tack room—"I'll call you if I need you."

Ducci shrugged. "Whatever you say," he said gruffly.

With him out of the way, Valerie turned her attention back to the stall. On its door was a brass plaque with the horse's name engraved on it: Storm Warning. *How appropriate,* she thought. She unlatched the stall door and stepped inside confidently but quietly. She stood staring at the magnificent creature a few moments before getting down on her knees beside him, steering clear of his hindquarters. The horse was in severe distress. Stroking his head, she began talking to him in a soft, gentle voice. Her eyes swept his body as she continued, assessing his general physical condition, seeing if he appeared to present with anything other than what she thought. After her cursory examination, she continued to stroke and talk to him for another minute before slowly getting to her feet and retrieving her medical bag and carryall.

She placed them near Storm Warning and got back down on her knees, speaking soothingly to him the whole time. Just as she opened her medical bag, there was a sudden crash of thunder and flash of lightning. The lights flickered for a moment, then went out, plunging the stable into complete darkness. The horses reacted to the violent weather with noises of their own, stomping, snorting, and whinnying.

"Dr. Rochelle?" Ducci called to her.

She stroked Storm Warning again. "Yes?" she replied.

"You okay?" he asked.

"I'm fine," she said. "Have you got a lantern or something?"

"I'll be right there," he answered.

She heard him moving about, feeling in the darkness. "There," she whispered, as her hands stroked the horse's slick, well-groomed coat. "You'll be okay, Storm Warning. We'll have you better in no time."

The minutes seemed to stretch interminably in the pitch black of the stable, but she soon heard Ducci approaching from the direction of the tack room.

"I'm on my way," he called. He appeared in the stall a moment later, lantern held high in one hand.

"Is there some place to hang that?" she asked.

He hooked it over an iron hanger in the wall. "Right there."

"Good," she said. "If you don't mind, there's a box of supplies in the back of my Jeep. It's on the left-hand side, right inside the door. Could you get it for me, and another lantern, if you've got it?"

"Right away," he replied. He sensed that she knew what she was doing and turned to go, carrying a flashlight to light his way.

In the halo of light cast by the lantern, Valerie rummaged around in her medical bag until she found what she was looking for. Then she proceeded to work on Storm Warning. First, she felt his neck, ascertaining where his jugular vein was. Then she injected him with Rompun. The sedative worked quickly, putting the horse at some ease, as well as making the rest of her work less difficult. Ducci returned and stood in the doorway with the box and another lantern.

"Is there another hanger for the lantern?" she asked without looking up.

"Right over here," he said, indicating the wall to the left of the door.

"Hang it there if you would, please," she said. "And you can set the box down next to my medical bag."

"I can hold the lantern for you."

"That won't be necessary," she replied. "I think Storm Warning and I will be better off alone."

"Whatever you say." He set the box down and hung the lantern up, then turned to leave. "You want me to wait for you?"

"It's okay," she said. "If you have something to do, go ahead."

"I'll be in the office for a minute," he said. "Need to check on things at the house."

She didn't reply but resumed her running whispers, trying to soothe the nervous animal, readying him for another injection. This one was a painkiller, Banamine, and it was injected, like the Rompun, in the jugular vein. She would wait a bit and give the sedative and painkiller time to ease the magnificent horse even more before she performed the next procedure.

The storm ended almost as quickly as it had begun. The stable fell silent as the thunder died out and the animals resettled themselves for the night. She didn't stop stroking Storm Warning or whispering her litany of soothing words until he seemed to be in less pain and somewhat lethargic. Then she retrieved the supplies she needed from the medical box and got busy again. She passed a nasogastric tube through one of his nostrils and down toward his stomach. Through the tube she poured mineral oil. It would act as a laxative, relieving the horse's painful cramps. She focused on her work in the quiet, losing track of the time. She was almost finished when suddenly the hair at the nape of her neck stood on end, and she felt a chill clutch at her heart.

Somebody's watching me, she thought.

Jerking her head up, she looked behind her into the pitch black of the stable. She could have sworn that she saw a figure suddenly step back into the darkness, but she couldn't be certain.

"Ducci?" she asked. "Is that you?"

There was no reply, and after a moment she shook her head as if to clear it and turned her attention back to the horse. *I guess the stormy night and the power failure have me spooked,* she thought. *Just like the horses.* She felt silly because ordinarily mere power failures and storms didn't affect her in the least. They were common in the country.

Maybe it's simply the situation, she thought. *My first time at Stonelair. All of the crazy rumors about the owner. And the giant, Ducci himself, though he seems harmless enough. I wonder what happened to him anyway?* Then it occurred to her that an estate like Stonelair, as lavish as it must be from the look of the stables, surely had a backup generator system.

She quickly finished her work on Storm Warning, giving him the last of the mineral oil, then easing the nasogastric tube back out of his nostril. She sat for a few minutes more, whispering to him and rubbing him with long, patient strokes. Satisfied that he was resting comfortably, she got to her feet. Taking first one lantern, then the other, she set them down outside the stall. Finally she repacked her medical bag and carryall and box of supplies.

At the end of the brick walk between the stalls, the glow of a flashlight appeared, and Ducci hurried toward her. "Sorry," he said, "I've been trying to get the backup generators going, but didn't have any luck yet."

"That's okay," she said. "I'm done here."

"What's the problem seem to be?" he asked.

"Severe colic," she replied. "I've given him a sedative and painkiller and mineral oil as a laxative. Let me know if there's no improvement overnight."

"Okay," Ducci said.

"And if you don't mind, could you help me get my things back out to the Jeep?" Valerie asked. She shouldered her carryall and picked up her medical bag.

"No problem," he replied. He leaned down and turned off the lanterns, then picked them up along with the heavy box of supplies.

"Just follow me," he said, leading the way with the flashlight.

When they reached the office, he held the door open for her, and she saw that several candles had been lit. But Valerie didn't linger. She headed toward the door that led out to the parking area.

"Dr. Rochelle?" Ducci called from behind her.

She turned to face him, her eyebrows raised in a question. "Yes?"

"Should I give you a check now or—?" he began.

"That's not necessary," she said, shaking her head. "The clinic will send a bill. If you've got a business card with the billing address, let me have one. I'll call tomorrow to check up on Storm Warning, by the way."

"Great," he said. He went over to the big desk, where he set down the lanterns, then flipped open a small wooden box and extracted a card. He handed it to her, and Valerie took it and tossed it into her carryall.

"Thanks," she said.

He walked her out to the Jeep and opened the cargo door for her. She shoved her medical bag in, then Ducci set the box down in its corner and closed the door.

"Thanks a lot, Dr. Rochelle," he said.

"It's okay," Valerie said. "Keep an eye on Storm Warning, but I think he'll be fine."

She went around to the door on the driver's side, tossed her carryall in, then climbed in after it. As she glanced down toward the stable, a light caught her eye, visible through the outside stall doors. It moved slowly from the end near the tack room, down to the middle of the stable, and stopped in the area where Storm Warning was housed.

Weird, she thought. *Maybe Ducci and I weren't alone in there.*

She started the Jeep and nodded at Ducci, who stood watching her leave. Going back down the drive the way she'd come in, she wondered if that had been Stonelair's new occupant who'd been going to visit the horse.

But why so mysterious? she asked herself. *For that matter, why didn't he come down and introduce himself to me? Why wasn't he hovering around, like most horse owners would, while I was working on Storm Warning?* She decided she didn't have a particularly high opinion of an owner who would have an underling deal with a sick animal and not participate in its treatment himself.

Her headlights shone off the huge gates that guarded the entrance to the estate, and before she could wonder how to open them, they began to slowly glide apart as the car approached.

"Open sesame!" she said aloud. She drove through and on toward the country lane that passed the entrance to Stonelair.

What a weird place, she thought as she pulled out onto the road. Mr. Clean, the giant who'd give anybody the creeps. The storm and then the darkness. The feeling that she was being watched.

She reached over to twirl on the radio. "I could use some music after that," she said. "Maybe some loud rock and roll." *Anything,* she thought, *to shake away this creepy feeling.*

The man had watched Santo take her to the office. Then he'd stepped out of the empty stall across from Storm Warning's and gone across the brick walk to the sick horse's stall. He'd stood staring into it, unable to see the horse in the darkness. When he'd heard them leave the office and go to her car, he'd gone to the office and gotten one of the lanterns, lighting it and returning to Storm Warning's stall.

He opened the door and hung up the lantern. Then, much as he'd heard her do, he got down on his knees and whispered soothingly to the enormous animal, stroking him lovingly all the while. He'd always treated his animals with such affection—who didn't?—but he'd never seen anyone with her ability to calm an animal. Certainly not a high-strung horse like Storm Warning.

It's as if she could really communicate with the animal, he told himself. *Well, that's not so unusual, is it? But it's almost like she's got some kind of weird magic touch.* Then he smiled. *Maybe it's that whopping big sparkler of a ring she was wearing,* he thought. It had picked up the lantern light and flashed it all around the stables. "Maybe that whopper has healing powers," he whispered to Storm Warning.

Chapter Three

Valerie turned off the highway and began the drive up to the veterinarian clinic, perched on top of a hill, overlooking summer fields of green and verdant woods. It was a cool morning, and a mist still hovered over the ground. The grass was soaking wet with dew, but she knew that the mist would soon burn off, and the ground would be quickly dried by a scorcher of a summer day.

She pulled into her customary parking spot in the back of the clinic and killed the engine. She was tired for a Monday morning, and that did not sit well with her. She was usually bright-eyed and bushy-tailed when she went into the clinic, eager to get to work. But not today.

It wasn't because she'd been on call this weekend. There'd been only the one emergency at Stonelair and five or six telephone consultations on Sunday, an easy weekend. It was spending the weekend with Teddy that had been exhausting, she decided. And not because of their vigorous physical activities, either. No, it was the emotional toll that dealing with Teddy had taken out of her that had left her feeling wrung out, limp, and ineffectual. That and her own weakness in handling the situation. She had come to realize that she and she alone was responsible for her actions, and she felt that she had failed herself this weekend. In spades.

"Elvis," she said, turning to look at the mutt in the passenger seat, "I've got to snap out of it. I've got a busy week ahead, and

I've got to be on my toes." Elvis turned and looked at her, wagging his tail sluggishly.

Valerie smiled and patted him, then put her car keys in her carryall and got out of the Jeep. She held the door open, allowing Elvis to jump out behind her. Letting herself in by the staff door, she headed down the hallway toward the reception area, where the door to her office was located. Elvis bounced along beside her, exhilarated as usual by being here in one of his favorite domains.

When she stepped into the reception area, the chatter she'd heard in the hallway suddenly stopped, and there was complete silence as four heads turned to stare at her: Daphne Collins and Charles Bradford, fellow vets, and Tami Reeves and Annie Wolsky, who doubled as secretaries and receptionists.

"Well, well, well," said Charles Bradford, who was also the owner of the clinic, in a hostile voice, finally breaking the silence, "we hear you've been out to the infamous Stonelair."

Valerie nodded in response.

"So it's true?" Daphne chimed in. "Our little Valerie has met the mysterious Mr. Conrad."

Valerie smiled brightly even though she was puzzled by Daphne's obvious sarcasm. It was an unusual tone for the very pretty, very blond Daphne to take with her. Valerie had always liked her and assumed that the feeling was mutual. They weren't best friends, but their relationship had been amicable from the start.

"Yes," she replied evenly, "I had to go out to Stonelair Saturday night. A horse—"

"What was he like?" interrupted Charles in a clipped, imperious manner.

"Oh, yes, Val," Daphne said, "tell us all about him." She ran her fingers through her hair in a nervous gesture and shifted her weight on her feet. She appeared to be waiting anxiously to hear what Valerie had to say.

"This Arabian stallion—" Valerie began.

"No-body cares about the horse, Val," Daphne said. "Tell us about Conrad!"

Everyone laughed, including the dapper Dr. Charles Bradford, who seldom ventured so enthusiastic a response.

"I didn't meet him," Valerie replied.

"What?" the three women cried in unison.

Valerie noticed that even Charles appeared to be perplexed by her response. He took off his glasses and began to clean them on a handkerchief, as if his hearing had been affected by dirty lenses.

"Sorry," she said. She smiled and shrugged apologetically.

"Damn," Daphne swore. "You mean you didn't even get a glimpse of Conrad himself?"

"No," Valerie said. "Some guy who works for him met me at the stable, and I never saw him."

"Was it the big muscley one we hear so much about?" Daphne asked.

Valerie nodded, looking at her. "Yes," she said. "He looks sort of like Mr. Clean."

"You didn't see anybody else?" Charles asked. "Nobody at all?"

"No," Valerie answered, shaking her head. "He was the only person around."

"What was he like?" Daphne asked. "Is he . . . well, I've heard he's really kind of creepy."

"He was strictly business," Valerie replied. "I didn't really get to know him. You know, I was dealing with the horse, and—"

"Oh, hell," Daphne said. "You're worthless, Val. No useful information at all."

The telephone rang, and Tami picked up. "Animal Clinic," she said in her pleasant professional voice. She listened for a moment, then said: "Hold, please."

She looked up at Valerie and held the telephone out over the top of the reception counter, a triumphant gleam in her eyes. Everyone looked over at her.

"It's for you, Dr. Rochelle," Tami said. "It's Mr. Santo Ducci at Stonelair. Line one."

"I'll take it here," Valerie said. She reached for the receiver at once rather than retreating to the privacy of her office to take the call. She wondered if Storm Warning might have taken a turn for the worse.

"Dr. Rochelle," she said.

"Good morning, Dr. Rochelle," the giant said. "This is Santo Ducci at Stonelair."

"Yes, Mr. Ducci," she replied. "Is there a problem with Storm Warning? Is he okay?"

"He's doing great," Ducci said. "Really great. There's no problem there."

"Good," she said, relieved.

"The reason I called," Ducci continued, "is that Mr. Conrad would like for you to take care of all the animals here at Stonelair. I mean you personally."

Suddenly Valerie noticed the four pairs of eyes on her. Now she wished that she'd taken the call in her office. "I appreciate that, Mr. Ducci," she said, "but that's not clinic policy. Generally speaking, we have a share-and-share-alike rule here. It depends on who's on duty. We do make exceptions, but I'd have to discuss it with the other veterinarians."

"I see," he said. "Well, I'm sure Mr. Conrad would make it worth your time if you agreed to see to his animals personally," Ducci went on. "He likes the way you handled Storm Warning, and there are a lot of animals out here to take care of."

Valerie could see that Ducci—or Conrad—was not to be easily rebuffed. "I'll see what I can do, Mr. Ducci."

"I'd appreciate that," he said. "I mean, surely the other vets there would understand if somebody wanted your services."

"I'll have to discuss it with my colleagues and get back to you," Valerie said.

"Good," Ducci said. "We'll be waiting to hear from you."

"Okay."

"And thanks again, Doc."

"You're welcome," Valerie said. When she was certain he'd hung up, she handed the receiver back over the reception counter to Tami. "Thanks, Tami."

Valerie saw the questioning looks from everyone in the reception area. Charles Bradford broke the silence once again. "That's the guy who works for Conrad, I take it?"

Valerie nodded.

"So, what did he want?" he asked, his cold gray eyes boring into hers.

Valerie hesitated before answering, then plunged ahead. "He said they'd like for me to take care of the animals out at Stonelair," she said.

"You mean you personally?" Daphne said. "Not the clinic?"

"That's what he said."

"He must've liked your looks," Charles Bradford snapped, his tone burning with scorn. He slapped a medical chart against his thigh and strode out of the reception area toward his office, his slightly long gray hair flipping up in the breeze he created as he walked.

Valerie felt her face flush with embarrassment.

"What's wrong, Val?" Daphne asked, seeing the look on Valerie's face. "Did Charles hit a sore spot?" Without waiting for an answer, she turned and, like Charles, headed for her office.

Annie suddenly looked very busy behind the reception counter, but Tami gave Valerie a look of understanding and concern.

Valerie felt like screaming, but instead, ears burning with indignation, she quickly got a cup of coffee from the communal coffeemaker, then went to her office, Elvis trailing along behind her. She closed the door, and Elvis immediately went to his bed under her desk, where he curled up to nap. She heaved her carryall onto the desktop, then sat down heavily.

She had become accustomed to Charles's behavior, but she couldn't fathom this sudden sarcasm in Daphne. *Jeez!* she thought. *How much longer can I take this crap?* She knew that Charles was miffed because time and again clients asked for her to see to their animals rather than anyone else at the clinic. And time and again, she'd had to endure Charles's resentful, jealous remarks.

Charles had singlehandedly established the clinic and built it up into the very successful practice that it had become. Valerie realized that he had a right to feel proud of his accomplishments, but did he have the right to be so demeaning toward others? He relished his role as the boss and treated her as a Johnny-come-lately underling who should always defer to him. Perhaps he felt threatened by her in some way, particularly by her popularity with patients. He had always been the "face" of the clinic, and he wanted to keep it that way.

Daphne was another matter. She had moved up from the south only three years ago, her arrival surrounded with rumors of a torrid affair gone bad. Valerie had never learned if there was any truth to these stories, but they had gradually died down anyway and were replaced by gossip about the obvious sexual interest that Charles had in Daphne. She had quickly become the clinic's most valued employee since Charles was determined to get in her pants. As Valerie and Daphne became friendly, she'd had several opportunities to see Daphne fend off Charles's advances. She naturally assumed that Daphne had no feelings for Charles and was perhaps still stinging from the wounds of her last relationship. But she didn't really know. For as friendly as they became, Daphne never revealed much of her personal life. Theirs was an easy friendship that had grown over the past three years. Or at least that's what Valerie had thought. Today made her wonder.

"Shit, shit, shit!" she said aloud. To have to take abuse from Daphne as well as Charles was too much. *When is this ever going to end?* she thought. But she knew the answer to that question, in theory at least: *When I have my own clinic and I'm my own boss, that's when.*

There was a knock at the door, then it opened before she could answer.

"Here," Tami said, her hand extended. "You forgot your schedule for today."

"Thanks, Tami." Valerie took the proffered sheet of paper.

"You're welcome," Tami said, eyeing her curiously before closing the office door.

Valerie took a sip of coffee and looked down at the schedule, but she didn't really see it. *I can't concentrate,* she thought miserably. She realized that her defenses were at a low point this morning and that the catty remarks had bothered her more than usual. Suddenly she felt almost overwhelmed by worry and fear and had a powerful urge to cry, but she was determined not to.

I'm not going to let them get the best of me, she thought.

It had all started with Teddy this weekend—her worries and fears—with his proposal and her own stupid response. Now it was only getting worse, and here at work, which she'd always thought of as a sort of haven.

Her vision of working in a veterinarian clinic, caring for animals, had always been one of a peaceable kingdom where concern for animals was of paramount importance. She hadn't envisioned the office politics, the games of one-upmanship. She had never dreamed of the sometimes callous attitude that doctors and staff displayed toward the animals and their owners. Nor had she imagined that it would take her years to pay off the tens of thousands of dollars she owned in loans that she'd taken out to get through school.

Elvis growled in his sleep, and she reached down and stroked him gently. *I've got to snap out of it,* she thought. *Self-pity will get me nowhere fast.* She picked up the daily schedule and took a sip of her coffee. She could see that it was going to be a busy day, and she was glad of that. It would keep her mind off of her troubles. The telephone rang, and she idly picked up the receiver, still perusing the schedule.

"Hello," she said.

"Valerie, dear," the cultured, dulcet voice of her mother intoned.

"Hi, Mother," she said, wishing now that she'd told Tami to screen her calls—and feeling guilty about having such a thought.

"How was your weekend, dear?" her mother asked.

Damn! Valerie thought. *I wonder if Teddy's already talked to her, and she knows about the ring.* "It was okay," she replied mildly.

"That's all?" her mother asked pointedly. "Okay?"

"Yes," Valerie replied. She decided she would not let her mother push her around this morning.

"I see," Marguerite de la Rochelle said. She paused momentarily, then continued. "I phoned because I want you and Teddy to come to dinner tonight."

"But today's Monday, Mother," Valerie said. "Teddy's gone back to—" Then she remembered that Teddy was taking the week off. He was staying out in the country.

"I should think you would know better than that," Marguerite said with reproach. "I spoke to him early this morning. He's staying at Apple Hill all week, and he'll be here for dinner."

Valerie's heart sank. *They're ganging up on me,* she thought.

The two of them are in cahoots as usual. "I wish you'd discussed this with me first," she said. "I have a very busy day and need to get a lot of things done at home tonight."

"I'm sure that whatever it is you have to do at your little home can wait," Marguerite said disparagingly. "I'll expect you around eight, dear."

Before Valerie could answer, her mother had hung up. *Shit,* she thought as she replaced the receiver in its cradle. *Why do I let her do this to me? And why does she always make me feel like a naughty child who is guilty of something? Why does she always make fun of my little house? The house I've worked so hard to buy?*

She wanted to scream for the second time that morning, but restrained herself, gritting her teeth. *I'd like to choke them both,* she thought. *Teddy and my mother!* She could already envision tonight's dinner. First, Marguerite would have to see the ring and swoon and coo to Teddy about it. Then Teddy and Marguerite would laugh and talk amiably, like old lovers, gossiping about mutual friends and acquaintances, the latest antics among the bluebloods in Manhattan and here in the country, and finally coming to focus all of their considerable energies on *her.*

Pressuring her into setting a date. Pressuring her into putting her house on the market and moving in with Teddy. Pressuring her to accept Teddy's offer to build her a clinic of her own and pay off her loans. Pressuring her into giving up nearly all the independence and self-reliance that she'd worked so long and hard to achieve. Soon enough, they'd be pressuring her into having babies and working part-time or giving up her work altogether.

And never once taking into account her own thoughts and feelings on anything. Never once giving her any credit for having an opinion, discounting out of hand any that she might express. It was as if she didn't matter in all of the elaborate plans they'd worked out for her.

Some things never change, she realized. Growing up, Valerie had been an outsider even in her own family. Marguerite was a vain and beautiful woman, obsessed with her own physical appearance and, equally as important, the image that the de la Rochelle family presented to the world. She was still incensed that Valerie had chosen to drop the "de la" from her name and go simply by Rochelle, failing to understand that Valerie had done it for simplicity's sake. Valerie de la Rochelle was a mouthful for some of her clients, and actually created a sort of barrier between her and others. Besides, she thought, we're no longer living in the Dark Ages when such distinctions came about and might have actually meant something.

Her mother, however, didn't see it that way at all. The de la Rochelle family could be nothing less than perfection at all times—in looks, behavior, and manners. They were also to be perceived as having healthy, happy—perfect!—relationships with one another and the coterie of rich, old-money families that made up their social circle.

In this and nearly every other respect, Valerie had been a miserable disappointment to her mother—and her father, for that matter. While he'd been alive, he'd been in league with Marguerite just as Teddy was now. Armand de la Rochelle had always dressed well, behaved well, and played the role of the wealthy gentleman heir to the fortune he'd inherited—and had managed to increase by his marriage to the equally rich Marguerite de Coligny.

Like Marguerite, Armand had been obsessed by appearances, and until the end, people had been fooled into believing that the world of the de la Rochelles was perfect in every way. Beautiful, tasteful, elegant, to the manor born.

She had loved her father dearly and missed him still, but she couldn't fool herself into believing that it had been reciprocated. He'd been as disappointed in her as her mother, with many of the very same complaints.

"Why must you keep your nose buried in that book, Valerie, dear?"

"Why don't you play with the other young people, Valerie, dear?"

"Why must you devote yourself to those filthy animals, Valerie, dear?"

"Why must you be all elbows and knees? So unattractive, so *ugly*, Valerie, dear?"

She could hear their voices as if it were yesterday. Both of them, Mother and Father, denigrating her from the time she was old enough to understand what they were saying to her. Perhaps they hadn't meant to be cruel; perhaps they had been challenging her to be her best. Whatever the case, the result had been to make her retreat into herself, to shy away from a world that also thought she was a gangly, awkward, four-eyed bookworm.

Virtually friendless and scorned by her beautiful parents, she had eventually found solace in animals. From an early age she had made friends of her pets, confiding in them, playing with them, telling them her joys and sorrows, her deepest secrets, caring for them in a way that others found eccentric. As she'd grown older, she'd begun to nurse her pets and any other sick or injured animal she came upon. Birds, dogs, cats, even a racoon and a chicken.

She had discovered that she could communicate with her pets on a level that most people would consider amazing—or, more likely, frightening. She'd kept this knowledge to herself, knowing that her family would disapprove anyway. She had decided early on that she wanted to be a veterinarian, a profession that would draw an equally unenthusiastic response from the powers that be.

She was expected to go to the "right" schools, blossom into a beautiful debutante, and eventually marry the "right" man. If she must work, she must do something genteel. Charity committee work, board directorships, perhaps something in the art or publishing worlds, if not too commercial, might fill the bill.

Valerie had gone to the "right" schools. Just before Armand died, she had even been presented to society in a New York City debutante ball. All to please her parents.

It was about this time that Valerie began to blossom. The gangly, awkward girl who'd been all knees and elbows with no breasts to speak of was gradually turning into a swan. Suddenly young men began to pay attention to her, but Valerie, who'd spent her childhood and youth alone, didn't really know how to cope with the attention. She had no use for small talk, was terrible at the social niceties, and really preferred the company of her menagerie, who understood her as she understood them.

When the question of college came up, Marguerite, newly bereaved, insisted that Valerie attend one of the Seven Sisters or, preferably, go to an exclusive finishing school in Switzerland. Valerie, however, had defied her mother for the first time in her life, choosing instead to go to Cornell and prepare for veterinarian school.

"Then you'll pay for it yourself," Marguerite had said. "You could be in Switzerland learning the proper way to be a wife and mother and a social figure of importance. Besides which, you would inevitably meet young ladies of your class and an appropriate young man to marry. But Cornell! I won't give you a penny for such nonsense."

"I'll find a way," Valerie had responded.

And she had, working part-time and taking out student loans, year after year. She never once asked her mother for anything, and her mother never volunteered it. Nor had Marguerite deigned to come to her graduation ceremonies.

Now, sitting in her office, Valerie imagined that her mother would be very pleased if she knew how miserable she was this morning. She caught herself laughing suddenly, amused by the situation. *Well,* she thought, *I'm not going to give her a reason to gloat. No way! I've succeeded in doing what I set out to do. And if I stick it out, I know I can do the rest.*

An image of Storm Warning abruptly came into her mind. She could see the stallion, panicked at first, rolling in his stall, covered with sweat, scared for his life. And later, after her gentle care, she could see the trusting look in his eyes. She could still sense the bond that had been formed between them, and it made her feel good.

Then she remembered the shadowy figure she'd seen while she'd been working on Storm Warning. Was it Conrad? she wondered. And, if so, why the secrecy? For that matter, why hadn't a single person hereabouts laid eyes on the mystery man since he'd bought and renovated Stonelair?

She felt a sudden twinge in her stomach, an uncomfortable feeling that she couldn't quite describe. All thoughts of tonight's dinner and unpleasant office politics were swept away, and she felt a new sense of uneasiness that she couldn't explain. It was something about Stonelair, of that she was certain, but what was it that had her so spooked?

Chapter Four

Wyndhym Ashley Conrad III slowly paced back and forth across the library's faded Portuguese needlepoint rug, a mug of coffee in one hand and an unlit cigarette in the other. A black baseball cap partially hid his long, slightly curly raven-black hair and all but obscured the thoughtful expression in his velvety dark brown eyes. The sleeves on his long-sleeved black T-shirt were rolled up above his elbows, revealing strong, muscular forearms and powerful-looking hands. Matching sweatpants, cinched tightly against the flat plane of his stomach, hung loosely on his muscular legs.

As he paced, four enormous Irish wolfhounds watched his every move. Two of them, both gray, were ensconced on tufted antique leather sofas that faced one another in front of the French limestone fireplace mantel. The other two, one brindle and the other brown, had arrayed themselves on the rug near the hearth. On their alert faces were looks of equal parts devotion and curiosity.

Wyn, finally weary of his aimless strides, sprawled on the cracked leather of an ancient Georgian wing chair and looked over at Santo Ducci, who was talking on the telephone behind Wyn's desk, a Louis XV *bureau plat*. He took a sip of his coffee and grimaced. It was already cold.

He tossed his unlit cigarette into a crystal ashtray and got back up, walking over to an ornate gilded console and draining the coffee mug in an orchid plant on the marble top. Then he walked to the minibar that was concealed behind a jib door near the fireplace and poured himself a fresh cup of coffee from the coffeemaker there. He retraced his steps, sipping the hot black coffee as he went, but before he could sit back down, Santo quietly hung up the telephone and looked over at him.

"That was the vet, right?" Wyn asked.

Santo shook his head. "No," he replied. The sun, which streamed through the French doors behind him, shone off the top of his shaved head.

"No?" Wyn said irritably. He glared at Santo, but the giant couldn't read the look in Wyn's eyes because of the long shadow cast by his baseball cap. "Didn't I tell you to call her first thing this morning?"

"And I did," Santo said mildly. He gazed at his boss dispassionately, his hugely muscled arms folded across his chest, his feathers completely unruffled by Wyn's irritation. "That was somebody else," he added.

"Oh," Wyn said, frowning. "Well then, tell me, Santo. What the hell did the vet say?"

"They share and share alike," Santo said. "She said it was usually against clinic policy."

"Against clinic policy?" Wyn stormed. "That's a crock of shit."

Santo held his hands out, gesturing at Wyn to hold on a minute. "Chill out," he said calmly. "She said she'll discuss it with the other vets and get back to me. It's a possibility."

"I never heard of anything so stupid," Wyn groused.

"I told you, she said they have a share-and-share-alike policy," Santo countered.

"What the hell is that supposed to mean?"

"It's simple. You don't normally get to choose a particular vet," Santo said. "You get whoever's on duty."

"That's ridiculous," Wyn spat. "This isn't a third-world country."

"Maybe not," Santo said, "but that's the usual policy."

"Damn!" Wyn sat down in the big wing chair and slammed his mug of coffee on the table next to it. Coffee sloshed out onto the table's highly polished walnut surface, but he ignored it. "Find out who owns the fucking clinic," he demanded, casting a scowl in Santo's direction.

"That's what I just did."

"And?" Wyn asked impatiently.

Santo looked down at some notes he'd scratched out on a pad. "A guy named Charles Bradford—he's one of the other vets," he said. "Owns it lock, stock, and barrel. Rochelle is just a salaried employee."

Wyn looked disgruntled. "Aw, shit," he said.

"Look," Santo said, trying to placate his unhappy boss, "don't get yourself so worked up. I bet it'll work out. She said she'd discuss it with the other docs, so she must be interested, Wyn. Right? She wouldn't bother talking to them if she wasn't. She'd have just said no." He looked at Wyn for some indication that he was satisfied. *Jeez,* he thought, *the guy's acting like a spoiled rich kid that has to have it his way, or else. What's worse, lately he's been carrying on like a genuine nutcase.* Santo was patient, however, because he figured that with all of Wyn's worries, he'd be pretty much a basket case himself.

Wyn finally nodded. "I guess you're right," he agreed. He looked thoughtful for a moment, then added: "Call her back and tell her that, if she does it, there'll be a bonus in it for her. A bonus that the others don't need to know about."

"If you say so."

"I say so," Wyn said emphatically.

But before Santo could pick up the telephone, it rang, and he answered it. "Stonelair," he said.

He listened for a minute, then said: "I'll have to put you on hold for a moment."

He punched the hold button and looked over at Wyn. "It's Arielle."

Wyn shook his head. "I'm not available," he said. "But put her on the speaker so I can listen."

Santo punched the hold button again, then the speaker button, after which he replaced the receiver in its cradle. "I'm sorry, Arielle," he said. "He can't come to the phone right now."

"You're lying to me, Santo." Her disembodied voice filled the room, its smokiness tinged with anger. The Irish wolfhounds pricked up their ears at the sound of their former mistress's voice.

"No, Arielle," he replied, "I'm not lying."

"You bastard!" she cried nastily. "You sound like you're in a garbage can. You put me on the fucking speaker so that shit can listen."

Santo looked over at Wyn, whose lips formed a smile.

"Let me speak to him," Arielle shouted.

"I told you, Arielle," Santo said in his most patient voice, "he can't come to the telephone now."

There was an audible sigh of resignation from the speaker. Then in calm and measured tones, Arielle said, "Tell him that his monthly support check hasn't arrived yet, and it's overdue. As you well know. I called Goldman's office, and his secretary said they haven't received it yet."

"I'll pass the word along," Santo said.

"You do that," Arielle replied, a bit more vinegar in her voice. "And while you're at it, tell him that they told me he hasn't sent back the signed divorce papers yet."

"I don't know about that," Santo said.

"I just bet you don't," she snapped. Then she sighed loudly again, as if suddenly realizing that she must take a different tack. Being demanding and unpleasant was getting her nowhere with Santo, and certainly wouldn't with Wyn, that she well knew. Thus, the hint of the helpless, little-girl plea that crept into her voice.

"Oh, Santo, please," she said rather sweetly. "You've got to help me. You're the *only* person who can. I don't know what I'm going to do. First the monthly support check's late, and now I find out he hasn't signed the divorce papers yet."

"I'll see what I can do," Santo said.

"Yes, please, Santo," she begged. "You know they won't release the final settlement check until he's signed everything, and I really need it. I mean, Christ, until the measly support check comes"—a sob that might arguably have been genuine caught in her throat— "it's all I can do to eat!"

Wyn almost laughed aloud when he heard this, but restrained

himself. He knew that she was fairly certain he was listening, but he wanted to keep her guessing. If nothing else, it compounded her misery, and that gave him no end of pleasure.

"I'm sick and tired of the whole mess," Arielle went on. "I just want it over with, and I thought he did, too. It's time we both got on with our lives, you know? Even all the therapists say so. This isn't doing either one of us any good."

"I hear what you're saying," Santo said. He looked over at Wyn again and saw a twisted smile on his lips. *He's really enjoying this,* Santo thought. *Sick fucker.* He cleared his voice. "I'll do what I can, Arielle."

"Please do, Santo," she whined. "I mean, I always thought we were friends, you and me, and I really need your help." Her voice choked up again.

Was it real? Wyn wondered with amusement. *Or had her acting abilities improved?*

"Oh, Jesus!" she managed to cry. "If you only knew! They started to turn off the electricity today. It's that bad."

"I told you, Arielle," he said, "I'll do what I can. I promise you that."

"Well . . . thanks, Santo," she whimpered girlishly. "Talk to you later. Ciao."

They heard her hang up, and Santo reached over and turned off the speaker. The room was once again silent but for the collective breathing of the dogs. It was momentary, however.

"Of all the women I had back in those days," Wyn said rue-fully, "I had to go and pick Arielle. What a joke." He began to laugh. It was a laugh that began somewhere deep down within him, gradually swelling up and out, filling the room with a roar. It was an evil sound, this laugh, and Santo turned and stared at his boss as did the wolfhounds.

He looks like a man possessed, Santo thought, almost mesmer-ized by Wyn's gleeful laugh. *Possessed by a demon straight from hell.* Sometimes lately, he'd begun to think that Wyn really had gone off the deep end.

Santo stared out through the French doors toward the swim-ming pool in the distance. He didn't want to be a witness to a scene that was, to his mind, sick, even perverse. It made him feel somehow unclean and stirred something deep down inside him, something frightening and inexplicable in his own nature that he'd yet to face.

When Wyn had at last exhausted his well of laughter, he got to his feet and padded over to a big Sicilian rococo gilt console. On its marble top were dozens of bottles—liquor, wine, seltzer, tonic, mixers, soda, and mineral water—a sterling ice bucket, and crystal glasses of every kind. He picked up a large crystal glass, plopped a few ice cubes in with tongs, and poured himself a glass of mineral water. He took a slice of lime from an ornate silver bowl and squeezed it into the drink, then tossed it in. Taking a crisp linen cocktail napkin from the stack that was replenished daily by Gerda, his Austrian housekeeper and cook, he nestled the glass in it, then turned to look at Santo. He took a sip of his water, staring at the giant's back across the room.

"You don't like it, do you, Santo?"

"Like what?" Santo said without turning around.

"This divorce business," Wyn said. "Making sure the monthly support checks are late and all that."

"It's none of my business."

"Then make it your business," Wyn said. "Tell me what you think."

Santo turned around and looked over at his boss. He could hardly make out Wyn's face at all beneath the cap. "Well, if I were you," he said, "number one, I'd send her monthly support check out. I could overnight it, you know. Number two," he went on, "I think you ought to go ahead and sign the papers and get this whole thing over with. You're spending a fortune on the lawyers as it is, and there's no advantage in dragging it out any longer."

"Oh, yes, there is," Wyn said with merriment.

"What?"

"It makes the bitch that much more miserable," Wyn said.

Santo sighed and rolled his eyes. "Well . . . yes," he agreed. "But—"

"Shut up, Santo," Wyn said. He took a long, leisurely swallow of the mineral water. "I'll sign the papers when I get good and ready. She's just in a hurry because she wants the settlement check."

He walked over to the table beside the wing chair and picked up the unlit cigarette from the ashtray, then stuck it in his mouth. "*And* she's in a hurry for the settlement check not only because she's a greedy little bitch but because she wants to tie the knot with that South American dude with the big equipment."

Santo sat down in the chair behind Wyn's desk. "Are you just pissed off and trying to punish her because she's found somebody she wants to marry?" he asked.

Wyn looked at him. "Maybe." He nodded. "That and a lot of other things."

"I still think you ought to let it go," Santo said. "It'd be the best thing for both of you. Get the whole thing over with. Besides, you know she's going to marry him no matter what."

"Maybe," Wyn agreed. "But I want to watch them squirm a little while longer." He smiled widely, a smile that even Santo could see from across the room. "It'll be interesting to see if her stud decides to stick around or vamoose for richer territory."

"Maybe they're really in love," Santo suggested.

"Aw, Jesus, Santo," Wyn said with exasperation. "They're both like sharks on the prowl, seeing what they can finagle out of each other. Sometimes I think you're as stupid as you are ugly. *Love!*" He barked a laugh. "Sex and money make the world go around," he said, pointing a finger at Santo. "Love's got nothing to do with it, my friend. And don't you forget it."

Santo stared at him, then cleared his throat. "I'm not ugly."

"Yeah, well, I didn't mean that," Wyn said. "What I meant was . . . menacing. You look menacing."

Santo smiled. "Menacing," he said, as if tasting the word on his tongue. "I like that. Yeah, I can deal with that. Menacing."

"I would hope so," Wyn said. "It's one of the reasons you work for me." He got to his feet and stretched. "What time is it?"

Santo looked at the gold Rolex on his wrist, a gift from Wyn. "About ten."

"It's time," Wyn said.

Santo nodded. "I'll be right back." He rose to his feet and strode in a ripple of muscles out of the library.

Wyn walked over to one of the French doors and stood gazing

out at the pool, thoughts of Arielle swirling in his head. Paddy, one of the wolfhounds, bounded off the couch and edged up to his side, nuzzling him. Wyn idly stroked the massive dog's head.

"She may be a beauty, Paddy," he said thoughtfully, "but she's also a bitch. And she's got it coming to her . . . anything I dish out. She's got it coming to her."

Santo returned to the library. In one hand he gripped a black leather bag that he placed on the desk. He opened it and extracted a bottle of rubbing alcohol and a paper packet containing a cotton swab. Setting them aside, he delved back into the bag and withdrew a glass, rubber-topped medicine bottle and a still-packaged disposable syringe and needle.

From the French doors, Wyn turned and watched as Santo tore the wrapper off the syringe, then inserted the needle in the rubber-topped glass container. The syringe filled with a colorless fluid. When Santo was finished, he looked over at Wyn.

Wyn walked to the desk, loosened his sweatpants, and pulled down his jockstrap. He put both hands on the desk and bent over, exposing his bare buttocks to the air. He jerked involuntarily as the cold alcohol hit his ass, then gradually relaxed. He didn't tense up when he felt a prick of pain as the needle plunged in. He waited a moment, the breath caught in his throat, and there it was. That almost instantaneous—he was always amazed that it only took mere seconds—feeling that washed over him as the drug's powerful effect began to work on his body.

As he straightened up, he could feel himself already begin to drift. He bent down and pulled up his jockstrap and sweatpants. Then he turned around, his eyes blinking slowly as they swept the magnificence of the mahogany-paneled library. Santo came to his side, and a faint smile touched Wyn's lips.

He began walking, slowly and deliberately, toward the spiral stairs that led up to the balcony, which ran around three walls of the library. When he reached the balcony, he went through a hidden jib door built into the balcony bookcases, and on down a hallway to his bedroom. Santo was right behind him, shadowing his every step, following him to the bedroom, to make certain he got there.

Even before they reached the darkness of his inner sanctum, Wyn felt himself begin to float, detaching from this place as if he were a balloon let loose to drift in the sky. Floating above it all up to a better place, a place with no pain, a place with no harsh realities. Floating, floating.

Chapter Five

Teddy de Mornay was comfortably sprawled in the office desk chair at Apple Hill Farm, his feet propped up on the desk. There was a glint of mischief in his eyes as he hung up the telephone, and he smiled widely when Lydia Parsons, his part-time secretary, click-clacked into the office on zebra-print stiletto heels.

"Hey, Lydia," he said. "How are you this morning?"

Lydia Parsons, her hair dyed a flaming red and set in huge swirls that looked as if they'd been fixed in place with cement, returned his smile, revealing big, yellowing teeth. "I'm fine, Teddy," she said. Her eyes narrowed as she looked down at his feet on the desk. "I see you've been out riding this morning."

"Yep," he replied, knocking his cowboy boots together.

"What's the big occasion?" she asked, knowing he despised horses.

"Oh, you know Val," he replied. "She claims old Kaiser doesn't get enough exercise and says I ought to ride him more."

"Aha," Lydia exclaimed. "So you're trying to impress your honey, doing all these things you hate to do."

"Huh," Teddy grunted noncommittally, although trying to please Valerie was exactly what he'd been doing. He'd gotten up early this morning, put on worn cowboy boots and old Levi's, and taken a short ride up into the hills. It had been beautiful, and he'd hated every single minute of it.

"Bet you two had fun this weekend," Lydia said with a lewd wink.

"That, too."

"Good," she said. "Because you've got a busy week ahead of you."

"What's up?" he asked.

She walked over to her desk and picked up a clipboard. "Let's see," she began. "Today we've got the pool cleaners. No big deal. The nursery guys are coming to do some general garden mainte-nance and see about that big maple that was struck by lightning. Then the painter's supposed to be here to do an estimate on paint-ing the guest house, but that's Sammy Burke—" she looked over at him meaningfully—"so you never know if the son of a bitch will show up. He might be on a bender."

Teddy laughed.

She looked down at the clipboard again. "Then there's a stack of paperwork to sign, a bunch of checks to get out, some money transfers to take care of . . ."

"Never mind," Teddy said testily. He reached over and uncere-moniously jerked the clipboard out of her hands, failing to notice the bright purple nail polish with little gold stars she'd had applied at the mall beauty parlor over the weekend.

Lydia stared at him, one hand on a hip, as he perused the clip-board briefly, then tossed it on the desk.

"Damn," he said. "There's a lot to do. And I've got to have dinner with Mrs. de la Rochelle to boot."

"Well . . . ," Lydia said, brushing imaginary lint off of her leopard-print blouse, "there's nothing here that I can't handle by myself, Teddy. Except for signing some of the paperwork. You could do that later or tomorrow. You don't have to stick around."

Teddy looked off into the distance, then back up at Lydia, really seeing her for the first time this morning. *She looks like a circus clown,* he thought uncharitably. *All that makeup: blue eyeshadow, red, red rouge, purplish lipstick. Big red hair. And those clothes! Leopard blouse with tiger skirt. Lots of cheap costume jewelry. Zebra-print stiletto heels with little leopard bows. She's sixty going on sixteen.*

He kept his thoughts to himself, however, because Lydia Parsons was an ace secretary, a great organizer, knew everybody in the area, and was fearless. She could get almost anything she wanted out of anybody. Plus, she was utterly devoted to him, and, he was certain, would hop into the old sack with him at a moment's notice. Not that he wanted her. God, no.

"Do you think you could hold down the fort for the next couple of hours?" he asked at last. "Just till after lunch, say?"

Lydia laughed good-naturedly, bending over his desk, exposing a couple of inches of cleavage. "Sure," she said. "It's done." She eyed him fondly—and conspiratorially. "You never could keep that thing in your pants, could you, Teddy?"

He shrugged. "Why should I?"

"Never was a truer word spoken," she countered with a cackle.

He got to his feet, leaned down, and planted a noisy kiss on Lydia's cheek. "You're an angel from heaven," he said, tapping her on her ample butt.

"And you're the devil from hell," she retorted. "But I love you anyway."

"See you in a bit," he said, already heading out to his car.

"Yeah," she said. "See you." She watched through the window as he hopped into his silver Jaguar convertible and fired it up. The top was down, and as he drove off, his blond hair was tossed about in the wind.

Jeez, she thought, *he is a vision. I wouldn't mind a little of that myself.* But she knew better than to pursue it because she and Teddy had a good thing going as it was. Strictly business. And sometimes, Lydia had decided wisely, that was the best way to keep things. *Besides,* she thought, a smile of wicked pleasure on her purple lips, *I've got Randy, and he's more than enough for one woman to handle. Twenty-three years old and just full of energy!*

Teddy's Jaguar spewed gravel as he pulled out of the drive and onto the highway. It was only five or six miles down the road to the little clapboard cottage that Tiffani Grant leased from him—at a greatly reduced rent—but he was in a hurry to get there. Monday was her day off work, and he didn't spend many Mondays in the country.

When he'd called her after his horseback ride, she'd picked up after several rings, sleep still in her voice. He could just see her, still in bed, bleached blond hair disheveled, a sexy nightie or, better yet, nothing at all on, a sheet draped over those big breasts, curled up in a big warm bed waiting for him. Teddy could feel a rise in his pants just thinking about it, and stepped on the gas.

When he neared the dirt road that led to the old cottage, he began to brake, then made the right turn off the highway and sped the hundred feet or so to the house, the car leaving a dust cloud in its wake. Circling around in the back to park, he drove across the lawn and pulled in close to the house where his car wouldn't be visible from the highway. Even though he owned the property, he didn't want anybody to see his car parked there for too long a time.

No need to give any of the old biddies around here an excuse to talk, he thought. *They all think I'm a perfect gentleman with real class. One of the few city people who treats the locals with the respect they deserve.* He laughed aloud. If they only knew! He loved fooling them, and he loved the sneaking around. That was part of the fun for him, because he had a real taste for the illicit. In fact, he had never really enjoyed sex much unless it involved some kind of subterfuge.

He hopped out of the car and bounded up the wooden steps to the back door, knocking on it a couple of times with his knuckles. When she didn't respond immediately, he tried the knob. *Damn!* he thought. *It's locked.* But before he could dash around to the front, he could hear Tiffani hurrying through the kitchen, headed to the door.

After fumbling with locks, she opened the door a crack and looked up at him. "Teddy," she said, smiling lasciviously.

He pushed his way in, then turned around and pulled her to him. She had a big pink towel wrapped around her voluptuous body, and her long, bleach-streaked hair was still wet from the shower.

"Hey, Tiff," he said, his hands already on her buttocks, pushing her hard against him. His mouth was on her neck then, kissing and licking and nibbling.

"Wait, Teddy," she said, trying to wriggle out of his grasp. "Just a minute."

He lifted his head and looked at her. "What is it, babe?" he said.

She smiled again, then slammed the door shut behind her and jerked off the towel. It fell to the floor in a heap.

Teddy stared at her body, his eyes sweeping her up and down, widening at the sight of her large creamy breasts with their raspberry nipples, lingering momentarily on her firm creamy thighs, fixing themselves hungrily on the completely shaved honeypot that lay between them. He groaned aloud, then threw himself against her, his hands everywhere at once.

Tiffani giggled gleefully and struggled against him. "Come on, Teddy," she gasped. "Not here. Let's go into the bedroom."

He followed her across the kitchen's worn linoleum, through the little dining room and living room, and down a hallway to one of the two bedrooms, getting out of his his polo shirt as they went. In the bedroom, he quickly pulled off his cowboy boots and tossed them on the floor, then loosened his belt and took off his jeans, throwing them on top of the boots.

Tiffani watched him, taking delight in his long, lean torso and his well-defined musculature. He was so unlike most of the men she knew. Teddy was so clean and blond and hard, in shape but not a steroid freak either. Most of the men she'd been with in the last few years—and there'd been too many to count—had been former football players gone to fat; hairy, dirty bikers with big beer bellies; or rangy, raw, or clumsy farm boys or tradesmen who didn't really give her much pleasure. There'd been more than a few of the local bodybuilders, and she liked their bodies, for sure. But they seemed more pleased with themselves than anything she could offer them. With most all the men, Tiffani often reflected, it had been the old in and out, slam, bam, thank you, ma'am. Except most of them had omitted the thank-you. She could count the real good lovers—the ones who wanted to give her pleasure as well as get it—on one hand.

Teddy was so different. She watched, entranced, when he

started to take off his jockey shorts, but quickly stopped him with a hand and a knowing look and went down on her knees in front of him. She slowly began pulling his shorts down with her long, pink-lacquered fingernails, looking up at him reverentially for a moment, then straight ahead at the prize between his legs.

As it sprang free, her tongue darted out and began licking his cock slowly, delicately, and lovingly, all the while gradually easing his jockey shorts down to the floor. He stepped out of them and put his hands on her head, guiding it onto his engorged phallus. Tiffani took it, going down as far as she possibly could, then began to suck on it furiously.

"Ahhhh," Teddy groaned, thrusting himself at her, "Tiff, you're going to make me come."

She eased her mouth away and stood up facing him. Teddy reached over and took a breast in each of his hands and began stroking them, thrumming her nipples with his thumbs. Tiffani gasped and pushed up against him, reaching down for his cock. He slid one hand down between her thighs and began stroking her soft shaved mound, excited by its nakedness, then slowly put a finger in her, feeling her wetness.

Tiffani trembled and whimpered. "Oh, please, Teddy," she begged. "Please."

Unable to wait any longer, he pushed her onto the bed and mounted her, her legs spread wide to welcome him. They were both in a frenzy of desire, and Teddy began thrusting away like a man possessed, Tiffani grinding against him with all her might. It was over almost as quickly as it had begun, Teddy bellowing as he heaved against her in release, and Tiffani squirming wildly against him, squealing ecstatically, kicking her legs as she contracted with one climax after another.

He collapsed on top of her, then rolled off onto his back, the two of them gasping for breath. When she could speak, Tiffani rolled to her side and kissed his cheek. "Can you stay a while?" she asked.

"An hour or so," he said. Then he looked at her. "Why?" he asked. "You got something special in mind?"

Tiffani giggled. "Maybe," she said. She sat up in bed and threw her legs over the side, her back to him. She reached over to the bedside cabinet and opened a drawer, rummaging around inside it. When she turned back around, she held up a small glass vial of white powder. A tiny metal spoon was attached to the top of it.

"Lookee what I've got," she said, wiggling her hand.

Teddy's eyes were riveted to the vial of white powder. "Wow, baby," he said, sitting up. "You won the lottery or what?"

Tiffani's brown eyes gleamed with mischief. "Something like that."

"Come on," he said. "Where'd you get it? I know that's not any of my stuff."

She spread out on the bed, and he stared down at her. "A little birdie," she said teasingly.

"Aw, Tiff," he cajoled. "Where?"

"You know that bar where I used to work?" she said.

He nodded. It was a local joint that catered to a crowd of hard partyers, mostly in their twenties to forties, a lot of them divorced and on the make, most all of them hourly workers.

"Well, I was in there the other night, just having a drink. You know. Anyway, this guy I used to know—he was a regular customer when I worked there—he gave it to me."

"You mean he just *gave* it to you?" he asked incredulously.

She stared at him a moment. "Why not?" she asked. "We're friends, sort of. You're not jealous, are you, Teddy?"

"No," he said, dropping onto the bed beside her. "That's stupid. Why would I be jealous?"

"Oh, I don't know," she said coyly. "You just don't look very happy suddenly."

"You're crazy, Tiff," he said. "But it doesn't make sense, does it. This guy just *gives* you a couple of hundred bucks worth of coke? Don't tell me he doesn't want something for it."

"If that's what you're thinking," she said, "you're wrong. He's just being nice to me 'cause I used to fix him up with girls. Besides, he's always got lots of coke 'cause he's a dealer."

Teddy's eyes sparkled with glee, then he laughed. "You know some interesting characters, Tiff."

"I guess so," she said. She sat up and unscrewed the bottle cap, then spooned out some coke, carefully holding it steady. "Want some?"

Teddy sat up on one elbow and, when she had the spoon under his nose, took a deep snort, a finger closing one nostril while he sucked the precious powder up the other. The taste was terrible, medicinal, but he knew the effect would be highly pleasant.

He lay back and watched as Tiffani snorted some, then replaced the cap on the bottle. She slid out of bed and turned to him. "I'll be right back," she said.

He watched her walk toward the bathroom. *Amazing body,* he thought. *Straight from heaven.* She never ceased to arouse him, even though she wasn't exactly the brightest woman he knew. She was pretty dense actually. But what the hell?

Tiffani was great for sex. Loved a little kink, too. She was like forbidden fruit, now that he thought about it: from the wrong side of the tracks, too much makeup, too much hair, cheap sexy clothes. Completely unsuitable for somebody like him and just his cup of tea. A lot like Lydia must have been forty years ago, except Lydia was smart. Beyond that . . . well, she was only amusing in bed, but that's all he wanted her for.

Tiffani came back into the bedroom, her large breasts bobbing against her rib cage. She slid onto the bed and put an arm across his chest. "You're so quiet," she said. "You tired, baby?"

"Had a rough weekend."

"Ah," she said. "Did that horse doctor fuck your brains out?"

"No," he said, irritated that she would bring Valerie into the conversation. "She had an early night yesterday because she was up nearly all night Saturday. At your boss's place, as a matter of fact."

She lifted her head and looked down at him. "You're kidding, really?"

"Really," he said.

"What did she say about him?"

"Nothing," he replied. "She didn't even see him. Just that muscle freak who works for him."

"God," she said, shivering involuntarily, "that guy's so weird. He scares me half to death. But the whole place scares me."

"Why?" Teddy asked without any real curiosity. "That sounds pretty stupid to me."

"It's not stupid!" Tiffani replied. "I've been working there part-time ever since they bought that place. Conrad bought it three years ago, and he's lived there for a year. And you know what? I still haven't seen him, the owner, except maybe if you count one time when I think I saw him at the window, staring outside."

"What did he look like?" Teddy asked idly. He could feel the cocaine begin to work its magic.

"Who knows?" Tiffani said. "All I saw was a man standing there. Not Santo 'cause I could tell if it'd been him." She lay back on the pillow again and slowly ran a finger down Teddy's chest.

"And you know what else?"

"What?" he asked, indulging her.

"I've never even been in that house. I've never been anywhere but the office in the stable," she said. "That creepy Santo runs the place like some kind of Nazi. I never see anybody but him and that awful old man Helmut. Sometimes his wife."

"Who's that?" Teddy asked.

"Helmut Reinhardt," she said. "He and his spooky wife, Gerda, live in a little house on the estate. They moved in when Conrad bought the place. At least I guess they did."

She ran her fingers through Teddy's hair. "Helmut, he's like a handyman, and his old lady's the cook and housekeeper. They're both real quiet, like the walking dead or something. Real zombies."

"Yeah," Teddy said, "but so what?"

"Think about it, Teddy," she said passionately. "You've got Santo, who's like some kind of weirdo giant freak with his shaved head and earrings and muscles and tattoos. You've got Conrad, who might as well be a ghost. Then you've got the old zombie couple, Gerda and Helmut. You're not there, so you don't see how creepy it is."

She paused and looked at him with a pouty expression. "But you know what the worst thing is? They don't give me the time of day. Any of them. It's like I'm garbage or something as far as they're concerned."

"You shouldn't pay any attention to them, Tiff," he said, taking her hand and moving it down to his crotch. "Conrad probably has them under his thumb. Probably doesn't like for the help to get to know each other too well. He's just another paranoid rich jerk," Teddy went on, easing a hand between her thighs.

"Everybody says you're rich, too, Teddy," she said.

"Huh? I do all right." He frowned. "I'm sure not rich like that creep. But then I'm not into drugs or the Mafia or whatever his game is."

"I just don't understand why he's so secretive," she countered, now stroking Teddy's cock firmly.

"Probably doesn't want you to see all those hot chicks he's got tied up down in the cellar," he said, grinning at her. "All of them just waiting to fulfill his every command."

Tiffani laughed. "God, I wouldn't doubt it," she said. "But I think that's what *you'd* like." She squeezed his penis.

"Hey," he said, "watch it! That's not replaceable, you know."

Tiffani laughed again. "But seriously, Teddy, it gives me the heebie-jeebies just to think about it. All that money. I've never seen so much come in and go out of a place in my life. It's hard to imagine being that rich. And the horses! Some of them worth a fortune. But you know what?"

"What?" Teddy rasped, completely losing interest in the conversation as she aroused him.

"I've never even seen him ride one," she said. "I've never seen anybody ride one."

"Probably can't," Teddy said, working a finger inside her. "They're just a hobby or something. Anyway, who needs him and his horses?" he said. "Look what we've got here."

She looked down between his legs and giggled. "Boy, are you so right, Teddy."

"I think we can make you forget all about Conrad and the freaks out there, Tiff," he said in a whisper. He pulled her to him and began kissing her ardently, his hand working between her thighs. "I love that shave job, babe," he whispered. "Really turns me on."

"I'm so glad you did it," she said. "It's turning me on, too."

"It's a beginning."

"Oh, yeah?" she said, pushing harder against him, totally

immersed in the moment, thoughts of Stonelair already out of her mind. "Oh, Teddy," she cooed, "you make me feel so good. You excite me so much."

"That's what it's all about, babe," he said, shoving himself up inside her.

"Oh, God," she moaned, "I'm so lucky. How'd I ever get so lucky?"

Chapter Six

The summer sun was still bright when Valerie drove up the long, twisting gravel lane that led to her mother's house, a rambling Italianate Victorian. The house was perfectly sited in a heavily wooded copse atop a hill that sloped gently down to lush meadows and a meandering stream. The Berkshires, clothed in their summer greenery, were visible from its eastern windows, and the Catskills, on the far side of the Hudson River, rose regally to meet the eye from the west.

This evening, its majesty seemed more depressing to Valerie than usual. *Maybe it's just that I'm not in a very good mood*, she thought, dreading the dinner she was about to have with her mother and Teddy.

She drove around to the parking area in back of the house and pulled in next to Teddy's silvery Jaguar. *So*, she thought, *he's already here, no doubt enjoying himself immensely, telling Mother every detail of last weekend that she doesn't already know*. Valerie wasn't surprised, although she couldn't help being miffed, because Teddy and her mother had long since formed a mutual admiration society. They seemed to genuinely enjoy one another's company.

Valerie quickly checked her reflection in the rearview mirror, patting down her unruly hair. It was pulled back into its customary long braid, the end of which fell across one shoulder onto her breast, but the top and sides had managed to create a frizzy halo about her face as usual.

"Ah, well," she said to her reflection, "you'll just have to do. Even if Teddy and Mother would like to see you coiffed to perfection with a real ladylike 'do."

She swung out of the Jeep and began brushing dog hair off the black linen pants and blouse she'd changed into. It had been her hope that the outfit would match, and thus conceal, Elvis's hair, which invariably managed to attach itself to everything she owned. No such luck, she noted. Elvis, whom she'd left at home in deference to her mother's wishes, was decidedly blacker and shinier than the black linen she wore.

Oh, well, she thought. *This too will have to do. Love me or leave me!*

She heard familiar voices in the garden and walked over to the iron gate that led into it and peered inside. Teddy, dapper as usual in a dark blue blazer, crisp white linen trousers, and a light blue shirt with a daring apricot-colored tie, and Marguerite, a vision of loveliness in a cream suit with emerald trim and an emerald blouse, were strolling toward her, arm in arm, their voices animated in conversation. Teddy's hair, she noticed, was sunny blond perfection, and Marguerite's, a stunning silvery white, was fixed in an elegant French twist. Neither of them had a hair out of place.

Of course, she thought with wry amusement.

Suddenly Teddy looked up. Seeing her, he began waving and calling to her. She waved back.

"We'll be in shortly," she heard her mother call. "Get yourself a drink."

"Okay," Valerie called back, nodding. She turned and walked to the big screened-in back porch and on through it into the kitchen.

"Well, look who's finally here," Effie said, wiping her hands on a towel. She tapped a dark cheek with a finger. "Right here," the tiny, white-haired woman said.

Valerie leaned over and kissed her on the cheek where she'd indicated. "You look great, Effie," she said, straightening up. "And whatever you're cooking up in here smells terrific."

"It's a surprise," Effie said, "so don't ask. I'm just glad you and Teddy came to dinner. It gives me a chance to do some real cooking. Your mother eats like a bird, so I hardly get to do much."

"I guess she's on one of her diets," Valerie said.

"She's always on a diet," Effie said grumpily. "One more disgusting than the next. It's a wonder she doesn't make herself sick, she's so skinny."

"Some things never change," Valerie said, and, she reflected, they really didn't. Effie had complained for as long as she could remember about Marguerite's eating habits, among many other things, but had remained devoted to her nevertheless. "I'm going to get a drink, Effie. Do you want me to mix something up for you?"

Effie grinned. "Thanks, Val," she replied, "but I already had a little nip of gin."

"Aha!" Valerie said. "I should've known, but I won't tell." Effie's nips of gin were a deeply guarded secret between Valerie and the old woman, a secret that everyone knew about.

"You better not," Effie replied, "or I'll tell Teddy some of your secrets."

"Blackmail!" Valerie cried with a laugh. "I'll see you in a bit," she said, heading out the kitchen door to the butler's pantry.

Scanning the bottles there, she quickly decided on a vodka and tonic, with lots of vodka. She didn't often drink anything other than wine, but tonight, she thought, a little fortifying medication was in order. *My mother by herself is excuse enough,* she told herself, *but Mother and Teddy conspiring together ought to make drinking straight out of the bottle permissible.*

Taking her drink, she began to roam the big quiet house, going from room to room, sipping as she went. Her eyes swept over the antiques with their beautiful silk, velvet, and leather upholstery. She scanned the walls, hung with luxurious silks from Lyons or the finest hand-blocked papers from Zuber in Rixheim. She glimpsed the elegant chandeliers of crystal and ormolu that hung suspended from the ceilings of nearly every room, and eyed the paintings that decorated the walls. Family portraits from France, Denmark, England, and America were rivaled by fine landscapes from all over Europe; plus drawings and watercolors, some of them nearly five hundred years old, hung chockablock in virtually every room.

Like the art, bibelots and treasures of all kinds covered almost every surface. Chinese and Japanese porcelains, Meissen and Sèvres, ormolu mounted vases, flower arrangements made of semiprecious stones and gold, photographs in fantastically carved silver or gilt frames.

The house was an Aladdin's den that would make an auctioneer's pulse race, she'd often thought. Many of the treasures had come from the big apartment in New York City that they'd sold after her father died. Memories of her childhood—both in the formal city apartment and here in the more casual atmosphere of the country—always swept over her when she came here. It was almost as if her entire past were contained in this one house.

Perhaps, she thought, *that's why I stay away from here as much as possible.*

A familiar sadness began to pervade her usually bright spirits, infusing her with a sense that all of this material beauty was part of a world gone by, a lifestyle that had all but ceased to exist, and a way of life that she had once been part of but never really belonged to. Even the familiarity with every object her eye rested upon did not dispel the feeling that she was an interloper.

In one of the drawing rooms she lingered over a favorite drawing, a Berthe Morisot of a field. Then she picked up an old black-and-white photograph of her father on horseback. He looked so handsome in his riding habit, she thought as she replaced it on the table. She meandered on into the music room and lightly stroked the ivory keys on the antique Bösendorfer, the same piano on which she'd learned to play. She climbed the curving stairs and went down the hallway to her old bedroom, where she sat on the lacy canopied bed that had once been hers. Looking at the antique dressing table, its surface still cluttered with crystal bottles of different scents and a monogrammed silver dressing set, she remembered the countless times she'd sat before its mirror, trying to make herself into the woman that her mother wanted her to be. To no avail.

No, she thought idly. *I was never the girl she wanted and haven't become the woman she wanted me to be. But then, I never really felt that I belonged here or that I was even an important part of life here.*

There had been a time when she would have given anything to fit in with these people and what most thought was their fabulous lifestyle. She'd really struggled to be the daughter her mother and father wanted her to be.

But no more. *I don't want to live like them. I want to live my own life, the way I want to live it. I want to be* me.

It sounded so simple, she thought, but she'd found it very difficult to break the bonds. It had been hard to see the disappointment on her parents' faces, to hear the recrimination in their voices, to deal with the constant pressures that they exerted on her. But despite all the battles, she was finally living her life in a way that she found fulfilling.

Her thoughts were interrupted by the tinkling of her mother's laughter and the sound of Teddy's doting voice. She took a sip of her drink and sighed. *Might as well go face the music,* she decided. She retraced her steps downstairs.

Teddy and Marguerite were standing in the marble-floored entrance hall, drinks in hand, and looked up at her as she came down the stairs.

"Hi, you two," Valerie said cheerfully.

"Hello, dear," Marguerite said, her eyes sweeping appraisingly over her daughter's appearance. She offered up a cheek for a kiss.

"It's good to see you, Mother," Valerie said.

"I'm glad you could fit me into your busy schedule," Marguerite said with a light laugh.

Valerie didn't reply, but kept a smile fixed on her face.

"Hi," Teddy said, brushing her lips with his, then putting an arm around her shoulders and hugging her to him. "We've been out looking at the garden," he said unnecessarily. "It's incredible what your mother does practically by herself."

"Oh, Teddy," Marguerite said, "you don't have to humor me. I know it's a disaster, but what can one do?" She spied Effie out of the corner of her eye. "Oh, look," she said, "Effie's ready to serve. Shall we go in?"

"Let's," Teddy said, offering Marguerite his arm. She took it, and he winked at Valerie. "Can you manage?" he asked.

"It's twenty or thirty feet, but I think I can manage it," Valerie joked.

Darkness had descended outside, and in Marguerite's dining room the silver and crystal sparkled in the candlelight. They had finished Effie's delicious feast of chilled avocado and cucumber soup, tiny stuffed Cornish game hens grilled with a ginger and plum sauce, fresh asparagus drizzled with Hollandaise sauce, wild rice with Portobelo mushrooms, and a salad of micro-arugula, endive, radicchio, and baby oak with a balsamic vinaigrette. She had just served the dessert, homemade ginger ice cream topped with fresh organically grown strawberries and raspberries smothered in a syrupy kirsch sauce.

"Thanks, Effie," Teddy said, "this looks delicious. Everything was really wonderful."

"Thank you, sir," Effie replied as she headed back into the kitchen.

"She never ceases to amaze me," Valerie said appreciatively. "I don't know how she does it. Cooking and cleaning and—"

"She *is* good," Marguerite interjected, "but I'm trying to teach her to rely less on sauces. They're so awfully rich, don't you think?" She glanced at Teddy speculatively, and he didn't disappoint her.

"Everything was very rich," he readily agreed. "You certainly couldn't eat like this all the time."

"Indeed not," Marguerite said. "It would spell certain ruin for both your health and your figure. And as for her cleaning, Val, dear"—Marguerite looked at her daughter pointedly and shrugged—"well, she barely hits the high spots with a feather duster anymore. I do think it's awfully sweet of you to be so loyal to her, but I sometimes think that Effie is taking advantage of me."

"Oh, Mother," Valerie burst out in barely concealed astonishment. "Effie's devoted herself to you for over forty years. I hardly think that if she slows down a little bit at her age, you should call that taking advantage of you."

Marguerite haughtily ignored her daughter's outburst entirely. She turned her attention back to Teddy. "The wine was divine," she said, "and perfect with this meal."

"Why, thank you, Marguerite," he said. "I have a fairly good cellar now, but it'll take a long time and a lot more money to get it where I want it. The Puligny Montrachet was a . . ."

Valerie withdrew into herself, eating the ice cream and berries and watching the easy exchanges between her mother and Teddy. *He's just her type,* she thought somewhat resentfully. *Handsome, rich, and charming to boot.* But equally as important was that Teddy came from the same background and class that they did. Her marriage to him would be considered an alliance between two descendants of the same gloriously aristocratic French Huguenot heritage, and any foibles he might have would be overlooked by her mother because of that illustrious background. Her father, she knew, would agree wholeheartedly about Teddy. Valerie, while not disrespecting her lineage, held it in no particular regard. It seemed so remote in time and meaning to her that she really never gave it a thought.

It's no wonder she and Teddy get along so well, Valerie thought, nibbling on the kirsch-soaked berries. *He's as much of a snob about his lineage as she is. Too bad Mother's not younger.*

She saw Marguerite adjust one of the cabochon emeralds at her ears and regarded her more closely. Despite the resentments she harbored toward her mother, Valerie had to admit that Marguerite Louise de Coligny de la Rochelle was a woman every bit as formidable as her name implied. Even though she was sixty-five years old, she had a flawless and creamy, if subtly lined, complexion. She had prominent, elegant cheekbones, a high forehead, a straight nose, and wide lips that were just full enough. Her silvery hair, even white teeth, trim figure, and immaculate grooming made her seem almost ageless.

Her vanity about her appearance had always astounded Valerie. Her mother spent hours at the dressmaker's, choosing fabrics and being fitted, as she had all of her clothes custom made. They were usually faithful and expensive copies of Chanel and other great designers. Then she spent hours with the hairdresser, the pedicurist, the manicurist, and untold time at home grooming,

grooming, grooming. She went to bed slathered virtually from head to toe in some lotion or other, and never permitted the bright sun to touch her skin.

Yet Marguerite had told Valerie she would never submit to the surgeon's knife or dye her hair. She considered women who did beneath her, contemptible really, slaves to unintelligent and ill-formed notions about beauty. These poor women, willing victims, she averred, were products of the brash, tacky, and utterly taste-less view of beauty promulgated by an aesthetically impoverished mass media.

"Valerie, my dear!"

Marguerite's cultured voice interrupted her reverie. She found her mother staring at her quizzically.

"I'm sorry," Valerie said. "I missed what you were saying."

"You haven't been paying any attention to us, dear," Marguerite said in a chiding manner. The emerald on the finger she pointed accusingly at Valerie glinted in the light. "How like you. We were discussing Teddy's business, Val. Something I should think you would take an interest in. He's been having a wonderful year with the stock market."

"Oh," Valerie said, "that's great, Teddy." She wondered why he never discussed his business with her.

Teddy smiled indulgently, as if Valerie couldn't possibly be capable of comprehending the complexities of this business-related conversation.

"You're so clever, Teddy," Marguerite enthused, "and I think you're to be congratulated."

"Well, trading definitely has its ups and downs," Teddy replied. "But I *have* had an extraordinarily good run recently. Of course, the way the market's been lately, Marguerite, who wouldn't?"

"Yes," she allowed, "but not everyone knows how to take advantage of it the way you do, Teddy. I guess bloodlines always tell, don't they? It's all in the genes."

Teddy laughed. "Maybe," he said. "But I doubt if I'll ever be the investment guru my father was."

Marguerite tinkled laughter. "Well, my dear, I think your father would be very proud of you."

"Well, thank you," Teddy said with an amiability that he didn't feel. He really didn't know or care what the late, great Theodore de Mornay would have thought. He'd hated the son of a bitch while he was alive and had grown to like him no more in death. The same with his mother, Claudine, who'd been nothing more than an apparition to him, coming and going in ball gowns, jewels, and expensive perfumes before spending the last of her fifty-odd years a virtual prisoner in her own bedroom, addicted to prescription drugs and alcohol.

"I wish Dockering Wainwright did so well by me," Marguerite said, worrying the emeralds at her neck with long slender fingers. She looked over at Valerie. The significance of the look was not lost on her daughter.

Valerie cleared her throat and placed a smile on her lips. "Dock's been handling your affairs forever, Mother," she said, "and he seems to have done a fine job. Dad always thought so," she added. She looked at Teddy. "That's not to say you wouldn't, Teddy, but Dad always had Dock do it . . . and, well . . ."

"I wouldn't think of encroaching on the great Dockering Wainwright's territory," Teddy quickly interrupted. "I'm sure he's a great investment advisor."

"Nevertheless," Marguerite said, "he certainly doesn't seem to get *your* results, Teddy. If you ask me, he's half asleep at the wheel."

"I think Dock's on top of things," Valerie said. "He may be old-fashioned and conservative, certainly he's not a risk taker, but he's astute and dependable nonetheless."

"Is he?" Marguerite asked. "I may be an old woman who knows very little about these things," she continued in an overweeningly self-deprecating manner, "but it seems to me that my little portfolio has hardly grown in value at all. Needless to say, it naturally follows that my dividends haven't either. And in a market that everybody knows is going great guns. Why, half the real estate sold around here is for cash! Total asking price, if not more. It's all these smart young men like Teddy from New York." She paused and looked directly at her daughter.

"Maybe you're right, Mother," Valerie conceded, "but I've never heard a complaint against Dock." She looked directly at her mother then. "Anyway, it's really not for me to decide who handles your affairs, is it?"

"No," Marguerite said, "it certainly is not." Her focus shifted back to Teddy again. "I think it's high time I gave old Dock a little goose," she said. "I suppose we all get a little complacent at times, don't we?"

"It's easy to do," Teddy said. "Especially when it's not your own money you're handling. Or if you don't have some sort of special interest in your client's welfare."

"Well said, Teddy," Marguerite pronounced. "I'll get on the telephone to Dock tomorrow, then give you a call to let you know what he has to say for himself. If that's okay with you, that is."

"Of course, Marguerite," Teddy replied. "I think it's a sound idea."

"Good, that's settled, then," Marguerite said. She took a sip of water, the huge emerald on her finger catching the light again, then set the glass down and turned the full wattage of her gaze on Valerie. "Valerie, my dear," she said, "I think there's something you haven't told me."

"Told you?" Valerie knew right away what her mother was talking about, but she decided to play dumb. She knew it would antagonize Marguerite if she didn't give her the satisfaction of an immediate answer. She also knew that she was being petty, but she decided to make her mother weasel the answer out of her. That would punish her and Teddy for discussing the engagement ring behind her back. "What's that, Mother?" she asked. "What haven't I told you?"

Marguerite's eyes took on a steely expression, but it was fleeting and quickly replaced by a laugh of amusement. "Valerie, my dear," she said, "you've been working far too hard with those filthy beasts. I can't think what else would make you forget something so important."

Teddy cleared his throat and smiled. "Val," he said, "she might be referring to a little something that happened over the weekend. Remember?"

Valerie decided to quit playing her little game. "Oh!" she cried. "How could I!" She looked at Teddy, who smiled endearingly at her. "Oh, Teddy, I'm sorry," she said. "I feel like such an idiot."

"Don't worry about it," he said good-naturedly.

Valerie glanced over at her mother. "Teddy and I . . . we . . . he gave me an engagement ring last weekend," she finally managed. She couldn't bring herself to say, We're engaged.

"Splendid," Marguerite pronounced, as if surprised. "Absolutely splendid." She reached over and touched her daughter's hand. "I'm so pleased for you," she said. Then she reached over and patted Teddy's hand. "Both of you. It's wonderful news."

Valerie nodded. "I'm glad you're happy, Mother," she said in a quiet voice.

"You must show me your ring, Val, dear," Marguerite said.

"Uh, well," Valerie sputtered, feeling herself blush hotly. "Oh, I . . . I forgot to put it on."

"You what!" Marguerite exclaimed. She stared at her daughter in disbelief.

"Oh, Val," Teddy groaned. "I noticed you weren't wearing it, but I thought that surely you had it tucked away in your handbag or someplace to surprise your mother."

"I'm sorry," Valerie murmured. "I was in such a rush to change clothes and get here after work, and besides"—she shrugged and smiled—"I'm just not used to it yet."

"No harm done," Teddy said in a forgiving voice.

Valerie turned to her mother. "It's really beautiful, Mother," she said. "And huge! You'll love it. I promise to come by with it one day this week after work."

"I do hope so," Marguerite said, not adding that Teddy had shown her the ring the day he'd bought it. "Teddy's made such an effort on your behalf, and I should think you'd be terribly happy with so generous a gift."

"I . . . I've just been so busy and everything," Valerie said. "I was on call at the clinic this weekend, and there was an emergency. And—"

"That clinic," Marguerite said with a frown of distaste. "It's always that clinic. I knew it. You spend far too much time there. And what sort of emergency could possibly make you forget you'd become engaged?" She looked at her daughter questioningly.

"Stonelair," Teddy said grimly, not giving Valerie the opportunity to answer for herself. "The mystery man."

"Oh, dear, no," Marguerite said, visibly shaken. "Don't tell me you've been out to that dreadful place, Val, dear. I've been told on the best authority that he's some sort of drug baron or something. Is it true?"

Valerie shrugged. "Who knows?" she replied. "I was taking care of a sick horse. I didn't even meet the man." She paused, then added jocularly: "But I didn't see mountains of drugs or guns or anything."

No one laughed.

"Well," Marguerite said in her most indignant voice, "it seems to me it would almost have to be drugs or something equally disgusting to support a place like that. Not even the young Wall Street tycoons that are buying everything in sight around here could afford that place." She paused, looking at her daughter significantly. "Besides," she continued, "nobody of any importance knows him as far as *I* know. And he's so secretive that I'm certain something evil is going on out there."

"I don't know anything about any of the gossip you've heard," Valerie countered defiantly, "but they've asked me to take care of all their animals. Personally."

"Oh, dear," Marguerite said, her eyes widening in alarm.

"You're surely not thinking of taking them up on their offer," Teddy said.

Valerie didn't answer him at once.

"Well, you're not, are you?" he prodded.

"I don't know yet," Valerie replied. But it was at that precise moment that she made up her mind to accept Conrad's offer and become Stonelair's exclusive veterinarian. She would make certain to discuss it with the clinic staff tomorrow.

"You don't know yet?" Marguerite parroted. "I must say I'm surprised by your cavalier attitude. I shouldn't think you would even entertain the notion." Her voice and demeanor were disdainful in the extreme. "He must be some sort of horribly evil Mafioso or some such thing. Why, I'm told that the beastly man has turned down every invitation that's been extended to him."

"What's so evil about that?" Valerie asked. "I mean, how does that make him a drug lord or Mafioso? Maybe he just doesn't like to mingle."

"Well, it makes him antisocial if nothing else," Marguerite said. "Which is highly suspicious, if you ask me."

"I haven't seen the place," Teddy interjected, "but I've talked to a couple of local guys who've been in there to do work. From what they say, the guy's spent millions on the place. Brought all the labor from down south, Florida or someplace. He sure seems to have bottomless pockets. I know that I couldn't even begin to do what he's done to that place."

Valerie had been watching Teddy, and she couldn't help but detect the somewhat cocky manner he assumed when he felt bested. Nor did she miss the distinct note of resentment in his voice. *He's jealous of Conrad, she realized. Jealous of his money, if nothing else.*

"Well, enough said about such an unsavory and frightening subject," Marguerite announced. "Let's have coffee on the porch, shall we? It's lovely out." She smiled at them both.

"Just what the doctor ordered," Teddy said.

Marguerite rose, and Teddy followed suit, taking her arm to lead her out to the screened-in porch. Valerie trailed along behind them. Effie had already lit candles on the porch, and it looked invitingly casual after the formality of the dinner. Teddy saw Marguerite to her chair, and Valerie spread out on a big, comfortable, old wicker sofa.

"I'll be right back, ladies," Teddy said, excusing himself to the bathroom.

The instant he was out of earshot, Marguerite turned her gaze on Valerie. Even in the dim, flickering light of candles, Valerie could see her mother's look of determination.

"I hope you're giving Teddy the attention he so richly deserves," Marguerite said. "I must say, you certainly seem somewhat lackadaisical about your engagement."

"I've just been very busy, Mother," Valerie answered defensively.

"Busy! That tiresome excuse!" Marguerite leaned toward her daughter. "You must not forget that Teddy can give you everything any young woman could ever want. He has money, Val, and what's more, he's very good at making more. And it doesn't hurt that he's also extremely popular. Everybody adores him."

"Or fears him," Valerie said.

"What?" Marguerite looked shocked. "You're being fanciful. Ridiculous. Why would anyone fear Teddy?"

"Well," Valerie said, "from what I hear, he's not so popular with some of his tenants, Mother."

"Perhaps they don't pay their rent on time," she countered. "Anyway, how could you possibly concern yourself with what some tenant would say?"

"They're people, too," Valerie said quietly.

"Humpf!" Marguerite dismissed her daughter's remark and straightened her shoulders for another assault. "And how could you forget to wear your engagement ring, Val? That's positively insulting. Teddy tells me that you won't set a date for the wedding yet. What in heaven's name is wrong with you?"

"Nothing's wrong with me," Valerie said with rising anger. "I'm just not ready yet."

Her mother's eyes caught hers once again. "It's inevitable, Valerie, dear," she said with a quiet forcefulness. "There's nobody else, and Teddy is ideal. Certainly more of a man than I would've ever dreamed it possible for you to attract."

Valerie swallowed, determined not to lose her temper, but she couldn't allow her mother's last remark to pass. *That was the old Valerie,* she told herself. *The Valerie who would sit and take whatever her mother felt like dishing out.*

"Why do you always have to put me down?" she asked.

Marguerite was taken aback for a moment, then plunged on. "Well, face it, Val, dear," she said, "you were never a great beauty. Now that you're older, you do have a certain . . . appeal, I must admit. But you didn't have that growing up. Besides which, you were always a little . . . strange . . . a little peculiar. That hasn't changed."

She smiled at Valerie, a smile that a stranger might assume was sweetness itself, but that Valerie knew to be filled with scornful disdain. "You certainly weren't very social," Marguerite went on, "with your nose always in a book. Or playing with your precious pets instead of other children."

Valerie digested her mother's diatribe in silence, wounded by the dispassionate way in which she described a shy little girl starved for love. *Despite all of my resolutions to the contrary*, she thought, *I still want this woman's approval and love. And no matter how independent I tell myself I am, I still let her hurt me.*

She finally cleared her throat and replied. "If you'll remember, Mother," Valerie said, "there weren't a lot of girls you'd let me play with. You didn't think that most of the ones I tried to make friends with were good enough."

"One has to protect a child from the . . . less desirable elements in society, Valerie," Marguerite replied. "And you seemed drawn to that element."

"Then when I got older," Valerie said, "you always made me feel like I wasn't pretty enough or clever enough. You always made me want to run and hide from other girls—and boys—my age because you thought they were so much brighter and better-looking than me."

"They usually were," Marguerite said firmly. "I pointed them out as examples for you to follow. Don't you see, Val? I was trying to get you to make something better of yourself. But no, you couldn't be bothered with your hair and clothes, could you? You couldn't be bothered with making yourself attractive to suitable young men. Thank *God* Teddy came along. And thank God you'd become a more presentable young lady by then and outgrown some of your silly shyness and backwardness. At least Teddy could see the possibilities."

Valerie was growing increasingly furious but decided to hold her tongue. She knew that any further argument with her mother would be an exercise in futility.

"Ah," Marguerite exclaimed with delight, "here comes our handsome young man now. I was just talking about what a wonder you are, Teddy."

"Me?" he asked in an amused voice. He stood by Valerie, waiting for her to make room for him on the wicker couch, then sat down next to her and took one of her hands in his. "I hope your daughter feels the same way," he said.

Valerie looked at him and smiled. "I think I'll keep you guessing," she replied. But deep down inside, she was beginning to feel as if Teddy was anything but the wonder her mother thought he was, and she wanted nothing more than to get up and go home to Elvis.

They sipped their coffee, chatting a while longer, until Teddy pointedly looked at his watch. "It's getting late," he said, "and I'm afraid we've kept you up past your bedtime, Marguerite."

"Not at all," she said. "I've enjoyed every minute of it."

"Well, I've got a very early morning," Valerie said, "and I'd better get going."

"I forgot," Teddy said. "Being up here all week loafing around, I tend to forget that you have a job to go to."

"It's too bad you couldn't arrange to be off this week, Val dear," Marguerite said.

Valerie rose to her feet and stifled a yawn. "It was impossible, Mother," she said. "Things are too busy at the clinic."

Teddy got to his feet and put an arm around Valerie's shoulders. "We can see ourselves out, Marguerite," he said. "Keep your seat."

"Thank you, Teddy," she said, "but I think I'll go on in now."

He removed his arm from Valerie's shoulder and extended Marguerite a hand. She rose and offered a cheek for him to kiss.

"I'm so glad you could come," she said. "And I'm thrilled with the news."

"Thanks, Marguerite," Teddy said.

"Good night, Mother." Valerie kissed her cheek. "Dinner was delicious."

"I'm glad you enjoyed it, dear," she said. "And I hope to see more of you both."

They walked to the porch door, which led out to the parking area, and Marguerite patted Teddy on the back. "We'll speak soon," she said.

"Yes," he said. "I hope so."

For a moment, Marguerite watched as they walked out toward their cars, then she snuffed out the candles and went inside.

In the parking area, Teddy turned and put his arms around Valerie, then kissed her deeply, running his hands up and down her back. She drew back and looked up at him. "I'd better run, Teddy," she said. "It's late, and I'd better get home."

"What?" he said testily. "I thought you'd spend the night with me."

"I can't, Teddy," she said. "I've got to take Elvis out."

"Then why don't you go home, take the ugly mutt out, and then come on over to my place?" he cajoled, brushing her neck with his lips.

"Not tonight, Teddy," she said. "I've got a very early morning and a really busy day ahead."

He continued nuzzling her neck. "Come on," he whispered. "We'll have a real good time, Val. We could fuck all night long."

"Teddy!" she said. "I just told you that I have to get up very early, and I have a long, hard day ahead of me."

"Call in sick," he said, his hands pressing her buttocks to his groin.

"No can do," she said. "I mean it."

"Aw, Val," he whined, "come on. You can do it. Let the dogs and cats and horses take care of themselves. Just this once."

"No, Teddy," she said firmly, trying to wriggle away from his arms. "I've got a job to do. Now, let me go. I've got to go take care of Elvis."

Teddy finally let her loose. "Then go," he said. "Go take care of your fucking mutt."

She looked at him challengingly. "I will," she said. She opened the door to her Jeep and climbed in, closing the door after her. She fired up the engine and gazed at him, standing alone next to his Jaguar. He looked like a little boy who hadn't got his way, as he increasingly did these days.

Well, too bad, she thought. *Nobody who calls Elvis a fucking mutt and doesn't apologize is going to get to sleep with me.*

She started down the long gravel lane to the highway and home to Elvis.

"Bitch!" Teddy snapped under his breath as he watched her taillights disappear. Then he got in his car and headed straight for Tiffani's, hoping that she would be home. *If not,* he thought, *I'll find somebody else. No problem.*

Chapter Seven

A rielle Conrad's high-heel, magenta leather mules, festooned at the toe with a bouquet of lemon-yellow flowers, click-clacked against the purple bougainvillea-draped coral stone and marble loggia that adorned the rear façade of her palatial Palm Beach mansion. The Atlantic Ocean, its breakers rhythmic and muted, slapped lazily against the pristine beach just beyond the walled-in perfection of the lawn, and the steady offshore breeze was refreshing in the summer night's steamy torpor.

Arielle, however, took no solace from her grand estate with its manicured gardens. Tonight, the luxurious trappings of her life seemed to her no more than a stage set for a tragedy. A Boodles gin with tonic in one hand and a thin brown cigarillo in the other, she paced restlessly from one end of the columned loggia to the other, pausing occasionally to run long, tanned fingers with magenta-lacquered nails through her platinum-streaked hair.

Catching sight of her reflection in an enormous mother-of-pearl-framed mirror, she saw how tousled her hair was. The candlelight was flattering, and she was pleased with what she saw. Her long hair had that sexy just-had-a-roll-in-the-hay look that so many women spend small fortunes to achieve but that for Arielle seemed just another of her many desirable, if not altogether natural, assets. Her face was perfectly made up, as usual. Her heavily mascaraed eyes were thinly lined with black and shadowed with a honey hue accentuating the shards of amber that streaked through the topaz brown of her irises. A terra-cotta blusher accentuated her high, prominent cheekbones, and glossy magenta lipstick adorned her full, sensuous, and cosmetically enhanced lips. Bee-stung lips, she thought, and sexy as hell, with a come-hither look.

She turned from the mirror and resumed her nervous pacing, puffing on her cigarillo, secure in the knowledge that, if nothing else, she looked appropriately beguiling. Then one of her heels caught on the weathered marble, and she lurched forward, just managing to catch herself before she fell to the hard stone.

Shit! she thought, looking down at herself. *Just my fucking luck.* She'd slopped gin and tonic onto the sheer orange silk blouse that she wore unbuttoned to the waist, where it was tied in a lav-ish knot. Somehow, she'd managed to miss all that lovely exposed flesh.

I must be getting a little drunk, she thought. *No, not drunk,* she amended. *Just getting a buzz on.* She quickly click-clacked to the big marble table where trays of liquor and mixers stood in atten-dance. Putting down her drink and cigarillo, she grabbed a nap-kin, dabbed it with club soda, and began brushing her blouse vigorously.

There, she thought after a few furious strokes, *that's better.* She tossed the napkin onto the table, picked up her drink and cigar-illo, and went over to a chaise longue, where she spread out, kick-ing off her mules and making herself comfortable. She picked up the latest issue of French *Vogue* and idly flipped through its glossy pages, but lost interest after a few minutes and tossed it to the marble floor with a sigh.

Where is the son of a bitch? she wondered, taking a sip of her drink. *He should've been here for dinner ages ago.* She took a long draw off her cigarillo. *Now, of all times, he's decided to disappear on me. Maybe I should call the club.*

She smashed out her cigarillo in the ashtray at her side, then pulled another one from the pack that lay there, lighting it with her gold Cartier lighter. *Yes,* she decided, *that's what I'll do. I'll call the club.* She was reaching for the cell phone on the table when she heard his distinctive heavy boot heels on the marble. She looked up as he sauntered toward her from the French doors that led out from the drawing room. He was still in his polo gear and looked sweaty and dusty.

"Lolo!" she cried, sitting up. "I've been worried sick about you. Where the hell have you been?"

Lolo's darkly tanned face lit up at the sight of her. Then his dark brown eyes became concerned when he heard the distress in her voice. "What is it, Arielle?" he asked in his heavily accented English, rushing to her, the sound of his heels resounding off the loggia's stone floor and walls.

"What is it?" She glared up at him malevolently. "You're late!" she cried. "And just when I need you, Lolo!"

"I'm on Spanish time," the handsome young man joked, his teeth sparkling white against his dark skin. He put one hand on each side of her face and leaned down and kissed her lips. "You know how Argentinians are."

She grimaced at his attempt at humor. "Why're you so late?" she asked, patting the chaise longue next to her and scooting over to give him room to sit down. She leaned back again, looking up at him.

He eased his muscular body down next to hers, and shrugged his massive shoulders. "I was out at the polo grounds till dusk," he said. "Like I told you I would be." He leaned over and kissed her lips, a hand moving to one of her easily accessible breasts, taking great pleasure in the feeling of her nipple as it began to harden under his touch. After a moment, he sighed with satisfaction and sat back up. "Then Palmer Johnson wanted me to look at some new polo ponies of his, so I went over to his place—"

"Oh, fuck Palmer Johnson," she said.

"Arielle," he said softly, looking into her eyes, "don't take your anger out on me. I've done nothing wrong. I'm just a little late. Whatever it is that bugs you—"

She sat up and threw her arms around his neck, hugging him to her tightly, relishing the feel of his hard, sweaty body next to hers. "Oh, it's not you, Lolo," she said contritely. "You're right. I'm sorry. It's that horrible Wyn." Her eyes became flinty with hate. "I could kill him, Lolo. I really could."

Lolo heaved a sigh. "What's the asshole done now?"

"It's the same old story," Arielle said, removing her arms from around his neck. "He hasn't signed the damned papers yet, and he knows good and well I can hardly make ends meet on that stupid temporary allowance the court decided on."

"Did it come today?" he asked casually. "The check, I mean?"

"No," she said, gritting her teeth.

"Jesus!" Lolo spat. "I'd like to go to New York and kill the son of a bitch myself. And I mean it, Arielle."

"I wish you would," Arielle countered, assessing him, wondering if he really did mean it. "That would solve all of our problems."

She paused and took a sip of her drink. It certainly wasn't the first time she'd thought about killing Wyn. "If I thought you could get away with it," she said, "I'd ask you to do it. I wish I could do it myself. I hate him." She tapped a fist against Lolo's chest. "I hate him, hate him, *hate* him!"

Lolo took her fist in his hand and brought it to his lips, kissing it. "You know, Arielle, he's stalling just to torture you," Lolo said. "To torture both of us."

"Yes, I know," she replied. "But knowing that doesn't help, does it? The torture just goes on and on."

"He'll sign soon," Lolo said. "He has to. Don't worry." He put a finger under her chin and lifted it, looking into her eyes. "Then all of our troubles will be over. We'll have everything we need. Everything. You'll see." He leaned down and began planting kisses on her beautiful face, first her forehead, then her nose, eyes, each cheek, and chin.

Arielle responded to his tenderness, her lips and tongue brushing over his neck, his ears, and face, until their lips met. They hungrily began kissing, their hands roaming over one another's bodies. Lolo gently pushed her back down against the chaise and drew himself up next to her, grinding his loins against her perfect body, moaning aloud at the feel of her sweet, soft femininity against him.

Arielle ran her hand over his chest and down to his thigh, then around to his hard bubble butt, reveling in his masculine odor, his sweaty riding gear, the dusty skin-tight polo jodhpurs and boots. "You're soaked," she murmured, almost shuddering with desire.

Lolo drew back. "Maybe I'd better go shower and change," he said, knowing that she wouldn't want him to.

"No, don't. I like you like this."

He laughed softly. "And I like you like this." He ran a hand inside her blouse again, rubbing a nipple between thumb and finger.

"Ummm," Arielle murmured. "That feels soooo good."

Lolo brushed his lips against hers. "Let's make this last a while," he whispered. "Let me get us both a drink? Huh?"

"Ummm . . . ," she murmured again, pulling him to her. "I think that's a great idea." Then she gradually released him. "Let me do it for you," she said, looking into his eyes. "I want to make a drink for my Lolo."

She swung her legs off the chaise and got to her feet, then slipped into her mules and click-clacked to the marble drinks table, casting a kittenish smile at him over her shoulder. She got two clean glasses, put ice cubes into them, then poured in healthy portions of Boodles. Finally, she added a tiny splash of tonic and a squeeze of lemon to each.

She walked back over to the chaise, putting a little extra swing in her step. "Here," she said, smiling. "Just the way you like it."

Lolo's eyes traveled up and down her body before he took the proffered drink. He held it up and Arielle clinked hers against it. "*Salud,*" he said.

"*Salud,*" she echoed, then took a sip of her drink and let out a breathy sigh.

"Suddenly you don't sound very cheerful," Lolo said, running a hand up her leg.

Arielle slumped down onto the chaise and stared into her glass. Lolo was right. She didn't feel very cheerful. Thoughts of Wyn and the nasty divorce had crept back into her consciousness, like an irritating itch that wouldn't go away. There'd been a time, back in the beginning of their marriage, when she'd thought she was the luckiest woman alive. With all the women Wyn had—and there'd been a lot—he'd chosen her above all the rest. She'd never forget the blonde that was determined to have him, then left broken-hearted when Arielle had won out. *What a bitch she was,* Arielle thought. She'd taken a special pleasure in seeing that one leave, crushed by the weight of what she'd lost. But the triumph Arielle had felt then gave her little comfort now.

Lolo set down his drink and slid an arm around her shoulders. "Come here to me," he said, pulling her toward him. "Don't look so sad, Arielle," he said. "Your Lolo is here for you."

His lips brushed up her neck, and he began nibbling her ears. "I know he's a real prick," he said in a near whisper, "and he's messing everything up now. But it won't be long before the lawyers will tell him he can't stall anymore."

Arielle took a long sip of her drink, then sighed again as she set it down. "I know," she said, "but in the meantime it really is making things difficult. I can hardly afford to pay the help, and I can't afford to entertain. Thank God I can charge everything at the shops and the club."

He pressed a finger to her lips. "Shhh," he whispered. "Don't think about it now, Arielle." He began gently kneading her neck and back.

"That feels so good, Lolo," she said with the hint of a smile. "I've been so . . . tense about all of this. I mean, what the hell are we even doing here tonight? We shouldn't even be here."

"What do you mean?" he asked.

"It's summer," she said. "We should be having fun in Southampton or Europe or at least the place up in the Adirondacks. Anywhere but here in the summertime. Nobody's in Palm Beach in the summer."

He took both of her hands in his, kissing them tenderly. "At least we're together, Arielle."

"Thank God for that," she said. "If it weren't for you, I don't know what I'd do."

"I wish I could do more," Lolo said, looking into her eyes. "But you know they don't pay me that much for riding. If I had my own money and a stable it would be different—"

"No, no, no!" Arielle said earnestly. "That's not what I mean, Lolo. I don't expect financial help from you. That's the last thing in the world I would expect. I know that Palmer Johnson's just like Wyn and all the rest of the rich bastards that play polo. They practically starve their star players." She looked into his dark eyes. "Like you," she said, "the best of them all."

He grinned, his white teeth flashing. "Well," he said, "one of the best anyway."

"I think you're the best," she said with pride in her voice, "but it's your being here that's even more important. It's what keeps me going from one day to the next."

His face became serious. "You really do feel bad tonight, don't you, Arielle?" he said. "Much worse than usual." He reached over for his drink and took a sip, waiting for her to speak, knowing that she needed to talk a while.

She sighed again. "I never would have imagined that my life would go this way. I wouldn't have believed—not in a million years!—that Wyn could be so cruel and spiteful and selfish. He wasn't like most rich men I knew. Money was never an issue. He wasn't a tightwad like most of them, you know? God knows, we threw it around like there was no tomorrow."

She reached over and shook a cigarillo from the pack on the table, and Lolo picked up her lighter and held its flame for her. "Thanks," she said, exhaling a streamer of blow.

"Go on," he said. "Tell me what's on your pretty mind."

"Well," she said. "That was one thing I liked about Wyn. He didn't really care about all that money and let me spend whatever I wanted to. That's what it's for, he always said. He's got so much he doesn't know what the hell to do with it." She took another drag off of her cigarillo and looked at Lolo, her eyes suddenly flashing anger. "But, Jesus, has the son of a bitch ever changed his tune. And there's no reason on earth he should be so horrible and mean."

"It'll all be over soon," Lolo said, not knowing what else to say. "Maybe . . . maybe I could get some kind of job or—"

"No way!" Arielle said. "No fucking way!" Then she laughed. "I can just see that. No more clubs, no parties. No trips. Early to bed, early to rise. No, Lolo." She poked his chest with a finger. "You and I weren't meant to live like that. That's for all the losers out there." She reached over and stroked his handsome face with her hand. She felt much better now, having talked about her woes.

"Somehow we'll make out," she said. "At least I have you all to myself. And it's fun to see you drive all the horny divorcées around here mad with jealousy." She kissed his nose.

Lolo grinned. "You make the men a little crazy yourself," he said. "I think every man in Palm Beach wants you, Arielle."

She tossed her head and laughed. "You think so?" she asked.

"You know it," he replied. He reached over then and pulled her to him. "And that includes me," he added. He began kissing her roughly, passionately, and hungrily, his hands exploring her body. Serious talk was over, and it was time for some serious play.

Arielle responded immediately, the fires of her desire rekindled by the feel of him against her. She ran her hands over his hard-muscled shoulders and arms, down his tight stomach, and slid one between his thighs, feeling the tumescence straining at his jodhpurs. She moaned with pleasure as Lolo began licking her breasts with his tongue, teasing her nipples between his teeth. She gasped aloud when she felt his hand between her thighs, fingering her wetness.

In one furious movement, Lolo jerked her shorts and panties down and off her legs and unzipped his jodhpurs, releasing his throbbing manhood. He mounted her then, entering her up to the hilt suddenly and quickly, and began pumping away at her as if possessed by a demon.

Oh, God, Arielle thought in an ecstatic swoon, her entire body shuddering against his. *Just when I thought it was all over for me, the man of my dreams comes waltzing into my life. And what a man he is! Not like that beast, Wyn Conrad.*

Chapter Eight

"Colette!" Valerie exclaimed, looking up from her desk, where she was filling in a chart. "It's good to see you." Elvis, who was in his bed, wagged his tail furiously.

Colette Richards, Valerie's elderly neighbor, swept into the office, her exotic perfume preceding her. She snatched off her sunglasses, and Valerie could see that her bright blue eyes were wide with alarm.

"Oh, Val, darling!" Colette cried, her voice at once whispery and throaty. "I'm *so* glad to see you, too. You've no idea, my darling." She spied Elvis in his bed and blew kisses in his direction.

Valerie rose to her feet and gave Colette a kiss on the cheek, then motioned her to a chair. "Here, Colette, sit down," she said. "Is it my imagination, or are you upset?"

They both sat down, Colette putting a large, expensive-looking straw tote with leather handles in her lap, then placing her arthritic hands, which were bedecked as always with huge jeweled rings, delicately across the top.

"Oh, Val, darling," the old woman gasped, "where to begin?"

Colette's habitual manner was so dramatic, Valerie thought, that she wasn't especially distressed by the elegant and arty woman's histrionics. Then it suddenly occurred to her that Colette didn't have Puff Puppy curled across an arm, yapping and snarling and otherwise making a nuisance of himself. How odd, she thought. Colette took the petite snow-white Maltese everywhere with her, as if he were a fashion accessory.

"Colette," she asked, "where's that little scoundrel, Puff Puppy?"

"At home, darling," Colette replied.

"Then what's the matter?" Valerie asked. "I saw your name on the list and assumed that something was wrong with him."

"Oh, Val, darling," Colette said, tears springing into her large eyes. Valerie grabbed the box of Kleenex she kept on the desk for distressed pet owners and pulled out a couple. "Thank you, darling," Colette said. "I'm sorry to be such a blubbering old nuisance, but it's . . . it's Hayden!" Tears began to roll down her rouged and powdered cheeks.

Valerie quickly grabbed more Kleenex and handed them to her, then got to her feet and put a hand on Colette's shoulder, stroking her gently. "Who's Hayden?" she asked softly.

She blew her nose with the Kleenex. "Oh, Val, darling," she said, looking up at her with watery eyes. "I didn't tell you?"

"No, Colette," Valerie replied.

Colette looked momentarily perplexed, then patted Valerie's hand. "Oh, do sit down, darling. And thank you for your moral support. I need all of it I can get these days." She dabbed at her tears with a fresh Kleenex.

Valerie sat back down in her chair and looked over at her old friend. She was clad all in white today, white artist's smock, white pants, even white shoes, and wore several strands of large pearls at her throat with matching bracelet and earrings. On her head was a huge straw sun hat. One glance was enough to see that the woman had been a stunning beauty in her youth, and she still had about her an air of youthfulness and vitality that belied her advanced age. Absorbed by everything around her, she found life endlessly wondrous and exciting. She was also coquettish and accustomed to having attention lavished on her. Her white hair, always perfectly coiffed, appeared to be in slight disarray beneath the sun hat, and makeup was now streaked down her cheeks.

"I simply can't believe I haven't told you about him before, but then I haven't seen much of you lately." She caught her breath before continuing. "Hayden, my darling, is right here with me, and it's high time you met." She opened the straw tote on her lap and carefully lifted out a tiny bundle.

A towel? Valerie thought. *What in the world?*

Colette delicately held the bundle in one hand and opened the towel with the other. "This is Hayden," she announced, holding her hands out for Valerie to see.

Valerie got out of her chair and stepped over for a closer look at the tiny creature Colette cuddled in her hands. "Oh, my God, Colette," she exclaimed, "he's tiny. And so precious." She slowly extended a hand toward the creature and stroked his coat of quills, very lightly with a single finger. He made a ball of himself and trembled all over, his eyes blinking suspiciously.

"He's an African pygmy hedgehog," Colette said. "Isn't he divine?"

"Oh, he's adorable," Valerie said, stroking him some more. "What does Puff Puppy think of him?"

"Puff Puppy adores him," Colette replied, "but I'm afraid the feeling isn't mutual. I can see that he likes you, though," she went on. "I can hardly believe it. Normally he has a fit if anybody touches him but me."

"Well, he doesn't seem too happy with me," Valerie replied. "May I hold him?"

Colette held her hands out, and Valerie took him into hers, careful not to drop him or let him escape. "Where on earth did you get the name?" Val asked.

"Why, he's named after Sterling Hayden, the actor, of course," Colette said, her eyes wide and her eyebrows arching in surprise. "The love of my life that man was, though I never knew him personally. Soooo romantic, you know. So handsome. Sun-bronzed. A sailor. A real adventurer. Not like these men nowadays who spend fortunes playing at being adventurous. You know the sort. Always have a safety net. Not so, Hayden. He sailed the seven seas. Oh, Val, my darling, he was of a dying breed. Sooo sexy!"

Valerie laughed. She didn't find it surprising that Colette Richards, who she knew was in the neighborhood of eighty, was still consumed by romantic notions at her age. She was a woman with quite a past.

"Well, what seems to be the problem with our little adventurer here?" Valerie asked.

"I'm not certain," Colette said worriedly, "but he hasn't been himself lately. Not at all. He has a lovely cage with a heating pad to sleep on—they love heat, you see—and I play with him every night before my bedtime. They're nocturnal, you know, and after we play for a while, he gets on his wheel and spins, spins, spins! He adores the pocket of my bathrobe and my smocks, so I carry him around the house with me."

"Has he been eating properly?" Valerie asked.

"Funny you should ask, Val," she said. "Now that I think about it, Hayden went off his food a few days ago, so I make him this delicious turkey soup that I found out they like."

"Did he like it?" Valerie asked.

"Adores it," Colette cried. "Gobbles it right up. Broth, turkey, vegetables, and all."

Valerie carefully turned him over, examining Hayden's tiny body. He was no more than five inches long. She delicately felt along his entire body. It wasn't an easy task, considering his quills. After studying his eyes for a long time, she carefully opened his mouth and searched there for any clues. She was just about to abandon her examination when she stopped.

"What?" Colette asked.

"Look, Colette," Valerie said quietly. "I think we've found the culprit."

Colette held a wrinkled hand to her heart. "Oh, dear, Val. What?" she gasped in a whisper.

"His teeth," Valerie replied.

"His *teeth*?" Colette exclaimed.

"Yes," Valerie answered, nodding her head. "I'm fairly certain that I can see the beginnings of gum disease."

"Oh, darling Val," Colette exclaimed. "What are we to do?"

"We'll have to clean his teeth," Valerie responded, still absorbed in studying the creature's tiny mouth.

"Clean his teeth? Imagine!" Colette said. "But can you do that, Val? I mean, how—"

"I'll have to administer anesthesia," she said, "but it can be done. I'll have to be very careful adjusting the dosage."

"Oh, my goodness," Colette said. "Val, darling, you're a marvel."

"In the meantime, we'll have to start him on a course of antibiotics," Valerie said.

"Antibiotics," Colette echoed. "And when can you do the cleaning?" she asked.

"The sooner the better," Valerie replied. "Let me look at the schedule. I definitely want to do it in the next few days."

"Oh, Hayden," Colette cooed. She reached over and stroked him with her fingers.

"Here," Valerie said, "take him for a minute while I check my schedule." She gently transferred him from her hands to Colette's.

Valerie looked at her date book, then rose to her feet. "I'll be right back, Colette," she said. "I'd better check at the desk and see what's scheduled on the clinic book."

She returned quickly and stood observing Colette and Hayden. "Friday it is, Hayden," she said. "You'll have to have him here around seven o'clock."

Colette looked up. "In the morning?" she asked.

Valerie nodded.

"Oh, Hayden," she said, looking at the tiny hedgehog, "we'll have to have an unusually early night, won't we, darling? And we're both such night owls." She carefully bundled him back up in his towel and placed the bundle in her tote, closing the leather strap over the top. "Thank you, Val, darling. I don't know what we'd do without you."

"It's my job," Valerie said in her self-effacing manner.

"Ha!" Colette exclaimed. Then in a near whisper she added. "If only your colleagues cared half as much as you, the world would be a *far* better place. I wish my own doctor cared as much as you do, but I'm old so I don't matter. One foot in the grave, you know . . ."

Valerie laughed and patted her on the back. "Not quite yet, I don't think."

Colette turned and started out with Hayden. "Anyway, dear, we'll be here bright and early Friday morning. In the meantime, don't be such a stranger. I've missed our little talks lately."

"Me, too," Valerie said. "I've just been so busy."

"I know, darling," Colette said with a wink. "Teddy's been away on weekends, so you've been catching up in the garden and around the house."

"Yes," Valerie said. "Anyway, I'll see you Friday, and maybe we'll be able to visit beforehand." She held the door open for her.

"Ta-ta," Colette said, and she swept through the lobby area on her impossibly high heels, trailing heavy perfume in her wake, waggling the fingers of one hand at Annie and Tami, who were seated behind the reception desk. At the front door she stopped and blew kisses at Valerie, who'd stepped into the reception area.

Valerie waved, and Colette headed out the front door.

When she was gone, Annie looked over at Valerie. "I don't know how you put up with that crazy old bat," she said.

"She's not crazy, Annie," Valerie said in Colette's defense. "And she's not an old bat, as you so unkindly put it. She's just different, that's all."

"Could've fooled me," Annie said, giggling.

"Dr. Rochelle," Tami piped up from behind the reception desk, "you've got a call on line three."

"Who is it?" Valerie asked.

"It's somebody at Stonelair Farm," Tami replied. "You want to take it or have them call back?"

"I'll take it now," Valerie said. She retraced her steps to her office and closed the door, then looked down at Elvis, who was snoring quietly. She punched line three on her telephone. "Dr. Rochelle."

"Dr. Rochelle," the man's voice said, "this is Santo Ducci at Stonelair."

"Yes, Mr. Ducci," she said. "What can I do for you?"

"All of our dogs—four Irish wolfhounds—need checkups, and their Lyme disease vaccinations," he said. "Plus, there's the cat. The sooner the better because they're behind schedule. We were hoping you could make a house call. It's sort of a problem to bring in four big Irish wolfhounds, you know."

"I understand," she said. And she did. Irish wolfhounds were like small ponies. It wasn't at all uncommon in the country to make house calls for big animals. That's why she usually spent half her days on the road, ministering to everything from horses to llamas.

"Hold on just a minute, Mr. Ducci," she said, "and I'll see what's scheduled and exactly when I'm scheduled to do house calls. They may send somebody else, you know."

"Either you do it," Ducci said, "or skip it."

Valerie was stunned by his bluntness, then said, "I'll see what I can do, Mr. Ducci."

She put him on hold and pushed the button for reception, where Tami picked up. "Tami, can I fit in a house call either this afternoon or tomorrow afternoon? Say, an hour at the most?"

"Let me see," Tami said.

Valerie waited patiently while Tami looked at the schedule.

"You can do it today between three-thirty and four-thirty, but you'll have to be back before four-thirty for sure for clinic appointments," she said.

"Great," Valerie said. "Put me down for a house call at Stonelair Farm."

"Gotcha," Tami said, hanging up.

Valerie punched Ducci's line. "Mr. Ducci," she said.

"Yes," he replied somewhat gruffly.

"I'll be there at three-thirty."

"Thanks," he said, his voice all politeness now, "that's great."

"How many dogs did you say there are?" she asked.

"Four," he replied, "and a cat."

"Okay," she said.

"By the way, Dr. Rochelle," Ducci said, "you never did get back to us about taking care of our animals."

Valerie felt a pang of guilt for not having returned his call, but she'd been putting it off. She'd dreaded discussing it with Charles.

"I assume you still haven't discussed it with the owner," Ducci continued, "since you said somebody else might be coming out here. You know, we've been waiting to hear from you. We have a lot of animals, and their health is very important to us."

"I understand, and I'm sorry about that," she replied. "I promise you that I'll discuss it with my colleagues as soon as possible."

"I'd think that the clinic would be glad for the business you'd be bringing in," Ducci said with unerring logic.

"I suppose you're right," Valerie said, "but I'll still have to discuss this with them. I'll try to speak to them today and get back to you, either this afternoon when I see you at Stonelair or sometime tomorrow."

"Good," Ducci said. "We'd appreciate that."

"Okay, then," Valerie said. "I'll see you at three-thirty. Good-bye."

Santo Ducci didn't respond because he'd already hung up. "Thanks to you, too," Valerie said, replacing the receiver in its cradle.

She glanced at her watch. It was noon already. Where had the time gone? It seemed as if she'd just gotten there. *Well,* she thought, looking back over her morning, *I guess it's no wonder.* First, there'd been a slightly premature birth at Breezy Hills Farm very early this morning. A beautiful foal. Then there'd been a llama with a leg injury at Maplecrest. She'd also seen a horse with parasites at Silver Fox, and a horse with gastric ulcers at Stream-side. Two dogs and one cat here at the clinic. Fairly routine stuff. Then Colette with Hayden.

And now I'm supposed to be perfection itself and meet Teddy for lunch at his place, she thought wearily.

She sat there for a moment, reflecting. It'd been nearly a month since he'd given her the ring and gone back to New York City, and he hadn't been up here on the weekends. He'd had important dinner parties with big-shot clients in the Hamptons the previous weekend, but he'd called her frequently. Now he had come up for part of the week to relax—just when she was at her busiest.

Funny enough, she thought, *I really didn't miss Teddy the last month, and I really would just as soon not see him for lunch today.* But she'd promised him, and she wasn't one to go back on a promise.

She rose to her feet and stretched, then took off her lab coat and hung it up. Elvis immediately roused himself from his bed and yawned, knowing that it was lunchtime. "Give me a minute, Elvis," she said, reaching down and giving him a few strokes.

She grabbed her shoulder bag and went into the bathroom and flipped on the light. Looking into the mirror, she applied fresh pale pink lipstick, then a little blusher. She was so tanned from being out in the sun working in her garden that she hardly needed any makeup. Her hair, in its single long plait, was rolled into a knot at the nape of her neck.

Take it down or leave it? she asked her reflection. She knew that Teddy didn't like her practical work look, especially her hair, but she decided to leave it exactly as it was. She had to return to work, after all, and Teddy would simply have to learn to like it. That or quit complaining about it. She flipped off the light and went back into her office. "Let's go, Elvis," she said, and stooped down and put his leash on.

Daphne Collins was in the reception area, tapping a chart against the desk. "Hi, Val," she said with a smile on her face. "I hear that Colette was here."

"Yes," Valerie replied. "Her African pygmy hedgehog."

"Oh, really!" Daphne replied. "I wish I'd seen her and the hedgehog. She's so wonderful. I bet it was as adorable as she is. What will she think of next?"

"There's no telling," Valerie replied. "By the way, have you got a minute?" she asked. "I need to have a quick word with you and Charles."

"I'm getting ready to go to lunch," Daphne replied, "but I can give you a minute, if Charles isn't busy." She turned to Annie. "Does Charles have a patient?" she asked.

"No," Annie replied. "He's in his office."

"Let's go," Daphne said, already heading down the hallway to Charles's office.

Valerie followed her with Elvis, and when they reached the door to his office, Daphne knocked and went on in without waiting for a response.

Charles looked up from the desk. In his gray eyes there was an expectant expression.

"Val needs a word with both of us," Daphne said.

"What is it?" Charles asked.

"The people at Stonelair want me to take care of their animals," Valerie replied.

"You mean you exclusively?" Daphne asked.

Valerie nodded.

The news did not sit well with Daphne. She turned to try to hide the disgruntled expression on her face, but Valerie didn't miss it.

Charles took off his glasses and looked at Valerie. "You know we don't generally operate that way," he said. "Except under special circumstances."

"Of course," Valerie said, "but they're pressuring me to ask about it, so—"

"This has happened time and again," Daphne said abruptly, her voice tinged with anger. "I don't know why you don't recommend one of us so that the workload is more spread out."

"I made it clear that we have a share-and-share-alike policy," Valerie said, "but they don't like that. They want to see one vet consistently, and since they've met me . . . well, they want me to handle it. There are a lot of animals out there, and it would generate a lot of income for the clinic."

Daphne stared at her, her brows knit crossly, but Charles barked a laugh. "You must've made quite an impression on the Mafia guys out there," he said. "What did you do for them, Val?"

She decided to ignore his remark, but could feel her face blushing heatedly. *Well, I am not going to stand here and be insulted,* she thought.

"Yes or no?" she finally said, her voice steely with determination.

"What do you think, Daphne?" Charles asked.

"I don't like it," Daphne replied. "She knows—"

"If I don't agree to do it," Valerie interjected, "Stonelair will take its business elsewhere. They won't use this clinic at all."

Daphne's mouth opened in a silent gasp, then snapped shut. She crossed her arms over her chest and looked at Charles. "Well, it would generate a lot of income," she said. "Like Val said, there're a lot of animals out there. Think about it, Charles."

As if taking a cue from her, Charles looked thoughtful for a moment. "I suppose so," he finally said. Then he smiled. "It's not a bad idea at all, come to think of it. Valerie here would be taking care of their animals, and we wouldn't have to deal with the slimy people." Charles nodded. "I think you're right, Daphne," he said. "But there'd have to be a couple of conditions."

"What?" Valerie asked, keeping strictly to business.

"We'd have to triage emergency situations," he said. "You

wouldn't be able to drop everyone else for those people, you understand. You'd still have your usual duties."

"Of course," Val said.

"So if more than one emergency arises at a time," he went on, "you'll have to make a decision about which is more urgent and see to it first. And it may not be theirs."

"Yes," Valerie said, becoming impatient since he was stating the obvious.

"And don't forget," Daphne added, "if you're away for some reason, on vacation or whatever, then they'll have to agree to use one of us. Isn't that right, Charles?"

He nodded. "Absolutely."

"I understand," Valerie said. "Is that all?" she asked.

Charles looked at Daphne, and a silent signal seemed to pass between them.

"I believe so," Charles said.

"Thanks," Valerie said. "Let's go, Elvis." She turned on her heel and left the office quickly, then heard the door slam with a loud bang when she got farther down the hall.

Jeez, she thought, *the sooner I get my own practice the better. I can't take this crap much longer. They are jealous, plain and simple, and want to put me through hell.*

In the reception area, Tami called to her.

"What is it, Tami?" she asked.

"If we're not too busy here this afternoon," Tami said, "I wondered if I could go with you out to Stonelair and help."

"I don't mind at all," Valerie said with a smile, "if Daphne and Charles agree to it."

"It would be sort of special to me," Tami said.

"Why's that, Tami?" Valerie asked.

"Well, you know, when I was little we lived out in the woods near there," Tami said, "so my brother and I used to play there a lot."

"At Stonelair?" Valerie asked, surprised.

Tami nodded. "There wasn't anybody but a caretaker, and Jimmy and I knew how to get in and out of the place through the fences in the backwoods. We even got in and out of the house without anybody ever knowing it."

Valerie laughed. "Then you're the only person I know who's ever been there," she said. "Talk to Daphne and Charles and see what they say. I'll be glad for you to come along, even though it wouldn't be much of a learning experience for you. It's just vaccinations and stuff like that."

"That's okay," Tami said. "I'd just like to see the place again."

"Well, if you can't come this time," Valerie said, "there'll be others, because I'm going to be taking care of all the animals out there."

"Great!" Tami said.

"I'd better run," Valerie said. "I've got a lunch appointment."

"Teddy?" Tami asked, smiling.

"Yes," Valerie replied, already heading to the door.

"Have fun," Tami called after her.

"I'll try," Valerie said.

She hurried out to her car, and began to wonder what she'd gotten herself into with this Stonelair deal. *Stonelair,* she thought. *A truly forbidding place.* And why did this Conrad guy insist on her? She didn't think she'd ever actually felt so pressured into handling a person's animals before. And certainly not for a person she'd yet to meet or see. *I guess the mysterious Mr. Conrad thinks he's too important to take care of mundane affairs himself.*

Suddenly she began to wonder about all the rumors that swirled around Conrad and the goings-on at Stonelair and if there was any truth to them. *But so what if they are true?* she thought. *I'm only the vet. How could they hurt me?*

Chapter Nine

At Apple Hill Farm, Valerie and Teddy sat under the protection of a large market umbrella out by the sun-drenched pool. Hattie had set the big weathered teak table for lunch, which she was serving. No fool, Elvis was stationed between Valerie and Teddy, ideally positioned to beg. At his most charming, his eyes shone with gleeful greed, and his tongue was stuck out, making his mouth look as if it were spread in a giant smile. His blue-black tail swept the stone terrace at regular intervals, anticipation in every swipe.

"Thanks, Hattie," Valerie said, "this looks delicious."

"You're welcome," Hattie replied. "Do you want me to take Elvis inside with me?" she asked tentatively. "I can give him a little something in the kitchen."

"Well . . . ," Valerie stalled, reluctant to say yes, for she knew that Hattie would let him have anything he wanted—and a lot of it. "I think he'll be all right out here, Hattie."

"Oh, come on, Val," Teddy prodded. "Let him live a little. It's not often he gets to eat really good food."

Valerie laughed. "Is that a reflection on my culinary abilities, Mr. de Mornay?"

Teddy smiled. "I know how you feed him at home," he said. "Yourself, too. Shall we just call it exceedingly healthy?"

"Oh, okay," Valerie conceded with a growl. "Elvis," she said, looking down at her attentive treasure, "you go with Hattie. Have a party."

"Let's go, Elvis," Hattie said, beckoning to him as she started toward the house.

He immediately sprang to her side, knowing what was in store for him.

Valerie watched them leave, convinced that Hattie and Teddy prearranged these little trysts to get Elvis out of the way. It worried her, because Teddy didn't seem to really like having Elvis around. Oh, he did a good job of pretending, she supposed, extending his generosity to Elvis as he did almost anyone around, but she sometimes wondered if Teddy actually liked animals—any animals—at all. He didn't have any pets, and poor Kaiser, his horse, went largely ignored.

Teddy picked up the chilled bottle of Pouilly Fuissé that was sweating in its silver wine coaster and was about to pour some into Valerie's wineglass, but she quickly put her hand over it. "Unh-unh. Not for me, Teddy," she said. "I've got a long day ahead of me yet."

"Christ, Val," he groused. "Just a glass?"

"No," she said firmly. "I'll stick with the mineral water."

"What? You afraid you'll butcher a poodle or something?" he joked.

"Not funny, Teddy," she replied. "What if your doctor had a couple of drinks before . . . say . . ."

"Okay!" He laughed. "Let's don't go there."

"Thought you might see it my way," she said.

"Well, cheers, anyway," he said amiably, lifting his glass.

"Cheers," she echoed, lifting her glass of water and clinking it against his wineglass. "This looks yummy," she said, gazing down at her plate.

"Hattie loves to cook for you," Teddy said, forking up a large bite of lobster salad.

Valerie buttered a cheddar-scallion biscuit, one of Hattie's specialities. "I'd forgotten about these scrumptious little goodies," she said before taking a bite.

Teddy smiled, taking pleasure in her delight. "I'll have to live on rabbit food when I get back to the city," he said. "Between the

food here and the food out in the Hamptons the last few weekends, it's going to be time for lettuce, lettuce, and more lettuce."

"Maybe so," Valerie said, "but you're really lucky to have Hattie. She's not only a treasure around the house, but she clearly
adores you like a favorite son."

"She could be your treasure, too," Teddy said.

Valerie's fork paused midway to her mouth, but then she continued eating, deciding not to respond to that remark.

Teddy continued to watch her as he took a sip of wine. "Just
think, Val," he continued. "Hattie would do all the cooking and
cleaning. Lydia would run the office, pay all the bills, hire all the
workmen and everything. You wouldn't have to do a thing
because it would all be done for you. You'd just have to show up."
He took another sip of wine. "You'd be the queen of Apple Hill."

Valerie felt her stomach lurch. *The queen of Apple Hill?* she
thought. *That is so ridiculous. I'm a veterinarian, for God's
sake.*

"The queen of Apple Hill, huh?" she said with amusement. "I
don't think I'd look too good in a crown."

With that, Teddy launched into the joys that her future life at
Apple Hill would entail, reiterating what he'd just said, but
embellishing with great detail the host of benefits she would enjoy
being the mistress of such a perfect estate.

She tuned him out almost entirely, picking at her food. She
knew exactly where this conversation—or monologue, she cor-
rected—was headed, and she didn't like it. She didn't need this
pressure from Teddy. Not now.

She expelled a silent sigh, pretending to listen to him, while at
the same time she began to feel an unpleasant sensation of guilt. *I
swear,* she thought, *he learned his techniques at my mother's knee.*

She realized that, in effect, she'd been leading Teddy on for a
long time now, unwilling to discuss her feelings with him, letting
their relationship just coast along as if there were nothing wrong.

When they'd first started dating in college, she was so thrilled
with his pursuit of her that she'd genuinely confused her feelings
for him with true love. As they gradually became an item, their
relationship was prodded along by their families and friends, who
viewed them as an appropriate match. Later on, while he'd

worked on his MBA and she'd gone to veterinary school, their relationship had continued long-distance.

There'd been the occasional boozy weekend and holiday parties that had been exciting and fun for her, opening up a whole new world of sophisticated acquaintances. Teddy was extremely popular and good-looking, and her acceptance by his friends had helped give her more confidence in herself. She had also blossomed physically, that gangly, gawky body maturing into an enviable tall and elegant beauty. She had gradually begun to see that there were myriad possibilities for her out there. Possibilities other than Teddy de Mornay.

She took a sip of her mineral water, then dabbed at her lips with a napkin, catching pieces of his monologue, all of it a familiar rehash of conversations past. She looked over at him with a fixed smile on her face, but her mind ranged elsewhere, analyzing their fractured relationship, even as he talked of permanently sealing it, cementing them into a marriage that everyone seemed to think was inevitable.

Since college, she thought, this sense of inevitability had only increased. For the last four years while building up her practice, they'd spent most every weekend together—always at his place, even though she now had hers—and everyone assumed that marriage was the next step.

She'd thought the same thing for a period of time, but she had become increasingly disenchanted with the idea as her love for Teddy—whatever kind of love it might be called—had diminished with time. She couldn't place the blame—at least not entirely—on Teddy himself. He hadn't really changed all that much. Over the years she definitely had begun to recognize behavioral patterns that she hadn't detected at first but that had always been there. Teddy, she'd come to realize, was a great charmer, a great actor.

Finally, she put her fork down and looked across at him, waiting for a pause. When it came, she quickly took advantage. "Teddy," she said in an even voice, "we've been over this, time and again. And I still feel the same way. I can't help it." She shrugged. "I want to wait a while."

He attempted a smile, but his eyes weren't smiling. As he

poured more wine into his glass, she continued. "You know that I appreciate everything that you've offered me. I really do. But I've also explained to you repeatedly that what I have to concentrate on now is building up my clientele and starting a practice of my own. Plus I want to get out of debt. I've still got huge student loans to pay off, and now I've got a mortgage. I just—"

"Oh, Val, for Christ's sake," he said, disgruntled. "Sometimes I think you actually forget who you are. You're a de la Rochelle. You're descended from French aristocracy. Even your very name, Valerie, is on the list of names approved by the French court, and don't you ever forget it."

She looked at him in disbelief. He was sounding increasingly like her snobbish mother.

"You shouldn't even be thinking about mundane things like that," he went on. "You know I'd pay off your crummy student loans for you. And when we get married, you could sell that little house you bought. That'd take care of the mortgage. Hell, Val, you could sell the house now. Move in here." He glared at her for an intense moment. "You didn't have to buy it to begin with, you know."

"Oh, yes, I did," she countered. "We talked about that, and I told you that I wanted to try living on my own for a while." She sighed audibly. "Don't you see? I want to be able to stand on my own two feet, Teddy. And I don't feel like I'm ready to get married until I can do that. I want to wait a little while longer and—"

"You told me Christmas," he said emphatically. There was a smile on his lips, but there was no missing the edge in his voice.

Valerie's face burned with the truth of his words. "I think I said probably, didn't I?" she said, in a futile attempt at levity.

He didn't laugh but continued staring at her with the expression of a petulant child.

Christmas, she remembered, had seemed so far away at the beginning of the year when she'd told him she thought she'd be ready to settle down by next Christmas. Now, of course, summer would soon be over, and she'd accepted his engagement ring.

"You're right," she said, "I did say that, and I meant it at the time. But—"

"But what, Val?" he said angrily. "You're not putting me off

again, are you? What's the big deal about getting married anyway?" He held a hand out and starting counting off points on his
fingers. "You spend nearly every weekend with me." One finger
down. "All of our holidays." Two fingers down. "We see each
other, maybe get to eat lunch or dinner together, practically every
day if I'm up here during the week." Three fingers down. "We're
like a married couple now, for Christ's sake." Four fingers down.

*If we are indeed like a married couple now, and if this is what
marriage is like,* she thought, *then I don't want any part of it—
ever.*

She said: "You're right again, Teddy. It's just . . . I don't
know . . ."

Teddy realized he was pushing too hard. He reached across the
table and took one of her hands in his. "Oh, God, Val. I'm sorry,"
he said contritely. His familiar harsh stare had become that familiar puppy's beseeching plea. "I . . . I guess I just love you so much
that waiting is . . . well, it's really such hell."

"I'm sorry, too, Teddy," she said softly but firmly. "You know
that I really have feelings for you. Right now I just feel as if I'm
being pushed from all directions."

Teddy quickly nodded in agreement. "You're right, Val. Don't
worry about it. "Now, let's eat," he said, digging into his lobster
salad with renewed gusto.

Valerie picked up her fork and began eating again. The salad
was delicious, but she'd almost completely lost her appetite.

"Did you have a busy morning?" Teddy asked after taking a
large sip of wine.

Valerie nodded. "Yes. A very busy morning. All the usual, and
Colette, too."

"Colette!" he exclaimed. "Oh, God, what's her problem?"

"She has a pet African pygmy hedgehog that's having trouble,"
Valerie said. "So we're going to fix him up."

"I can't figure her out," Teddy said. "She's smart as a whip,
sophisticated, all that, and loaded to the gills with money. But"—
he thumped a hand on the table—"she won't let me handle her
portfolio."

"You asked her?" Val said, surprised to hear this news.

"More than once," Teddy said. "But she won't give an inch.

Says she's quite happy with her present money managers. I can't figure it," he said. "She's known my family forever, but she just refuses to see reason and switch."

"I didn't know," Valerie replied. "She hasn't mentioned anything to me at all."

"If she does," he said, "let me know, will you?"

"Sure," Valerie said, thinking that she probably wouldn't.

"You have a busy afternoon coming up?" he asked.

"The usual late-afternoon office appointments, plus I've got to go out to Stonelair."

"Stonelair?" he said with alarm. "Again?"

"He's got four Irish wolfhounds," she said, "and they all need the Lyme vaccine plus heartworm medication and checkups. And there's a cat."

"So why are you going out there?" he asked. "Why doesn't he bring them into the clinic?"

"Teddy!" she exclaimed. "It would take a horse trailer to bring them in. They're Irish wolfhounds. You know, practically ponies."

"Well, I hope you know what you're doing," Teddy said ominously. "Getting mixed up with weirdos like that."

"There was nothing weird the night I saw the horse," Valerie said defensively. "I think all this talk is just that. Talk."

"There's usually a reason for it," Teddy said. "And from what I've heard, things are really strange out there."

"You sound like my mother," she said.

"Maybe so," Teddy said, "but your mother's got very good instincts, I think. And she smells a rat." He sat looking at her for a moment. "By the way," he asked, "did she give old Dock Wainwright a call?"

"I don't have any idea," Valerie said, looking at him curiously. "Why?" she asked, although she thought she already knew the answer to that question.

Teddy shrugged nonchalantly. "Just wondered," he replied, swirling the remains of his wine around in the glass. "She talked about it at dinner that night. Remember?" He looked over at her. "Old Dock's twiddling his thumbs. Just letting her account sit there gathering dust. He probably nods off reading financial reports."

"So now you want to get your hands on my mother's money," Valerie said teasingly.

He gazed at her seriously, ignoring her joking tone. "Well," he began, "I don't see why not, Val. Your mother certainly seemed interested in my handling it. She knows what the market's like, and she knows Dock's not doing anything for her. The way he invests money, it probably doesn't even keep up with the rate of inflation."

For a long time now, she'd wondered when Teddy would approach her mother about handling her money. For some reason she couldn't put her finger on—perhaps, it was simply an instinct—she didn't like the idea of Teddy becoming involved in her mother's finances. She couldn't shake the feeling that it would be a mistake, even though she realized that she was probably being irrational.

I guess I'm being silly, she thought. After all, Teddy was a supposed to be a great moneymaker, wasn't he? And he certainly did live like one. The lavish bachelor pad in New York City, the meticulously restored showplace up here, the new Jaguar for himself and a truck for the farm every year. A gazillion-dollar wardrobe. Those expensive weekends in the Hamptons.

Suddenly she realized that Teddy had asked her a question.

"What?" she asked.

"You're not listening to me," Teddy said. "You're already thinking about all those poor dogs you've got to neuter."

"Oh, stop with the dumb vet jokes," she said with good humor.

"I was just asking if you had any idea how much money she's got invested with Dock," he said.

"I don't know anything about that," Valerie replied, surprised that he'd asked something that personal. Teddy was aggressive, but usually a lot more subtle than this. "That's strictly *her* business," she added, "and she doesn't talk to me about it." She looked down at her wristwatch. "Anyway, I'd better get going," she said.

"Don't you want dessert?" Teddy asked. "It's just some fruit, but—"

"Too many donuts at the office this morning," Valerie glibly fibbed, already getting to her feet.

Teddy followed suit and walked around the table to her. He slid an arm around her waist and gave her a kiss on the cheek. "I'm glad you came," he said. "I've missed you the last few weekends."

Valerie smiled and nodded. "I . . . I'd better hurry and go get Elvis," she said.

"I'll go with you," he said.

They strolled up to the house in silence, but when they reached the door, Teddy turned and stared into her eyes.

She looked at him with an expectant smile.

"You're not wearing your engagement ring," he said softly. "Why, Val?"

She felt a blush rise to her face. "Teddy," she said, "think about it for a minute. I don't think it's a good idea to wear it to work. At least not my work. I mean, it's not the kind of thing you wear to help give birth to a foal, is it? Or set a llama's broken leg? I don't think you want to see it covered up with blood, do you?"

"Well . . . no," he said, "but you could've had it handy for lunch."

"I'm not about to carry around a ring like that and take it on and off," Valerie replied. "I'd lose it in no time. Or have it stolen."

"You're probably right," he agreed.

"I know I am," Valerie said. "Besides, it's so big, I'd never be able to fit my surgical gloves over it."

Teddy laughed. "You may have a point there, too," he conceded as he opened the door. "You going to be able to come over tonight?" he asked as she headed into the conservatory. "I'm going back to New York tomorrow, you know."

Valerie kept walking toward the kitchen. "I really shouldn't, Teddy," she said. "I've got a lot to do when I get home tonight."

"But—" Teddy began, then he immediately thought better of trying to persuade her to spend the night. *Pressure,* he remembered. *Lay off, Teddy, old boy. You don't want to chase her away now.*

"But what?" she asked.

"Nothing," he replied. "I was thinking out loud. About all the work Lydia's got lined up for me in the office."

"See?" she said. "You've got a lot to do, too, so I don't have to feel guilty."

In the kitchen, Elvis happily greeted them, reluctantly leaving Hattie to prance proudly alongside Valerie back out to the car. Teddy watched as she opened the door for Elvis, then started to get in herself.

"Aren't you forgetting something?" he asked.

Valerie turned and looked at him.

He held his arms out, and she went into them, letting him embrace her. He gave her a quick kiss and let her go. "I know you're in a rush to get back," he said. "I'll give you a call tonight, okay?"

"Sure," Valerie replied. "Talk to you tonight." She got in the Jeep, Teddy closing the door after her. She started the engine and backed out of the parking area, turning around to head down the drive. She waved as she left, and Teddy stood in the driveway waving back until she was out of sight.

Oh, Lord, she thought. *Why is it becoming more and more of a trial to see Teddy? And why, oh why, don't I feel like a woman who's supposed to be getting married to the perfect man at Christmastime? Why don't I have the courage to do what I know I must eventually do?*

Lydia had gone out to lunch, and in the privacy of his office, Teddy picked up the telephone and punched out the number. The machine picked up after the fourth ring.

"Hi, this is Tiffani," her disembodied voice answered. "I'm not here right now, so leave your number and a message. Oh, and wait for the beep. Thanks." Her voice sounded perky and sexy, he thought. Just like her.

After the beep, he said, "Hey, babe, it's Teddy. I got hot just listening to your voice. What about me coming over there after you get off work? We could have a real good time. I've got a little candy for you, babe. Give me a call when you get in."

He replaced the receiver in its cradle and smiled, thinking about Tiffani, that voluptuous body of hers, the things they could do. He knew she'd call back. *She's really into me,* he thought. *Really gets off on it.* Besides, she wasn't about to turn down the chance to snort a little nose candy.

Chapter Ten

Valerie drove the Jeep toward the big iron gates at Stonelair, stopping at the post in the middle of the drive to push the intercom button.

"Who is it?" a voice asked. *The not so jolly bald giant,* she thought.

"Dr. Rochelle," she answered.

"When you get to the split in the drive, veer to the right," the voice said. "To the house."

"Okay," she said, noting once again that video cameras, mounted on the stone piers to which the gates were attached, swiveled toward the Jeep. Must be motion sensitive, she thought. She had the urge to wave at them and stick her tongue out, but decided that would look pretty silly on the monitors. Not very professional, either.

The gates swung open, and she drove through, anxious to see Stonelair in the daylight for the first time. On her last visit in the darkness and driving rain, she'd seen virtually nothing but the stable compound. The mile-long drive was beautifully landscaped, bordered on both sides by giant old conifers, with ancient maples and oaks behind them. Rhododendrons, mountain laurel, and azaleas were massed along the edge of the drive and banked around the bases of the big trees. They were long past their blooming stage, but it must be spectacular in the spring, she thought. The place was like a beautifully kept park.

She came to the split in the road and veered to the right, following Ducci's instructions. When she finally came within sight of the house itself, her first glimpse was of massive chimneys and a slate roof reaching to the sky above the treetops. As she rounded a bend in the road, the house itself came into full view. She slowed down and looked at it with awe.

My God, she thought, *it's a small château!* Built of limestone, it loomed in the near-distance like a great fortress, albeit an elegant one. She'd heard about it all of her life and seen very old photographs of it, but nothing had conveyed the monumental reality of the house.

She knew that it had been built by one of the great robber barons before the turn of the century, a railroad tycoon, as she remembered. Then it had descended to one family member after another, none of them staying there for more than a month or two a year. Sometime back in the early sixties the family had boarded it up, their fortune largely squandered over the course of the last century, until finally they'd sold it to Conrad.

The drive led into a courtyard in the center of which was a large fountain, its bronze horses spouting sprays of water. She drove up to the wide stone terrace that led to the front door. Killing the engine, she got out, grabbing her large carryall, then went around to the back of the Jeep, where she retrieved her medical bag from the cargo compartment.

Valerie looked over as one of the massive wooden doors across the terrace opened. Santo Ducci, giant that he was, didn't quite fill it. He quickly strode across the terrace toward her, his entire body seeming to ripple as he approached.

"Here," he said as he reached her, "let me take that for you."

"No need to," Valerie said, looking up at him with a smile. "I'm used to it."

"Have it your way," he said, shrugging.

He led her across the terrace and into the entrance hall, where their shoes echoed loudly on the stone floors. Valerie glimpsed a limestone fireplace and neoclassical *boiseries* on the walls. Over the ornately carved *boiseries* hung old oil paintings, their picture lamps casting little pools of light in the dimness. She caught only a fleeting glace at them before Ducci gestured her to the left and down a long gallery, its lefthand wall hung with more paintings and the right punctuated with French doors, which led out onto another stone terrace that gave onto acres of manicured lawn.

They finally arrived at a set of double doors, and Ducci stopped, gesturing for her to enter. "The dogs are in here," he said, "and probably the cat." He smiled.

"The cat may be on the prowl, huh?" she said.

"You never know," he replied, "but she hangs out with the dogs a lot."

Valerie stepped just inside the doors and found herself looking into a library, a cavernous double-height room with a balcony running partway around it. Bookshelves lined the walls both beneath and above the balcony, and a spiral staircase led up to the balcony's walkway. On one wall was a huge fireplace similar to the one in the entrance hall, and another wall was set with French doors that gave onto the stone terrace she'd seen from the gallery. Two matching Dutch baroque brass chandeliers were suspended from the ceiling, and the fireplace wall was hung with oil paintings, hunt scenes and horses galore and several dog portraits. Bronzes, primarily of horses, stood atop bookcases and on the shelves, and needlepoint carpets covered the floor. Despite its grandeur, the room had an air of being truly lived in.

She stepped on into the room and was surprised—and delighted—to see that amid this incredible luxury four giant Irish wolfhounds lounged in various positions, two on the rug looking out toward the lawn and two spread out on old leather couches in front of the fireplace. That explained some of the room's lived-in feeling, she surmised.

The moment they became aware of her, all four sprang to their feet, bounding over to greet her. She immediately set down her bags and began stroking their somewhat wiry coats, talking to the giant beasts all the while, her face beaming with joy at their sheer size and friendliness.

"Oh, they're beautiful," she exclaimed.

"Thanks," Santo said. "They're a handful sometimes."

"I bet you are," she said to the dogs, trying to divide her attention equally among the four.

"What are their names?" she asked Santo.

"Paddy, Katy, Sheila, and Seamus," Santo replied.

Valerie couldn't help laughing. "So they're Irish through and through," she said.

He nodded. "Yeah," he said. "We got them when they were pups. From a breeder in Castleknock, outside Dublin. Flew them over here."

"I can see why," she said. "They're such great beauties. Which is which?" she asked.

"Paddy and Katy are the grays," Santo replied, "Shelia's the brown, and Seamus is the brindle."

Valerie continued letting the dogs get a good scent of her, stroking them and crooning all the while until suddenly she caught a movement out of the corner of her eye. She looked up. An enormous cat, a fat, long-hair calico, was not so much walking down the steps from the balcony, Valerie thought, as descending them grandly, her every step measured and regal.

"Ooooh," she cooed, "and who do we have here?" The cat strode toward Valerie, her feet practically invisible beneath her fat, furry body, and continued through the veritable thicket of dogs' legs, rubbing herself up against Valerie when she finally arrived at her feet. She was totally comfortable with the dogs, ignoring their friendly sniffs and licks at her. Valerie leaned down and stroked her silky fur, noticing her huge green eyes.

"That's Mina," Santo said.

"Oh, Mina, you are a beautiful lady," Valerie said. "Quite the *madame,* aren't you? And you look like you have a lot of Maine coon in you."

"We think so, but we're not sure," Santo said. "Wyn—Mr. Conrad—got her at the pound several years ago."

"She's certainly brave with these dogs," Valerie said.

"She's fearless," he replied. "She had a Mexican standoff with a six-foot-long snake once. I don't think she's due any shots, but you can check her chart. I have all their medical charts here."

Valerie looked up at him in surprise. "They usually send them to us," she said.

Santo looked stony-faced. "I had them sent to Mr. Conrad overnight so you'd have them today. You can take them with you when you leave."

I guess Mr. Conrad gets whatever he wants, she thought. "That's great," she said. "Could I take a look at them?"

"Sure," he said. "They're over here." He walked over to an enormous French *bureau plat,* and she picked up her bags and followed him, the dogs and cat trailing behind her.

Santo indicated the pile of charts on the desk, then placed them on a corner, where they were easily within her reach.

Valerie set her bags down and studied the charts for a while, then neatly placed them in a stack on the desk's old burgundy leather surface and looked up at him.

"You're right about Mina," she said. "She's up-to-date on everything." She turned around, looking at the dogs. "So it's just you guys," she said. Then turning back to Santo, she asked: "Okay if I set up here?"

"Sure," he replied. "Whatever's best for you."

Valerie set her leather medical bag on the desk, opened it, and started pulling out supplies: four syringes, already filled with fluid, swabs and alcohol, and several boxes of medication.

"I'll help hold them for you," Santo said, starting to straddle Paddy's huge body with his own.

"No," Valerie said. "Just leave them be. That won't be necessary."

"Uh, I beg to differ," Santo said. "I think you're going to be a very sorry lady if you don't let me help you out here."

She shook her head. "No," she said emphatically. "Trust me on this."

Santo saw that she meant what she said, just as she had down at the stables some weeks ago, and reluctantly backed off. "Okay," he said, "but I think you're making a mistake."

Valerie paid no attention to him as she picked up an alcohol-soaked swab, looking over at the pack of tail-waggers. "Okay, who's first?"

The dogs looked at her expectantly.

"Aha," she said, "I think Katy wants to be first. You know the old rule, don't you, Katy? Ladies first."

She began stroking Katy's neck, talking to her softly and reassuringly, all the while rubbing the alcohol-soaked pad on the back
of the neck where she wanted to give her the injection. After a
moment, she put down the pad, picked up the syringe, and then
deftly plunged it in. Katy looked around, but her attention was
diverted by Valerie's constant crooning.

Santo watched as she repeated the process with the three
remaining dogs without experiencing any difficulty whatsoever.
When she was finished, he shook his head. "I don't believe it," he
said, "not a single complaint."

Valerie smiled and continued petting the animals. "You're all
good boys and girls, aren't you?" she said. "Okay, now we'll have
our first heartworm pill. That's nothing. It tastes like a real treat."

She opened one of the boxes on the desk and tore off four of
the large chewable pills. "They should have one of these a
month," she told Santo, opening the blister packs one by one.
"Here's a magnetized calendar you can put on the refrigerator or
wherever to keep track of when they should have them. You can
mark down today's date and go from there."

"Thanks," he said, taking it from her.

When she was done, she gave each of the dogs one of the pills,
and all four returned to their favorite spots to chew them.

With a tiny meow, Mina jumped up on the chair at the desk,
then onto the desk itself. "Oh-ho," Valerie said, "are we jealous?"
She stroked the big cat, then looked at her more closely. "Oh,
Mina," she said. "You have a tiny tick on your chin."

"What?" Santo said, looking at the cat.

"Yes," Valerie said. "See right there, just below her lower lip? A
tick."

"I hadn't seen it," Santo said, apologetic.

"Well, it's easy to miss," Valerie said. "It's barely begun to feed.
I'll just get rid of it." She reached over a thumb and finger, prepared to pinch off the tick.

"Don't do that!" a voice boomed out authoritatively from
somewhere above her.

Valerie jerked around, looking up, but she didn't see anybody.
She did see all four of the Irish wolfhounds spring from their var-

ious positions and go bounding toward the spiral steps that led up to the balcony.

"You'll either have to put her under or heavily sedate her to do it," the voice continued, its volume now lower, but still commanding.

Valerie's eyes followed the dogs to the spiral stairs, where she finally spotted a figure standing up on the balcony at the opposite end of the room. There her eyes rested, trying to make out the distant figure, his body silhouetted against the sunlight pouring in through the window behind him. He appeared to be very tall and lean. His polo shirt revealed powerfully built arms, a neck thickly corded with muscle, and hinted at an imposing chest. Other than that, she could tell almost nothing about him because he was wearing a baseball cap pulled low over his face, casting it in shadow.

The elusive Mr. Conrad? she asked herself. *Obviously,* she decided. *Who else around here would issue orders from on high?*

"I think I can take care of the problem," she finally replied in an even tone.

"Then I don't think you know the animal," he said challengingly.

"And I don't think you know me," she retorted without thinking.

"You're right about that," he said, "but I know Mina extremely well."

She flushed in anger and embarrassment. Who the hell did he think he was, questioning her abilities like this? First the man all but begs her to come out here and treat his animals, and now he insults her about those very abilities he is willing to pay for.

"Mr. Conrad," she said, making an effort to control the irritation in her voice, "if you *are* Mr. Conrad, I think I know what I'm doing. And I don't think I need your help."

There was the sound of Santo catching his breath, then dead silence in the vast room. It was finally broken by a chuckle coming from the balcony.

"It's your hand," the voice finally said. "Bloody it if you will."

Valerie heard the amusement in his voice, and wasn't certain whether to be further insulted or somewhat placated. She wished she could see his face so that she could read the expression on it, but the man didn't move from his spot. His face was still in complete shadow.

"But don't tell me I didn't warn you," he continued. Then he paused a moment before saying: "And, by the way, I *am* Conrad. Wyn Conrad."

Valerie still felt flustered, but replied cooly, "And I'm Dr. Rochelle." *Not Valerie Rochelle to you,* she thought.

"Pleased to meet you, Doc, I'm sure," he said.

"And now I'd better get about my business, if you don't mind, Mr. Conrad," she said.

"Don't let me stop you, Doc," he replied.

Valerie turned back to Mina then, stroking and caressing her gently.

"You'd better hold her tight," Santo said.

But Valerie ignored his advice and continued stroking the huge cat. Then, using her thumb and finger, she reached down and, in the blink of an eyelid, grasped the tick and removed it with apparent ease.

Mina didn't even react to the procedure, but simply continued her contented purr, obviously enjoying Valerie's gentle strokes on her back. Out of the corner of her eye, however, Valerie had seen Santo flinch, then relax. She couldn't help but feel satisfied with herself, perhaps even a bit smug. She had accomplished the simple deed Santo and Conrad seemed to believe was impossible without risk of bodily injury.

"I never saw anything like it," Santo exclaimed in wonder. "I . . . I don't believe it. She won't let anybody touch a tick on her. Not even a burr." He looked up at the balcony, where Conrad still posed, though he had stepped forward a pace to get a better view. "Did you see that?" Santo asked.

"I saw it," Conrad said. He sounded a little disgruntled.

"She looks awfully well groomed for a cat that won't let anybody take a burr or tick off her," Valerie said with irrefutable logic.

"Well," Santo said, "she lets Wyn—Mr. Conrad—brush her. In fact, she goes to him every day after lunch to be groomed, and she won't let anybody else groom her. I mean *nobody.*"

So the mighty Mr. Conrad stoops so low as to groom a cat, Valerie thought. *I'd like to see that.*

"But," Santo continued, "and this is a big but, she won't even let him pull off ticks or burrs."

She smiled and gave Mina a final stroke. "Well, I guess I'm finished here," she said, pleased. "So I'll be on my way. I'll get their charts updated and filed, so you'll get notices about vaccinations and so on from now on. Let me know if you need anything else."

"Thanks a lot," Santo said. Then he picked up the animals' medical records and put them in a large padded envelope. "I think everything's here."

"Thanks, Mr. Ducci," she said, taking them from him.

"Santo, please."

Valerie nodded slightly. "Santo, then."

"And by the way, I sent copies of the medical records for all the horses over to your office this afternoon," he said.

"Great," she replied, disposing of the syringes in a special plastic carrying case she'd brought. This little case she would have to put in the biohazard garbage back at the clinic, from where it would be picked up, along with all the other biohazardous materials, and sent to Canada for disposal. She closed her leather bag with a snap, shouldered her carryall, and turned to leave.

She glanced up toward the balcony, and Conrad quickly retreated a step backward. "Nice to meet you, Mr. Conrad," she said gaily.

He nodded from his distant perch. "You too, Doc," he said, then he did an about-face and disappeared down a hallway.

"Do you want a check now?" Santo asked.

"The office will bill you."

"Okay," he said. Santo indicated the door they'd used to enter the huge room. She followed him back through the long gallery to the grand entrance hall. She noticed a few of the paintings appeared to be by George Stubbs, arguably the greatest painter of horses, and several that she was certain had been painted by Alfred Munnings.

Suddenly she stopped, drawn by a tiny, postage-stamp-size drawing of a horse's head. She stood, entranced, studying the remarkable image. It was exquisite, rendered in charcoal, and signed by Stephano della Bella. She shook her head in wonder.

"Mr. Conrad's an art collector, I gather?" she casually said to Santo, who had stopped with her.

Santo nodded. "Sort of," he replied. "He inherited a lot of the stuff and now and then he'll pick something up to add to it. Like the drawing you just looked at. He got that himself."

"It's truly beautiful," Valerie said.

"He thought so."

They reached the front door, and Santo opened it. "Thanks again, Dr. Rochelle," he said. "I've got to hand it to you. You did a good job."

Valerie smiled. "You're welcome," she said, accepting the compliment with ease. "If there are any problems, let me know."

"Will do," he said.

She walked across the stone terrace and down the wide steps to the driveway and her Jeep. She stowed her medical bag in the rear compartment, then went around to the front door, opened it, and climbed in with her carryall bag.

Santo waved from the doorway as she pulled out, and she waved back. Slowly going back down the long drive, she was rounding a curve, then almost slammed on the brakes to bring the Jeep to a stop. She took a deep breath. *Shit!* she swore. She was certain she'd glimpsed a figure about to step out into the drive. But no. The figure—not an apparition, she told herself—rushed behind a stand of hemlocks.

She felt goose bumps rise on her flesh, and her heart began to race. She almost pulled the car over to relax a minute, but then she thought better of it.

I'm getting out of this weird place, she thought, as fast as possible.

She gunned the engine and swiftly arrived at the entrance gates, where she was buzzed through automatically. On the highway at last, she pulled over for a moment and took a few more deep breaths. *What's going on in that place?* she wondered. *And why is Conrad like some kind of ghost? Staying up on the balcony, watching me from a distance?*

She checked for traffic, then pulled back out onto the road. *I don't think I'll be going back there,* she told herself. *It just makes me feel too uneasy.* Despite her laughing at all the silly rumors, she had to admit that the atmosphere was somehow . . . eerie.

On the other hand, she told herself, the animals were well adjusted and happy. *Conrad must love them,* she thought. *But,* she asked herself, *what can I really make of what I know?* He had appeared to be quite an impressive specimen from what she could see. She wished she could have seen his face, seen if it matched the rest of his body. She had to admit that his insulting sergeant-major behavior and then his amusement at her obvious anger should have been a real turnoff. Men like that were generally for the birds as far as she was concerned. But for some reason she couldn't put her finger on, she couldn't shake her curiosity about him.

Suddenly she realized that she wanted to know more about him. She had become intrigued by the old place and its owner. Despite just deciding that she didn't want to return, she realized that she couldn't wait until the next time she was called back.

Chapter Eleven

Arielle's head jerked wildly from side to side as Lolo thrust away at her like a man possessed, sweat flying off his body, his grunts like those of a rutting animal. Then she screamed, her nails sinking into his back, as she felt him release a flood tide inside her, his body in an arc of rigid muscle atop her, his bellow of spent passion almost like a wail of pain.

He fell on top of her, and flushed and panting, they threw their arms around one another, their sweat-soaked torsos meeting as they peppered each other with kisses. They lay gasping for breath amid a tangled mass of Egyptian cotton sheets, discarded silk lingerie, and polo gear ripe from the practice field. On the table next to the bed were half-empty gin and tonics.

The air was pungent with the aromas of her Caron perfume, the lavender water her sheets were laundered in, and the sandalwood-scented powder that she lavished on her body. Intermingled with the sweet scents of her boudoir was the sweaty leather of his polo boots and knee pads, and the faintest hint that remained of the spicy vetiver cologne he'd used much earlier in the day. But overpowering all of these scents was the indisputable smell of their sex.

"Oh, my God, Lolo," Arielle gasped in a breathy voice, "that was fantastic stuff." She barked a short laugh and hugged his hard muscularity. "*You're* fantastic stuff."

Lolo stroked the perfect length of her nose with his fingertip and smiled, his teeth gleaming against his darkly tanned flesh. "I think I'm beginning to love everything in Palm Beach," Lolo said, a hand stroking her buttocks.

"Well, I hope not everything," Arielle said. "Maybe just me."

"Yeah," he said. "Just you." He reached over to the bedside table for a package of Arielle's cigarillos and her gold lighter. Sitting up in the bed slightly, he took two of the long, thin cigarillos out, placing both of them in his mouth. He lit them and handed Arielle one.

She took the cigarillo and sat up next to him. "Thanks," she said, kissing his cheek.

He draped an arm around her shoulders and held her close, proprietarily, but he smoked in silence, blowing lazy plumes of gray fog toward the ceiling, staring off in the distance.

Arielle watched him, aware of his unusual silence and his thoughtful expression. Normally they were chatty after sex, oftentimes sharing their dreams for the future they wanted to build together, the future they would have after the divorce was finalized and the settlement was paid.

"You're awfully quiet, Lolo," she finally said, unable to bear his distance any longer. His silence frightened her.

Still, he smoked silently, not responding to her remark. The lazy whorls of smoke streamed toward the ceiling, shifting about in the breeze coming in off the ocean.

"Come on," Arielle cajoled, her voice rising with concern. "What is it? Why the silence? Something's wrong, isn't it?" She stubbed out her cigarillo in the ashtray, grinding it hard against the crystal with nervous fingers.

He shrugged and sighed loudly, exhaling smoke at the same time. Then he looked into her eyes and smiled wanly. "I'm sorry, Arielle," he said. "It's just that . . ." He sighed again, and all of the energy seemed to seep out of his body with its sad, defeated sound.

"Come on," she said with alarm. "You can tell me, Lolo. You know that. You can tell me *anything*."

"Well," he finally said, averting his eyes from hers and looking off into the distance, "it's just that"—he flashed a look at her—"I don't have the money for the car payment on my Ferrari this month."

She looked at him in confusion. "You mean the fucking thing's not paid for?" she cried in horror. "I can't believe this." She slapped the bed with both of her fists, and her pretty face contorted in a mask of fury.

Lolo had known she was going to be outraged, but there was no avoiding the issue. Not if he wanted to keep the car. A few more days and the fiery red Ferrari would be hauled off right out from under him.

Finally, he ground out his cigarillo and turned to look into her eyes again. "I'm sorry, Arielle," he said. "I should've told you before. I just didn't want you to worry about it."

His expression was so genuinely contrite that Arielle melted. "Oh, darling Lolo," she said softly, placing her hands on his cheeks. "Nothing you could do would worry me." She leaned toward him and kissed his lips, then sat back and looked at him lovingly.

He tried to smile, but the effort was too much. He looked down at the bed hopelessly.

"Tell me how this happened," she said, stroking his cheek with a long magenta-lacquered fingernail. "I thought you paid for the Ferrari when Palmer gave you the bonus for signing up to play for his polo team."

Lolo shook his head slightly, then his downcast eyes rose to meet hers. "No," he said. "I made a down payment with part of it," he said, "and they let me finance the rest."

Arielle slumped despite herself. Jesus, she thought, *what's this going to cost? And where the hell did the rest of the money go?* "What happened to the rest of the money, Lolo?" she asked calmly, trying not to sound distressed.

"It's all gone," he said.

"All of it?" she replied in astonishment.

He nodded.

"But . . . but what the hell did you do with it?" she asked, her voice becoming strident in spite of herself.

"I had to pay some bills," he said sheepishly. "You know. Clothes and stuff."

"What?" She looked at him in amazement. "Clothes and stuff?

Jesus, I've charged a fortune in clothes for you. In every fucking shop in Palm Beach! What the hell could you've bought that took that kind of money?"

He looked at her with a sulky expression. "Shit, Arielle," he said irritatedly, "you know what custom-made polo gear costs? One pair of new boots over two thousand—"

"Why the hell didn't you get Palmer to cover those costs?" she snapped angrily. "You're playing for him, for Christ's sake!"

"You know I can't ask that of him," he replied, the irritation gone from his voice and a softness replacing it. "I'm expected to have all of that or get it with my bonus."

She looked at him, studying his face, his splendid torso, and those hard-muscled, inviting arms. She knew that his machismo would prevent him from admitting to Palmer—or any other man—that he couldn't afford new polo boots, or anything else for that matter. Hell, she thought, he could hardly afford a polo shirt, but he would never let on. She also knew that this wasn't unusual in the rich and rarefied world of polo. Like many South American players, Lolo was one of those penniless, uneducated guys who'd learned to play on the *estancias* of the very rich, then been recruited by wealthy American team owners who brought them north and kept them on a very tight rein.

"I understand," she finally said, nodding her head. And she did, too. Lolo wanted it *all,* just like she did, and he wanted it *now,* not tomorrow or the next day, also like her.

She ran her fingers through her disheveled hair, then reached over and idly began running them through Lolo's. He was looking at her expectantly, but she was silent, lost in thought, twirling his damp black curls around her fingers. Then she leaned in and placed her smeared, collagen-enhanced lips against his.

"I'm sorry, Lolo," she said. "I really didn't know. I just assumed—"

"You think I do nothing to contribute," he said. "That I just use you."

"Oh, no," she cried in a pleading voice. "That's not true. You make me so happy. Oh, my God, I don't know what I'd do without you." She leaned over and kissed his lips again. "Please. Let's don't argue, Lolo. I'm sorry. I just wasn't thinking. Please forgive me."

Lolo remained silent for a moment, his eyes averted from hers, then he turned his gaze to her. "Okay," he said, nodding. "But that still doesn't solve the problem of the Ferrari."

"No," she said with a sigh, "it doesn't." She swiveled around and lay back against the pillows, staring at the ceiling thoughtfully for a minute. "I guess I could pawn some jewelry," she finally said.

"*No!*" Lolo said. "I won't let you do that, Arielle."

"I don't mind," she replied, stroking his face. "Not for you, Lolo. It'll only be for a little while. Till that shit Wyn comes through with my money."

"It always goes back to him," Lolo replied. "The stingy bastard."

"Yes," she said, nodding her head. "It always goes back to him." Her features suddenly screwed up into an ugly, angry mask. "God, how I hate him!" she cried furiously. "He's the cause of all our problems. If it weren't for him—" She slammed a fist against the bed.

Lolo grabbed her arm and pulled it to him, kissing her hand, trying to placate her. "Don't worry," he cooed. "It won't be much longer. Maybe I can hold off the car dealer long enough." Then he looked into her eyes. "I've been thinking about something," he said.

She looked at him with curiosity, her eyes brightening. "What?"

"If you like," Lolo said, "when we go up to Saratoga, I could go and see Wyn and try to talk some sense to him."

She jerked up. "I'd forgotten about Saratoga," she exclaimed. She ignored him for a moment, her eyes seemingly focused on the Venetian mirror atop her dressing table, as if its baroque beauty held the answer to all of their problems.

"What?" Lolo asked, tugging at her arm. "What is it, Arielle? I can tell you're thinking of something important."

"I'm just thinking," she replied. Then she slowly turned to him. "Yes, maybe seeing him in Saratoga is a good idea," she said.

"I would like that very much," he said. "We could have a man-to-man talk."

"I'm sure that Bibi and Joe Whitman will fly up in their jet," she said excitedly. "We could hitch a ride with them. Or the Connollys. Even if I can't stand that bitch Peggy Connolly." Her eyes began to brighten even more, and she rubbed her hands together.

Lolo watched the transformation in her demeanor, and his eyes began to widen. "What—what do you have in mind, Arielle?" he asked quietly.

"Oh, I don't know," she replied cagily.

"Arielle," he said. "I know that crazy look." He tugged at her arm again. "What are you thinking of doing?"

She turned to him and smiled widely. "Me?" she asked innocently. "Why would you think I would be up to something?"

"Come on," he cajoled. "What have you got on your pretty mind? What are you thinking of doing?"

Her eyes glittered with an intense flame that seemed to Lolo to be a mixture of excitement, wrath, and perhaps a little madness, and it frightened him, for he knew that Arielle was capable of doing really crazy things.

"It's not what *I'll* do," she said evenly, staring into his dark eyes steadily. "It's what *you'll* do, Lolo." She jabbed his muscular chest with a painted fingernail.

He stared at her curiously for a moment, then sat up beside her. "Wait a minute," he said. "Tell me what you have in mind."

She smiled secretively, then lay back on the pillows and stretched out on the bed. "Let's have another drink," she said, her hands reaching down between his thighs to stroke his much-talked-about equipment. "And have some more fun." She stroked him gently, pleased to see that her hands could excite him as they did. "Then we'll talk about it."

Lolo expelled a deep breath, his eyes running up and down the length of her magnificent body. All thoughts of his Ferrari and Saratoga were swept out of his mind as if by magic, his body surging with renewed desire.

He smiled and began stroking her breasts, slowly and gently, then more urgently as he felt her rise to his touch. "Ah, what a future we'll have, Arielle," he whispered as he fell on top of her.

If you only knew, she thought. *If you only knew.*

Chapter Twelve

Dusk was settling and Wyn Conrad walked alone toward Stonelair's stable block. *It's a perfect late summer evening,* he thought.

He approached a bend in the path and heard footsteps and soft-pitched voices nearby. *Helmut and Gerda Reinhardt,* he thought, *taking an evening walk.* He rounded the corner, and there they were, walking briskly along the path that led from their cottage to the parking area at the stables. Gerda had changed out of her customary uniform and was wearing a big flowery print blouse and shorts. Helmut wore baggy shorts and a pale short-sleeve shirt. Both of them wore sandals. They were holding hands like teenagers, he observed, though they were well into their sixties.

"Ah, good evening, Mr. Conrad," Gerda called to him, her English, like her husband's, heavily accented with the inflections of her native German.

"Mr. Conrad," Helmut said, nodding respectfully.

After all these years, Wyn thought, *they still insist on being so formal, so Old World in manner.* He'd asked them repeatedly to address him by his first name, but he'd long since learned it would never happen. They considered themselves employees, and he was their boss. Apparently, never the twain would meet.

"Hi, Gerda," Wyn said, "Helmut. Taking a walk?"

"We're going to a movie," Gerda said.

"Have you got my medication?" Helmut asked his wife.

"*Ja*, Helmut," she responded. She lifted an arm. "Right here in my *Beutel*." She held up a small vinyl bag with drawstrings. It looked almost as old as she did. "The cell phone, too, Mr. Conrad," she said, nodding at Wyn. "We always have it with us in case you need us, just like you've told us."

Wyn smiled. "You two have a good time."

"I'm sure we will," Gerda said.

"We'd better hurry," Helmut added, "or we're going to miss the beginning."

"See you later," Wyn said.

He watched them hurry on toward the lighted parking area, feeling a twinge of envy. They were a taciturn, thrifty, and childless couple with little if any sense of humor, and they seemed to get little joy from life, at least that he could see. He was surprised that they were allowing themselves a trip to the movies. But, he realized, they were also exceedingly hardworking and loyal to him. They were also devoted to one another and had been for over forty years, something of a record among the people he knew.

He shot a last glance in the direction of the parking lot, where they were already driving out in their old Volkswagen, then resumed his walk, trying to shake the sense of loneliness that had come over him. Gazing out in the direction of the surrounding forest, toward a clearing to the north, he noticed that Santo's cottage was in darkness, except for a dim porch light. He'd probably gone into town to the gym to work out as he sometimes did, even though there was a well-equipped gym here. Or maybe, Wyn thought, he'd gone out to a bar in one of the nearby towns. He wasn't really certain how Santo spent his free time, other than working out, but he imagined that he went out seeking company. Santo might appear to be nothing more than a muscle-bound steroid freak, practically inhuman to strangers, but Wyn knew that he must grow tired of the monotonous days and nights of virtual imprisonment at Stonelair. He never discussed it with him—in fact, he'd never given Santo's personal life much thought—but he trusted him implicitly. He'd stayed by his side through thick and thin for the last decade, never asking questions, never making demands, and always doing as he was told. Loyal, like the

Reinhardts, he thought dismally, but then that was part of what they were all paid for, wasn't it?

He reached the stable office and flipped on the lights, then went on through to the tack room. He flipped on the lights there, revealing all the mementos of polo seasons past, artfully arranged on the pine-paneled walls: crossed mallets, team photographs, and trophies. He walked over and looked at an old framed polo shirt of his, hunter green, the letters and numbers in white. On the sleeve was his number, 1, and on the chest the TC logo, for Team Conrad. The shirt was ripped nearly to shreds and was stained a dull brown all over. Dried blood.

He averted his gaze and looked at some of the team photographs. A few of the familiar ones from the more recent years were missing because Santo had carefully edited out those that had Arielle posing with the team as well as those in which Lolo appeared with Team Conrad or the opposition. His eyes swept over some of the photographs briefly: the Paris Open at the Polo Club of Paris at Bagatelle, the Prince of Wales Trophy at the Royal County of Berkshire Polo Club, the Royal Windsor Cup, and the Queen's Cup, all in England, shots from Greenwich, Houston, Sante Fe, Santa Barbara, Wellington, Saratoga, and on and on. In most of them he was soaked with sweat, splattered with turf, and smiling with utter joy.

Those days are over, he thought bitterly. The loneliness that had descended on him earlier only became more acute. Any magic these mementos might have held for him turned to nothing more than a terrible reminder of the drastic changes in his life. *There's no one to share the beauty of the summer night with,* he thought sadly, *but then there's nobody who could stomach living with what I've become.*

He looked longingly at the saddles and tack, all of it polished and displayed, ready for immediate use. He remembered the feeling of the air on his face and the exhilarating sense of freedom when he rode. *Damn,* he thought, *I'm sick of being bored, sick of being cooped up, sick of all of my problems. And I'm the only person who can do anything about it.*

With that he turned and strode over to the dressing room, flung the door open, and flipped on the light. He sat down and took off his sneakers, then stood up and pulled off his Levi's. *This is crazy,* he thought giddily, *but I'm going to ride. It's been far too long.*

He quickly slid into riding jodhpurs before he could change his mind, then grabbed boot hooks and a pair of the custom-made riding boots that had been gathering dust. He sat down and slid the boot hooks through their loops and pulled them on, then stood back up to ease his feet completely into the boots.

Suddenly a woozy feeling overcame him, and he sat down again for a moment to wait for it to pass. *It must be that last shot,* he thought. He took several deep breaths and wiped away the beads of sweat that had popped out on his brow. *I really must be crazy,* he decided. *In my condition, with all the drugs in my system—*

He wouldn't think about that now. No, he was going to do this no matter the consequences. He got back to his feet and snatched the first helmet he saw, put it on, and went back out to the tack room, where he grabbed a bridle, reins, and girth off wall hooks, then took an English saddle and quilted saddle pad off a rest.

In his weakened condition the saddle was heavy, but he manhandled it through the door to the horse stalls, eased it down on the bench there, and flipped on the light. He would saddle up Demon. It had been too long since he'd been on the old hellion. He began walking down the length of the stalls, peering in at the horses, stopping to talk to them and stroke their necks, something he used to do on a daily basis, but lately had neglected.

He took his time, lingering at one stall after the other, until he finally reached Demon. He eyed the magnificent Arabian admiringly, then began stroking him as he had the others, talking to him in almost a whisper. Demon had been his favorite for a long time now, and he couldn't wait to saddle him up.

He had started to open the stall door when a sudden noise made him stand still and listen. After a few seconds of hearing nothing more than the usual sounds of the stable at night, he reached for the stall door again. And heard the strange noise again.

What the hell? he wondered. He stood listening once more. He walked down past Demon's stall, being as quiet as he could in his riding boots, and heard the sound again, unmistakably to his right this time.

He looked into the stall from which the sound had emanated. His eyes grew wide with alarm and then growing disbelief and horror as he stared at the horse that stood staring back at him from within the stall. It was a horse that Santo had purchased only a few days ago, Layla by name, and she was in acute distress, of that there could be no mistaking. The sounds had been her whinnies of pain.

Opening the stall door, he stepped in for a closer look. Her nose was bleeding profusely, and her legs were horribly swollen, as was her neck. Then he noticed something else. Her coat was covered with a wet, slicking-looking secretion. *I've never seen anything like this in my life,* he thought. *What the hell could it be?*

He went down on one knee to get a closer look at her swollen legs. They were white, and he could clearly see where she was hemorrhaging beneath the skin. He felt her swollen throat. It was as if she had the mumps. His mind began to race, and his heart was sick, for he knew the horse must be in great pain. He stroked her neck for a moment, then backed out of the stall and closed the door.

Gone were all thoughts of riding tonight as he ran toward the office telephone. He would have to call the vet immediately to see to Layla. Then it occurred to him that he was alone here at Stonelair. Santo was gone. The Reinhardts were gone.

It's okay, though, he thought. *They'll have their cell phones. I'll call Santo first and get him back here as quickly as possible. Then he can handle the vet.* He reached the office and lunged toward the telephone there. He picked it up and punched in Santo's number. It began to ring.

Darkness was descending, and Valerie had spread out on a chaise longue on the screened-in porch at the back of her house. Elvis was curled up on the floor beside her, sleeping soundly. She idly gazed out at the pale moon's reflection on the small pond in the garden. *It's such a perfect late summer night,* she thought.

Her eyes shifted to the approach to the pond and the flower

beds bordering the stone steps that led down to it. The whites and silvers of the moon garden she had planted were beginning to reflect the moon's light, as the pond reflected the moon itself. She'd worked hard planting it, not quite believing that it would be as effective as Colette had sworn it would be. She'd been delighted to discover that Colette had not only been right, but that it held a magic she would never have anticipated. It was like looking at a particularly complicated painting, mysterious and secretive, not wanting to give up all of its details, compelling one to delve deeper to discover what lay hidden in its combination of darkness and light.

She squeezed herself with her arms, aware of the fact that she felt somewhat lonely, despite the beauty of the night. She didn't have to be alone tonight. Teddy had called to tell her that he was coming up and was going to stay over a couple of nights since he couldn't be here over the weekend. He had to spend another weekend with important clients, this time in Connecticut. He'd wanted her to come over and stay with him, but she'd begged off.

Frogs, along with unseen creatures of all sorts, had begun singing their nightly chorale, but she took little comfort from their cacophony. She had to admit that company would be nice, human company preferably, but was determined that she wouldn't let her loneliness drive her to Teddy.

Suddenly she heard a noise around at the side of the house. Elvis scrambled to his feet and barked. For a moment she was alarmed. Then she realized that it was simply the creaking of the hinge on the front garden gate.

Colette, she thought. With the exception of her mother and Teddy—both of whom would call first—Colette was the only person who would come around that way rather than ring the doorbell at the front first. Elvis had quit barking and stood wagging his tail at the door that led onto the porch. Valerie smiled somewhat ruefully. *I'm going to have company after all,* she thought.

"Val, darling?" Colette's near whisper was like an exotic sigh carried by the late summer breeze. "Are you there?"

"I'm here, Colette," she replied. "On the porch."

"Am I a bother?" the older woman asked.

"You know better than that, Colette."

From out of the darkness, the older woman's snowy hair appeared, and Valerie watched as she took deliberate little steps on the stone path that led to the porch.

"Wait, Colette," she said. "Let me turn on the light for you."

"No, no, my darling," Colette said. "Don't break the spell. It's so lovely like this. So romantic."

Valerie rose to her feet and went out onto the path and took Colette's arm. "Here," she said. "Let me lead the way at least."

On the porch, Colette settled herself in a chair, petting Elvis while Valerie lit several candles on the dining table.

"Would you like a glass of wine?" Valerie asked.

"Oh, lovely, darling," Colette said. "My grandfather, a doctor, always said a glass before bedtime was just the ticket."

"I'll be right back," Valerie said.

She stepped through the open French doors into the kitchen and got a crystal wineglass out of a cabinet, then retrieved a bottle of chilled white wine out of the refrigerator. She set Colette's glass on the table next to her chair, then filled the glass.

"Oh, Val," Colette enthused, "you are a saint for putting up with an old ninny like me."

Valerie laughed. "Don't be silly," she said. "You know you're welcome here anytime, Colette."

Valerie refreshed her own glass of wine and sat back down. She took a sip, staring at one of the candles, ringed by moths, its honey-suckle scent pleasant in her nostrils. She felt Colette's eyes on her, but didn't break the silence.

Colette lifted her goblet delicately by the stem, swirled the wine in the glass, then took a tiny sip. "Delicious," she pronounced, setting the glass back down. "Heavenly on the palate."

Valerie turned to her slowly and smiled. "It is, isn't it?" she agreed. "Teddy gave it to me." She paused a moment, her gaze shifting back to the candle. "He knows so much about wine," she continued, "and always makes such good choices. He doesn't trust me to." She laughed lightly, but there was no humor in it.

"Teddy does have excellent taste," Colette said, "but that's not everything, is it?"

Valerie looked at her, and Colette cocked her brow. Valerie

laughed again, but it was genuine this time, full of mirth. "You're a pistol, Colette," she said.

"And you're unhappy," the older woman said, picking up her wineglass again. The large rings on her fingers flashed brilliantly in the candlelight.

Valerie started to reply, but clammed up instead, watching Colette sip the wine, thinking about what she'd said. A lot of people thought of Colette as a supercilious woman, capricious to a fault, eccentric in her ways, and spoiled by money, and Valerie realized that all of that was undeniably true. It was not all that Colette was, however, and Valerie would never underestimate her friend. For among her other assets, Colette was extremely observant, worldly wise, and had a wealth of experiences and knowledge. *In fact,* Valerie thought, *she's probably the sharpest person I know.*

Much of Colette's eccentricity, Valerie had decided, was part of a pose that the old woman had long ago perfected, a protective pose that she had developed to keep the world at arm's length. On the surface, Colette appeared to be carefree and fun-loving, a bit zany and daring, and she was all of those things. But she'd also been wounded by life and chose to keep her disappointments to herself.

Valerie decided not to brush off Colette's remark, and at last asked, "Why do you say that, Colette?"

Colette turned sharp eyes on her. "It's simple, Val. I don't see the blush on the peach that ought to be there when one is deeply in love," she replied. "You're not excited by Teddy. That much is clear. To me at least."

Valerie felt her face burn with embarrassment. *Is it that obvious?* she wondered. She looked off into the distance, then cleared her throat and turned to Colette. "I . . . I guess you're right," she said in a small voice. "I've been seeing Teddy so long that I guess he's . . ." She stopped and searched for words.

"Teddy's become a habit," Colette supplied. "And why not? He's handsome and has charm. He has money and connections. He's well-bred, and . . . he's a dreadful bore. At least, to you. And, I daresay, to me as well."

Valerie erupted into laughter.

Colette smiled. "Am I on the mark, darling?"

Valerie nodded her head and ran her fingers through her hair. "I guess you are, Colette," she said. She looked over at her friend. "Oh, hell," she said with a laugh, "you've hit the nail on the head, as usual."

Colette nodded knowingly, her eyes still on Valerie.

Valerie took a sip of her wine, then set the glass down. "But I don't know what to do about it," she said with a sigh. "I feel so damn guilty. We've gone together for so long, and he's so determined. And so is Mother, of course."

She paused and her eyes took on a faraway look before continuing.

"I used to think that I was really in love with Teddy. He is good-looking and sweet and considerate, most of the time at least. All those things you said." She smiled ruefully at Colette. "But I'm beginning to realize that he was really the first man that paid any attention to me. I guess I felt so grateful that I thought I was in love."

Colette reached an arm over and brushed Valerie's cheek with her fingertips. "These things happen, Val darling, and they're unfortunate and sad. But you mustn't allow it to drag you down and make you unhappy. If you really think it's over with Teddy— and it certainly sounds as if that's the case to me—then the thing for you to do is end it." She sliced a hand through the air. "Like that!" she exclaimed. "Cut the cord. If you don't, the pain—yours and his—will go on and on. You're just prolonging the inevitable. Don't you see?"

Valerie shifted uncomfortably in her chair. She knew very well that Colette's words were true, but they were difficult to hear nevertheless. It was a problem she simply didn't want to face.

"I just . . . I guess I'm just a chicken," Valerie said at last. She looked over at Colette. "I don't want to have to deal with this. I'm . . . I'm . . . scared, Colette. Especially since I accepted his engagement ring."

"Oh, darling," the older woman sighed, reaching over and squeezing Valerie's hand in hers. "I understand that perfectly, and I'm so sorry. I know I come on like a virago sometimes, but I *am* thinking of you. I hate to see you unhappy, and you haven't been happy with Teddy for quite a long time, I think."

Valerie nodded.

"The only cure for your problem is being honest. With yourself. And Teddy. A tall order, I know, but the sooner the better, I say." She looked at Valerie steadily, those large blue eyes glistening in the candlelight.

"You've got everything going for you, Val," she went on. "Everything. You have an unusual beauty. You have a wonderful career. You have a marvelous personality, and even with all your assets, you manage to be down-to-earth. You're a good person, Val, a very good person. And they're hard to find."

Valerie shifted in her chair again. She appreciated the compliments, but sometimes she still had a difficult time accepting them as the truth about herself.

"And," Colette said with emphasis, "someone, someday soon, I expect, will come along for you. A man better suited to you. I'm sure of it."

Valerie looked at her. "Do you . . . do you really believe that, Colette?" she asked.

Colette nodded dramatically. "Absolutely," she said. "Someone whom you'll be happy with." She paused and sipped her wine. "Oh, realistically speaking, we all have to make concessions at times. We have to compromise, Val, don't we? But that doesn't mean you have to align yourself with a man who makes you unhappy, even if he has a lot of good qualities. Think about five years down the road. Ten. If you're unhappy with Teddy now, think of years of it."

"Oh, Colette," Valerie groaned. "I know you're right, dammit."

"And I refuse to believe that a man won't come along who'll help make your life more joyous," Colette said.

"You make me feel so much better," Valerie said. "And . . . a little bit less afraid, too."

"Remember, darling," Colette said, "Teddy may be a man, and a strong and forceful one at that, but what's he going to do?" She shrugged expansively. "He has no ironclad hold over you. You're not married, after all, and this sort of thing happens all the time.

So I expect he'll fuss about for a while, lick his wounds a bit, then get on with his life. There'll undoubtedly be harsh words because of his disappointment, some unpleasantness to deal with, but that won't last long. You'll see."

Valerie stared out toward the moonlight on the pond and the silvery flowers surrounding it. Its beauty held her attention for but a moment. For all of Colette's well-intentioned efforts to make her feel better and to give her courage, her last words had had a chilling effect.

Over the years she had come to realize that Teddy was a much needier man than she would ever have expected, and that from this neediness sprang a desire to control and manipulate everything—and everybody—around him, including Valerie herself. And that's where his ruthlessness came into play. For he ruthlessly pursued what he wanted—she could see that now—and would stop at almost nothing to get it. Woe be to anything or anybody who got in his way.

She suddenly wrapped her arms around herself and shivered slightly.

Does that include me? she wondered. *Will Teddy refuse to let me go?*

She quailed inwardly at the thought. She was glad, however, that she and Colette had had this conversation. For if nothing else, the realization that had been gradually asserting itself in her consciousness—that she didn't love Teddy and didn't want to marry him—had become crystal clear. She knew now that she must talk to Teddy as soon as possible. Colette had given her the courage to act on her feelings.

Still, a pervasive sense of dread made her uncomfortable with this knowledge. She would have to handle Teddy with kid gloves, of that she was certain.

"You're awfully quiet, Val," Colette said. "Have I disturbed you terribly with my unsolicited advice?"

"Oh, no, Colette," she replied. "I'm really grateful to you for being honest with me." She reached over and squeezed her friend's hand. "You've made me feel more sure of my own feelings. Thank you."

Colette smiled tenderly. "I love you, Val. You know that."

"I know," she replied, "and I love you. I've sometimes wished that you'd been my mother."

Colette sputtered with laughter. "As much as I love you, I would never, not in a million years, want to compete with Marguerite for that honor."

Valerie laughed with her. "How's Hayden doing, by the way?"

"Ah, he's doing beautifully," Colette exclaimed. "I just made him a new batch of turkey soup. I make a lot, then freeze it in ice trays and microwave a cube for him. He's positively addicted to it. He turns up his piggy nose at mealworms, which is what all his hedgehog friends love. I suppose Hayden's an iconoclast, which doesn't surprise me in the least. Do you want to say hello?"

"What?" Valerie asked. "You have him with you?"

"Of course, darling," she replied. "He's right here in Mummy's pocket." With one hand she reached down into one of the large pockets in her smock and carefully lifted Hayden out, holding him for Valerie to see.

"He loves my pocket," Colette said. "So he travels about the house with me."

Valerie reached over and carefully stroked the pygmy hedgehog's quills, surprised once again at their sharpness. He quivered for a moment, but then settled down as he seemed to recognize her through his excellent sense of smell.

Elvis stirred on the floor when he heard that particular cooing sound of Valerie's voice.

"Oh, ho," Valerie said. "Maybe we'd better put Hayden back in your pocket before Elvis gets too interested."

"I do let Puff Puppy have a little sniff," Colette said, "but I can't honestly say that Hayden really enjoys it half as much Puff Puppy does. Perhaps I should tuck him back in." She carefully replaced Hayden in her smock pocket, then stroked him for a while with a single finger. "It's odd, isn't it," Colette said, "the things that can give us pleasure?"

Valerie nodded in agreement. "It never ceases to amaze me. Especially in the animal—"

The telephone on the table rang loudly, its shrill man-made sound slightly unnerving them both in the quiet.

"I have to get that," Valerie said. "It could be the service calling."

"Of course, darling," Colette said. She picked up her wineglass and took a sip.

Valerie lifted up the receiver. "Hello?" she said.

"Dr. Rochelle?" a familiar voice asked.

"Yes?" she replied.

"It's Dotty at the service. Sorry to bother you, but there's been an emergency call from a place called Stonelair."

Valerie felt an involuntary chill go up her spine. *Uh-oh. Can I handle a call out there tonight?* she wondered. *But of course, I can,* she told herself.

"What seems to be the problem, Dotty?"

"Something with a horse," the operator answered. "I didn't get it all. Something about swelling and bleeding. The man sounded very upset, and I do mean very upset."

"You don't remember anything else?" Valerie asked.

"Sorry, Dr. Rochelle," she replied. "He was talking so fast I just couldn't get it all."

"Okay, Dotty," Valerie said. "And thanks a lot. If he calls back, tell him I'm on my way."

"Will do," the woman said and hung up the phone.

Valerie let out a sigh and turned to Colette. "I've got to go out to Stonelair on an emergency," she said.

Colette's eyes registered alarm. "Nothing serious, I hope?"

"I'm not sure at this point," Valerie said. "Whoever called the emergency in was very distressed, and Dotty didn't get all the details. Anyway, it's a horse, so I'd better get cracking."

"Indeed, darling," Colette said. "Hayden and I will vanish in the bat of an eyelid."

"Why don't you sit and finish your wine?" Valerie said. "You know you don't have to leave just because I am."

"Well, perhaps we will sit a tad longer and keep Elvis company," she said. "Then we'll toddle along home."

"Be right back," Valerie said. "I have to get some things." She dashed through the open French doors and into the kitchen, then on into the hallway, where she grabbed a clean lab coat from out of the closet. Then she sat down and quickly laced on a pair of sneakers. There, she thought. That will do it. She already had on jeans and an old T-shirt, so none of her good clothing was in danger of being ruined, and there was always that possibility when going on an emergency call. She grabbed her carryall and dashed back out to the porch.

"Ready?" Colette asked.

"Ready," Valerie replied. "But you and Hayden stay as long as you want," she added. "Elvis will love the company."

"Fine," Colette said. "Off you go."

Valerie dashed through the screen door, down the steps, and around to the gate that led to the front yard and her car.

Colette heard her start the Jeep and spew gravel as she pulled out of the driveway, rushing off to help a horse in some sort of distress. She took another sip of her wine and reached down and gave Elvis a few strokes. "Valerie will be back soon, Elvis," she said. She looked at her watch then and saw that it wasn't that late, around ten-thirty, if her eyes served her correctly.

The telephone shrilled again, and Colette stared at it. *Should I answer it?* she wondered. She reached over and picked up the receiver. *What's to lose?* she thought.

"Hello," she said. "Dr. Rochelle's residence."

"Who's this?" a man's voice demanded.

Colette did not appreciate the edge she heard in the words. "This is Colette Richards, Dr. Rochelle's neighbor."

"Oh, you."

Colette listened and heard nothing but heavy breathing.

Then the man spoke again. "Where's Val?" he demanded.

"She's on an emergency call," Colette replied, thinking that she recognized the voice now.

"Jesus!" the man exclaimed. "She's always on an emergency."

"Is that you, Teddy?" Colette ventured.

"Yes," he said, his voice almost a snarl.

"Oh, how nice to speak to you," she said. "I haven't seen you in forever, it seems."

"I've been busy," he said imperiously. "Very busy. What's the big emergency tonight?"

"Stonelair," Colette said. "There's an unfortunate horse in distress of some sort."

"Stonelair!" Teddy almost shouted. "I told her not to go out to that damn place. That guy's some kind of mobster or something."

"I think Valerie is old enough to take care of herself, Teddy," Colette said calmly. "This is a professional call, and she is highly trained to handle it."

"Yes, well, maybe so," he snapped, "but she's not trained to handle trash like Conrad."

"Oh, I think you underestimate our Valerie, Teddy," Colette said. "I think she's capable of handling a lot more than you can imagine, and I think she should be respected for it."

"What the fuck do you know?" Teddy spat.

Colette was shocked by his language. *He's been drinking,* she thought. *Or using some sort of drug.* Whatever it was, he was quite obviously in an altered state. His words were rushed, clipped, and at the same time breathy. He certainly wasn't the ever-charming and proper young man with the perfect manners everybody seemed to love. *Why am I not surprised?* she asked herself.

"I think I know Val," she finally said. "And furthermore, I don't think you know her very well at all." Colette clapped a hand over her mouth after her last statement and rolled her eyes. *Oh, dear,* she thought. *Now, I've gone and done it. But I don't care. The little weasel deserves it.*

"You don't know what you're talking about," Teddy said. "Are you drunk or something?"

"Not yet," Colette said in an amused voice.

"Just crazy," Teddy said.

"Maybe," Colette said, "for having this ridiculous conversation with you."

"You . . . you . . . never mind," Teddy spat. "You'll be sorry." Then he slammed the telephone in her ear.

Colette carefully replaced the receiver in its cradle. For a moment she felt a bit giddy. *I guess I got that brat's goat,* she thought. *And a brat he most certainly is.*

Colette took a long swallow of wine and set the glass back down. *I'm going to have to find out as much as I can about Teddy and what's going on with him. Yes, I need to stay on top of this if I'm going to be of any help to Val. And help, I'm afraid, she's definitely going to need.*

Chapter Thirteen

Valerie clipped along the dark highway at a steady pace, driving fast but not recklessly, her mind torn between the conversation she'd had with Colette and the emergency call she was on. When she reached the gates to Stonelair, she pulled over to the intercom post and slammed on the brakes. She reached out the open window and pushed the intercom button.

"Dr. Rochelle?" the man's voice asked. It was not Santo, of that she was certain. Was it Conrad himself?

"Yes," she replied.

"Through the gates and down to the stables, where the driveway veers off to the left," the man said. "I'll be there."

"Okay," she said.

The gates began opening at once, and when they had fully opened, she sped past the big stone piers and on down the drive until she could see the well-lit parking courtyard in the stable area. Racing to it, she pulled over and parked the Jeep. She gathered up her big canvas carryall and her heavy medical bag.

No one had come out to greet her, so she headed toward the office where she'd been the first time she was here. She could see that lights were burning in there and in the stables, too. When she reached the office door, it was open, and she went on in. There was no one about.

How strange, she thought, *especially with an emergency going on.* Often in an emergency situation, the whole family and staff, if there was one, would be on hand, letting her know what had happened, offering to help. But there was an unearthly quiet here, as if nothing were amiss at all.

"Mr. Ducci?" she called.

There was nothing but silence.

"Mr. Ducci?" she called again, louder this time.

Still there was no response.

She walked on through to the tack room, where the lights were burning brightly, but there was nobody in there either. *Must be in the stable,* she thought. The main overhead lights in the stable weren't turned on, but she could see that the lanterns on the outside of each stall were lit, as was the small overhead in one of the stalls down toward the end of the stable. But she could see no one about in there, either.

"Mr. Ducci?" she called out again.

"He's not here, Doc." A man's voice, Conrad's obviously, answered from somewhere farther down the length of the stable. "You're going to have to deal with me."

"Gladly," Valerie responded. "But who are you, and where are you?" She knew who it was, of course, but couldn't resist making him tell her.

"It's Conrad," the voice replied, oddly quiet and noncombative, "and I'm down here at the tenth stall on your right. Where the light's on."

"I'm on my way," she said, and began walking down the length of the stable. When she got to the tenth stall, she set her medical bag down, then her carryall, and stepped into the stall.

"Oh, God," she whispered, looking at the horse that stood before her, tethered to the stall. The first thing that caught her eye was the horse's profusely bleeding nose. She very carefully felt its neck. It was quite obviously swollen, as if the horse had the mumps. She stroked all around the horse's neck, studying it.

As she took her hands away, she looked down at them in consternation. They were covered with a secretion from the horse's coat, the likes of which she'd never seen. She wiped them off on her lab coat, wondering what on earth was going on.

She looked down and noticed the horse's forelegs. "Ahhhh . . . no," she whispered to herself. She bent down on a knee for a closer look, then scooted around to examine all of the horse's legs. They were enormously swollen, and because they were white, she could clearly see hemorrhaging through the skin, up and down the length of the legs. Touching them delicately, she could feel the same secretion here as on the neck. She wiped her hand on her lab coat again and stood back up, a puzzled look on her face.

She reached out and stroked the horse's body in various places. The secretion was everywhere, oozing from its pores. She stood back, her eyes still searching its body for clues. *What is going on?*

Only then did she become aware of Conrad, leaning against the wall in a darkened corner of the stall, his arms crossed and his head down. He was in riding gear, even with his helmet still on, she noticed, its visor casting his face in darkness. All she could make out distinctly were his riding boots, the light reflecting off of their highly polished leather. She was startled, so intent had she been on examining the horse that she'd forgotten all about him. Now, his silence in the darkened corner perplexed her even further.

"I didn't see you," she said.

"I've just been watching," he said quietly. And he had been, appreciating her sensitivity to the animal and its condition. Marveling at her composure in the light of the horror story that the horse presented. Perhaps it was to be expected, he thought. She was a professional, after all, accustomed to the blood and guts that her work sometimes entailed.

"Well, we've got a real problem here," she said.

"I know we do," he replied. "I was going out for a ride and heard Layla here making some strange whinnying noises. The blood in her nose, I guess. So I called your office."

"You found her like this?" Valerie asked, discomfited that she could see him only in shadow.

"Exactly like this, Doc," he replied.

"Okay," she said, thinking, still puzzled by the horse's condition. "What do you know about this horse's history?" she asked.

"Nothing," he said. "Santo bought her for himself about a week ago from some people at a farm near Saratoga."

"Do you have her medical records?" Valerie asked.

"Uh . . . jeez," he said. "I really don't know. I'm sure Santo must've gotten them, but I don't really know anything about it."

"Is he here?" she asked.

"No," Conrad said somewhat testily, "and I haven't been able to get him on his cell phone. I don't know where the hell he is or why he isn't picking up."

"I really need to see this horse's records," she said, "or at least get some idea of its history. I know you keep copies of medical records here," she went on, "because Santo told me you did since he does some of the vaccinating himself. Where would the medical records be?"

"In the office," he replied.

"Could you please show me?" she asked.

"Well, I . . . I could tell you where they might be," he said hesitantly.

"Oh, come on, Mr. Conrad," she said angrily, irritated by his manner. "Layla is a very sick horse, and if you give a damn about your animals, you'll get those medical records for me. Or take me in there, and *I'll* help look for them. The answer to her problem may be in those records, and I've got to find out what's going on with her before it's too late."

Wyn glowered at the stall's straw-covered floor. He hadn't given the horse's medical records any thought because he'd been in such a panic trying to get Santo or the Reinhardts on the telephone. When he couldn't get anybody, he'd finally decided he'd have to handle the problem himself. He couldn't under any circumstances let the horse suffer. But now—this. What the hell was he going to do?

"Come on, Mr. Conrad!" Valerie cajoled. "The sooner we get those records, the closer I'll be to solving Layla's problems. You don't want her to die, do you?"

"No!" he said emphatically. "Aw, shit! Let's go get the records."

What is his problem? Valerie asked herself. *You'd think I was asking him to give me all his gold.* She stepped back out of the stall and turned toward the office, waiting for him to join her.

Wyn shoved himself out of the darkened corner, stalked around

Layla and out the open stall doorway, then rushed past her in a blur. "Follow me," he said without further preamble.

Valerie was taken aback by his abrupt behavior, but she followed along behind him, wondering what on earth could make a man so disagreeable and rude.

When she reached the tack room, he had already passed through it, presumably, and had switched off the lights on his way. *What a creep,* she thought. *Is he one of those filthy-rich misers who resents every kilowatt of electricity burned?*

She entered the office and saw that he'd turned off most of the lights in here, too, leaving only a small banker's lamp lit on the desk. His back was turned to her, and he was bent over a file cabinet searching through folders, virtually in the dark. *Well,* she thought, *he can search in the dark if he wants to, but not me.* She reached over and flipped on the wall switch, flooding the room in light from the ceiling fixtures.

Conrad jerked up and turned around.

Valerie started to tell him that she needed the light, even if he didn't. Then she glanced over at him and instantly started to scream.

BOOK TWO

The Beast

Chapter Fourteen

In the split second before he did an about-face, hiding his head away from the harsh overhead lights, she understood everything. His aversion to the outside world, his desire for complete privacy, and his unwillingness to interact with a stranger. *No wonder he has Ducci act as his go-between,* she thought.

Her initial horror dissipated, and she felt sorry for him. She wanted to reach out and enfold him in her arms and tell him that it was okay. But she couldn't do that, of course, for she would only antagonize him. Some instinct told her that he was not a man who wanted to be pitied, that he was in fact a man who despised pity.

Her mind reeled with what she should say now that she had learned his secret, and the only conclusion she could come to was to behave as naturally as possible. She swallowed hard, took a deep breath, and spoke. "Do you want to search for the file alone?" she asked, giving him an opportunity to be by himself, away from her outsider's eyes.

"No," he said after a moment's hesitation. "It's . . . okay, Doc. You've got a job to do. I guess you need the operating room lights."

She heard a note of irony in his voice. Apparently he had a sense of humor, even if macabre, about his situation.

"All right," she said, "you want to show me where to look?"

"Sure, Doc," he said. "Why not?" He slid a filing cabinet drawer open, then gestured toward it. "Ought to be in there," he said. "Help yourself. I'll be right here if you've got any questions." He sat down in a chair over in a corner, his head turned slightly sideways.

Valerie quickly thumbed through the files to get an idea of how they were arranged. It was the simplest system possible, using each animal's name for a file folder, arranged in alphabetical order. It looked like the four dogs, the cat, and a number of horses were there, no more than twenty-five or thirty files. She searched for Layla's file, and found it exactly where it should be. She pulled the file out and began looking it over in silence.

She saw that Santo Ducci had bought the horse only a week previously from a couple named Hurley. It listed their address and telephone number. Then she saw that Santo had vaccinated the horse himself only yesterday. It was the usual vaccination against multiple horse diseases, except rabies. Nothing unusual there at all. An owner was permitted to vaccinate against everything except rabies. She stood puzzling over the record, forgetting about Conrad, who remained silent.

There was nothing in the record that could explain the horse's condition. Then suddenly it occurred to her that the problem might lie in that fact itself: there was nothing indicating any past vaccinations or diseases or conditions.

Valerie put the file down. "I've got to call the previous owners," she said, thinking out loud.

"What seems to be the problem?" Wyn asked.

Valerie turned and looked at him, still preoccupied with thoughts of the horse. Her initial fright at his appearance had become almost like a distant memory as she'd become caught up in the mysterious nature of the horse's plight.

"I don't know," she said frankly, "but there's no history in her file. So what I need to do is get in touch with the previous owners. They may have the key to her problem."

"How so?" he asked, intrigued.

"I'm not sure," she replied, shrugging her shoulders, "but the file contains absolutely nothing to go on except for the vaccinations."

"It's strange," he said.

"What?" she asked.

"That Santo would've bought a horse like that," he replied. "I mean, without a lineage, let alone without any records at all."

"I guess it is," she agreed, "especially when you consider the other horses. They all have impeccable bloodlines." She picked up the file and flipped it open. "It's getting late, but I'm going to try to call these people, the Hurleys, anyway. If I wake them up, so be it. I need to find out everything I can about this horse."

She looked down at the telephone and saw that there were several lines, then glanced over at him. "Do I have to dial anything special on this telephone or just punch in the number?" she asked.

He came over toward the desk and peered down at the telephone. "Just dial the number," he said. "A button is already pushed for an outside line."

She looked at the file again, then keyed in the telephone number, all the while aware of the fact that Conrad was gradually becoming more comfortable in her presence. *Maybe he realizes that I don't think he's some kind of a monster,* she thought, *even if the initial shock* was *disconcerting.*

The telephone rang several times but was finally picked up. "Hello?" It was a woman's voice, sleepy and annoyed.

"Is this Mrs. Hurley?" Valerie asked.

"Yes," she replied. "Who's this?"

"This is Dr. Valerie Rochelle," she answered, "and I'm over at Stonelair examining a horse, Layla, that Mr. Santo Ducci purchased from you last week."

"What's wrong with it?" the woman asked. "There wasn't anything the matter with her when he bought her. I wouldn't sell a man a sick horse."

"No, of course not," Valerie said. "I didn't mean that. Anyway, I'm not really certain what's wrong with her, and that's why I'm calling you." She was making an effort to choose her words carefully. She might alarm the woman, especially if the horse hadn't been properly cared for, and then she would not find out anything.

"Mr. Ducci failed to get any medical records for the horse at all," she went on, trying to shift the onus to Santo, "and I thought you might be able to fill me in on her history."

"I'll tell you whatever I can," Mrs. Hurley said. There was the sound of relief in her voice now that she realized she wasn't being accused of anything.

"Has Layla ever had any diseases or conditions that I should know about?" Valerie asked.

"Well . . ." The woman seemed to be thinking. "I can't think of—oh, wait a minute. I do remember something now. She got colicky on us once, but it wasn't anything serious. That was sometime back. I don't remember exactly when."

"Can you think of anything else?" Valerie persisted. "It's really important. She's got a badly swollen neck and her legs are, too, and—"

"A swollen neck?" the woman broke in.

"Yes," Valerie said. "Why?"

"I just remembered," the woman said. "She was the one that had strangle. Her neck was all swollen up then. She had abcesses in her throat."

"You're certain about that?" Valerie asked excitedly.

"Sure," the woman said. "Had to call the vet."

"Who saw her?" Valerie asked. "Which vet?"

"Old Dr. Kramer," Mrs. Hurley said. "It was right before he retired."

"Thank you, Mrs. Hurley," Valerie said. "I'll try to get hold of him. You've been a great help."

"I hope so," the woman said. "She was healthy as could be when that man bought her."

"I know," Valerie said, "and we want to get her back in good health. Thanks again. I'd better hurry and get hold of Dr. Kramer. Good night."

" 'Night," Mrs. Hurley said.

Valerie replaced the receiver in its cradle. Conrad was looking at her expectantly. He'd been listening to her every word, guessing at the other end of the conversation, but had remained silent, letting her handle the situation.

"From the sound of things, you're on to something," he said. "What'd she have to say?"

"I've got to call Dr. Kramer before I'm sure," Valerie said, "but I think I may know what's going on. Mrs. Hurley says that Layla had strangle sometime before Dr. Kramer retired. If that's the case, then we've got our culprit."

Wyn nodded knowingly. "Because if the horse has had strangle and Santo vaccinated it against strangle disease . . ."

"Then the vaccination is what's caused the problem," Valerie finished for him. "The strangle vaccine would set off a chain reaction in the horse's system, causing the swelling and hemorrhaging."

Strangle itself wasn't rare, Valerie knew. She'd seen it many times. It was caused by a bacterium, *Streptococcus equi,* which caused abcesses in a horse's neck. Layla's condition, however, was entirely new to her. She'd never seen a horse that had been vaccinated for the disease *after* it had already had the disease. Apparently, this was what had happened. Santo hadn't known the horse had once had the disease and gave it the vaccination.

"I've got to call Dr. Kramer," she said to Conrad. "Just to confirm that Layla's had strangle."

Conrad nodded. "You want some coffee?"

"That would be great," Valerie replied. "If it's not too much trouble."

"Not at all," he said. "There's everything we need right here. I can do that while you're on the telephone."

Valerie watched as he went over to the bookcases that lined one wall of the office and opened two narrow doors of "books," leather book spines that had been glued to the doors, making them appear to be part of the bookshelves. The open doors revealed a minibar, complete with a small refrigerator, microwave, coffemaker, sink, and cabinetry.

He started making coffee while Valerie held for information. She jotted down Dr. Kramer's telephone number when she got it, then dialed in his number. He surprised her by picking up on the first ring.

"Hello?" he said.

"Dr. Kramer," she said, "it's Valerie Rochelle."

"Hello, my dear," the veterinarian replied. "How're you doing, or need I ask if you're calling an old man like me at this time of night? An emergency, eh?"

She laughed. "You hit the nail on the head."

She related the problems with Layla and her conversation with Mrs. Hurley. Dr. Kramer confirmed what Mrs. Hurley had told her. "It was right before I retired," he said. "Last October. So I imagine with the vaccination, antibodies are racing around in that horse's system, creating havoc."

"Exactly," Valerie said.

"Well," Kramer said, "I won't insult you by asking if you know how to handle it because I know better."

"Yes," Valerie said, "I know what to do, but I do appreciate your help. Thanks a lot."

"Anytime, Val," he replied. " 'Night."

"Good night," she said.

She hung up the telephone again and turned to Wyn.

"Dr. Kramer confirmed what Mrs. Hurley told me," she said to him.

He looked up from the minibar. "So how do you proceed from here?" he asked.

"Massive doses of IV antibiotics and steroids," she replied. "And keep our fingers crossed." She smiled.

He returned her smile. "It'll only be a minute till the coffee's made."

"Great," she said. "I'm going to run back to the stall and see what I've got with me in the way of medication."

"How do you like your coffee?" he asked.

"Two sugars and a little cream," she replied on her way into the tack room.

"It'll be waiting," he said.

When she left the room, he poured their coffees, stirred in her sugar and cream, then set hers on the desk and sat down with his. He took a sip. It was hot and strong and tasted especially good tonight. *In fact,* he thought, *it's been a long time since anything has tasted this good.* But he knew why. It was because Valerie Rochelle had so quickly recovered from her shock. So she couldn't be that horrified by what she saw.

Valerie came through the tack room door, her carryall in hand. "Well," she said, "it looks like I'm going to have to make a run to the clinic."

"Why don't you have some coffee first?" he offered, indicating the cup on the desk.

She sat down on the desk chair, dropped her carryall, and took a sip of the coffee. "Aw," she said, "this is perfect. Thanks."

"Just what the doctor ordered," he joked.

She smiled. "Exactly," she replied. "A horse doctor, anyway."

They sipped their coffee in silence for a minute before Wyn broke it. "Do you think Layla's going to be okay?" he asked.

"I can't promise anything, Mr. Conrad," she said without hesitation.

"Hey," he said. "Back up there a minute. It's Wyn to you, please."

Valerie felt herself redden slightly with a blush that she hoped he didn't see. "Okay," she said, "Wyn it is. And I'm Val, all right?"

He nodded. "Val," he said, drawing it out as if testing the word on his palate. Then he smiled. "Sorry to interrupt you," he said. "Go on."

"Well, I think Layla stands a very good chance if I get her on the antibiotics and steroids right away." She looked thoughtful for a moment, then asked: "I guess Mr. Ducci, Santo, is going to be upset. Is he very attached to her?"

Wyn shook his head. "I don't really know," he said. "I knew he'd picked up a horse for a bargain, but we never did get a chance to discuss it. He's gone out tonight, so I won't get the full story till later or tomorrow." He took a sip of coffee, then looked her square in the eye.

"You know what surprises me the most about you, especially being a doctor of sorts, is that you've shown the restraint not to ask what happened to me."

Valerie didn't know how to respond to his comment.

"Don't you want to know?" he asked.

"I want to know what you want to tell me," she said.

He nodded. "Good answer."

"But before you tell me what you want to, *if* you want to, I'd better run to the clinic and pick up that medication," she said.

"Of course," he said.

"Want to come along?" she asked.

"No," he said emphatically, shaking his head. "I'll stay here with the horse."

She rose to her feet and picked up her carryall, then went to the door. "I'll hurry," she said.

Chapter Fifteen

S anto stood, his back leaning slightly against the bar, his legs spread wide apart, his huge arms across his massive chest, a beer clenched in one meaty paw. Even in the dim light, his shaved head shone, his gold earrings twinkled, and his tattoos—bands of barbed wire around his right biceps and chains around the left— were real attention-getters, rippling with even the slightest movement of the powerful muscles in his arms. His T-shirt revealed only a hint, but a tantalizing one, he thought, of the tribal tattoos that decorated his shoulders, chest, and back.

He knew he wasn't flattering himself to think that he'd attracted a lot of attention in the bar. *The women have been coming on to me ever since I walked through the door,* he thought.

He took a long swallow of his beer, emptying it, then turned and put the bottle on the mahogany bar. The place was packed, but the bartender immediately caught his eye and came his way. Santo shoved his empty bottle of Heineken toward the bartender and threw a five on the counter. The bartender nodded wordlessly, retrieved another bottle from the cooler, opened it, and placed it in front of Santo with a fresh napkin.

Santo turned back around, facing out toward the crowd in the bar again. Everybody seemed to be having a great time, but he knew better. Many of them were just as lonely as he was, of that he was certain, eagle-eyed and on the make.

Nothing like a night of hot sex, he thought, *to drive that lone wolf feeling away.*

He was definitely feeling it tonight. Working for Wyn had been a lot easier in Palm Beach. The town, while so very proper, immaculately clean, and morally upright on its surface, had a filthy underbelly. There was a lot of money there, and a lot of idle people.

He missed it, and although he understood why Wyn had done it, he wished that his boss had never decided to make the move up here to the hinterlands. He missed the glamour, the flash, the constant stream of parties and clubbing, and that whole underclass of servants like himself who often had very interesting lives of their own, intertwining as they did with the rich and powerful. He missed Arielle with her incessant teasing, her unreasonable demands, and her spoiled bitchiness. She'd been a real pain at times, but she flirted with him constantly.

Damn, he thought, *if only all this mess with Wyn and then the divorce hadn't happened.* He knew he could've gotten another job in Palm Beach like the one he had now. It would've taken all of about fifteen minutes with his experience. But there was one drawback to that, and it was a major drawback. Wyn Conrad had written him into his will—for his faithful service, he'd told him—for sticking with him through thick and thin. Now the son of a bitch had him hooked like a fish on a line.

What was he going to do? Walk away and give it up? No way. When Wyn kicked, Santo would be able to buy a little condo down on Lake Worth or someplace close by. He'd be set for life. He didn't know how long that would be, but the way things were going, Wyn might kick at any time. He might OD on drugs. Stoned as he got, he might fall down the stairs or drown in the swimming pool. He might even off himself. He wouldn't put it past him or blame him if he did. Wyn was a very unhappy man, and living up here, the way he did, it was hell. *Shit,* he thought, *I might even accidentally give him too much one day. Or not be there to drag his ass out of the pool. Or pick him up off the floor.*

He smiled to himself. He might be a fairly well-off man sooner than he'd thought. In the meantime, he had to do something to keep his sanity intact, to stay cool and bide his time.

The blonde he'd been talking to earlier sidled up to him. "Got a light?"

Santo shook his head. "Matches at the bar though," he said. He twisted around and snagged a book of them, then turned back around and struck a match.

The blonde looked at him, then took Santo's big hand, stuck the cigarette into the flame, lighting the cigarette, eyes never leaving his.

She was a real exception to the rule up here. *This number could even pass muster in the dens of iniquity down in Palm Beach,* he thought. Up here, he hardly saw a soul, except for Wyn, the Reinhardts, and Tiffani, the girl who helped out in the office.

"You said you had a place to go, right?" Santo asked.

"Yeah, I got a place. Not too far away, either," the blonde said.

"Why don't we take a ride?" Santo said.

"Let's split."

The blonde took his great bear paw and led the way out, through a throng of watchful eyes, some of them registering surprise, many of them envious.

In the parking lot she put an arm around his waist, and he let himself be guided toward what must be her car. When they reached it, the blonde turned to him. "Get in."

"Shouldn't I follow you?" Santo asked.

"No. You ride with me," she said. "I'll bring you back to get your car."

Santo nodded. "Okay."

The blonde unlocked a big Range Rover with a remote and opened the passenger side door.

"Nice car," Santo said. "You must be loaded." *Like I'm going to be someday before too long.*

The Reinhardts had returned from the movie, and they both became terribly upset and embarrassed when Wyn, alone in the stable, had asked them why they hadn't answered his telephone call.

"*Ach, Gott in Himmel!*" Gerda had cried, her hands flying to her face. "The cell phone was in my *Beutel.*" She brandished the ancient vinyl drawstring bag that she carried with her everywhere. "I left it in the car when we went into the theater."

Wyn calmly assured them that it was okay, but he made it clear that he didn't want it to happen again. Tonight, he'd told them, it so happened that he hadn't needed their help after all. The future might be another story.

They walked on to their cottage, Wyn listening to their argumentative voices carrying on the wind.

Shortly afterward he heard Valerie drive in, and they headed for Layla's stall immediately. Finally, after Valerie reexamined the horse and started her on massive doses of antibiotics and steroids, Valerie and Wyn sat down in the stable office. He offered her a glass of wine from the minifridge, and she accepted.

"I can't believe I'm doing this," Valerie said with a laugh.

He smiled. "I'm glad you are."

"But I've got to be up early in the morning," she said. "I've got a lot to do."

"Stay for a glass," Wyn cajoled. "I haven't gotten to talk to anybody on the outside in a long time." Then he laughed. "I don't think I've ever gotten to talk to anybody like you, for that matter."

"What's that supposed to mean?" Valerie asked, her voice one of mock anger. "I'm some kind of freak or something?"

"No," he said. "You're different, and in a most delightful way, but you most definitely are not a freak." He paused and looked down into his glass, then back up at her. "I'm the freak. I've been one ever since I was in a polo accident and got dragged across the field."

Valerie shook her head and then, unbelievably, she let out a short laugh.

"What?" he asked, intrigued with her reaction. He'd expected sympathy, assurance, pity, anything but a laugh.

"No, Wyn," she said, finding it easier to use his first name now, "you're not a freak at all. You're just a very unlucky polo player who let a polo pony practically plow a field with him. And now you look a little bit like the creature from the black lagoon."

"Creature from the black lagoon, huh?" he responded, smiling now. "That bad, eh?"

She nodded. "Only uglier."

"You . . . you . . . ," he began, but then he laughed and didn't finish.

Valerie laughed again, too, then became more serious. "At first I didn't know quite what to think," she said honestly. "With that black mask covering all the bandages on your face, it looked almost like you were wearing some kind of gruesome S&M mask like you see in the movies. All I could see were your eyes and your mouth peeking out."

"Very spooky, I know," he said.

"Very spooky," she agreed. "I think you should dispense with the mask, Wyn. Black, I might add, was a bad choice of colors for it."

"Maybe I should go for something flesh colored?"

"Maybe," she said. "Or just get rid of it. The bandages couldn't look worse."

"Maybe you're right," he said.

"Anyway, then I noticed the scar tissue on your neck and arms and hands. I thought maybe you'd been in a horrible fire or something. To top everything off, there was your secrecy and your gruff attitude. I guess I was prepared for the worst."

"Gruff attitude, you say?" he said grumpily.

"For sure," she replied. "You haven't exactly been the most polite and charming customer up to now."

"Can you blame me?" he asked. "My so-called friends don't want anything to do with me, even a lot of the longtime ones. They think I'm some kind of monster now. Hell, even my wife couldn't stand being around me. She didn't want to have to look at me."

"Can't say as I blame her," Valerie joked.

He smiled. "You're a tough broad, aren't you? You don't pity me at all, do you?"

She shook her head. "I think what happened was horrible," she said, "but with time and operations you'll be good as new. Maybe not as handsome as you look in those polo pictures I saw in the tack room, but I think you'll be fairly presentable. At least in appearance."

"What does that mean?" he asked. " 'At least in appearance.' "

"I think you could work on your manners a little bit," she said. "Maybe not come on to people like some kind of authoritarian dictator or something."

"Well, you haven't seen the way people react to me," he said seriously. "I freak them out. They stare at the bandages or the mask, if I'm wearing it. They stare at my arms and neck and hands. It makes me feel like . . . well, it makes me feel like Quasimodo or somebody. Like something in a sideshow at the circus. And I'm serious when I say my best 'friends' abandoned ship after this happened."

"That's terrible," she said sympathetically, "but I don't doubt it. Most people don't want to face the possibility of what could happen to them. Just look at Christopher Reeve. A lot of people wish he wouldn't make personal appearances. He's too painful for them to look at. Part of it's because of their own fears, I think, and part of it is because it's really not a pretty sight."

The expression in his eyes was understandably glum, but he didn't say anything.

"The bright side," Valerie went on, "and there really is one, is that with a few more operations, as painful, time-consuming, and tedious as they may be, you're going to have a lot of your old self back."

"That's what the doctors in New York told me after the last operation," he said. "But I don't know, Val, I really don't. It's so slow and painful. Sometimes I feel like giving up, you know? Sometimes it doesn't seem like it's worth it. I mean, even when all these great doctors are finished, I'm still going to look like one big skin graft. My face. My neck and arms and hands. Some of my chest and thighs. When I fell, that polo pony dragged me from one end of the field to the other, and after it was all over I'd lost nearly all the skin on the front of my body. *Down to the bone, Val.* They couldn't even suture me up in most places because there wasn't anything to suture." He grimaced with the memory. "My nose . . ." he began.

"You'll have a nose," she said. "It's amazing what they can do nowadays, and it sounds like you've got the best surgeons money can buy."

He hung his head, staring down into his glass again. "I know you're right," he finally said. "It's just so damn hard to have to accept the fact that I'm never going to look like I used to. To have to deal with walking around with scar tissue and grafts for the rest of my life."

"Yes," she said softly. "It's not going to be easy to accept that. In a way it's like aging, Wyn. We have to come to accept what our bodies inevitably become because none of us, no matter how hard we fight it, will remain the great-looking eighteen-year-old kids we once were."

He looked at her. "You really are one tough cookie," he said.

She reached out and touched his hand, and he jerked slightly. "And so are you," she said, patting it. "You're too much of a man to let this defeat you."

From a dark corner of the parking area, someone had been watching and waiting, biding time. Now, after seeing them part company, the watcher felt blood boil in heated veins. From outside, the interloper had listened to part of their conversation, catching bits and pieces of it, easily filling in what couldn't be heard. Then witnessed their sweet, reluctant parting at her Jeep.

Still as a statue, a white-hot anger raging inside, the interloper saw Wyn make his way toward the house. Quickly processing this new development, wondering how it might change things, having to figure a new person into the equation so carefully worked out, well, it was infuriating and scary, and the interloper didn't like it at all.

No! I don't like this business one bit, and I might just have to see what I can do about it. Fists clenched into tight balls. *Goddammit! Nobody's going to fuck up my chances! Nothing and nobody's going to come between me and what I want. I've worked too hard to get it!*

When Wyn finally disappeared into the house, the interloper quickly darted down a path toward the woods, mind already spinning with possible solutions to this problem. It was a problem that needed to be nipped in the bud.

Chapter Sixteen

Teddy poured himself a few fingers of vodka, paused a moment and looked into the glass, then drank it straight down. He shivered from the taste and fire of it and quickly chased it with a glass of water. "There," he said aloud, almost gagging, "that's better."

He crossed to one of the big couches and sat down. A smile came to his lips. On a small mirror on the coffee table were the two long, thin lines of cocaine he'd cut, along with the sterling silver straw a friend in New York City had given him. Although he was alone in the conservatory at Apple Hill, he instinctively looked around him before picking up the straw. Bending down, he snorted up both lines, one up his right nostril, the other up his left.

Dropping the straw, he sank back into the downy comfort of the couch and took a few deep snorts of air, making sure he got all the coke up there. Then he let his mind drift, relaxing after a busy day and grueling dinner. *Whoa,* he thought after only a few mintues. *This is powerful stuff.* Seemingly of their own accord, his feet had begun tapping on the floor and his fingers were beating an erratic tattoo on an invisible drum.

He looked over at the telephone, then glanced at his watch. Tiffani surely would be home soon, he thought, and he could hardly wait. The evening had been a terrible bore. He'd called Linda and Barry Miller, clients of his who lived up here, to discuss their stock portfolio. When he let slip that Valerie was busy and wouldn't be coming over to his place, they'd very kindly invited him to dinner. He thought the Millers were loathsome, if cultivated, nouveau riche, and he hated their endless discussions of art and music and politics and civic responsibility. He'd gone, however, and been his most charming, of course, because they'd invested a lot of money with him. And he was after them to invest a lot more.

Well, he thought, *at least I managed to insult that old witch, Colette Richards.* He laughed aloud. He really didn't care because, although she was one loaded old lady, he knew he'd never get his mitts on her money. She had blue-chip, blue-blooded money managers on three continents.

He wondered what she would tell Val about the call, but then decided he didn't really care about that either. He could always pull the wool over good, trusting, naive Val's eyes, couldn't he? Always had, he told himself.

He looked at his watch again, then reached over for the telephone. He punched in Tiffani's number.

"Hello?" she answered.

"Hey, babe," he said, "where you been? Why didn't you call me? I've been waiting for you."

"Oh, Teddy," she cooed, "I'm so glad you called. I just listened to my messages and was getting ready to call you. I went over to Billy's. You know, the bar where I used to work."

"Yeah?" he said. "What were you doing over there?"

She giggled. "Just having a few drinks with the girls. You know, ladies' night out."

"Yeah?" he said. "Well, what about spending a little time with a man?"

She giggled again. "I'll be ready and waiting."

"I'll be over there in about fifteen minutes," he said.

"I'll be here," she replied.

Teddy went back over to the drinks table and poured himself another few fingers of vodka. *One good thing about coke,* he thought, *is that you can drink and drink and never feel drunk.* He downed the vodka, shivered as before, then quickly drank a big swallow of water. He set the glass back down on the table and retraced his steps to the coffee table. He picked up the mirror, silver straw, and the little plastic bag of cocaine, and shoved them into his trouser pocket.

He could already feel his body responding to his excitement about the night that lay ahead. Just the thought of seeing Tiffani, hearing her voice, thinking about what they'd do—he never failed to get aroused. He strode to the entrance hall, grabbed his keys off a console there, and sauntered out to the Jaguar.

Troubles? he thought, smiling with pride at his sleek machine. *What troubles? Teddy de Mornay doesn't have a worry in the world. Not tonight he doesn't.* He laughed aloud again and got in the car. *No, siree. He's got a hot date. That's what he's got.*

Arielle put the remote telephone up on the swimming pool's coral stone coping and turned around to face Lolo, her arms spread out on the coping, her breasts bobbing on the water's surface. She looked at him teasingly, her sensuous lips parting in a smile. "Guess what?" she said, flipping water at him with a finger.

"What?" he asked.

"Bibi and Joe Whitman are flying us up to Saratoga," she said. "We're invited to use their guest house as long as we want."

"Great!" Lolo responded. "When are they leaving?"

"They're already there," Arielle said. "They're sending their jet down to pick us up tomorrow."

Lolo swam over and placed an arm on each of hers, pushing his body up against hers in the water. "You know what that means, don't you?" he said.

"What? That we have to hurry and pack?" Arielle asked with a laugh.

Lolo nibbled at her neck. "You know what I mean," he said. "The jet has a nice bedroom, and we can have fun all the way to Saratoga."

Arielle laughed again. "I knew you'd be thinking about all of the really important logistics," she said. She kicked her legs out and scissored them around his ass.

"That's me, for sure," Lolo said. "Always practical." He buried his head in her breasts, licking and kissing her, underwater, then above the water's surface.

"Hmmmmm," Arielle moaned. "That feels so good, Lolo."

He came up for air and placed his lips on hers, kissing her hungrily, pushing himself against her, his desire for her precluding any further conversation.

Arielle threw her arms around his neck, pulling him against her greedy body, abandoning herself to pleasure. He was already aroused, and she gasped when she felt his manhood brush against her nakedness.

Lolo moved his right hand down between her thighs and began rubbing her there. His breath became more rapid, his desire mounting as he felt her distended readiness. Putting his arms under her knees, he lifted her legs, then entered her, and Arielle trembled all over as she felt him inside her.

Lolo began moving in and out, slowly at first, teasing her with long strokes of his engorged cock, taking his time, enjoying the little whimpers and sighs and moans that escaped her lips as he moved in and out, in and out, until he couldn't hold off any longer. He suddenly began to speed up, pumping at her with more vigor, and Arielle began to moan louder, then begged him for more, her desire for him overcoming any urge to hold back. She gave herself up to him entirely, her body starved, and began moving wildly against him as he began to thrust into her with abandon, his body demanding release.

Suddenly he groaned hoarsely and rammed into her, virtually impaling her on his throbbing cock as he heaved his juices into her in explosion after explosion. Arielle screamed when she felt his release, and her entire body spasmed against him in a monumental climax, wave after wave of contractions sending her into an orbit she had never known before. They clung to one another, gasping for breath and shuddering with pleasure, their lips meeting again in a kiss before their bodies parted.

When he could finally speak, Lolo said, "See what we have to look forward to in the jet tomorrow?"

Arielle sighed with pleasure. "Oh, yes," she breathed. "And tomorrow and tomorrow and tomorrow."

And she thought: *Yes, Lolo, my love. There'll be plenty of time for this, a whole lifetime. I'll see to that. But we have a mission, too. Only you don't know it. Not yet.*

Chapter Seventeen

Wyn poured himself a cup of coffee in the library and began pacing the floor, lost in thought, as he sipped from the steaming mug. He was still worried about Layla. It was early in the morning, not long past dawn, but he had already been down to the stables and checked on the sick horse. She appeared to be somewhat better, perhaps less swollen and not in as much distress, but he wasn't really certain.

He strode over to his desk and started to call for Santo when the giant lumbered through the library door.

"I was just getting ready to call you," Wyn said, looking over at him.

"You're up awfully early this morning," Santo said somewhat grumpily. He was hung over from his night out and would have liked a little time to himself this morning. He'd already taken some aspirin to help chase away the incessant pounding in his head, and now he needed a lot of coffee before the day's activities began.

"I want you to get on the phone and get hold of that vet," Wyn said. "Valerie Rochelle."

"Now?" Santo asked. "The place isn't even open yet, Wyn."

"Then leave a message for her," Wyn said. "I want her to take a look at Layla this morning as soon as possible."

"What's the problem with Layla?" Santo asked.

"Oh, I forgot you weren't here last night," Wyn said pointedly. "When you bought her, she'd apparently had strangle. Then you vaccinated her, and now she's having a massive reaction to the vaccination."

"Aw, jeez," Santo said, his headache suddenly getting worse. "I had no idea—"

"That's why things like lineage and medical records are so important in this business, Santo," Wyn said sharply.

"I'm sorry," Santo said, "but I had no idea. She looked—"

"Just get on the phone and get that vet here as soon as possible," Wyn interjected.

Without another word, Santo picked up the address book on the desk and flipped through it until he found the clinic's number. He picked up the telephone and dialed. When the service answered, he left a message for Dr. Rochelle to call as soon as possible regarding Layla. He hung up and shrugged. "I left a message," he said. "There's nobody in yet."

"Okay," Wyn said. "I'm going to go upstairs and get cleaned up and change clothes. When she calls, you tell her to get out here pronto. Got it?"

"Yes," Santo said, "I've got it."

He watched as Wyn climbed the spiral stairs to the hallway that led to his bedroom. *What the hell's gotten into him?* he wondered. *He's hardly worn anything but sweats for months and doesn't bother cleaning up half the time.* It did not look like a promising day at Stonelair.

Valerie parked near the stable office and, carryall and medical bag in hand, she strode to the door, hoping that Layla hadn't taken a turn for the worse.

Santo Ducci stood up when she entered the office. "Good morning," he said.

"Good morning, Santo," Valerie said. "Layla's in her stall, I take it?"

He nodded. "You can go on back."

"Thanks," Val said. She went through to the tack room, then

on into the stable, walking down the length of stalls to Layla's.

When she got there, the stall door was open, and Wyn was sitting on a stool intently looking at Layla. "Hi, there," Valerie said.

He looked up. "Hi, Doc," he said, standing up.

Valerie was momentarily nonplussed. He had taken off the mask and left his bandaged face exposed. She wanted to study it closely in the light to see how serious the damage was, but she didn't say anything. *Not now,* she thought. *First things first.* Her immediate responsibility was to Layla.

"Okay," she said, "what's going on here? Has Layla taken a turn for the worse?"

"That's why I called you," he said. "I don't really know. I came down here early this morning and then again a little while ago, but I can't be sure if there's any change or not. I don't mean to be an alarmist, but I want your opinion."

"I don't think you're being an alarmist," Valerie said. "She was in acute distress last night. Let me just have a good look." First she examined Layla's neck, then she got down on all fours and studied each of her legs in turn, gingerly feeling for swelling and looking for signs of hemorrhaging.

When she was finished, she stood back up and looked at Wyn. "You know what?"

"What?" Wyn asked.

"It's working," Valerie said happily. "The swelling has already gone down considerably and the hemorrhaging has stopped completely. I think she's going to pull through with flying colors."

Wyn breathed a sigh of relief. "Thank God," he said. "I was making myself crazy trying to decide, but I honestly couldn't tell whether there was any difference this morning or not."

"It's not an easy call in such a short period of time," Valerie replied, "but I'm more than satisfied with her progress overnight. She'll pull through."

"Thanks, Doc," Wyn said. "I really appreciate you coming all the way out here."

"That's what I'm here for," Valerie said.

"Well, as long as you are here," Wyn said, "could I offer you a quick cup of coffee or something?"

Valerie didn't even take the time to think about it, though she had a busy schedule today. "Sure," she said. "I'd like that."

"Why don't we go up to the house?" Wyn suggested.

"Okay."

They sat on a big couch in the library, the four Irish wolfhounds lounging on the floor around them. Sunlight streamed through the French doors, and Valerie could see his face clearly now. He wore a bandage across his forehead, a large one across his nose, and one eye was completely bandaged over.

"You look a lot better without the mask," she said quietly.

"Do you mean that?" he asked.

She nodded. "Definitely." She paused a moment, then asked, "Do you mind if I take a closer look?"

"No, I don't mind," Wyn said, surprising himself.

Valerie set her mug on the coffee table, then scooted across the couch. She examined his face closely, lightly brushing her fingertips across the exposed skin. "Very light scarring," she concluded. "Dermabrasion would take care of most of it, if you wanted to bother. Personally, I wouldn't even bother with that."

"Are you serious?" he asked.

"Absolutely," she said, nodding her head. "May I look at the bandaged areas?"

"Go ahead," he said, deciding to trust her. "You've gone this far."

Valerie lifted one end of the forehead bandage, looked at the wound beneath it, then carefully secured the bandage again. She followed suit with the other bandages, making certain they were properly replaced. When she was finished, she sat staring at his face for a while.

"What is it?" Wyn asked. "What do you think?"

"You're healing remarkably well," she said, "and I don't think there's going to be much evidence that you ever had an accident. Very minor scarring, if any."

"You don't have to try to let me down easy, Doc," he said. "I can take the truth."

"That's exactly what I'm giving you," she said seriously. "Oh, your nose may look like you've been in a fight or something, but other than that . . ." She shrugged. "Your looks are hardly going to have changed. I might add that you've got great plastic surgeons."

He sat in silence, digesting her words. "You really do mean that, don't you?" he finally said.

"I think that it's not half as bad as *you* think," she said, carefully choosing her words. She reached over and touched his hand. "I think that there are other, more serious scars you've got to deal with, and they're making these seem a lot worse than they are."

He looked down at her hand on his and sighed heavily. "Maybe you're right, Doc," he said softly. He looked up at her. "Maybe you're right."

Wyn showed Valerie to her car, watching until the Jeep had disappeared from view. He walked back to the library and sat down at his desk, where he booted up the computer. *It's time I e-mailed the men out West,* he thought. *See what's going on. Stay on top of things.*

Santo stood at one of the French doors, staring at his boss. He noticed that Wyn wasn't wearing the mask or his customary baseball cap and that his hair was carefully combed. Then he took in the clean knit polo shirt, the crisp chinos, and shiny loafers.

Something's definitely going on, Santo thought. *Something I don't think I like.*

He stepped into the room and approached the desk. "Want to go over today's schedule now?" he asked Wyn.

"Sure," Wyn said. "It'd be a good idea before I start my E-mails."

"I'll go get your meds first," Santo said, starting for the spiral staircase.

"Santo," Wyn called to him.

Santo turned around and looked at him. "Yes?"

"I don't want the shots anymore," Wyn said.

"You—?"

"You heard me," Wyn said. "No more shots. You can get rid of the stuff."

Santo stood, rooted to the spot. *Is it that damn vet?* he wondered. *Could she be causing all these changes? Could some bitch like her waltz in here and waltz away with everything, Wyn included?*

He had some serious thinking to do, some very serious think-ing. About his future. Wyn's future. And Valerie Rochelle's.

Chapter Eighteen

Marguerite gave Effie strict instructions. She was to serve lunch on the screened-in porch as she normally would, then disappear for the duration of the afternoon. She was not to serve dessert, nor was she to clear the table. Marguerite would see to these things herself.

"I don't understand," Effie protested, unaccustomed to any variation in her work routine. "I always serve the dessert and clean up afterward. Why are you—?"

"Shush!" Marguerite commanded, a long slender hand held straight up in the air. Her eyebrows were arched, and her emerald eyes glistened with intensity. "You are not to question me, Effie. You are to do as I say. As soon as you've served lunch, leave. Go into the village and shop or go have a drink somewhere."

"A drink! But—" Effie started to protest.

"Oh, do come off it," Marguerite exclaimed. "I know you swill gin half the day, and I really don't care. But I do want you gone this afternoon. I don't care where you go, just go!"

Effie would do as she was told, though she pouted in the kitchen until Teddy had swept in to say hello when he arrived for lunch. "Oh, I'm so glad you're here," she told him, looking him up and down with pleasure. He was wearing a jacket and tie, an outfit most would consider overkill for a lunch in the country, but not Marguerite de la Rochelle or Teddy. "You look nice," Effie said.

"And you look worried," Teddy replied. "What's going on?"

"I don't know what's gotten into her," Effie said, nodding her head toward the parlor where Marguerite was, "but she sure could use some cheering up or something today."

"Why?" Teddy asked. "She seemed fine when we spoke on the telephone."

"I don't know why," Effie said, "but I'll tell you one thing. She's been acting strange ever since that fancy-pants cousin of hers, Mr. James de Biron, got here day before yesterday. And today, she's being meaner than a snake to me. She's making me clear out till after you leave."

"Oh, well, Effie," Teddy said reassuringly, "you know she doesn't mean any harm. Whatever it is, she'll get over it. Maybe she's just a little nervous because her cousin's visiting from France."

"Humpf!" Effie said. "I don't wonder. He may be real good-looking and always have a big smile ready, but if you ask me he's a snake in the grass. And he's not even French. He just lives there. Imagine her wanting me out of here."

Now Teddy understood perfectly well why Marguerite had banished Effie from the premises. She didn't want Effie to be privy to what she'd planned to discuss with him and Jamie de Biron. There was always the chance that Effie would overhear something, and Marguerite knew that Effie would go straight to Valerie with the information.

Marguerite, Teddy, and Jamie convened on the big screened-in porch. She always had summer lunches here rather than at a table in the garden because her beautiful skin was shielded from the sun's damaging rays and they were protected from the plethora of bothersome insects.

Soon they were enjoying the warmth of the summer heat and the remnants of dessert, sliced mango topped with a mango and papaya sorbet.

Teddy put his spoon down and smiled. "That was delicious, Marguerite," he said, "but then your food always is."

"Marguerite's always done everything perfectly," Jamie added, smiling at his cousin. Like Teddy, he was dressed casually but elegantly in a navy blue blazer with gold buttons, white trousers, and a blue-and-white striped shirt with a yellow tie. His very blond hair was short, almost in a military cut, and contrasted sharply with his darkly tanned skin. It was obvious that he was in excellent physical shape.

"Thank you both," she replied. "I'm so glad you could be here with us today, Teddy, so that you could meet Jamie and we could have our little discussion in privacy." She paused and delicately sipped her mineral water, then looked directly into Teddy's eyes. "But you mustn't forget that not a single word of this is to reach Val's ears."

"There's no danger of that, Marguerite," he replied. "I think— no, I know—that we're of a single mind on this. You and I know what's best for Val, even if she sometimes doesn't, and in this case it's best that she doesn't know anything."

"Exactly," Marguerite said. "I think you and I will get along very well, Teddy. We always have, and I see no reason why that shouldn't continue. We do see eye to eye. Certainly about my daughter." She shifted her gaze to Jamie. "And you've known her practically all of your life, Jamie, so it goes without saying that you understand why I'm doing what I am."

Jamie set down his wineglass and nodded. He had consumed several glasses of wine over lunch, Teddy had noticed, but it didn't seem to have affected him in the least. "You don't have to explain a thing to me, Marguerite," Jamie said. "I know exactly how Val is—always has been—and the only difference I see is that she's become more . . . independent, I guess is the word . . . in the last few years. Somewhat out of control, I would say."

He looked over at Teddy and smiled warmly. "I think you're perfect for Val, by the way, Teddy," he said. "And I'm so glad the two of you are going to get married. She needs somebody practical, with two feet planted firmly on the ground. Marguerite can tell you that I love Val dearly, but Val's never had any respect for her heritage or family, and she's always dillydallied with . . . well, *outsiders,* if you know what I mean."

"Never was a truer word spoken," Marguerite said, "and that's one reason I'm delighted that the two of you could meet. I think that the three of us together can make certain that everything of

Armand's and mine will be taken care of properly. I don't have to tell you that I've become increasingly concerned about Val's behavior lately. She's getting more independent, as you so aptly put it, Jamie. She's even become somewhat distant and headstrong. Quite frankly, I'm worried that when I'm gone, she'll take everything that Armand and I worked so hard to keep and auction it all off, then give the proceeds to an animal shelter or something."

"I don't think you have to worry about that now," Teddy said, his square chin jutting out authoritatively. "Between Jamie and myself, we can handle whatever might come up. And don't forget, Marguerite," he added, "I will be her husband."

Jamie laughed. "You can whip her into shape," he said.

"Easier said than done, I'm afraid," Marguerite said seriously. "This eccentric streak of hers runs awfully deep. I don't know where it came from, but it's there, and it's powerful." She looked over at Teddy. "You'll draw up the paperwork soon, Teddy?" she asked.

"I'll have it done tomorrow," he said. "When I go home, I'll get my secretary on it right away. I'll give you a call tomorrow when it's all ready. If you like, I can run it over here, or you and Jamie can come over to my place for a drink and sign everything while you're there. Whichever you prefer."

"Wonderful," Marguerite said enthusiastically. "Why don't we do the signing at Apple Hill? I would love for Jamie to see what you've done with it, Teddy." She turned to her cousin. "He's done an absolutely marvelous job of renovating the place. It's in perfect taste, and I think you would love it."

"I'm game," Jamie said.

"Good," Teddy said. "Why don't you plan on coming over about five o'clock? I'll make sure everything's ready by then. There will be loose ends to tie up with Dock Wainwright, but we can get most everything done right away. In the meantime, I hate to eat and run, Marguerite, but I'd better get back there so all the paperwork can get started." He picked up the folder of papers to the right of his place setting.

"That's fine," Marguerite said. "The sooner, the better." She rose to her feet, and the men followed suit. "We'll see you promptly at five, Teddy."

She turned to lead them out to the parking area. Jamie held the door for her and Teddy, then followed them out.

Teddy got into his Jaguar and started the engine.

"You didn't leave all the papers, did you, Teddy?" Marguerite asked.

Teddy lifted the folder off the seat next to him. "I've got everything, Marguerite," he said, "so don't worry about a thing."

"Good," she said.

Teddy roared off, and Marguerite turned to Jamie and took his arm. "Let's stroll for a moment in the garden, Jamie," she said.

They went through the nearby gate and down the path, summer blooms spilling out of their beds onto it from both sides. The warm air was filled with butterflies and sweet scents.

"What do you think of him, Jamie?" Marguerite asked.

"He's absolutely appropriate," Jamie replied without hesitation. "He's one of us. Our kind."

"Yes," Marguerite agreed. "He is indeed."

They strolled on in silence for a while, admiring the garden.

"Are they in love?" Jamie asked.

"Love!" Marguerite exclaimed. Her green eyes widened, and she shrugged her thin shoulders. "What a silly question, Jamie."

He laughed lightly. "I was just curious," he said. "It's been known to happen, you know. Mostly among the lower orders."

"Oh, I think there's been an attraction of sorts," Marguerite conceded. "In the beginning anyway, as there so often is, but I think that initial attraction has worn off for both of them. For Val more so than Teddy, surprisingly."

"Oh?" Jamie said. "Do you think she's interested in someone else?"

"No, no, no! It's nothing like that at all. I don't think she has much interest in men. Just animals."

"What about him?" Jamie asked. "You say he's still attracted to her."

"I think he's more interested in marriage than she is," Marguerite said. "I don't know that he's particularly interested in her physically. Oh, they spend a lot of weekends together, but neither of them seems all that . . . sexually charged, shall we say . . . over the other."

"Well, it sounds ideal," Jamie said. "If she gets bored, she has her animals."

"Exactly," Marguerite said, squeezing his arm. "I'm so glad you feel that way. I only wish Val knew how fortunate she is to have us taking care of her this way, but she can't know anything about our plans. It's too bad really that she doesn't know all the trouble we go to on her behalf." She looked up at him, her expression almost wistful. "It's really too bad that she doesn't know how much we love her."

Lydia was typing at the computer when Teddy came through the office door. She paused and looked up at him severely. "You've got several messages," she said, "and some of them need to be answered ASAP, Teddy. And I do mean ASAP. Like a couple of banks and a couple of brokers in New York City?"

"Don't worry about it, Lydia," he replied, smiling. "I'll get to them."

She was surprised by his nonchalant response to her urgent message. "You look like the cat that caught the canary," she finally said, a speculative smile hovering at the edges of her lips. "Must've been some lunch with that hateful old bitch, Mrs. de la Rochelle."

She was fishing for information, and Teddy knew it. He decided to let her suffer a few minutes. "I've got to make some telephone calls, Lydia," he said. "Then we'll get to those messages of yours."

She scowled. He wasn't going to be forthcoming about lunch. "Sure, Teddy," she said, her voice clipped. "Whatever you say." She looked back down at the keyboard and began typing very quickly, hitting the keys with an extra punch to try to irritate him.

Teddy ignored her and sat down at his desk. He flipped through the Rolodex until he saw the number he wanted, then picked up the telephone and dialed it. He waited for someone to answer, feeling especially self-satisfied. On the third ring, a secretary picked up.

"Dockering Wainwright's office," she said.

"Hi," he said jauntily. "This is Teddy de Mornay. I need to speak to Dock Wainwright right away."

"I'll see if he's in," the secretary said.

"It concerns Marguerite de la Rochelle," Teddy added.

"Yes, sir," the secretary said. "Just a moment."

Teddy waited patiently, although he was anxious to speak with Dock Wainwright. He could hardly wait to hear what the old man would have to say.

"Dockering Wainwright here," the older man's voice intoned. "How are you, Teddy?"

"I'm fine," Teddy replied. "And you?"

"At my age," Wainwright said, "I have no reason to complain."

"That's great," Teddy said.

"What can I do for you, Teddy?" the older man asked. "You say this has something to do with Marguerite de la Rochelle?"

"Yes," Teddy said. "I've just come from a luncheon meeting with her and her cousin, James de Biron."

"Ah, yes," Wainwright said. "I see."

"Marguerite, and Jamie, and I," Teddy went on slowly, drawing out his news, "had a long discussion at lunch about the de la Rochelle estate."

"That so?" Wainwright replied, clearly wishing that Teddy would get to the point.

"Marguerite," Teddy said, "has decided to give me control of all of her investment accounts." There, he'd dropped his bomb on the old man.

"I see," Dockering Wainwright replied calmly. He cleared his throat. "Her entire portfolio?"

"Yes," Teddy replied almost gleefully. "All of it."

"I see," Wainwright repeated.

"I've got the paperwork here," Teddy said, "powers of attorney and such, and I'll have it sent over to you just as soon as everything is ready."

"Yes," Wainwright said. "I'll have to have a signed statement from Mrs. de la Rochelle to that effect, of course."

"I've got it right here," Teddy said smugly. "It'll be with the paperwork I send over." He paused, then added: "She wants you to send a check over to me as soon as possible, with any commissions due you deducted, of course."

"Certainly," Wainwright said stiffly. "I'll get on it as soon as I receive the necessary paperwork."

"Thanks a lot," Teddy said. "You can expect a messenger in the morning."

"Yes, well, . . . good luck with it, Teddy," Wainwright said, forcing cheer into his voice.

"Thanks," Teddy said. He wanted to tell the old man he didn't need his good wishes and started to hang up, but thought better of it. *Never burn bridges,* he told himself. *You never know when you might need them, and Dock Wainwright, old as he was, might be very useful in the future. The near future, anyway.*

"I hope there'll be no animosity on your part," Teddy said. "I think the only reason Marguerite's doing this is because Val and I are going to get married."

"Well, that's wonderful news," Wainwright said. "I hope you're both very happy."

"Thanks," Teddy responded. "I'll be talking to you."

"Good-bye, then," Wainwright said. "And please give my regards to Val."

"I will," Teddy replied. "Bye." He replaced the receiver in its cradle, then looked up. Lydia had stopped typing and was looking at him with a curious expression.

"What is it?" he asked.

"We're just full of news today, aren't we?" she said.

"Yes," he answered. Then he opened the file of paperwork he'd brought back with him from Marguerite's. He withdrew an envelope and opened it, staring down at the papers in his hand. "Tomorrow morning," he said, "stop on your way in and deposit these in the bank." He got up and handed the checks over to Lydia.

She looked down at them, and her eyes lit up brightly. "Je-sus!" she said. "I thought old Dock Wainwright had all their money."

"These are just quarterly dividend checks," he said. "They'll be coming straight to me in the future."

"My God," Lydia cried, "I didn't know they had that much money. De Mornay Investments is going to have a lot to play with."

"No," Teddy said. "Deposit them in my personal account."

"But-but these—" she began.

"Never mind, Lydia," he said firmly. "Deposit them in my personal account for the time being."

"If you say so," Lydia said with a frown.

"I say so," Teddy said.

"But how am I supposed to enter these on the books, Teddy?" she asked.

"I'll handle that," he said. *And I will, too,* he thought. *Marguerite de la Rochelle and Jamie de Biron aren't going to miss a dividend check right away. Especially not with the switch over from Dock. Besides,* he thought, *I'll be replacing them before they even receive statements from my investment company. There's nothing wrong with my making use of them for my personal needs for a short time, is there? It wasn't my fault if the technology stocks bottomed out, was it? In the meantime, this money will more than take care of my margin calls. It'll shut up the banks and the brokers.*

"Now then," he said, looking at Lydia. "What are these so-called urgent messages you've got for me?"

Chapter Nineteen

M rs. McDougall," Valerie said, "I don't think you have anything to worry about. Lexi is doing very well."

"I don't know that I agree with you," Mrs. McDougall said, "but we shall see." She picked up the tiny mixed-breed dog and held him in her arms.

"If you have any problems, let me know," Valerie said.

"Of course," Mrs. McDougall said.

Valerie held the door open for her, then followed the tall, thin woman out into the reception area. She waved good-bye to her and went on into her office to fill out Lexi's record. *There's really nothing wrong with Lexi,* she thought as she scribbled her examination notes. *It's Mrs. McDougall who needs the doctor. And a good and patient psychiatrist at that.* The woman had been bringing the dog in for three years, together with a laundry list of ailments that no one at the clinic had been able to discern. Lexi was perfectly healthy, if a bit neurotic, but that was to be expected in an animal that was smothered with so much attention.

Valerie finished her notes, then went out to the reception area to give them to Tami to file.

"Here you go, Tami," she said. "Lexi's file."

"Thank you," Tami said, taking the file from her. "The dog with all the phantom ailments, right? What is it this week?"

"It's a limp," Valerie said. "For about the twentieth time."

Tami rolled her eyes and laughed.

The telephone rang, and Annie picked it up. "Hold on a moment," Valerie heard her say. Then Annie looked up at her. "Val, it's for you. Mr. Conrad at Stonelair on line three."

"I'll take it in my office," Valerie said. She turned and went back to her office, unaware of the curious eyes that followed her.

She sat down at her desk, pushed the button, and picked up the receiver. "Hi, Wyn," she said. "What can I do for you?"

"I was wondering if you could have another look at Layla," Wyn said. "This afternoon, if possible."

Again today? Valerie thought, but she said, "Sure. Let me check my schedule. Can you hold on a minute?"

"Okay, Doc," Wyn said.

Valerie pressed the hold button and sat in puzzled thought. *I don't think Layla really needs a follow-up visit today,* she decided, *but Wyn Conrad obviously does.* She realized that she'd opened the door to friendship and felt as if she must follow through. More than that, she discovered that she wanted to.

She quickly checked her schedule, then got Wyn back on the line. "How about around six o'clock?" she said. "That's when I finish up here today."

"That'd be great," Wyn said. "I'll see you then."

"Okay," Valerie said. She hung up the receiver, still curious about the call, wondering if her instincts were on the mark. There wasn't time to think about it now, however, because she had a busy afternoon ahead of her.

Valerie parked and walked toward the stable office and saw that no one was behind the big desk. *I guess he's with Layla,* she thought. She went through the tack room, then on out into the stables. Down the row of stalls ahead of her, she saw Wyn, standing with two horses saddled and bridled, ready to ride. As she approached him, she saw him grin.

"What's this?" she asked.

"I thought we'd take a ride," he said.

"But I thought you wanted—" she began.

"Layla's doing great," he said, "but I thought the two of us could use a little recreation. How about it?"

Valerie couldn't help but smile. "I think it's a great idea," she replied, "and I sure am glad I'm wearing pants and sneakers."

"This is Dixie," Wyn said. "She has a lot of spirit, but she behaves herself."

Valerie set down her carryall and medical bag and stroked the beautiful Arabian's neck. "She's a real looker," she said.

"And this is Demon," Wyn said.

"Appropriately named, I take it?"

Wyn nodded. "But I can handle him." He held Dixie's reins out to her. "Ready?"

"Yes," Valerie replied. She took Dixie's reins and mounted the horse with ease, then watched as Wyn mounted Demon.

Together they rode out of the stable's open doors and toward a trail that led through Stonelair's lush meadows and on through the heavily wooded forest in the distance. When they reached the meadow, Wyn began a trot, and Valerie kept pace, enjoying the sun and wind and the feel of Dixie beneath her.

Wyn would catch her eye from time to time to make certain that she was okay. "You're a good rider," he called to her.

"You're not so bad yourself," she called back. *He's a terrific rider,* she thought. He sat a horse beautifully, in full command of himself and the handsome Arabian. *His body may be scarred but he has complete confidence on horseback.*

Wyn began a canter, moving slightly ahead of her, and Valerie followed suit as before, picking up speed, glad for the faster pace, and the opportunity to watch Wyn and Demon move. *They move as one,* she thought, *with a fluid grace seldom seen in riders, even competent, fully experienced ones.*

She caught up with him, but he put Demon into a full gallop, turning to grin at her as they headed straight toward the woods. She gave Dixie a kick, and off she went after him, determined to catch up with him again and blissful in her element.

Just as she drew up alongside him, Wyn reined in Demon and began a trot as they approached the forest trail. Valerie quickly did likewise, and they rode together along the path in the dappled sunlight.

When they finally returned to the stable, she had no idea how long they'd been riding, but she hadn't enjoyed herself so much in as long as she could remember. After they dismounted, Helmut Reinhardt appeared from within the stable and took the horses' reins.

"Helmut," Wyn said, "this is Valerie Rochelle, our vet."

Helmut Reinhardt nodded and practically clicked his heels together in an Old World manner. "I'm very pleased to meet you," he said in thickly accented English.

"I'm happy to meet you, too," Valerie said and watched as he disappeared into the stable with the horses. "That was wonderful," she said to Wyn.

"I'm glad you enjoyed it, Doc," he said. He hesitated, then added, "How about a drink or something before you go? Or do you have plans?"

"No," she replied. "That'd be great."

They sat on one of the couches in the library, sipping champagne that he had opened. The wolfhounds were sprawled about the room, all of them asleep. Valerie and Wyn talked enthusiastically about horses and their love for riding, sharing experiences and laughing together, unaware of the time. It was not until darkness approached and Wyn had to get up and turn on lamps that they realized they'd been sitting together for hours.

He returned to the couch and sat looking at her with an expression of complete happiness on his face. She returned his gaze, and her heart swelled with pleasure. She couldn't remember when she'd felt this happy, this . . . excited by someone.

He drew closer to her and said, "What are you thinking about?"

"I . . . I was thinking about what a great time I had," she said.

"I did, too," he said. "I . . . I didn't even think it was possible."

"I didn't either," she said. She reached over and touched his hand. "I didn't know it could be like this."

He grasped her hand in his, enjoying its feminine, yet strong, feel against his. *Oh, God!* he wondered. *Can this really be happening to me?* Then he thought: *To us?* He began to stroke her hand gently, reluctant to let it go.

Valerie felt her body tremble slightly at his touch, at the connection between them. She didn't know how to describe it. It was almost as if some chemical reaction had taken place between them, as if some force were operating over them without their control. It was frightening, this feeling and her knowledge of it, but simultaneously it thrilled her to the very core of her being.

She'd never felt this way before. Not with Teddy, not with anyone. *Was it merely sexual?* she asked herself. *Or was it something more?* She didn't know, but she suddenly realized that she was willing to explore it, to take a chance, to risk whatever may come to get to know this man better.

Wyn seemed mesmerized by her hand, stroking it, staring down at it, slightly embarrassed to look into her eyes, for fear that he would see mere indulgence there or, worse, rejection. But look up at her he finally did, unable to resist. His heart surged with a new-found joy when at last he witnessed the look of tenderness, perhaps even the disquiet of love or lust, in those emerald eyes. Hers was not a gaze of pity, nor was it mere empathy. It was much, much more, of that he was certain.

He set down his champagne glass and brought her hand to his lips and kissed it, barely brushing it with his mouth, all the while searching her eyes for meaning. He was not disappointed, for Valerie's lips quivered slightly at his kiss and her eyes watched him fearlessly, unblinkingly, and, he thought, a bit proudly.

When he released her hand at last, Valerie let out a deep breath. Her heart was racing, and she could feel her pulse beating a steady tattoo. She wanted to say something, but needed to recover her equilibrium first. It was as if she were under a magic spell and couldn't quite get out of its grasp.

"I want to see you again, Doc," he said softly. "Soon."

She nodded slightly and her lips parted. "Yes," she barely breathed. "Oh, yes."

After a few moments of staring into one another's eyes, she shook her head and sighed pleasantly, almost wistfully. "I'd better go," she said. "I really do have a big day tomorrow."

"I know," he said, "but I wish you didn't have to. I wish . . . well, I wish you didn't have to leave at all."

She nodded again, knowingly, understanding what he wanted, what they both wanted. She drew herself up and reluctantly relinquished the magic of the moment for the reality of what lay ahead.

"Walk me to the car?" she asked.

"You bet," he said.

They rose simultaneously, and Valerie retrieved her carryall and medical bag. Together they walked out to the Jeep, and she got the keys out of her carryall. She started to open the door, and, from behind her, his arms enfolded her in a tender hug.

She felt as if she could stay in his arms forever, just like that, and be happy, but she had to leave now or she didn't think she ever would. She turned to him and kissed his lips quickly, then turned again to the car.

"I really have to go," she said. "While I still can."

He grinned. "I'm glad you feel that way, too," he said.

She got in the Jeep and started it, then sat looking at him.

"I'll call you, okay?" he asked.

"Yes," she said.

"Tomorrow okay?"

Not soon enough, she thought. "Yes," she replied.

" 'Night, Doc." He touched his fingers to his lips and touched hers with his fingertips.

" 'Night, Wyn," she said.

She put the car in gear, pulled out of the parking area, and turned to drive down the long lane, already eager for tomorrow to come, already hungry for his touch, knowing in her heart of hearts that this was right and true and pure.

Wyn stood watching her taillights disappear down the lane, then began walking up to the house, his mind consumed with Valerie. He could hardly believe the evening that had passed, and felt the urge to shout his joy from the rooftops. But he walked on in silence, looking forward to tomorrow for the first time in many, many months. He couldn't help but grin. He'd never thought he would be able to think of such things again, not in the condition he was in. He'd never thought he would even *want* to think of such things, not after his miserable experience with Arielle.

Valerie Rochelle, he thought. *What an amazing woman.*

Chapter Twenty

There, Noah," Valerie said, giving the elderly husky a firm stroke, "I think you're as good as new." She looked up at Eddie Lowell. "He really is in great shape," she said.

Eddie smiled, his darkly tanned face a mass of leathery wrinkles. "You're like Wonder Woman, Val," he said. "I never would've believed a pacemaker would make such a difference. I didn't think he was going to last out the year, and now he's practically like a young pup again."

"Just like you," Valerie said.

"Oh-ho," he laughed. "I wish! Try telling Jonathan that. I can hardly keep up with him."

She looked at Eddie, somewhat surprised that the forty-something antiques dealer had mentioned his twenty-something boyfriend in what virtually amounted to an intimate manner.

"Maybe that's what keeps you so young, Eddie," she said. "Having a younger partner, I mean. You never seem to age at all."

"Well, you're sweet to say that, Val," he said, "but sometimes I feel like old Noah here did. Maybe a pacemaker would do the trick for me, too."

"I don't think so, Eddie," she quipped. "You'd have to have a heart first."

He laughed at her joke. "You're right," he said, "but I wouldn't be a successful antiques dealer if I did."

Valerie leaned over and gave him a peck on the cheek. "I know your heart's made out of pure gold, and you know I'm crazy about you," she said.

"And I'm crazy about you, Val," he said, beaming. "Are you coming by for that drink tonight?"

"Yes, I am," she said. "Fancy dress, right?"

"Oh, sure," he said. "As fancy as blue jeans or khakis get. Well now, I'd better get out of here and let you do your work."

She handed him Noah's leash. "I'll see you about six-thirty," she said, giving the dog another stroke.

"Good," he said, starting for the door. "Oh, and feel free to bring Teddy." Then he added, "If you want to, that is."

"Thanks, Eddie," Valerie replied, "but I think he's busy tonight, so I'll come alone."

"Okay," he said. "See you later."

She held the door to the examining room open for him and watched as he left. She quickly made some notes on Noah's chart, then left the examining room and went out to the reception desk. "Noah's chart for filing," she told Tami, handing it over the desk to her.

"Thanks, Val," Tami said.

Daphne rounded the corner from her office. "Was that Mr. Lowell with Noah I saw leaving?" she asked.

"Yes," Valerie said.

"I remember the last time I saw Noah," Daphne said. "He was really sick. He looks like a whole new dog, doesn't he?"

"He sure does," Val replied.

"Mr. Lowell must be so happy," she said. She looked at Val with a quizzical expression. "You seem to be very good friends with him."

"I've known him for a long time," Val replied.

"You're lucky," Daphne said. "You have so many nice friends like him."

"I am lucky to have Eddie for a friend," Val agreed. "I guess you can't have too many, Daphne."

"You know when I went over to his place on an emergency," Daphne went on, "I was amazed by the house. All those paintings and things. It was really beautiful. He must be rich."

"I don't know about that," Val said with a laugh, "but it is beautiful."

The telephone rang and Tami picked up the receiver. "Good morning," she said. "Animal clinic."

Valerie started for her office but turned back when Tami called out to her. "What is it?" she asked.

"I have Mr. Conrad at Stonelair on line two," she said. "He wants to speak to you."

"Thanks," Valerie said, feeling her heart begin to flutter. She had been hoping he'd actually call.

Daphne watched Valerie rush to her office, then turned and went back down the corridor to her own.

Valerie closed the door behind her and took a deep breath. She told herself that her reaction was absurd. *I'm not a teenager*, she thought. *What's happening to me?*

She went to her desk and heard Elvis's tail begin to thump against the kneehole's worn wood. "Hey, sweetie," she said, leaning down to give him a few strokes. Elvis gave her hand a lick, then settled back down to his nap. She pushed the button for line two and picked up the receiver.

"Valerie Rochelle," she said.

"Hey there," his deep voice replied. "It's Wyn Conrad. "How are you?"

"I'm fine," she replied automatically. "Busy as usual."

"I was just wondering," he began slowly, "if maybe . . . well, if you'd maybe like to have dinner with me?"

His voice sounded hesitant, she thought, almost as if he were a kid asking a girl on a first date.

"I would like that very much," she said.

"Great," he said. "I thought about seven-thirty, eight o'clock. How's that sound to you?"

"Let's make it eight. I have to make a stop on the way."

"Okay," he said. "I'll see you about eight."

"I'll be there."

She hung up, then slumped down in the chair at her desk. *I can't believe this*, she thought, feeling a little bewildered. *Mr. Wyn Conrad has actually asked me to dinner. I wonder if he . . . No*, she told herself, *quit thinking that way. You can't presume anything, Val. Maybe you misread him last night. Maybe he wants to see you to set the record straight. You don't have any idea whatsoever what he has on his mind.*

Still, she couldn't help but smile. He wanted to see her.

The telephone on her desk jangled loudly, and she jumped, so lost in thought was she. She picked it up. "Valerie Rochelle," she said.

"You've got another call from your other male admirer," Tami said. "Teddy this time. On line three."

"Thanks, Tami," she said, slightly annoyed at the secretary's tone. She hung up the receiver for a moment and stared at it. *What does Teddy want?* she wondered. *And what do I tell him if he asks to see me tonight?* Then she remembered Colette's advice: *Tell him the truth, sooner rather than later.* She felt her stomach begin to flutter unpleasantly. *I can't do that now. Not on the telephone,* she told herself, rationalizing. *I'll have to play it by ear.*

She picked up the receiver. "Hi," she said cheerily.

"What took you so long?" Teddy asked in exasperation. "I've been on hold."

"That's a nice greeting, Teddy," she said. "I *am* at work, you know."

"Sorry," he said, backing down. "I didn't mean to sound grumpy."

You sure have sounded grumpy an awful lot lately, she thought. "It's okay," she said.

"I guess I've just been awfully busy, and I've had a really rough week," Teddy went on quickly. "You know what?"

"What?" she asked.

"Some of my clients are being a real pain in the ass," he said, the words tumbling out in a rush. "Interests rates are going up, the market's pretty volatile, the goddamn soothsayers are predicting everything from Armageddon to a fantastic bull market without end, and I'm caught in the middle of it all."

"Lots of nervous clients, I guess," she replied.

"God, Val," he said, "you wouldn't believe it. These are people who've never lost a dime in the market. They've never seen anything but prosperity, and when something goes wrong, bam! It's like they lay everything on me. I'm some kind of monster or something."

"I'm sorry, Teddy," she said. *He sounds so wired,* she thought. She'd never heard him sound quite this troubled before, and she was puzzled. He'd always seemed to take the swings of the market in stride and to handle his clients with ease, laughing off their nervous reactions, never taking anything personally. "It must be very difficult for you."

"Yes," he said. "It is. Anyway, I decided not to go away this weekend. I couldn't take a whole weekend of Ned and Edyth Chamberlain. They're so fucking stuffy, you know?" He couldn't tell her that he was working double-time on her mother's behalf, nor was he going to tell her that he was entertaining her mother and her cousin Jamie.

"I've never met them," she said.

"Oh, I forgot," he replied. "Anyway, so what time are you coming over?"

"Coming over?" she said. "I-I made other plans. You'd told me you weren't going to be here."

"Other plans?" he exclaimed. "What do you mean, 'other plans'?"

Valerie couldn't help but feel irritated. Why was it he expected her to be at his beck and call on weekends? At least those weekends when it was convenient for him to see her? "I meant exactly what I said," she said firmly. "You said you'd come up early because you couldn't be here over the weekend. I made other plans."

"Then change them," he said.

She felt like exploding, but she forced herself to keep her voice even. "No," she said. "I've made other plans, and I don't want to change them. I don't like hurting people's feelings."

"What about my feelings," he said angrily.

"Teddy," she said, with more than a hint of exasperation in her voice, "you weren't going to be here. Remember?"

"And what other people?" he snapped, ignoring her. "Where're you going? What're these big plans of yours?"

"I don't like being cross-examined," she said testily.

She could hear him heave a big sigh. "I-I'm sorry, Val," he said, his voice calmer, though still distressed. "I just really had a bad week, that's all."

"I'm sorry, too," she said, "but I'm not responsible for your bad week, and I don't want it taken out on me."

"Please forgive me," he said. "I didn't mean to be so . . . demanding." He paused for a moment, then said, "I guess it's best this way anyhow. I need to get some sleep. Really rest up from all the pressure."

"It sounds like it," she said. "Maybe an early night would do you some good."

"Maybe so," he agreed. "I haven't been getting much sleep lately. Why don't you come over after you've been . . . well, wherever it is you're going?"

"I don't think so, Teddy," she replied.

"Ah, come on, Val," he said. "Just you and me. Late tonight. It'd be like having a late date."

"No, Teddy," she said. "I told you I've already got plans, and I don't want to change them. Besides, I'm on call this weekend, so I'd better have an early night."

"You're always on call," he groused.

"No, Teddy, I'm not," she said. *He sounds like a petulant child,* she thought. "You know very well that we take turns at the clinic."

"You said you had plans," he argued. "So you can do something else, but you can't see me?"

"Look, Teddy, I don't want to argue about this. You told me you weren't going to be here this weekend, and I made plans. It's as simple as that. Why can't you live with it?"

"Where are you going?" he asked heatedly.

Valerie really didn't want to tell him. He wasn't fond of Eddie and Jonathan, and she didn't want to have to listen to his asinine comments about them. And telling him she was going to have dinner with Wyn Conrad made her feel queasy. He would probably explode. Then it occurred to her, as it had repeatedly over the last few weeks, that Teddy had a right to know what she was doing. After all, they were engaged, for the time being at least.

Once again, she reminded herself of Colette's encouraging words, then drew a deep breath and plunged right in with the truth. "I'm going over to Eddie and Jonathan's for a drink," she said. "Then I'm going to dinner at Stonelair." There, the truth was out.

"You're what!" he exclaimed in astonishment.

"Do I really have to repeat myself, Teddy?"

"I can't believe my ears," he snarled. "I mean, I can believe you're going over to Eddie's. For some reason, you've always liked that old fag, but—"

"Stop right there," she said furiously. "Don't you ever belittle him like that again. You sound like some stupid twelve-year-old boy posturing in the locker room. Eddie's never been anything but nice to you, and he's been a real friend to me."

"Ah, come on, Val," he said, a bit contritely. "You know I didn't mean any harm. I don't mind Eddie."

"That's certainly not the way you sound," she said.

"Yeah, well, what I can't believe is that you'd go out to that weirdo's at Stonelair."

"I don't care what you believe," she snapped, still angry. "I've made plans, and they're not subject to your approval. Neither are the people I choose to see."

There was silence for a moment as Teddy digested her remark. Valerie felt as if all her senses were heightened, and she could feel her skin tingle. *The heat of the argument,* she decided. *And telling Teddy what I actually feel. Funny, now I really* don't *feel so bad. Maybe Colette was right. Maybe I should be honest more often.*

"I don't know what's happening to us, Val," Teddy finally said, his voice soft and hurt.

"I think we'd better continue this conversation another time," she said. "I'm too angry to talk to you."

"Well, I think we'd better continue it now," Teddy countered, "because I'm getting really worried."

"No," Valerie said, "not now." He was already trying to put her on the defensive, and she wasn't going to have it. "We'll talk tomorrow, Teddy."

"Val, I don't think—" he began.

"We'll talk tomorrow," she repeated. "Good-bye, Teddy."

"Val—"

She quietly replaced the receiver in its cradle, then, elbows on the desk, she held her head in her hands. *What have I done?* she thought. For a brief moment, she thought that she should pick up the phone and call Teddy back. *I should apologize and assure him that I'll spend time with him tomorrow.* Then she remembered his remark about Eddie, and her anger returned. *No way,* she decided. *If he's miserable, it's not my fault. He deserves it for being so thoughtless and nasty.*

The telephone on her desk jangled again, and she picked up the receiver. "Yes?" she said.

"Mrs. Sutherland is here with Happy," Annie said, a note of glee in her voice.

"I'll be right out," Val replied. *Just my luck,* she thought. *That vicious old Mrs. Sutherland with her equally vicious little Happy, a yapper and a biter and a whiner. He was just like his mistress.* She rose to her feet and took Happy's chart from the pile of today's patients on her desk. Elvis's tail thumped against the kneehole again. Leaning down, she gave him a few strokes. "Oh, Elvis," she said, "today's got to get better. It can't get worse."

Arielle pulled the chintz drapery panel aside and gazed out the window of the guest house toward the swimming pool and tennis court in the distance. No sign of life about, except for a grounds-keeper who was trimming hedges. Her eyes wandered to the mansion itself as she slowly sipped champagne from a crystal flute. "Oh, look, Lolo," she said. "Bibi and Joe are back. I thought I heard the car."

Lolo stepped up behind her and craned his neck over her shoulder toward the window, following her gaze. He spotted the familiar figures he'd often seen in Palm Beach, walking toward the terrace at the rear of their pristine white mansion. "They're not coming out here," he said, stating the obvious.

"No," she said. "The chauffeur said they would expect us for cocktails at six o'clock, so I guess until then we should stay out here. Bibi's a real stickler for protocol."

She felt Lolo's arms encircle her waist and his warm breath on her neck. "Good," he said. "We can have a little fun before dinner."

She let the drapery fall back into place and turned in his arms, facing him. She set her champagne glass down on a table. "Let's move away from the window," she said. "I'd hate for that old dragon lady to see us in our underwear."

"She can't see us from there," he said, nuzzling her neck with his lips.

"She'll probably have binoculars trained on the windows at all hours," Arielle said.

Lolo chuckled. "That's loco, Arielle," he said, snapping the waist of her flesh-colored bikini panties.

"Believe me," Arielle retorted, "Bibi's just loco enough to do it. She's probably even got this guest house bugged."

Lolo drew back and looked at her with genuine concern. "Do you really think she would do a thing like that?"

Arielle shrugged. "Who knows?" she replied. "I wouldn't put it past her. I do know that she puts up a good front, acting real prim and proper, but underneath all her stupid old-lady Chanel suits, she's really a horny old cow. Joe probably hasn't been able to get it up in years."

Lolo laughed. "*You're* loco, Arielle," he said, pulling her body up against his, relishing the feel of her silk panties and bra and firm tanned flesh against him.

"Maybe," she said, "but I'm sure not stuck with an old stuffed shirt like Joe Whitman." She pressed her pelvis against his crotch, then brushed her lips lightly across his. "Why don't we have some more champagne?" she said softly.

Lolo kissed her, then loosened his arms from around her. "That's a good idea," he said. "I'll get it." He picked up her glass, then walked over to the elegantly draped table, where his champagne flute sat nearly empty next to the sweating wine cooler.

Arielle padded over to the big sofa, sat down, and drew her legs up onto the floral chintz, watching Lolo pour their drinks. She yawned and stretched her arms. It had been a long day after a very late and raucous night of lovemaking, but she'd managed to nap aboard the Whitman's Gulfstream V. The trip had gone without a hitch, and Larry, the Whitmans' chauffeur, had been at the airport to meet them in Bibi's dark green Rolls Royce Phantom V.

"Mr. and Mrs. Whitman had to go out," Larry had explained, "and apologize for not being here to greet you. They will expect you at six o'clock for cocktails and then dinner."

When they'd reached Bibi and Joe's monstrous old house in Saratoga, Mildred, the housekeeper, had greeted them and shown them to the guest house, where a bottle of chilled champagne awaited them. The guest house was filled to overflowing with bowls and vases stuffed with beautiful flowers, roses mostly, and a cornucopia of fresh fruit sat in the center of the dining table. The kitchen was well stocked with an assortment of gourmet treats to satisfy any appetite: cheeses, patés, caviar, various cuts of pre-pared meat and fowl, and mineral water, mixers, sodas, and liquor galore.

Bibi, she reflected, was legendary for her exquisite taste and lavish entertaining, and deservedly so. Too bad Arielle didn't really like her or old Joe, but even the dragon lady and the stuffed shirt couldn't dampen her excitement at being here in Saratoga.

I'm only a stone's throw from Wyn, she thought, *and I can already smell all that lovely money.*

Lolo stood over her, a glass of champagne extended in her direction. She smiled and took it from him. "Thanks, Lolo," she said, moving her legs and patting the sofa with a hand.

He sat down next to her, then lifted her long, slender legs and placed them over his own. "What are you thinking about, my *loco* Arielle?" he asked, running a hand up one of her legs toward her thigh.

"Hmmm," she breathed, taking a sip of the champagne, then setting the crystal flute down on the marble-topped coffee table. She looked at him, smiled mysteriously, and withdrew a cigarillo from the pack on the table.

Lolo reached for her gold cigarette lighter and lit the cigarillo for her, looking into her eyes. Then he took one for himself and lit it. "You're up to something, Arielle," he said. "What is it?"

She took a long draw on her cigarillo. "Ooooh, just an idea," she said teasingly, smoke trailing from her nostrils.

"What?" he asked, running his hand back up her thigh again, his dark eyes searching hers.

"I thought . . . I thought we might pay a call on Wyn," she said.

"I mean . . . we're so close and all." She stared at him, her eyes gleaming with mischief.

His hand suddenly stopped moving, and his eyes bored into hers. "You're joking, aren't you?" he said, already knowing that she was deadly serious. "I told you that I would talk to him, man to man, but it's crazy for both of us to try to see him. He'd never see you, so I wouldn't get to him, either."

She had the merest hint of a smile on her lips. "Maybe you're right, but I'm not joking. I've never been more serious."

"But-but what are you thinking?" he stuttered. "What kind of plan do you have? This is really stupid, Arielle. Don't you see?"

Her eyes never left his as she slowly shook her head. "Nooo," she said softly, "I don't. In fact, I think it might be one of the smartest things I've ever done." She languidly tapped her cigarillo in the ashtray.

Lolo became agitated. "Arielle," he said, "what the hell have you got in mind? You know he doesn't want you there. It's crazy."

"He won't even know we've been there," she said, looking into Lolo's eyes. "If things work out the way I want them to." She smashed her cigarillo out in the ashtray, then reached toward him with her arms. "Come here," she said, sliding one of her legs around his back, the other still across his lap.

He set his champagne down and put out his cigarillo, looking at her anxiously. "I don't know, Arielle," he said slowly, shaking his black curls.

"Come here," she repeated, reaching for him.

He leaned toward her, letting her hook an arm around his neck, her legs scissored around his torso. Her other arm slid down to his crotch, and she eased her hand beneath his jockey shorts, encircling the growing tumescence there. "Kiss me, Lolo," she said. "Kiss me hard."

Teddy sat behind his desk in the office at Apple Hill, his feet propped up on its surface. He finished looking over the paperwork Lydia had left for him and flung it down unceremoniously onto his desk. He heaved an audible sigh of relief. The ups and downs of the last few days had almost gotten the best of him, that and having to be on perfect behavior with Marguerite and Jamie.

He knew that the nose candy had helped fuel the ups and had probably been responsible for the depth of the lows, but, hell, he didn't know how else to keep going. Between running his investment company, satisfying clients, trying to keep Val happy, and making certain that he and Tiffani had time for a little fun on the side—well, it had all begun to wear him down as never before.

But everything's in order now, he told himself grimly. He'd had a handful of investors who'd recently withdrawn all of their money from his investment service—thanks to the volatility in the marketplace—and he'd had to perform a number of intricate and time-consuming maneuvers to make certain that they were all fully recompensed.

Now at least those bastards are all out of my hair, he thought. There was no satisfaction in it for him, however. He'd been controlling a quarter of a billion dollars last week—chump change as far as a lot of high-flying Wall Street guys were concerned, but a tidy sum for him to work with—investing it for a small group of very rich clients. This week he found himself left with less than fifty million dollars, money entrusted to him by those investors who'd stuck with him despite recent losses in the market.

Thank God, Marguerite de la Rochelle and James de Biron hopped on board when they did, he thought for the umpteenth time. *And thank God Dock Wainwright came through with the paperwork and checks overnight.* Between himself, Lydia, and Dock, everything had been set up. He was in full control of Marguerite's stock portfolio now, and had a good chunk of Jamie's to boot. He'd needed all the capital he could get his hands on to repay all those investors who'd abandoned ship. Now he just had to make certain that when the time came, he could show Marguerite and Jamie that their money was not only intact but making a nice hefty profit under his brilliant and watchful eye.

I'll be able to do it, he told himself convincingly. *I've played the market successfully in the past, and I can do it again. I just need the chance to hit the right stock at the right time, and . . . voilà! I'm not only back in business but back in the black. I'll just have to be very careful dealing with Marguerite and Jamie.*

He knew they both appeared on the surface to be unconcerned with money, as if it were something dirty for others to deal with, but he also knew that beneath their sophisticated and aristocratic exteriors, they wouldn't hesitate to sacrifice him to the authorities if they detected the least impropriety on his part.

His thoughts turned to Valerie and the telephone conversation they'd had a little while ago. He considered telling Marguerite what had transpired. He knew that she was capable of instilling in Valerie a sense of duty and responsibility, if not outright fear, and he knew that she was his ally. She would certainly be mad to hear that Valerie had so offhandedly given her fiancé the brush-off.

He reached down and pulled open the bottom right-hand drawer in his desk and picked up the little box he had put there. He set it down on the desk and extracted the plastic bag of white powder and the silver straw. He ignored the mirror and razor blade as he had ever since he reached the country. Instead, he opened the bag, stuck one end of the straw in the powder and the other in his nostril. He inhaled deeply and held his breath for a long moment, then repeated the process with his other nostril. When he finished, he leaned back in his chair, enjoying the enhanced feeling of well-being that the drug rapidly induced.

He looked at the telephone, thinking that he would place that call to Marguerite, then decided to wait and talk to her when she and Jamie came over to sign paperwork. That might prove to be interesting, he thought, because Jamie de Biron was an enigma to him, and he needed to get to know him better. After all, the better he knew him, the better he'd know how to control him.

Whoa! Suddenly he realized the coke had really hit, and he felt almost as if his body had begun to vibrate with life.

I'll try to get hold of Tiffani, he thought. *Make sure we can get together tonight. He was off the hook with Val, so he might as well make the best of his time.*

He dialed her number and waited. After the fourth ring the machine kicked in. *Shit!* he thought. After the message beep, he said, "Hey, babe, it's Teddy. Call me as soon as you get in. Let's party tonight. I've got lots of toys to play with."

Slamming the receiver in its cradle, he frowned. *Where the fuck is she?* he wondered. *First Val, now Tiff. She's probably already out at that local dump of a bar with redneck friends.*

And now I've got to get ready to play host to Marguerite and Jamie, he thought. *Put my best foot forward.* But he knew they wouldn't be here long, probably no more than a couple of hours at the most. Tiffani probably wouldn't get his message until late. That left him at least a couple of hours alone.

Suddenly he decided what he would do with those two hours or so. He laughed aloud, then got to his feet and picked up the box on the desk, tucking it under his arm, grinning from ear to ear. *First I'll take a shower,* he thought, walking toward the office door. *Then change clothes for Marguerite and Jamie. Be my most charming self for them. When they've gone, I'll have a little bite of whatever it is Hattie's left in the kitchen for me. If I feel hungry. Then I'll get busy. I know what'll put the fear of God in Val for sure. And it'll serve her right, too. Serve them all right.*

Chapter Twenty-One

A table for two had been set on the stone terrace just outside the big library. In its center was a small bowl filled with daisies and other colorful wild flowers, and to either side of it, big glass hurricanes held candles that flickered romantically as the night darkened. The table was set with a colorful cotton Provençal cloth and simple pottery dishes with attractive but plain glassware and silver.

The table looked summery and beautiful, Val thought, yet casual and not too precious. Thank heaven it didn't look as if everything had belonged to some long-departed royal or immensely rich robber baron. She appreciated its simplicity all the more because of the grandeur of the house itself. She hadn't known what to expect, of course, but was hoping that the dinner wouldn't be as formal as what one might expect in such a mansion.

She'd been surprised not to be greeted by Santo Ducci, or see him at all. Wyn had answered the door himself, dressed in khakis, a crisp black linen shirt, and Top-Siders. She'd been doubly surprised when he'd mixed their drinks himself—a vodka and tonic for her, a scotch and water for him—then served the dinner without anyone assisting him, other than Val herself.

In the kitchen, he'd confessed that Gerda, Mrs. Reinhardt, had put together the simple fare: a delectable whole cold poached salmon with a creamy dill sauce; an unusual but delicious potato salad with bits of corn, tarragon, and lobster in it; fresh chilled asparagus in a balsamic vinaigrette; and tomatoes, right out of the garden, topped with a locally made buffalo mozzarella and garden-fresh basil, lightly drizzled with a heavenly tasting cold-pressed extra virgin olive oil.

Wyn had opened a bottle of delicious white burgundy that went perfectly with the meal. "It's an Antonin Rodet Château de Rully, '98," he'd said. "I think it'll go okay. I haven't really familiarized myself with the wine cellar here yet."

"It's delicious," Val had told him after having a taste.

Now she sat sipping at the wine on the candlelit terrace, enjoying the beauty of the late summer night. She was alone, surrounded by darkness, waiting for Wyn while he made the long trek to the kitchen to bring dessert. She'd insisted on helping, but he'd told her to sit still and digest a bit before he came back with the promised dessert: homemade vanilla ice cream with chocolate sauce.

A light breeze ruffled her hair slightly. She'd worn it loose tonight, with a lightweight cream cotton sweater and cream nylon clam-diggers with cream thong sandals, all of it casual but well-cut with a hint of the glamour that Armani knows how to do. Little diamonds glinted in her ears, and a pearl necklace—her paternal grandmother's—hung around her neck. At her wrist was her "dress" watch, a gold Cartier Santos that her father had given her many years before. She seldom wore it, not wanting to subject it to the wear and tear her work would inevitably cause.

When she'd arrived at Eddie and Jonathan's earlier, Colette had been there, and the three of them had all but applauded her appearance, giving her ego a tremendous boost. Their timing couldn't have been better, because her afternoon and early evening hadn't gone well. It was as if the telephone call from Teddy had left her with an unpleasant aftertaste that she hadn't quite been able to overcome, but she'd made an effort to dress for tonight—if not formal, at least elegant and sexy.

Her efforts had paid off, she thought. Eddie, Jonathan, and Colette had practically swooned over her appearance and had immediately demanded to know what the special occasion was.

When she'd told them she was going over to Stonelair for dinner, they'd all been intrigued and delighted and had quizzed her without any show of restraint. She'd told them about taking care of the animals at Stonelair and meeting Wyn, and when they'd asked her about his mysterious aloofness, she'd told them that he was recuperating from a polo accident. She didn't go into any detail, however, because she felt that she would be encroaching on Wyn's privacy.

"What about the money?" Jonathan had asked. "Do you think he's really some kind of drug lord or Mafioso or something?"

"That's ridiculous, Jonathan," Colette had snapped, glaring at him. "The man has too much good taste for that sort of thing. He'd never have bought Stonelair otherwise, and he certainly wouldn't have asked our Val to dinner. No, this is bound to be a man of discrimination. Why else would he be interested in Val?"

They'd all laughed at her remark, but Valerie had had to tell them that she knew nothing about the source of his wealth. "All I know is that he apparently lived very grandly in Palm Beach," she'd said, "because I saw a lot of polo pictures in the tack room."

"There!" Colette had exclaimed. "That proves my point. If he were really a gangster, he certainly wouldn't be playing polo in Palm Beach." Then she'd turned to Val and winked at her. "Val, darling," she'd said. "You remember our little conversation about your future? When we discussed Teddy and men in general?"

Valerie had nodded, certain of what was coming next. "Of course I remember it, Colette," she'd replied.

Colette had smiled brightly and knowingly, as if they shared a secret. "I think I already see a touch of the bloom on those lovely cheeks of yours."

Val had blushed, then laughed merrily, but she hadn't disagreed with Colette.

When she'd gotten out of the Jeep at Stonelair's front door, Wyn had opened it himself, before she could even ring the bell.

"Well, well, well," he'd said, looking her up and down. "No blood-smeared lab coat. I almost didn't recognize you."

"You're almost unrecognizable yourself," she'd replied.

"How's that?" he'd asked, looking puzzled.

"You're wearing a smile," she'd said. "I didn't know you had one in your wardrobe."

"*Touché, madame,*" he'd said, bowing slightly. He'd swung the door open wide and walked her to the library, where all four of the dogs and Mina, the cat, had greeted her.

Later, while they were eating, he'd complimented her appearance again, more directly and sincerely, if in a teasing manner. "You really do look beautiful tonight," he'd said, "especially considering how I usually see you."

"If that's a compliment," she said, "I'll accept it, and return it." She looked over at him. "You look better without the big nose and eye bandages. Almost human, in fact."

"*Almost* human?" he'd said.

"Well, maybe I'm stretching things a bit," she'd joked, "but I think I detect a faint resemblance to a human being. The eye patch is much more becoming than that huge bandage, and you look much better. You're cleaning up nicely."

Now, as she reflected about the last couple of hours in his company, she couldn't suppress the smile that came unbidden to her lips.

"Penny for your thoughts," Wyn said, coming through one of the French doors with a tray in his hands.

"Cheap, aren't you?" she said.

He smiled. "You're an expensive woman. How about a quarter?"

"I'll take it," she said. "But . . . oh, I wasn't thinking about anything really," she went on. "It's just so nice out tonight, and I'm enjoying myself."

"You didn't expect to?" he said, setting the tray down.

"No, it's not that," she said. "I guess I didn't know what to expect, and as it turns out, I don't know when I've had such a good time."

"Do you mean that?" he asked, taking a plate off the tray and putting it in her place.

"Yes," she said, nodding. "I'd almost forgotten what it's like to . . . well, just have a good time without any complications."

He sat down and looked into her eyes. "I feel exactly the same way," he said. "It's been like being let loose from jail for me. In more ways than one. It's not just that you know about my accident and the injuries and all that. It's more than that, Val."

She felt her heart quicken a beat and could feel the heat of her blood rush from her chest up to her face. "I-I think I know what you mean," she said.

He reached over and put one of his hands over hers, where it lay on the table, and held it there tenderly, then gave it a squeeze. She almost shuddered at his touch, so electrifying was it.

"We'd better eat this ice cream before it melts," Wyn said, grinning as he removed his hand.

"It looks yummy," she said, picking up her spoon.

"Gerda makes it," he said, "in one of those electric ice cream machines, and she makes the chocolate sauce, too."

Valerie took the spoon out of her mouth. "This is fantastic," she said, still savoring its taste on her palate.

"I'm glad to see that you have a good appetite," he said. "I like to see that in a woman."

"Maybe so," she said, "but I don't think you'd like to see the results of a woman eating like this all the time."

He laughed. "I guess you're right about that, but I really do like your digging in. My ex, or soon-to-be ex, ate like a bird. And that was when she really let herself live."

Val looked over at him. "Always diet-obsessed?"

He nodded. "Percentage of body fat was a chief topic of conversation in her set, and a pound either way would make her absolutely crazy. But I think the number one topic of conversation was plastic surgeons. Who did the best breasts, the best lipo, the best . . . well, you get the picture." He looked off into the distance, then back at her. "She was crazy anyway," he added.

Valerie hesitated before responding. Ex-wives were dangerous territory, she thought, and despite her natural curiosity, this was definitely not an area of his life that she wanted to pry into. But he did seem to want to talk about her. After all, he'd brought her up.

"What's she really like?" she asked, deciding to venture into the topic. "I know she isn't really crazy or you wouldn't have married her. I mean, bad crazy as opposed to a little bit crazy, which can be good, I think."

"She was always a little bit crazy. Good crazy, as you so aptly put it," he said. "But she started getting a little too crazy for my tastes. She came from a family near West Palm Beach that didn't have much. They weren't poor, but they couldn't afford luxuries. She's very beautiful and sexy and pretty damn smart and saw what Palm Beach had to offer—as opposed to West Palm."

"Upwardly mobile, I take it?" Val said.

"With a vengeance," he replied. "And I actually appreciated that in her. Nothing wrong with wanting to make a better place for yourself in this world, is there?"

"Absolutely not," she agreed, nodding.

"Anyhow," he continued, "she got a job as a secretary in Palm Beach, met an older rich guy from New York with a condo there, and ended up marrying him. Two years later, he had a massive heart attack, and she inherited almost everything."

"Is that when you came into the picture?" Val asked.

"It was around then," he said. "She had some money and started dating, mostly proper-type rich divorced men, then started giving a little money to charities so she'd get invited to their parties. She was also throwing parties at her condo for a wilder set and hanging out in clubs, that kind of thing. I was living pretty much like her. You know, quite the ladies' man, really wild, going from one woman to the next, sowing wild oats left and right. Anyway, some friends of mine introduced us at a party, and I liked her right off the bat. It wasn't just that she was beautiful. She was like a free spirit, you know? Not stuffy and preppy like so many of those rich Palm Beach women. She was sort of a renegade, a breath of fresh air. I found out she'd almost run through nearly every cent of poor old Sydney Goodman's money by the time I met her." He laughed.

"What was she going to do then?" Val asked, genuinely intrigued.

"She didn't have the vaguest idea," he said, shaking his head slightly. "She told me that she was sure something would work out somehow. And if it didn't? She wasn't afraid. Of anything. At least not then."

"That's a gutsy lady all right," Valerie said. "Most women crave security. I guess most everyone does. Money-wise and mate-wise."

"Yes," he agreed, "and her being different was definitely one of the things that attracted me to her. But things began to change after a couple of years of marriage."

"Did familiarity breed contempt?" she asked. "Or am I being nosy?"

"Not at all," he said. "Arielle got used to a lot real fast, if you know what I mean. I loved spoiling her, but then after a while, she just didn't seem to be able to get enough no matter what it was."

"Material girl, huh?" Valerie said with a smile.

"That too with a vengeance," he said. "Plus, I think that while I was off playing polo or taking care of business, she got bored and started to hang out with a party crowd that dabbled in drugs. She stopped going to charity flings and that kind of thing, and spent all of her time with this really wild set. And I mean wild. Mostly bored Eurotrash with lots of cash, and their hangers-on."

"She must not have known what to do with herself," Valerie said. "It sounds like she didn't have any real interests and was bored."

"I guess so," he agreed. "The first year we were married she traveled with me a lot to polo matches and even went on business trips. She really seemed to enjoy some of the polo trips. There was usually a lot of socializing, big parties, meeting people, and all that. The business trips were a bore for her, I know. I mean, looking at mines and mining equipment isn't much of anybody's idea of a good time. It's a filthy, stinking business. But for a while there, we went everywhere together." He paused and looked over at her. "Then she completely lost interest in me. In every way."

Valerie stared at him for a moment before replying. "You're still hurt, aren't you. I mean by her losing interest in your life . . . and you."

He nodded. "I have to admit that I am, Doc," he said, looking over at her with a tight smile. "She had already starting ignoring me before the accident, but it didn't help that she wouldn't have anything to do with me after the accident. And I do mean anything."

"I see," Valerie said. Obviously, Arielle, who had already lost any affection she might have had for him, couldn't cope with him after the accident. If she was as obsessed with looks as he said, then his injuries would've only made sex with him all the more unendurable.

"Why don't we have a little brandy?" he said, changing the subject.

"Just a smidgen for me," she replied. "I have to drive home tonight. Remember?"

"Yes," he said, "but I was hoping I could get you good and drunk and then keep you here all weekend and take advantage of you." He smiled.

"I'm on call at the clinic," she said, "so I'll have to let you do that some other time."

They both laughed.

"Want to have that drink in the library?" he asked. "The dogs have been so good about not bothering us tonight, I think we should reward them with our company."

"That's fine with me."

He got to his feet and came around to her chair, easing it back for her as she stood. Then he put an arm around her waist and led her into the library.

From their various positions, the dogs bounded to their feet and rushed over for attention as the two of them entered the room. While Wyn went to the drinks table and poured them each a snifter of brandy, Valerie alternated petting the four huge dogs until she'd shown them all an equal amount of affection. They finally returned to their napping spots satisfied and settled down.

"My God," she said, "they're all such pussycats."

"They are with you," he said, "but they're not that way with just anybody."

He brought her the brandy and indicated a seat on one of the big leather Chesterfield couches. "Oh, wait a minute," he said. "On second thought, maybe we'd better not sit there. You'll get dog hair all over your clothes."

"Oh, that's ridiculous, Wyn," she said. "I live in dog hair. Remember?"

"If you're sure," he said.

"I'm sure." She sat down on the couch, and he followed suit, leaving a little distance between them. He slipped off his Top-Siders and put his feet up on the coffee table.

"Make yourself comfy," he said.

"I am," she replied.

"But you've got your shoes on."

"Well, there is that," she said, slipping her sandals off and putting her feet up on the big marble coffee table, too. She wiggled her toes. "Now," she said, "I really am comfy."

"I knew it," he said. "I bet your mother and father could hardly keep shoes on you when you were little."

"That's right," she said, laughing. "And I guess I haven't changed all that much."

"Cheers," he said, holding up his brandy snifter.

"Cheers," she repeated.

They clinked glasses, looking into one another's eyes.

"This is a wonderful room," she said, breaking eye contact and looking around.

"I practically live in this room," he said, "and so do the dogs, as you've noticed. I eat and read and do all my telephoning in here. I even do all of my computer work in here," he said, indicating the laptop on the antique French *bureau plat*.

"What kind of computer work?" she asked.

"Stuff related to the mines mostly," he said. "Keeping track of production, sales, things like that, and of course I'm constantly e-mailing management."

"So you're into mining," she said.

He nodded. "My grandfather started the mines, then left them to my dad. When he died, I took over and started expanding into related areas. Chemicals and stuff. I'd worked there in the summers since I was fifteen anyhow, so I knew quite a bit about the business."

"And your mother?" she asked. "Is your mother still alive?"

He shook his head. "No," he said, "she lived about two years after Dad died. She was so lonely without him. They'd been a real team, you know? She didn't seem to want to live after he died."

"I'm sorry," she said.

"It's okay," he said. "It's been a few years."

"So you're left running everything on your own?"

He nodded. "The last few years I've been able to do nearly everything from home, but I go out west four or five times a year and stay a few days. It puts a face on the boss for the new people, and there's nothing like an up-close and personal inspection to make sure things are under control." He grinned.

"I bet you're a tough boss," she said.

"I am," he said without hesitation. "But I'm also fair, and I reward my employees accordingly. They also know that there's not a job there that I haven't personally done, so they know I'm not just some rich guy living off their labor. I've worked alongside some of them." He paused and looked at her. "That's enough about me," he said. "What about you?"

"What about me?" she said teasingly.

"I bet you had a coming-out party and went to one of the Seven Sisters," he said, "and your father set you up in a nice practice."

She laughed, almost sputtering brandy.

"What's so funny?" he asked.

"Your—your presumptions."

"I'm not wrong, am I?"

She nodded. "Yes and no," she said. "I did have a coming-out party. That part you got right. But I didn't really get into it. I wasn't part of that scene at all. In fact, I wore a borrowed dress, and I didn't go to a single party but the ball itself."

"You were doing what Mommy and Daddy wanted you to do, I bet," he said.

"Exactly," she said. "It was easier than arguing with them. As for school, I worked my way through Cornell."

"You're kidding," he said, a look of surprise on his face.

"No," she replied. "I worked in a bookstore, worked as a waitress, a dog walker, baby-sat, house-sat, all kinds of things. And I borrowed money. Lots of money. Student loans. Which I am still paying off." She laughed, and he laughed with her. "Sometimes I think I'll be in debt the rest of my life."

"Could have fooled me," he said. "You had a coming-out and all that, but your parents didn't pay your way through school?"

"No," she said. "My mother insisted on my going to a finishing school in Switzerland or maybe doing literature or French at one of the Seven Sisters. But I wouldn't do it. I wanted to be a veterinarian. So she said I'd have to pay for it myself."

"You're kidding," he said.

"Nope," she said, shaking her head. "But I don't think she actually thought I'd go off on my own like that, and I think she was just waiting for me to come running home."

He smiled. "Well, good for you," he said. "That shows a lot of spunk."

She shrugged. "I just knew what I wanted," she said, "and I was going to get it come hell or high water."

"What do your parents think about it now?" he asked.

"My father died before I went to college," she replied. "My mother . . . well, she still doesn't like it. She has this Old World idea that I should be married to someone from the same background and living the life of leisure. You know, like one of the ladies who lunch in New York. The charity circuit and all that. The way she lived until my father died."

"You'd wither up and die in that atmosphere," he said unhesitatingly.

She nodded. "I know," she said, "but try telling my mother that."

"It seems to me she ought to be really proud of you," he said. "I would be. I *am*."

Valerie laughed. "For what?" she asked.

"I've watched you in action," he said, "and I think you're a top-notch vet. And person."

Valerie felt herself blush again. "Thanks," she said. "I appreciate that."

"Now," he said, "tell me about whoever it is that's lucky enough to be engaged to you."

"Wha—?" She stared at him dumbstruck, unable to finish her sentence.

Slowly, somewhat reluctantly, the shadowy figure lowered the binoculars and let them hang loose on their neck strap. Fingers quickly rubbed tired eyes.

Watching them had been almost mesmerizing, as if observing some sort of forbidden ritual or an especially tantalizing pornographic video, not that there had been anything in the least bit lewd or lurid in their behavior. No, they had behaved in an exemplary fashion.

It's the invasion of privacy. That's why it feels so strange. Invading their privacy, watching them on their own turf, without their knowing anything about it. It's a real kick, though. A real sick kick.

Watching even the most mundane of activities could be fascinating if observed in this way, the interloper supposed, but that was not what this was about. No, this had a purpose, and an important one at that. In fact, seeing them together had driven home the fact that the situation held a lot more potential for danger than previously thought.

The way they'd chatted during dinner, all cozy and relaxed and laughing, with some serious-looking moments thrown in for good measure. The way he'd held her chair for her to sit down, then the way he'd slid it back for her to get up. The way he'd put a hand over one of hers during dinner, then the way he'd put an arm around her waist when they went inside together.

Now they sat together on the couch, their bare feet propped up on the coffee table like they were sweethearts, their bodies close together, nearly touching while they chatted on and on into the night.

Imagine their talk! Earnestly telling one another all about their lives, their histories, past and present, getting to know one another—all the ridiculous flotsam and jetsam about where they came from and who they were—before they made that inevitable leap into the old sack and onto each other's bodies.

It was enough to make you puke.

Spitting on the ground as if to expel a bad taste, then looking at the glow-in-the-dark watch, the figure in the shadows saw that it was a little after eleven. It was getting late, and there was work to do. It was getting to be time to do it.

"Who-who told you about that?" she finally stuttered, her mind spinning with a million questions at once.

"Nobody," he said, looking at her with a superior expression.

"What do you mean nobody?" she asked. "How could you possibly know about that?"

"It's simple," he said, breaking into a laugh.

Damn him, she thought. *He's playing with me and enjoying it.* "Tell me," she said. "What's so simple?"

"Remember the first time you came out here?" he asked.

She nodded. "Of course, I do," she replied. "Storm Warning had colic. Why?"

"I saw you that night," he said, suddenly somewhat sheepish. "I was watching you out in the stable. In the dark, so you couldn't see me."

"I see," she said with a nod, remembering the eerie sensation she'd had that night of being watched.

"I couldn't help but notice that you were wearing a real humdinger of a ring," he went on. "It practically lit up the stall when the lantern light hit it. And it sure did look like an engagement ring, at least to me, Doc."

She swallowed. It was true, she thought. That was the night that she had accepted the ring from Teddy, and she'd been wearing it when she came over to see about the horse. It was so new that she'd forgotten she was wearing it when she'd ministered to Storm Warning. Otherwise, she'd have taken it off to keep from getting it dirty.

She gazed over at him and nodded. "Guilty as charged," she said, smiling tightly.

"So you are engaged," he said, the look on his face undeniably one of disappointment.

"You . . . might say that," she replied.

"What's that supposed to mean?" he asked. "Maybe you are, maybe you aren't?"

Was she imagining it, or did she detect a hint of hope in his voice? "Well . . ." She looked up at the ceiling and shrugged. "Where do I begin?"

"The beginning's a good place, so they say," he replied, reaching over and taking her hand.

She looked down at his hand in hers and realized that it felt natural, comfortable . . . and wonderful. She looked back up at him.

"I've been going with the same guy for a long time," she said. "Since college. Everybody's always expected us to get married sooner or later. Including me." She sighed heavily, then continued. "Anyhow, to make a long story short, he gave me the ring that night. The night I came over to see about Storm Warning."

His eyes were glued to hers. "But I haven't seen you wear it since then," he said.

"You're . . . you're awfully observant," she said with a short laugh.

"I'm awfully interested," he said, smiling.

She was silent for a moment, and he prodded her with another question.

"So are you still engaged or what?" he asked. "You don't seem like an engaged woman to me."

She shrugged again, then said, "I guess you could say that officially we're still engaged."

"Officially," he repeated.

She nodded.

"In other words," he said, "you haven't . . ." His words trailed off into silence.

"In other words," she said, supplying words for him, "I haven't told him that I don't want to marry him."

"Aha," he said softly, a smile on his lips. "This is getting very interesting." He paused, then said, "So when are you going to tell him that it's a no-go situation?"

"I don't know," Valerie groaned. "It's . . . it's so difficult to do, and I'm such a chicken that I keep putting it off. But I know that I've got to do it sooner or later."

"Do it sooner," he said.

She looked at him with widened eyes. "What-what are you saying?"

"You heard me," he said. "And I think you know exactly what I mean."

"You . . ." She couldn't bring herself to express what she thought he might mean.

"I want you free," he said. "For me."

Valerie's body jerked, as if she'd been shocked by a bolt of electricity. She felt her heart begin to pump violently, and a pulse beat hard against her eardrum. She couldn't quite catch her breath, and she didn't trust herself to speak. It was a moment of truth.

He's in love with me, she realized, *and I am in love with him.*

Before she could respond, he reached toward her and pulled her to him. She acquiesced, easing into the warmth of his arms happily, as if she were going home to a place she belonged. He kissed her, and she felt a thrill rush through her body, even as her hands felt the soft naturalness of his dark hair and the alien scratchiness of the gauze bandages that were wrapped around part of it.

To think that anyone could ever be afraid of this man, she thought. *To think that he has sparked dark rumors as no one else around here ever has. And to think that he loves me.*

She kissed him passionately, forgetting all else, giving herself up to this moment. It was an unforgettable moment in time, occupying some unique and magical realm all its own.

When he finally drew back, he smiled at her and his eyes searched hers for any indication of what she was thinking and feeling. She returned his smile unhesitatingly, then whispered to him, "It'll definitely be sooner than later."

Chapter Twenty-Two

Valerie rolled over in bed and glanced at the clock on the bedside table. *Six-thirty! What the hell?* she wondered. The telephone had been ringing relentlessly, and she'd tried to no avail to block out its awful early morning cacophony in her tender ears. Then suddenly she remembered she was on call at the clinic, and she quickly reached over, grabbing the receiver.

"Hello?" she said, trying to clear the sleep from her voice.

"Valerie?" The cultured voice was clipped, imperious, and demanding all at once, immediately putting her on alert.

"Mother?" she asked. "What-what is it? Is something wrong?"

"Wrong?" Marguerite de la Rochelle repeated. "Certainly not. Not with me at least."

"Oh," Valerie said. "It's just so early . . . I thought maybe . . . well, I didn't know. You don't usually call this early on a weekend morning."

"I want you to come to breakfast," Marguerite said. It was an order, not a request.

"Breakfast?" Valerie said. "But . . . I-I've really got a lot to do around the house, and—"

"Breakfast will be served promptly at nine o'clock," Marguerite interjected, "and I want you here. There are some things we need to discuss. Your cousin Jamie is here, as you know, and you've made no effort to see him."

"I haven't been avoiding Jamie at all," she said in self-defense. "I was planning on having him over or coming out there to see him. You know I've been busy at the clinic, Mother, and I just haven't got around to it yet."

"No, indeed, you have not," Marguerite said. "You have no time for family, do you, Valerie? So this morning is ideal, isn't it? This *is* the weekend, and you're not working, so we can have a lovely breakfast."

"I'm on call at the clinic," Valerie said, "so I—"

"Damn that clinic!" Marguerite exclaimed angrily. "I think you can spare the time for breakfast with your mother and your cousin. Some sick dog will simply have to wait. Nine o'clock!"

Before Valerie could respond, there was a loud and resounding bang in her ear as her mother hung up on her. She looked at the receiver in her hand for a moment, then put it down. She sighed, wondering what on earth had brought this on. Then suddenly she began to laugh aloud.

Elvis, who was spread out on the floor at the foot of the bed, began to wag his tail furiously, excited by the sound of her laughter. She looked down at him, the laughter still rising in her throat, shaking her body and lifting her spirits. "Oh, Elvis," she said when she could finally speak, "she is not going to make me upset today. Nothing could upset me today." She hugged herself with her arms, thrilled with the memory of last night. Of Wyn Conrad.

Elvis looked up at her with what she was certain was a bright smile on his face, his tail still thumping against the floor.

She slid her legs over the side of the bed and rose to her feet, stretching her arms and back and shoulders, lifting herself up on her toes, reaching toward the ceiling. "No, siree, Elvis," she said. "Marguerite de la Rochelle is not going to get my goat today, no matter what."

She dashed into the bathroom, performed her morning ablutions, and padded into the kitchen on bare feet, still in the huge T-shirt she had worn in place of pajamas, Elvis trailing along behind her. She quickly filled his water bowl and fed him his breakfast— the usual dry food with a little of the tuna fish he loved mixed in— then she ground beans and got the coffeemaker going. She let Elvis out when he was finished, then rushed back into the bathroom and quickly showered. Afterward, wrapped in a bathrobe, she poured herself a mug of coffee and wandered out onto the screened-in porch to drink it.

The morning promised to be a beautiful one, and she regretted that she wouldn't be spending it out in the garden, puttering around, prettifying here and there.

She sipped her coffee, wishing that Colette would come tiptoeing into the garden with Hayden so that they could have a good gossip. She could hardly wait to tell her what had happened last night, but she would have to put it off until later in the day. It was too early to call Colette now. She finished her coffee and went back inside. She peered at the kitchen clock. Nearly eight o'clock already. She'd better start getting ready to face breakfast with Jamie and her mother.

She went back into the bathroom and put on a touch of mascara and eyeliner, then daubed lightly at her cheeks with the merest hint of blusher. Next, she carefully applied a little lipstick, a gingery color that she liked with her strawberry blond hair and green eyes. Finally, she brushed at her hair vigorously and then let it fall naturally into place. She stood back and examined herself in the mirror.

Not half bad, she thought, even though she knew that no matter what she did it wouldn't be enough to satisfy her mother. *No, she thought, Mother will manage to find fault somehow or other, and she'll let me know about it.* She smiled at her reflection.

Well, this morning, Marguerite, your criticism will fall on deaf ears, she told herself. *Because nothing, absolutely nothing, is going to take the shine off my day.* Then she remembered perfume and quickly spritzed herself with some of the Femme on the vanity.

Rushing back into her bedroom, she shrugged out of her bathrobe, slipped on her bra and panties, and rummaged in her closet. *Where the devil is my green silk tee?* she wondered. She liked it because it was a close match to her eyes. She opened and closed several dresser drawers, thinking that she'd folded it and put it in one of them. No luck.

She went back to the closet and rummaged some more. Still no luck. *Oh, well,* she thought, *just find something and put it on.* She grabbed a navy blue short-sleeved tee, silk like the green one, and quickly put it on, then donned a pair of cream clam-diggers almost identical to the ones she'd worn last night. She slipped into her cream thong sandals and went back out to the kitchen, where she grabbed her shoulder bag. *Ready,* she thought. *All except for Elvis.*

She went out to the screened-in porch and called to him, and he came prancing toward her from somewhere down near the pond. She opened the door and let him in. "Elvis," she said, "I'm going out to see Mother so I'm leaving you here." She leaned down and gave him several strokes. "I'm sorry to do this to you, but you and Mother both will like it a lot better this way."

She locked the porch door and left the kitchen one open for him. That way he could enjoy the porch or stay in the house, whichever he wanted. She glanced out toward the garden longingly, then turned and headed to the front door. *I really don't want to do this, but nothing can wipe the smile off my face today.*

Twenty minutes later, she pulled into the parking area behind her mother's house, and her face immediately fell.

Teddy's silver Jaguar.

Oh, no, she thought. *Why didn't she tell me? And what is he doing here this morning anyway?* But it didn't take an Einstein to figure out exactly why Teddy was here. Marguerite had asked him, of course, and most likely she'd arranged this breakfast *after* Teddy and her mother had had a little talk last night about her unwillingness to cancel her plans to be with him.

It would be just like Teddy to have called Mother, she thought. *Trying to get her help to keep me in line. Well, it's not going to work, folks.*

She stepped into the screened-in porch, where she noticed the table had been set for breakfast, then went on into the kitchen. Effie was bent over the oven door, sliding out a pan of croissants. When she heard Valerie, she turned around and smiled widely.

"I'm so glad to see you," she said, putting the pan down on the center island.

Valerie gave her a kiss and a hug. "You look great, Effie."

"You don't have to flatter me," the old woman replied, "but I'm glad you do." She stared at Valerie for a moment, then her eyes narrowed into slits. "You!" she said, pointing a finger at her.

"You're the one who looks great, Val. You're glowing from head to toe."

Valerie smiled. "Do you really think so?"

"You know you are," Effie said. She looked at Valerie with an expression of curiosity. "Tell Effie what you've been up to," she said. "Because I know that look, and it means something awful good's going on."

"Oh, Effie," Valerie replied, "I don't know what you're talking about."

"Come on," the old woman said, cajoling her. "You can tell me, young lady."

Valerie leaned down and kissed her cheek again. "I'll tell you all about it later on," she said. "When you and I can have some privacy."

"Promise?" Effie said, looking at her with widened eyes.

"Promise," Valerie answered.

Effie beamed. "I knew it!" she said. "I just knew it!"

"Where's Mother?" Valerie asked.

"She and the boys are out at the old swimming pool," she said. "I'm surprised you didn't see them."

"The swimming pool?" Valerie said. "What in the world are they doing out there?"

Effie shrugged. "Who knows?" she replied. "Since that cousin of yours has been here, he and your mother've been whispering around like a couple of conspirators. Like they were planning a murder. And they don't tell me anything."

Valerie frowned, then relaxed her features. "Well, it's probably nothing, Effie," she said. "They're probably just talking about old family secrets or something. Skeletons in the ancestral closet, that sort of thing."

"Humpf!" Effie said. "That wouldn't be anything new to me."

They heard the sound of approaching voices and turned toward the door. "We'll talk later," Valerie said, then walked out to the porch to greet everyone.

Her mother looked at her, her features set in a mask of amiability that didn't fool Valerie for a second. "Good morning, dear," she said, holding her cheek up for a kiss.

"Good morning," Valerie said, kissing the proffered cheek. "And Jamie! It's so good to see you."

Jamie hugged her and air-kissed each cheek in the European fashion. "You look great," he said.

"You look terrific yourself," she replied. "I see you've been working out a lot. I think the South of France agrees with you."

She felt Teddy's arm slide across her shoulder. "Good morning," he said, kissing her cheek.

"Good morning, Teddy," she said without looking at him.

Effie appeared from the kitchen, laden with a tray on which sat a pot of fresh coffee, surrounded by baskets and platters of food.

"Oh, I see Effie's got everything ready," Marguerite said. "Let's sit, shall we?"

Jamie held her chair for her, and Marguerite took her place at the head of the table, while Teddy held Valerie's chair for her. She sat down, feeling a slight sense of dread despite pumping herself up before arriving here.

Effie set the tray down and put out the food, then poured coffee for everyone. There were scrambled eggs, bacon and sausage, croissants and biscuits, fruit, and various condiments. Marguerite began helping herself, then passed the food around, and everyone began eating with gusto.

"This is so good," Valerie enthused. "It's been a while since I've had one of Effie's great breakfasts."

"You should try it more often, dear," Marguerite said, looking at her daughter pointedly. "Effie makes breakfast every morning, as you know."

Teddy laughed. "I bet Val has more food in the house for Elvis than she does for herself."

Valerie felt her face flush, but she decided not to say anything. *Let them think what they will. Nothing anybody can say or do today is going to hurt me,* she reminded herself.

"Marguerite has always known how to do everything perfectly," Jamie offered. "Whether for man or beast."

Breakfast continued with small talk centered primarily on the garden and then the swimming pool, which Valerie discovered her mother had for some reason decided to completely remodel. Even though she was curious about this turn of events, she didn't ask any questions and contributed very little in the way of talk, deciding to listen and then make as quick an exit as possible. Suddenly, however, she became the center of attention.

"Val, dear," her mother said in what Valerie recognized as her most condescending tone of voice, "I'm so glad you could come this morning. I think it's high time we discussed your wedding. Your cousin Jamie and Teddy and I have discussed it at length, and we've decided that it should be as soon as possible. You won't have to do a thing. We'll take care of everything for you."

Valerie listened to her mother with disbelieving ears. Yet she knew that there was nothing wrong with her hearing, and she also knew that her mother meant every single word she was saying. She started to interrupt more than once, but restrained herself, deciding to hear her out, for the time being at least.

"You know," Marguerite went on, "you and Teddy have been seeing each other for years now, living together for all practical purposes, so we think it's time you finally made it official. I'm certain that if your father were alive, he would feel the same way. Neither of us ever really approved of young people living together before marriage, but we always knew that you and Teddy would eventually marry." She looked at Valerie questioningly. She seemed genuinely surprised by her daughter's continued silence.

"I see," Valerie finally offered in a neutral voice, taking a sip of her coffee.

"Oh, good. I'm glad you do," Marguerite continued. "We've also decided that a big church affair and reception should be dispensed with at this point. A waste of time and money, really, and you both have such busy lives. Teddy with his career, and you with your little job. So unnecessary, don't you agree?" She looked at her daughter with lifted brows.

"Absolutely," Valerie answered.

"Wonderful," Marguerite said, clapping her hands together lightly. "We'll have an intimate family ceremony here at home as soon as possible. Effie can make a nice wedding luncheon or something. It's so fortunate that your cousin Jamie is here for it. He can give you away, don't you think?"

Valerie knew that she couldn't listen to much more of her mother's talk without exploding. Her mind was already reeling with the appropriate obscenities, but she didn't really want to use them. That these people would presume to plan her life for her was enraging, but that it should all be done behind her back was adding insult to injury.

Who or what do they think I am? she asked herself. *Some pawn in a chess game they're playing? Have I always been so . . . so spineless to their demands that they think they can actually railroad me into this marriage?*

Marguerite was staring at her, her emerald eyes glittering intensely, a smile on her lips, waiting for the expected response from her daughter. After a moment, Valerie noticed, she actually began to tap perfectly manicured fingernails against the tablecloth in her impatience. Then she saw that both Teddy and Jamie were watching her as well.

Like evil blond twins, she thought. *Only Jamie's more built-up and has shorter hair.*

Finally, she set her coffee cup down on the table and took a deep breath. She looked directly into her mother's eyes. "There will be no wedding, Mother," she said quietly but forcefully.

"Don't be absurd," Marguerite replied, laughing lightly. It was as if she'd heard the words but gave them no credence. She looked at Teddy and Jamie and shrugged eloquently.

"I'm not being absurd, Mother," Valerie said.

"What on earth can you mean?" Marguerite asked, the laughter gone from her voice now.

"Just what I said," Valerie replied. "There will be no wedding. Because I'm not getting married."

"Val, dear, don't—" her mother began.

"I'm sorry to have to say this in front of other people, Teddy," Valerie said, turning to look at him, "but I'm not going to marry you."

For a moment, there was a stunned silence around the table as the words actually sank in. Valerie noticed Effie in the doorway to the kitchen, a smile on her lips. Then Jamie broke the silence with a bark of a laugh.

"Oh, Val," he said, "you were always so . . . so different. I just love it. You're such a jokester."

"I'm *not* joking, Jamie," she said, turning her gaze on him.

"Val, I think we should discuss this in private," Teddy said, reaching for her hand.

She brushed his hand away. "There's nothing to discuss," she said softly.

She reached for her carryall on the floor beside her and rummaged around inside it for a minute, finally extracting the black box stamped *Bvlgari*. She put it down on the table and slid it across the tablecloth toward Teddy.

"I hadn't planned on doing it this way, Teddy," she said, "but I don't have much choice, do I? You've planned all of this without consulting me, and I'm left with little choice but to return your ring and call it off before you plan anything else behind my back."

"But we—" Teddy began, his voice angry and bewildered at once.

"You ungrateful child!" Marguerite exclaimed, interrupting Teddy, her voice quavering with rage. "How dare you go against my wishes! And what a terrible lack of manners! I can't believe you're my daughter! My own flesh and blood! To do such a thing to such a wonderful young man without taking him aside for privacy."

"Don't preach to me about manners," Valerie said in a barely controlled anger. "You and Teddy didn't have the decency to take *me* aside to discuss my wedding with me, did you, Mother? No! You invited me over here, thinking that your plans—and Teddy's—were a fait accompli. That I would do anything you asked me to."

Marguerite stared at Valerie as if she thought her daughter had gone mad.

"Well, surprise, surprise," Valerie said, scooting her chair back and rising to her feet. "I'm not doing what you want this time!" She reached down for her bag and slung it across her shoulder. Turning to Teddy, she said, "I really didn't want it to end in such a shabby way, Teddy, and for that I'm truly sorry. But your plotting behind my back was a little bit shabby, too, you must admit." She looked at Jamie and her mother. "Now, if you'll all please excuse me, I'll be going."

She walked to the door, but when she reached it, a voice stopped her.

"Val, dear?" her mother said.

"Yes?" she replied without turning around.

"The two of us will discuss this later."

"No, Mother," Valerie responded, turning to face her mother, her voice full of the determination she felt, "we will not discuss this later. Or ever again, for that matter."

She opened the door and hurriedly walked to her Jeep. She got in the car, fired up the engine, and pulled out of the parking area, heading down the long drive that led away from her mother's stately home atop the hill.

By the time she reached the highway, her eyes were nearly blinded by tears. Tears of shame and humiliation. Tears of relief. But most of all, tears of joy.

She opened the front door, and Elvis virtually danced before her, his toenails clicking on the entrance hall's wooden floor. "Oh, Elvis," she said, "I'm so glad to see you." She went down on her knees and hugged him. "You're so lucky you weren't with me, but now we can start the whole day over again. It can only get better, old boy."

She walked back to the kitchen, Elvis following her. She dropped her carryall on the center island and looked at the clock. A little after ten. She had a powerful urge to call Wyn at once to tell him the news, but she decided she wanted to calm down a bit first and digest the turn of events herself. She still felt unnerved from the scene at her mother's, and she didn't want to come across to Wyn as some sort of hysterical basket case.

Maybe I'll call Colette, she thought, *and we can have a cup of coffee and talk. I need to gather my wits about me, and that should do the trick.*

She started to pick up the telephone, and it rang just as she reached for it. *Maybe it's Wyn,* she thought excitedly. She grabbed the receiver.

"Hello," she said.

"Val, it's-it's Eddie," her old friend said in a strangely choked voice.

"Hi, Eddie. What is it?" she said, her antennae on full alert. "You don't sound like yourself." He was definitely upset about something.

"It's . . . it's Noah." He managed to get the words out before his voice collapsed into heart-wrenching sobs.

"Eddie, listen to me," Valerie said. "Try to tell me what the problem is."

"He-he-he's . . . d-d-dead," Eddie sobbed.

Dead? But that isn't possible, she thought. *He checked out perfectly okay only a few days ago.*

"Please, Eddie," she said, "tell me exactly what's going on."

Eddie took a few breaths and managed to control his sobs. "I let him out to do his business about ten or ten-thirty last night," he said, "and I left one of the French doors in the back open for him like I always do. This morning he wasn't in his bed like he usually is, so I thought he was outside. I went out and called him and called him. When he didn't come, Jonathan and I went out looking for him. I thought maybe he'd cornered a chipmunk or something and just wasn't paying any attention."

His voice choked up again, and Valerie waited patiently while he calmed down. "We-we found him down near the creek," Eddie continued. "Dead."

"You're sure he's not just injured, Eddie?" she asked.

"He's been murdered!" Eddie cried. "Somebody deliberately killed him!"

"Murdered?" she asked incredulously.

"I'm positive," he declared, indignant. "Somebody murdered Noah!"

"I'm coming straight over," she said.

"Oh, would you, Val?" he said, weepy again.

"I'll be there in five minutes," she said. She hung up the receiver and grabbed her carryall, then headed to the front door.

"I'll be back soon, Elvis," she said, leaning down and giving him a few fast strokes. "You guard the house."

She dashed out to the Jeep and hopped in, heading to Eddie's as quickly as possible.

Eddie and Jonathan were both standing outside their beautifully restored Greek Revival house waiting for her when she arrived. They had obviously been crying, their red and swollen eyes testament to their grief. She hugged them both, her heart aching for them, then immediately got down to business.

"Okay," she said. "Show me."

"It's this way," Jonathan said, pointing down toward the creek that bordered the property. "You want to wait here, Eddie?" he asked. "I can take Val."

"Oh, no," Eddie said. "I'm coming, too."

They walked through the lushly planted garden and then through the parklike grounds toward the rocky creek, Jonathan leading the way, Val taking Eddie's hand in hers.

"We didn't move him," Eddie said, "because I wanted you to see him first, Val. I don't know whether to call the police or what."

"We'll have a look," she said.

"From a distance, he looks like he's spread out just like he's asleep," Eddie told her, "and when I saw him like that, that's what I tried to tell myself. That he was just sleeping. But when I got closer to him, I could see that he definitely wasn't asleep."

They neared the creek, and Jonathan came to a standstill ahead of them. Val could see his shoulders begin to shake and a hand go up to his mouth. She and Eddie drew up to his side.

Noah certainly didn't look asleep, she thought. He looked very dead—and as if he'd died in terrible agony. Eddie really had been trying to fool himself at first. The handsome dog was on his back, his forelegs stiffly drawn back and slightly curled. His eyes looked huge, and his mouth was drawn back in a terrible rictus of death.

She went down on both knees and started to examine his body, but her eyes were drawn to a hideous, fly-infested, bloody-looking mass on the ground near Noah.

A chunk of meat, she thought, bile rising in her throat. *It must have been a roast or something.* Her eyes began to tear, but she quickly wiped them and tried to focus on Noah's lifeless body. She examined him, noticing that his eyes were widely dilated. *Poison, probably,* she thought. She turned to Jonathan.

"Have you got a freezer bag or any kind of plastic bag I could use?"

"Sure," he said. "I'll go get it."

"Thanks, Jonathan," she said.

"I'll be right back," he said, and he dashed off toward the house.

"He's been poisoned, hasn't he?" Eddie asked.

She stood back up and nodded. "Yes, Eddie," she said. "It certainly looks that way."

"Val, look at this," Eddie said. "The invisible fencing runs just along here." He was drawing a line along the property with an outstretched finger, then pointed to the bridge that crossed the big creek bordering his property. "Whoever did it probably came down the path from the bridge, then walked along the creek, and threw the meat over the invisible fencing to this side." He looked at her, studying her face to see what she thought of this scenario.

Valerie nodded. "It makes sense, Eddie," she said.

"Noah never crossed the invisible fencing, or at least he hadn't for years," Eddie said. "Two or three shocks when he was younger, and he stayed inside it."

"So somebody would've had to toss the meat over here to this side of the fencing to get him to eat it," Valerie said. "But who would do a thing like that? And why?"

Eddie stared into her eyes. "The most important question is, who would've done it that also knew where the fencing ran?"

Val gazed at him with an expression of curiosity. "Of course, whoever threw the meat to Noah didn't necessarily know about the fence at all. But if what you're saying is true, Eddie, it would probably be somebody who knows you pretty well."

"Exactly," he said, nodding his head.

"Do you have somebody in mind?" she asked. "Is there anybody you can think of that didn't like Noah for some reason? Or . . . you?"

Eddie looked at the ground. "I keep asking myself the same thing, Val," he replied, "but I keep coming up with zilch. Some of the local guys park up near the bridge and come down here to fish, and Noah would sometimes bark at them. But he always stayed on this side of the invisible fencing. He never bit anybody or anything." He shrugged. "I just don't know, Val," he said. "Nobody ever complained to me or anything, and I can't think of anybody who has a grudge against me."

Jonathan returned with a large freezer bag. "Will this do, Val?" he asked.

"Perfect," she said. She took the plastic bag from him, then went back down on her knees. She took several Kleenex out of her carryall, then picked up the chunk of meat with them and put it in the bag, along with the Kleenex. She fingered the Ziploc bag shut and rose to her feet.

"I'll have the lab analyze this," she said, "but I'm pretty sure we all know that there's some kind of poison in the meat." She looked at them. "I'm just so sorry," she added.

"Thanks for coming over, Val," Eddie said.

"You'll let us know what they find out?" Jonathan asked.

"Yes," she said. "I'll call you as soon as I find out anything. I'll put a rush on it, and it'll be sometime this coming week. In the meantime, what do you want to do about Noah?"

"I don't know if there's a law against it or not," Eddie said, "and I don't give a damn if there is. We're going to bury him here on the property. Down near the gazebo."

"I can help you," Val offered.

"No, Val," Jonathan said. "That's okay. We can do it."

"I'll be glad to help," she said.

"No, you've done enough," Eddie said. "Jonathan and I'll do it."

"Do you want to call the police?" she asked. "I can wait for them to come."

"I don't think so," Eddie said, a defeated sound in his voice. "We don't have a thing to go on, do we?"

"Just the fact that he was probably poisoned," she said. "And I'll know with what in a few days."

"I don't think they'll be able to accomplish anything," Eddie said. "I can't imagine who would do anything like this, so I couldn't be any help to them."

"Have you thought of anybody, Jonathan?" she asked. "Or any reason?"

"No," he said. "I can't think of anybody. Maybe not everybody's crazy about us, but I can't think of anybody who actually hates us this much. I think it's got to be some kind of nutcase. That's all I can figure."

"I guess you're right," she agreed. "It's just so hard to imagine. Anyway, I'll drop this by the clinic, but I'll be back home in a hour or so at the most. If you need anything, anything at all, let me know."

"Thanks, Val," Eddie said. "You're a champ." He kissed her cheek, and they hugged again.

She hugged Jonathan next. "I'll get on my way," she said.

"We'll walk you to the car," Eddie offered.

"No," she said, turning to leave. "That's okay. You two do what you have to do. I'm fine."

She walked through the grounds, on through the verdant garden, and then into the courtyard parking area. *I wish I really was fine,* she thought, shaking her head. But something about Noah's death—Noah's *murder,* she reminded herself—disturbed her deeply. Something she couldn't put her finger on.

Who on earth would do such a thing? she asked herself. *Perhaps Jonathan was right. Maybe it was some nutcase. A random act of violence. But why go to so much trouble? Buying the poison and the meat; parking at a distance so as not to be seen or heard; taking the path down from the bridge along the creek in the darkness of night? And what about the invisible fencing, if that was actually a factor? Some nutcase knew about that?*

She got in the car and started it, headed to the clinic to put the meat-filled bag in the freezer there. A shudder went up her spine. *This is so malicious,* she thought. *Why would anyone deliberately kill a dog?*

Chapter Twenty-Three

"A re you sure you'd rather not have dinner with us?" Bibi Whitman asked. "It's not a large party, just twenty or so." She
took a sip of her vodka martini, then set it down on the table next
to the white wicker chair on which she was perched. She sat
erectly, one leg crossed carefully over the other, one low-heeled
spectator pump planted firmly on the stone terrace.

"You're very kind, Bibi," Lolo said, "but I think after I get out
of this polo gear and get cleaned up, we'll take a nap and go out
for a hamburger or something. Make it an early night."

"Well, it's no wonder," she said, looking at him understand-
ingly. "You must be exhausted. You played like a demon, Lolo. I
bet every owner there wishes you were on his team. In fact, I bet
you get some nice offers after the way you played today."

Lolo grinned. "Well, thanks, Bibi," he said.

"Are you sure that Joe's okay?" Arielle asked.

"Oh, yes, Arielle," Bibi said. She trilled laughter. "It's just age,
dear. He tries to do too much. You know how men are. He'll be
fine after a little rest."

"Oh, good," Arielle said, "I was worried about him." Arielle
smiled at the older woman sweetly. *It's no wonder the old goat's
half dead,* she thought. *A dinner party every single night, a luncheon every day, mimosa-soaked breakfasts, and scotch-laced*

*teas—it's enough to kill a man half his age. On top of which he
has to put up with the dragon lady.*

Arielle took a cigarillo from the pack on the coffee table, and
Lolo lit it for her. "Thanks, Lolo," she said.

Bibi and Lolo began talking about the polo practice session,
analyzing it play by play, and Arielle planted a smile on her face
and tuned out, bored by the conversation. She'd decided she hated
polo, but she liked the men who played it.

She watched her hostess with fascination, convinced that Bibi
was flirting with Lolo, who seemed to be enjoying it enormously. It was all Arielle could do to keep from giggling aloud,
the idea was so ridiculous. Bibi's chestnut-dyed hair looked as if
it had been set with mayonnaise, and her perfectly made-up face
could only be described as horsey at best. Her couture-tailored
suit with matching everything only made her look older than
she was.

*She's somewhere north of sixty, and she looks like somebody's
maid playing dress-up,* Arielle thought unkindly.

She took a long drag off of her cigarillo and heaved an inaudi-
ble sigh along with a plume of smoke. It didn't matter one iota
how old or ugly the warhorse was, she thought. Bibi came from
big bucks, older and cleaner and better-connected than most, and
she could have looked like a walrus. The society columnists would
always kowtow, referring to her as a great beauty and legendary
hostess and style-maker extraordinaire.

Not like me, Arielle thought enviously. *I've had to work for
every dress, every piece of jewelry, every goddamn cent.*

"Well, I'd better go see to the details for dinner," she heard Bibi
saying, "but you two young lovers do whatever you want. Stay
out here and enjoy the terrace as long as you like, take a swim . . .
whatever." She smiled meaningfully.

"Thanks for a wonderful day," Lolo said. "I look forward to
the match tomorrow."

Arielle came to attention. "Tell Joe I hope he feels better," she
said.

"I will, dear," Bibi said. "Oh, and don't forget. The keys are in
that little Jeep. The dark green one. Help yourselves. Come and go
as you like."

"Thanks, Bibi," Arielle said. "You're a lifesaver."

"Don't mention it," Bibi said. She rose to her feet, and Lolo followed suit.

"We'll see you in the morning," he said.

"Ta-ta," she said, disappearing through an open door into the house.

Arielle stood up and stretched. "Let's go," she said.

"Finished with your drink?" Lolo asked.

"We can have another one in the guest house," Arielle said.

They strolled arm-in-arm through the lushly planted gardens toward the immaculate cottage that served as a guest house. "I think Bibi's taken a real liking to you, Lolo," Arielle said, her stiletto-heeled Jimmy Choo sandals click-clacking noisily on the stone path.

Lolo laughed. "You must be kidding."

"I saw the way she was looking at you," Arielle said teasingly. "I've been wondering why she's always so nice to me, and I thought it was just because I'm getting a big settlement out of Wyn." She pinched Lolo's ass. "But now I know that's not the only reason. She likes to look at you, and I don't blame her."

"You're crazy," he said, slipping his arm around her shoulder and kissing her cheek. Then he looked at her with a serious expression. "You know, I do think one reason she's so nice to us is because you're divorcing Wyn. Joe was sort of the undisputed king of the polo world until Wyn came along and got all the attention."

She laughed. "Joe hasn't played polo in a hundred years," she said. "I bet he hasn't been on a horse in fifty."

"Yes, but he owned winning teams," Lolo said, "and Wyn's teams came along and started beating his."

Arielle looked surprised. "I hadn't really thought about that," she admitted. "I guess you could be right. Bibi's a competitive old coot, and she wouldn't like to think her husband's team was losing."

"That's right," he said.

"So it's not just your body she's interested in?" Arielle teased.

"No," he said. "I don't think so." He leaned down and kissed her cheek again.

"That's better," Arielle said.

"And it'll get a whole lot better than that," Lolo said with a lewd look.

"Promise?" she replied.

"Have I ever failed you?"

"No," she said. "Not yet."

Arielle, her head on Lolo's shoulder, ran a fingernail down his muscular chest, on down past his six-pack abs, and into the dampness of the curly black mat at the base of his torso. She squeezed his heroic toy. "That was better than ever," she said. "I think playing polo makes you horny."

Lolo laughed. "I don't have a thing for horses, if that's what you mean."

"No," she said, "it's not what I meant. I think you're like old Bibi. You get a charge out of the competition . . . and the danger."

"Maybe," he said hesitantly, looking at her with curiosity. "I never really thought about it, but I guess I do."

"You like a challenge," she said. "Don't you?"

"I . . . usually do," Lolo replied, knowing she was leading up to something but uncertain as to exactly what it was.

"I know you do," she said, a fingernail trailing down his biceps and onto his forearm. She took his hand in hers. "Lolo, you've got to help me with something," she said. "Maybe something challenging." She looked up at him.

"What?" he asked. Then he frowned. "Jesus, Arielle. Don't tell me. You've still obsessed with this crazy idea of going to Wyn's. Right?"

She nodded. "Not exactly," she said. "I called Santo yesterday, and we—"

"You what?" he exclaimed, sitting up.

"I called Santo," she said, sitting up next to him, "and we had a *very* interesting conversation. I'm supposed to meet him tonight."

"I don't believe this," Lolo said, looking away from her. "The lawyers have told you to lay off and mind your own business. To wait. And you won't pay any attention to them."

"Lolo," she said cajolingly, "listen to me. You know and I know that Wyn's so rich he can drag this out in court forever. Do you want to starve in the meantime?"

"No," he said, his dark eyes fiery. "But I don't like the idea of you messing with Wyn. Or that creep Santo."

"Oh, I can handle Santo. He's just a big pussycat," she said. "At least with me. And there's no danger involved. I just want you there when I talk to him . . . as a witness."

"But what are you going to talk about?" he asked, exasperated. "How the hell can Santo help you?"

"That's exactly what we're going to talk about," she said. "How we can help each other."

"I don't like this, Arielle," he said, a hard look in his eyes. "I don't like it one single little bit."

She cupped his chin in her hand and turned his face to hers. "You're not scared, are you, Lolo?"

He stiffened. "Of course I'm not scared."

"Then, please," she said. "For me?" She stared into his eyes pleadingly. "I've asked for so little from you, and I love you so much. Don't you love me?"

His features melted immediately, and he wrapped his arms around her. "Oh, you know I do, Arielle," he said. "I love you very much."

"Then you'll go with me tonight?"

He sighed. "I think my plan to talk to Wyn man to man was a better idea, but I'll go," he said. "I don't like it, but I'll go."

"Oh, thank you, Lolo," she said, peppering his face with kisses. "You won't regret it. I promise."

"I hope not," he said thoughtfully.

Colette hung up the telephone and sighed. "Oh, Hayden," she said, brushing a finger across the tiny hedgehog's quills, "poor darling Val. We must go to her at once." She made kissing noises in his direction, then carefully placed him in the pocket of one of the big linen smocks she habitually wore around the house. She traipsed into the bathroom, flipped on the light switch, and looked at herself in the mirror. "Dear, dear, Hayden," she said. "We mustn't let anyone see Mummy looking like this."

She picked up a little case of blusher on the vanity and brushed at her cheekbones extravagantly. "Too much is not enough, Hayden," she whispered. "Not at my age." With a final flourish she finished, then snapped the case shut and picked up the tube of pale pink lipstick. She expertly applied it, then blotted her lips. "There," she said. "Mummy's almost ready. Just a bit more mascara." She picked up the bottle and unscrewed the top, pulling out the brush, then flicking at her eyelashes quickly. "Now," she said. "All better." She flipped off the light, closing the bathroom door behind her.

"Oh, Puff Puppy," she said. "There you are. I almost tripped over you." She leaned down and stroked the Maltese, then straightened back up. "Mummy must go next door. You be an angel, and I'll give you something special when I get back." She blew kisses in his direction.

Through the kitchen she hurried, then stopping near the back door, she grabbed one of the big straw hats on a coatrack there. She put it on, adjusted it just so, and rushed on through the doorway, out the porch door, and through her garden to the gate that led into Valerie's.

"Oh, darling, there you are," she exclaimed, seeing Valerie and Elvis walking toward her. "Kiss, kiss, Elvis," she said, bending over to give him a pat on the head.

"Oh, Colette, I'm so glad you could come over," Valerie said. "Do you have Hayden in there?"

"Yes, of course, I do, darling," Colette replied. "But do let's hug. Only carefully."

They embraced, then Colette stood back and looked up at Valerie. "I think we both needed a nice hug today."

Valerie nodded. "It's been one of those days."

"You must tell me all about it," Colette said. "I've already talked to Eddie, of course, and cried my eyes out. Poor, sweet Noah. It's such a tragedy."

They settled themselves on Valerie's screened-in porch with iced tea, and Valerie told her about the scene at Eddie's.

"What kind of monster would do such a thing?" Colette asked worriedly after she'd heard the complete story.

"I don't know," Valerie replied, "but it gives me the creeps."

"Me too, darling. I'm not letting Puff Puppy out in the garden without me," Colette said. "And Hayden will be with me at all

times. I don't suppose it was anything, but thought I heard someone or something outside late last night. I started to call you, then
saw that your car was still gone, so I didn't."

"You heard someone?" Valerie asked, looking at her. "You're
sure?"

Colette shook her head. "No, I'm not the least bit sure," she
said. "I didn't see a thing, so I guess it was just an animal of some
sort." She shrugged. "A racoon trying to get in the garbage or
something like that probably, but never mind that. I'm dying to
hear what happened this morning at your mother's." She paused
and looked at Valerie conspiratorially. "And last night at Stonelair, of course."

Valerie laughed. "I'll tell all," she said, "but I think I'll get this
morning over with first."

She told Colette everything that had transpired at Marguerite's.
She realized, even as she told Colette the story, that it was already
beginning to seem like a distant memory because of the terrible
scene at Eddie's that followed it.

"This is almost too much for one person to bear in a single
day," Colette said sympathetically. "It's horrible, of course, the
way Marguerite treats you, the way she's always treated you, but
there is one marvelous thing to come of it." She turned her beautiful blue eyes on Valerie and smiled. "It gave you the perfect opening to give Teddy the old boot to the backside."

"There is that," Valerie agreed. "It certainly wasn't what I had
in mind, but what could I do?"

"Exactly what you did do," Colette said. She seemed lost in
thought for a moment, then added, "I don't like Teddy, frankly,
and I never did. He always seemed too good to be true, and a lot of
things that seem that way are. But I hope he doesn't take it badly."

"Teddy's been really moody and irritable lately. Even nasty at
times. I guess it's just work and me being too busy to see him, but
I don't know. It's really sort of worrisome. And Mother, well, you
know her. I don't think either of them is going to take it lying
down."

"No," Colette said, "come to think of it, I'm sure you're right.
I think that underneath all those lovely manners they're both real

fighters who'll fight for the sake of fighting. But imagine! Those two in cahoots like that! And that stinking cousin of yours in on it, too. Well, they deserve each other, is all I can say."

Valerie smiled. "Somehow I don't think they'll find much comfort in each other."

"Ha! Cold comfort at best," Colette said. She took a sip of her tea, then looked over at Valerie. "How do you feel about it now, darling?" she asked. "Do you have regrets?"

Valerie shook her head. "None whatsoever," she replied. "I wish it hadn't happened the way it did, but I didn't plan it that way."

"Do you think you're going to be terribly lonely and blue?" Colette asked. "Any port in a storm and all that?"

"No," Val said, looking off toward the pond in the distance. "I don't think I'm going to be lonely at all." She turned and looked at her friend and couldn't help the smile that hovered on her lips.

Colette's mouth, too, slowly spread in a smile and her eyes brightened considerably. "Well, well, well!" she finally said. "I don't believe it. But I do! Yes, I do believe it." She clapped her hands together. "Is it the mystery man at Stonelair, Val?" she asked eagerly. "Who is he, or shouldn't I ask? You don't have to tell me a thing, but I'm dying to know."

Valerie was silent for a minute, then quietly said, "Yes, it's Wyn Conrad at Stonelair."

Colette's eyes widened enormously. "You-you don't mean it?" She clapped her hands together again. "It is the mystery man. This is better than I could've ever imagined. You must tell me all about it."

Valerie took a sip of her iced tea, then set the glass down. "I've been taking care of the animals out at Stonelair."

Colette nodded but remained silent, waiting for more.

"Well, when I first met him," Valerie went on, "I didn't get a good impression. In fact, he seemed like an imperious smart-ass. Then he told me about the polo accident and all, and since then, well . . . I've found out he's anything but the man I thought he was at first." She turned and looked over at Colette. "I feel like I've known him all my life."

Colette smiled dreamily. "Like an old shoe?" she said.

"Something like that," Valerie replied. "The first time we actually talked—not the first time when we just met each other—I think sparks began to fly between us. No, I *know* they did. Then last night at dinner, we got to know each other a lot better. It's just . . . fabulous." She looked at Colette again and shrugged. "So, there you are."

"I'm so thrilled for you, Val," Colette said. "This really is the best news, and the timing! Well, it couldn't be better, could it? It's almost as if it were planned this way."

"It is odd, isn't it?" Val agreed. "It almost makes you believe in some kind of fate."

Colette took a sip of her tea and sighed wistfully. "What's he like?" she asked. "I know he must be wonderful, or you wouldn't feel the way you do. And I know he must like animals or he wouldn't have them. But can you give me an inkling?"

"He's . . . oh, it's so hard to explain," she said. She decided she would confide everything in Colette, knowing that she could trust her discretion. "He had that terrible accident playing polo, like I told you, and it's going to take a long time for him to recover—in more ways than one. His looks have been affected by skin grafts and plastic surgery, and he's got to have a lot more."

"Oh, dear," Colette said. "Will he be permanently scarred?"

Valerie nodded. "Yes," she said, "and that's terrible, of course. But I think the worst damage it's done is to his ego. His pride. You can imagine. In places, his skin looks like a burn victim's. Most of that's hidden, but some of it does show. He'll have to live with it the rest of his life. There's no escaping it."

"Perhaps with time," Colette said, "he'll learn to cope with it, and perhaps . . . perhaps you can help him?"

Valerie felt herself blush slightly. "I hope so, Colette," she said. "He's still a very handsome man. Just a little rough around the edges, I guess you'd say. That's one of the reasons he came up to Stonelair. To get away from the world and have a place to recover."

"So that's it," Colette said. "Something so innocent, so harmless. And all this talk about drug lords and the Mafia and such."

Valerie laughed. "It really seems ridiculous once you get to know him." She went on to tell Colette everything she knew about Wyn Conrad, and about their dinner the night before.

When she'd finished, Colette said, "It's when wonderful things like this happen, Val, that I begin to suspect there might be a benevolent creator. That there might really be some great plan. It seems much more than a mere coincidence." She reached over and squeezed Valerie's hand in hers. "I'm so happy for you."

"Thanks, Col—" Valerie began. The telephone rang on the table next to her. "I'd better get that," she said apologetically as she picked up the receiver. "I'm on call at the clinic."

"Of course, darling," Colette said.

"Hello," Valerie said.

"Val?"

Her heart skipped a beat at the sound of his voice, and she suddenly wished she were alone. *Thank God for portables,* she thought, getting up out of her chair. "Wait just a second," she said. She pressed the hold button.

"Colette, I'll be right back," she said.

Colette smiled knowingly. "Should I go?"

"No," Valerie said. "I'll just be a minute." She stepped through the door into the kitchen, then went on down the hallway to the living room, where she curled up in a chair. She pushed the hold button again.

"Hi," she said. "Sorry about that, but my neighbor's here and I wanted to have some privacy."

"That's okay," he said. "How are you doing today?"

"I'm all right," she said. "Actually, it was sort of hectic this morning. A friend's dog was poisoned, and I had to go over there and check that out."

"Poisoned?" he said. "That's horrible."

"Yes," she said. "It really was terrible, and I can't figure it out. Sometimes that sort of thing happens because of real grudges or revenge, but there doesn't seem to be any reason for this. The owner's a friend of mine, so it was really awful."

"I'm sorry," he said. He paused a moment, then added, "Maybe I can help make you feel a little bit better?"

She felt her heart leap with joy. *So this is what it's like,* she thought. *This . . . this wonderful feeling is what I've been missing with Teddy.*

"And exactly how do you propose to do that?"

"I can think of several things," he replied with a chuckle, "but I was thinking about a little dinner again tonight. For two."

"Think you can wine and dine me and win me over, huh?" she joked.

"I am sincerely going to give it my best try."

"Spoken like a true male chauvinist pig," she said. "So comforting."

"I thought so," he said. "I am putting up my best front for you."

"I'd hate to see your worst."

"How about if I show it to you after dinner then?"

"Sounds heavenly," she replied.

"About eight o'clock okay?"

"Perfect. I'll wear my new see-through Versace."

"We don't want to scare the horses," he said.

"You're one to talk," she said.

He was silent for a beat, then roared with laughter. "You're a mean and hateful and spiteful woman, and I can't wait to see you."

"Same here."

He hung up, and she sat there staring at the living room walls, not really seeing anything. She didn't think she'd ever felt so buoyant, so happy, so alive and full of hope for the future. She went back out to the porch, where she rejoined Colette.

"The look on your face says you have a date," Colette ventured.

Valerie nodded. "Yes." She sighed happily.

Colette reached over and patted her on the arm. "God bless you, Val," she said. "I suppose Hayden and I should run along home and let you spend your time getting—"

The telephone rang again, and Valerie looked over at Colette and shrugged. "What can I say?" she said. "I'm popular."

She picked up the receiver. "Hello?" she said.

"Val, I want to talk to you." It was Teddy, and he sounded like a sergeant major giving orders.

"Not now, Teddy," she said. "Colette's here, and we're busy."

"What do you mean you're busy?" he snapped. "What's that old bitch ever done but powder her nose?"

Valerie was stunned speechless by the vehemence in his voice. "I don't have to listen to this," she finally replied. "I'll be glad to talk to you when you're not feeling quite so offensive." She quietly replaced the receiver in its cradle and turned to look at Colette.

"Oh-ho," Colette said. "He's not playing nice-nice."

"No," Valerie replied. "Definitely not."

"Oh, dear," Colette sympathized. "If there's anything I can do, darling, you just say the word, and I'll gladly do it."

"I think Teddy and I'll just have to have a little talk," Valerie said. "After what happened this morning, I don't feel like I really owe him any explanations, but I guess I ought to try to smooth over some of his ruffled feathers."

"Well, you were friends for years, so it would be a shame for it to end really badly," Colette agreed. "But don't you dare let him browbeat you, Val."

Valerie shook her head. "No, Colette," she said, "don't you worry about that. I'm not going to let that happen. I'm really sick to death of being told what to do by him—and my mother. I'd like to be friends with both of them, but I'm really up to my ears with their ordering me around."

"That's the spirit!" Colette said. "I knew you had it in you."

"I guess you knew it better than I did," Valerie said, looking over at her friend.

"Well, you know it now," Colette said. "You've been very brave in the past, defying your parents to do what you really wanted to do, but still, you've been under their thumbs for such a long time—well, Teddy's and your mother's—that it's wonderful to see you sprouting wings."

"Speaking of which, I'm surprised Mother hasn't already called," Valerie said.

"Oh, she will," Colette said, nodding. "Knowing Marguerite, she's simply busy plotting away at her war table, drawing up new battle plans."

Valerie laughed. "You know her so well."

"Well enough to know she's not yet begun to fight," Colette

said. "Unfortunately." She opened the pocket of her smock and peered in. "I thought I felt Hayden stirring about, but I see he's sound asleep. I suppose I ought to take him home and put him to bed."

"He's got to have his rest, so he can play on his wheel all night," Valerie said.

"Oh, yes," Colette said. "They're completely nocturnal creatures, and that's nice for me because you know how nocturnal I am. Hayden keeps me company in the wee hours when I read or write letters or watch television. Puff Puppy sleeps away like a smart doggy should." She looked at her wristwatch. "Anyway, darling, I'd really better go. I know you want to get all beautified for tonight."

She eased herself out of the chair, then adjusted her big straw hat. Valerie rose to her feet to show her out.

"Darling," Colette said, "I'm so thrilled for you I can't find the words." She kissed Valerie on both cheeks. "I know you'll have a wonderful evening."

"I know so, too," Valerie said, "and don't worry, I'll keep you posted."

"Oh, I hope you do," Colette said. "It's so exciting." She leaned down and stroked Elvis. "Bye-bye, sweet boy," she said. Elvis thumped his tail in response.

Valerie held the porch door open for her, and Colette left, waving as she negotiated the stone path, the sweet scent of her perfume trailing behind her. *Thank God for Colette,* Valerie thought. *I couldn't ask for a better friend.*

She filled Elvis's water bowl, added some dry meal to his food bowl, and decided to take a long, leisurely bath. After making herself a light lunch, she had worked for a long time in the garden, weeding and deadheading mostly, before she had finally decided to call Colette to come over. Now she could feel her muscles, tired and sore.

Maybe I'll take a bubble bath, she thought. Then she laughed aloud. *This is really fun. This gleeful anticipation of the evening. Now I finally know what all those other women over the years were talking about before their big dates.*

*   *   *

Outside, the car cruised by again, slowly, but not so slowly as to look too suspicious to anyone who happened to notice it. Not that there was anyone about to see anything. There were only the two houses on this country lane. Then suddenly there *was* somebody.

The driver sped up slightly, but not before seeing Colette come through the garden gate that led to Valerie's and noticing her take something from the pocket of her smock, holding it up to her face, and making as if to kiss it before replacing it in her pocket.

What the hell? the driver wondered. *Does she think a creepy little thing like that even knows who she is? She must be crazy, the old coot, but at least she never saw me.*

Chapter Twenty-Four

They had dined together on the candlelighted terrace again tonight, but Gerda Reinhardt hadn't had a hand in preparing the food. With some assistance from Valerie in the mansion's big kitchen, the two of them had done everything together, sipping a dry white wine as they worked. Valerie gathered up the condiments—ketchup, mustard, mayonnaise, and pickle relish—then sliced tomatoes and onions and cheese and washed lettuce, while Wyn piled charcoal in the grill outside and lit a fire, then made big patties out of the hamburger meat and peeled and sliced potatoes for French fries.

"I'm not going to deep-fry these," Wyn said, "if you don't mind."

"What are you going to do with them?" she asked.

"Spray them with Pam, then put them in the oven," he replied. "I swear they're almost as good as the real thing."

"It sounds good," she said, "and healthier, too. I guess we should make *some* concessions to healthy eating, shouldn't we?"

"Well," he said, "a little here and a little there. I don't obsess about it."

"Good," she said, "because I don't think I could stand it if you did."

He laughed. "That's what I like about you," he said. "A woman who speaks her mind."

"If I don't," Valerie replied, "nobody's going to do it for me."

Out on the terrace, they enjoyed their hamburgers and French fries, and had fresh peaches for dessert. Then they sprawled out in the library with the four dogs and the cat, who'd decided to pay a visit. They were sipping coffee laced with a dollop of brandy.

"That was really perfect," Valerie said. "I love simple food."

"I do, too," he said. "I didn't realize how much I liked it until I went to one too many fancy parties in Palm Beach. All the hostesses try to outshine each other with delicacies and exotic ingredients."

"I think that trend has even hit the provinces," Valerie said.

"I finally decided I had pretty simple tastes," Wyn went on. "Not just meat and potatoes, but fish and fowl and veggies, too, only not played with so much. You know what I mean?"

Valerie nodded. "It's become almost like an obsession with some people, and I'm worn out with it. At first I thought it was funny, but I'm really tired of going to restaurants with micro this and baby that and infused the other." She stopped and looked at him. "And I'm really sick of the pyramids."

"Oh, yeah," he said, laughing. "Now everything on your plate has to be arranged in a pyramid. Whether it's an entree or dessert or whatever. I'm glad you noticed that, too."

"I guess it's just another fad," she said. "Something else will come along soon—maybe trapezoids?—but I'll still love hamburgers and French fries."

"You're my kind of girl," he said, looking into her eyes.

"You think so?" she asked.

He nodded. "I know so." He took a sip of his coffee, then said, "Which brings me to a ticklish subject."

"What's that?" she asked. "My feet?"

He grinned. "No," he said. "That's later." Then his face became serious. "Did you talk to that fiancé of yours yet?"

"As a matter of fact, I did. By default actually," she replied, her eyes sparkling with liveliness. She had hardly been able to restrain herself from telling him what had happened this morning, but had wanted to wait for the right moment. Now, she decided, was definitely it. "You're not going to believe it."

"Try me," he replied.

She repeated for him the events at breakfast that morning at her mother's. When she was finished telling the story, she looked over at him and said, "So you see, Mr. Conrad, I'm a free woman."

His dark eyes were boring into hers intently. "I don't know when I've ever heard better news," he said. "And I mean that, Val."

He slid an arm around her shoulders and pulled her closer to him on the couch. Then he tenderly kissed her on the cheek. "I've never meant anything more," he said. "You sparked my interest the very first time I saw you, then, well . . . you set off fireworks inside me. I didn't know it could ever be like this."

"I know exactly what you mean," she replied. "I-I've been . . . experiencing the very same thing. I guess . . . I don't know what to call it, but . . ." Her words trailed off into silence.

He kissed her cheek again, then whispered, "I think it's safe to say it's what they call love, Val."

She almost shivered with the thrill of hearing the word. It was a thrill mixed with fear, for she knew that with love came commitment and compromise, and having to give up a degree of the independence she'd fought so hard for. But she also knew that for this man she could overcome any fears. Every fiber in her being told her he was right for her, there was no mistaking it, that he was the one.

It is love, she thought, *plain and simple.* There was nothing else to call what she was feeling for him, or he her, if what he said was true.

"You can say it, Val," he whispered. "I will."

She felt his arm tighten around her, and she looked up into his dark eyes.

"I love you, Val," he said. "It may be crazy, but I know I really do love you."

She felt her face flush with heat, and she nodded slightly. "I'm-I'm in love with you, too, Wyn," she said softly.

"There," he said. "That wasn't so difficult, was it? We're in love with each other." He hugged her closer still, then kissed her lips gently, staring into her eyes.

Valerie returned his kiss, hungry for him as she had never been for Teddy or anyone else. She put her arms around him, gingerly stroking his back, wanting to hold on to him with all her might, but afraid that she'd hurt some tender spot on his body unknowingly.

He seemed to sense her cautious restraint and leaned back and looked at her, a smile on his lips. "I'm not glass," he said. "I won't break."

"I-I'm just not sure how delicate you are," she said.

"Me?" he said. "I'm tough as leather, young lady, and don't you forget it." He smiled again. "Well . . . except maybe for my face right now."

"Aha!" she said teasingly. "So you've got a soft spot."

"For you," he said, "I've definitely got a soft spot."

He gently drew her to him again, and she felt herself melt into his arms. They began kissing once more, their hands exploring one another's bodies, their passion blossoming into urgency. Valerie forgot her concerns for any pain she might cause him and enjoyed the feel of his body, stroking him as he stroked her, wanting to get to know every inch of this man. She'd never felt the desire to merge with another as she did now. To become one with him.

When at last they parted, they were breathless.

"You look so beautiful, Val," he gasped. "You're glowing."

She suddenly realized she'd never seen his entire face at once without any bandages, except in the photographs hanging in the stable's tack room. "I'm glad I can see more of you," she said. "More of your face, I mean. I think that you glow, too."

"You're sure you like the way I look?" he asked.

"I love the way you look," she replied. "Besides, I wouldn't care if you looked like Freddy Krueger."

"You're certain about that?" he asked seriously.

She stared into his eyes. "Wyn, that's not the case, so it doesn't matter. You were handsome before, and you're handsome now."

He looked at her for a moment. "I'm still going to need some more operations," he said. "It'll take a long time. Do you think you could handle that?"

She playfully slapped him on the arm. "I'm a vet, remember?" she said. "Give me credit for knowing something about these things and being able to deal with them."

"Yeah," he agreed, "but you might enjoy leaving all that at work when you come home at night. You might get tired of coming home to more of it."

She shook her head. "Never," she said with fiery determination in her voice. "Not for a single minute. Not if I come home to you."

"You're very brave," he said. "Or very stupid." Then he grinned. "But I know you're not stupid."

"I'm neither," she said. "I'm in love."

He kissed her lips gently. "And I'm in love." He drew back and gazed at her steadily. "You know how I first knew?" he asked.

"When you saw me in my lab coat?" she joked.

He shook his head. "It was the stethoscope."

They both laughed, then he said, "I was certain when I stopped taking the shots."

"The shots?" she asked.

He nodded. "I was taking a lot of pain medication." He paused a moment, his eyes cast down, choosing his words carefully. "I think . . . I know . . . that I was overdoing it. I was lonely and depressed. And I felt like some kind of freak. The painkillers took me away from it all." He looked back at her. "Then you came along." He took her hands in his. "You changed everything, Val," he said. "You made me want to live again. To feel life again. Even if some of it is unpleasant and painful."

With his words, Valerie's heart surged with love and, she had to admit, a measure of pride. To think that she could have that sort of effect on a man was empowering.

"I was at a turning point in my life," she said, "or low point, I guess. I knew that I wasn't in love with Teddy, but in all honesty, Wyn, I was actually tempted to go through with the marriage anyway. It seemed easier than arguing, and I didn't want to be alone forever. I don't think anybody does. Then, guess what?"

"What?" he asked.

"You came along from out of the blue," she replied, looking at him and smiling. "The last thing I ever imagined."

"The old white knight or Prince Charming, huh?" he said.

"Well . . . ," she said, "more like Frankenstein."

He grabbed her and held her as she laughed. "You mean, mean woman." He kissed her passionately, almost roughly, wrapping his arms around her tightly. Within moments, they were breathlessly kissing, stroking, massaging, delving, probing, and exploring.

They finally parted, and it was Wyn who spoke first. "I-I don't know . . . how you—how you feel . . . about waiting," he stuttered, looking into her eyes, "but it's making me crazy already. I want to make love to you, Val."

"I may be a free woman," she said laughingly, still breathless, "but-but . . . you're still a married man, Mr. Conrad."

"You won't hold that against me, will you, Doc?" he asked.

"I might," she said. "I think I really should know what's going on in that quarter."

"You're right," he said. "It's only fair. After all, you've told me all about your ex." He paused. "Arielle and I are getting a divorce, you know, but we haven't arrived at a final settlement yet."

Valerie nodded. "And?" she said, coaxing him.

"And I'm playing hardball because I'm really pissed off with her," he admitted.

"I see," she said. "I would've suspected as much from you."

"You already know me pretty well."

"I think so," she said. "You're a wronged man, and mean as a snake."

He nodded. "You bet. I could get it over with quickly," he said. "All it would take is one little phone call to the lawyer, but I've been torturing her. Deliberately."

"Of course, just what I would've guessed. But!"

"But what?"

"Does it make any sense to go on torturing Mrs. Conrad if you want there to be a new Mrs. Conrad?"

"Are you proposing to me, Doc?" he asked, smiling.

"Darn right, I am," she said. "So you've got to unload some of your riches on the first Mrs. Conrad and tell her good-bye. Besides," she went on, "I think it'll improve your disposition considerably when she's out of your hair—and I'll have you all to myself."

"You think so?"

"I do," she replied.

"Well, Doc," he said, "I think you've got a point, but are you sure you want me to make an honest woman out of you?"

"I don't think either one of us wants to live life any other way. Honest living is the only way to go."

He sat grinning at her like a boy. "I'm going to call the lawyer tomorrow," he said, "and tell him to get it over with ASAP. Give the woman what she's asking for and get rid of her once and for all."

She stared at him through slitted eyes. "Honest injun?"

"Scout's honor," he said, holding a hand up.

"Cut your finger and sign it in blood?" she asked.

"For you, Doc, I would," he replied. "But somehow I don't think you're so mean you'll make me lose blood over this." He fell on her body again, tickling her until she shrieked, then he began kissing her until they were both moaning with passion.

The parking lot out behind the bar was dark, the only light coming from distant streetlamps. The roar of the dance music playing on the bar's powerful stereo system was reduced to a muffled bass beat out here, momentarily amplified when a parting customer flung open the door and came out the back way.

Inside the car, the three people sat deeply engrossed in discussion, their conversation abruptly ceasing altogether when the occasional patron passed close by.

"You're crazy," the huge bulk in the front seat said in a quiet but intense voice. He stared straight ahead, as if he wasn't addressing the two people in the backseat, as if they didn't even exist. The light outside reflected off the smooth back of his shaved head.

"No, I'm not crazy," the female in the backseat said. "It's a cinch. When you shoot him up with the painkiller, you give him too much, then the poor guy falls down the stairs or something. It's simple."

"You mean I throw him down the steps," the giant said.

"Exactly," the woman replied. "Make sure his neck is broken or something. I'll give you fifty grand."

"Oh, Jesus," the man in the backseat said, almost under his breath. "I don't believe I'm hearing this."

The woman turned to him, her eyes glittering angrily. "You have a better idea?" she said. "Maybe *you* want to do it for fifty grand? Is that it? What if I give you a gun? I've got one at the house, you know. I brought it with me. Will you go in there and do it? Earn your keep?"

"Shit." The man sighed, turning away from her and staring out the window, his face almost pressed up against the glass. "You've had too much to drink. You don't mean what you're saying."

"Yes, I do," the woman said. "I mean every word. I'll pay fifty grand up front, then fifty when it's done. I'd do it myself except I'd be suspect number one, and I'd have hell even getting in there."

"I'd be number one," the bulk in the front seat said. "I'm there nearly twenty-four hours a day, and I'm in the will."

"That's crap," the woman said. "Make it look like an accident, like I said. Tell the cops how he shoots himself up sometimes. Wanders around the house at night. Just make sure he's dead, then go on out to your cottage and go to bed. Those stupid fools the Reinhardts wouldn't know any different. Besides, everybody knows you've been totally devoted to him for years."

"One major problem," the giant retorted.

"What?" the woman asked.

"Since he's been seeing that vet, he's quit shooting up, unless he's doing it himself."

"That doesn't matter," the woman said, "he's got needle marks on his ass, right?"

The bulk nodded.

"So who's to know he quit?" she asked.

"You make it sound so easy," the man in the backseat said.

"It is," she said. "So why don't you give it a try if he won't? He could get you inside and back out again without any problem." She looked toward the front. "Right?"

The bulk nodded again. "I could do it."

"No way," the man in the backseat said. "No fucking way. I'm not going to have anything to do with this."

"Not even for me?" the woman asked, thrusting a clenched fist against her breast.

"No," the man said.

"And a hundred grand all your own?" she said tauntingly.

The man shook his black curls. "No," he said. "Don't ask me again. That's final. No!"

She looked toward the front again. "You've got to do it then," she said to the hulking presence at the steering wheel. "You've got to!"

The bulk sighed, then said, "I'll have to think about it. Think about how to do it. Maybe."

Tiffani frowned. "Why were you so late anyway, Teddy?"

"I just had a bunch of business stuff to do," he replied. He put the silver straw up his nose, then bent over the line of cocaine she'd cut for him, and took a snort up one nostril, then repeated the process with the other. He sniffed several times, making certain he'd gotten it all up into his nose, then looked at her and smiled. "Forgive me?"

"I forgive you," she said. "How can I be mad at a man with such good nose candy?" She giggled. She felt great. They'd already snorted several lines, made love, and had a long talk about something Teddy wanted her to help him with. *Imagine,* she thought. *Me, poor little Tiffani being able to help the rich Mr. de Mornay.* Only she wasn't so sure she wanted to get involved with this little project. *I've got to make sure there's plenty in this for me,* she decided.

"What're you thinking about?" Teddy asked her, putting a finger under her chin and turning her face to him. "You look like you're in another world, Tiff."

"Oh, I don't know, Teddy," she replied, shaking her long, copious curls. "I just . . . well, I mean, your idea sounds too dangerous to me. I don't even know my way around Stonelair except in the stable complex. It's, like, I drive there, park, go inside to the stable office and work, and that's it. Besides, that creep Santo's always there, and you never know when old man Reinhardt's going to come wandering in."

Teddy took a sip of the wine he'd brought over to Tiffani's, then set the glass down. "The stable complex would be enough for right now," he said, looking at Tiffani.

She stared back at him. "The stable?" she said quizzically. "But why the stable?"

He had to tell Tiffani that he was planning a surprise for Wyn Conrad and Valerie, but he didn't want her to know exactly what he had in mind. He'd have to keep her in the dark to some extent, or he'd never get her cooperation. Tiffani may have the hots for him, he realized, but he had the feeling that she'd only stick her neck out so far.

"Because," he finally said, "what I want to do can be done in the stables when nobody else is around." He slid a hand across her naked breasts, then ran his fingers up and down her torso gently, finally maneuvering it down between her thighs, where it rested on her warm mound.

He could feel the new line of coke kicking in, and he felt powerful, indestructible. "You don't have to worry about a thing, Tiff," he said. "It's a piece of cake. And I'll take good care of you for helping out."

"Hmmmm," Tiffani moaned. "You feel so good."

"You'll help me, won't you, Tiff?" he asked, leaning over and licking at a nipple with his tongue. "Please, Tiff."

"Ahhhhh, Teddy," she moaned.

His fingers began to work between her ample thighs, delving into her wetness, while his tongue flicked out at her nipples between words. "Please, Tiff," he said. "For me."

"But-but I don't know what you want me to do, Teddy," she said in a gasp. Her body began to quiver with delight, and she didn't want him to stop. Ever.

"It's no big deal," he said, momentarily taking his mouth off a nipple. "Nobody'll get hurt."

"You-you sure?"

"I'm sure," he said, removing his hand and sitting up.

"Oh, no, Teddy," she immediately complained. "That felt so good."

He got on his knees between her legs and spread them wide apart with his hands. "It's going to feel even better, Tiff," he said. "I want you to feel better than you ever have." His head plunged between her thighs, and his tongue replaced his fingers there.

Tiffany began to roll her head from side to side, moaning loudly, her legs alternately stiffening and spasming, her hands pushing down on the back of his head. "Ohhhh, Teddddy," she cried. "You-you're going to make me—"

His tongue plunged into her relentlessly. Then he suddenly withdrew and sat up again.

"Nooooo, Teddy," Tiffani groaned. "That was so—"

Paying no attention to her complaints, Teddy grabbed her knees with his hands, spread them wide and, without any further preamble, he plunged into her hard, up to the hilt of his fully engorged manhood.

Tiffani gasped and nearly levitated off the bed before she began to spasm again and again, her cries of pleasure and flowing juices driving him ever harder and faster, until he was bucking like a cowboy, and with a roar like a bull and a final plunge he exploded inside of her, his entire body jerking wildly.

He collapsed atop her, and the two of them lay spent, exhausted for the moment. It was a long time before Teddy rolled off her, pulling her with him so that he stayed inside her. He stroked her damp hair and looked into her eyes. "You'll do it," he whispered. "Won't you, Tiff? For me? Please?"

She nodded slowly. "If you promise me nobody'll get hurt," she said.

"You bet," Teddy said, grinning. Nobody *will get hurt, you stupid bitch,* he thought, *but that doesn't mean n*othing *will.* "Nobody'll get hurt, I promise."

She smiled. "And you promise we'll keep doing this, Teddy."

"Believe me, baby, I want to do this as much as you do," he said. *At least until something better comes along,* he thought. She was already getting tiresome, he'd decided. It was time to move on soon, explore new territory.

He took her in his arms and kissed her passionately, his tongue plunging between her lips, his cock stirring to life again inside of her. Tiffani responded immediately, grinding herself against him and moaning with pleasure.

Teddy's going to be mine, she thought. *All mine, and nobody else's. I just know it. I'm going to be the rich Mrs. Teddy de Mornay.*

It was late at night, but the shadowy figure didn't want to get too close to the house because the dogs might get alarmed. It wasn't necessary anyway. Not with such great binoculars. The lovey-dovey couple was sprawled out on a big Chesterfield couch in the library with the lights on. It was as if nothing or nobody in the world could harm them.

Ha!

While they made love to one another in that magnificent room, they were in a world of their own, protected from prying eyes.

Or so they thought.

They'd undressed one another, taking their precious time, seeming to savor every single minute of it. Tenderly caressing each other, running hands all over each other, nibbling, licking, and kissing.

How sweet and gentle they were.

Then, rutting like animals, devouring one another like starved, lovesick dogs. Moaning and groaning in ecstasy, no doubt, while they pawed and clawed at each other in a frenzy of carnal delight. Then resting, breathless, but unable to keep their hands off of each other after their great mutual and explosive climax. In sync, those two. Whispering sweet nothings to each other for sure, yapping about how great it was, and oh, yeah, professing their undying love.

We'll see about that.

Then going at it again. Like a horse at stud and a mare that had never had it before. Disgusting, really. They're nothing but animals. Dirty, filthy animals.

A shudder went through the watching figure. *And me? I've got nothing. Never had anything or anybody. Not like them. But I'm going to have to fix that one way or the other. I'll have to fix them.*

Chapter Twenty-Five

Colette awoke to sunlight streaming through her bedroom windows. *It's late,* she thought idly, sitting up in bed and rubbing her eyes. She looked over at the clock on the draped table at her bedside. *My goodness, ten o'clock.* Puff Puppy stirred at her feet, and she leaned down to pet him.

"Good morning, Puff Puppy," she said. "Your mummy overslept, and you didn't wake me, you naughty boy."

She slid her legs over the side of the bed and into damask-patterned silk slippers, then stood up, shrugged into a silk robe, and went into her bathroom. She quickly performed her morning ritual, gave her hair a few strokes with a brush, and dismissed her appearance in the mirror with one lifted eyebrow. "Later, alligator," she said to her reflection. "Yes, I'll fix you up later."

She snapped off the light and made her way to the kitchen, Puff Puppy following slowly along behind her. She opened the kitchen door, padded out onto the screened-in porch, and opened the screen door for Puff Puppy. "There, darling," she cooed. "Do your business for Mummy. I'll have your breakfast waiting when you get back."

She watched as Puff Puppy went out into the garden, sniffing here and there, and headed for one of his favorite spots. It was a patch of ferns that hid him entirely from sight, giving him a sense of privacy, she supposed. *He's awfully sluggish this morning,* she thought. *I wonder if something's wrong with him. He doesn't seem himself. I'll have to watch him,* she decided, *and if he continues behaving this way, I'll have to make an appointment with Val.*

Forgetting her promise to herself not to let Puff Puppy out of her sight, she returned to the kitchen and filled his water bowl with fresh water, then filled his food bowl with a mixture of dry food and leftover bits of chicken she'd deboned for him. That done, she ground coffee beans and filled the coffeemaker with water and aromatic coffee.

She heard Puff Puppy at the screen door and padded back out onto the porch and let him in. "Were you successful, darling?" she asked the quiet and still sluggish dog.

Puff Puppy made a beeline for his bed in the kitchen. He slumped down and immediately closed his eyes.

"Oh, dear me," Colette said worriedly. "If you're not yourself by noontime, I'm calling Val."

She poured herself a cup of the freshly brewed coffee, then mixed in a tiny spoonful of sugar substitute and a generous portion of nonfat milk.

Coffee cup in hand, she walked over to Hayden's big wire cage, which was entirely covered with a heavy blue cotton cloth that blocked out all light. That way the nocturnal creature wasn't bothered by the kitchen's bright daylight. She lifted the cloth and peeked in. "Hayden, darling," she cooed. "Did you have fun last night? Spinning away on your little wheel?"

She didn't see Hayden or any movement indicating that he was there. He was hidden by toys perhaps, or burrowed deeply under his blanket. African pygmy hedgehogs couldn't stand cold, and Hayden always slept on a heating pad burrowed under a little blanket. Colette straightened up and worriedly removed the cloth from over his cage entirely, putting it down on a chair.

"Hayden?" she called again. "Are you there, darling boy?" There was still no movement, so she opened the cage's door and carefully grasped his blanket, looking under it. Nothing. She took the blanket out and moved her fingers gingerly about the cage, searching in vain for the missing creature.

"Hayden? Hayden!" she began to cry. "Where are you, darling?" She removed her hand from the cage and closed the door. *How on earth?* she asked herself in a panic. *I'm certain I had the cage door secured when I went to bed last night. Or did I?*

Then another thought occurred to her. *Oh, dear! Maybe Hayden's loose in the house somewhere,* she worried. *He's very enterprising and may have ventured out of his cage.* She'd often let him out at night and let him explore the kitchen, so it wasn't altogether strange territory for him. But the kitchen door was open to the porch. She rushed over to it and looked about the screened-in porch. No sign of Hayden there.

She closed the kitchen door firmly and began searching the baseboards around the room. *He always seemed partial to the baseboards,* she thought, exploring the perimeter of the room. She looked and looked, but there was no sign of Hayden.

With a sigh, she turned to the notepad she kept on the kitchen counter to look at the list she'd started yesterday. All the things she had to do, the groceries and other items that she had to shop for.

Iced tea, she remembered. She had intended to make a big pitcher to have on hand for herself and Val, if she happened by later today. It was a green tea jazzed up with a delicious, rather rare kind of honey. She put the to-do list down and decided to get busy.

She retrieved a big glass pitcher on the ancient Welsh dresser, then going to the side-by-side refrigerator-freezer, she held the heavy pitcher in one hand and opened the freezer compartment with the other. She always filled the pitcher to the brim with ice cubes to start. Reaching her hand into the pile of ice that the ice-maker had churned out, she took a handful from the reservoir and put it in the pitcher. She took another handful and placed it in, then reached in for another.

"*Merde!*" she cried aloud. She must have nicked her hand on a sharp piece of ice. She removed her hand with the offending ice from the ice-maker's big reservoir and started to toss it in the pitcher, looking down at it first to make certain she hadn't gotten blood on it from her hand.

Suddenly her eyes grew enormous, and she dropped the pitcher of ice to the floor, where it shattered into dozens of pieces at her feet. Puff Puppy barked in alarm, but she didn't hear him. Her mouth widened into a blood-curdling scream of shock and fear and horror, and she dropped the piece of ice in her hand—*no, not ice!* she told herself—to the floor, where it landed amidst the broken glass and ice cubes.

Colette stepped back, the scream still rising from deep within her. Looking down at the floor, her screams turned to wails of anguish, then into sobs of utter despair. She clutched the lapels of her bathrobe as if hanging on to them would somehow protect her from whatever evil had done this. Tears began to pour from her old eyes, running down her face in rivulets of sorrow.

On the floor, atop the broken glass and ice, lay Hayden, frozen to death, his quills as hard and sharp as knives, his beautiful gray color frosted pale, his tiny dark eyes open in a look of eternal horror.

Colette covered her own eyes and continued to sob, choking on her sorrow, until she could finally make her way to the kitchen table, where she sat down heavily in a chair, the tears still flowing.

Who could do something so demonic? And why, oh, why? She had no answers to her questions, but they continued to roar at her.

She had no idea how long it was before she quietly rose to her feet and methodically took a tea towel from the kitchen counter, then picked up Hayden's lifeless little body and wrapped it in the towel. She placed the bundle in his cage and closed the door. Then, retrieving a broom and dust pan from a closet, she cleaned up the broken glass and ice. *Puff Puppy mustn't hurt himself,* she thought.

That accomplished, she picked up the Maltese, clutching him to her as if she were still on automatic pilot, and went out onto the screened-in porch and sat down, staring off into the garden. She had to call Val at the clinic, but she felt so dispirited that she decided to wait a while. Nothing Val could do would bring Hayden back. She would spend some time alone with Puff Puppy, trying to come to terms with the evil that she'd been forced to confront.

Valerie had just finished her morning rounds of the local horse farms and had gotten out of her dirty coveralls and boots and changed into a fresh lab coat and sneakers. She was washing up, getting ready for the rest of her day, when Tami rushed into her office.

"Val," she gasped, "it's your mother. She says it's an emergency."

Val's eyes widened in alarm. She turned off the water at the sink in the little bathroom. "An emergency?" she asked, stepping into her office. "What is it?"

"I don't know," Tami said, "but she seems to be in an awful state. She's on line three, okay?"

"Thanks, Tami," Valerie said. "Tell her I'll be right there."

"Will do."

Valerie quickly buttoned up her lab coat, then approached her desk with trepidation. *What could the emergency be?* she asked herself, wondering if there really was an emergency at all.

Seated at her desk, she pressed the button for line three and picked up the receiver. "Hello, Mother," she said as calmly as she could. "Tami tells me there's an emergency. What's going on?"

"I must talk to you at once, Val," her mother said in a voice that was uncustomarily anxious. "Before you cut me off, I must tell you that it's of the utmost importance."

"What is it, Mother?" Valerie asked.

"I thought you were going to marry Teddy," her mother began, "and—"

"I don't want to discuss that, Mother," Valerie said in no uncertain terms.

"That's not what I want to discuss, either," her mother hurriedly said. "*Please,* Val, hear me out for a minute before you rush to judgment. It's vitally important."

What on earth? Valerie wondered. "Okay," she said, "I'm listening."

"What I'm trying to say," her mother continued, "is that because I thought you were going to marry Teddy, I signed a power of attorney and turned over my entire stock portfolio for him to manage. I—"

"You what?" Valerie asked, not quite believing her ears.

"You heard me correctly," Marguerite replied with a heavy sigh. "Because I thought you were marrying him, I turned everything over to Teddy to manage. I took it all away from Dock Wainwright."

"I can't believe you did that," Valerie said. "Dock Wainwright has always handled the family's affairs. And quite conservatively, like Dad wanted him to, I might add. You know as well as I do that Teddy trades in dangerous territory. Maybe he's had success. I don't really know anything about it, but I do know that Dock always seemed to take very good care of you and Dad."

"Be that as it may," Marguerite said, "I've done what I've done, and now I'm . . . well, frankly, I'm a little disturbed. I don't think I would be if I knew you were marrying—"

"I said I don't want to discuss that," Valerie said with fire in her voice. "If you've made a decision you regret, I'm not taking the blame for it. And if you're trying to talk me into marrying him just because you've invested with him, then you might as well stop right there. There is not a chance in hell I'll marry Teddy."

"I'm well aware of that," Marguerite said, "although I don't think you have to use such harsh language to get your point across. In any case, that's not what I'm trying to do. I'm certainly not trying to convince you to marry him because I've invested with him." She sighed.

"Okay," Valerie said. "Then what is it? What can I do?"

"I'm telling you because I'm beginning to worry about the whole thing," Marguerite said. "I've just had a talk with Suzy Brooks. She and Harry have taken their account away from Teddy, she told me." Marguerite paused as if gathering the courage to go on.

"I guess people do that all the time," Valerie said. "I mean, you just did it with Dock Wainwright."

"Yes," Marguerite said, sighing again, "but in any case, Suzy said that Teddy had been handling a substantial amount of money for them, several million dollars, in fact. She said that everything had gone swimmingly for a while, but that lately their statements had been arriving late or not at all."

"You mean they hadn't been getting anything from him?" Valerie asked. "Are you sure?"

"Absolutely," Marguerite said. "Suzy would never have made this up. She said that when they asked Teddy about it, he assured them it was all due to some sort of new accounting procedure they were switching over to in the office. Anyway, to make a long story short, they finally decided to bail out, and it's taken them months to recover their money from him. They practically had to threaten to file a lawsuit against him to get him to pay up."

"I see," Valerie said, genuinely alarmed now.

"Not only that," Marguerite continued, "but when they got their final statement and check, all sorts of highly debatable charges had been made to their account, reducing it by several thousand dollars."

"Oh, my God," Valerie moaned. "Are they going to try to do something about it?"

"They haven't come to a decision," Marguerite replied. "But I have. I want my money to go straight back to Dock Wainwright and as quickly as possible. I was going to try and get Jamie working on it this morning, but I can't find him."

"What do you mean you can't find him?" Valerie asked. "Where does he go?"

"I . . . I don't really know," Marguerite confessed. "He has friends nearby, I know."

"Look, Mother," she said. "I'm sure it'll be just fine. He's only had your money a very short time, right?"

"Yes," Marguerite said, "but I can't help worrying after Suzy's call. I thought I was doing the right thing, and having Jamie as a sort of watchdog over everything, well, how could I go wrong?"

"Jamie as a watchdog?" Valerie asked. "What do you mean? How's he involved?"

"He was transferring some money to Teddy as well," Marguerite replied. "And Jamie knows a thing or two about money management, so I signed papers giving Jamie the power to make decisions regarding stock trades and such. He is supposed to be consulted before Teddy makes any final decisions regarding changes in the portfolio. That sort of thing. But I haven't been able to reach Jamie. He's visiting friends in Saratoga, I believe."

It gets more Byzantine by the minute, Valerie thought, but didn't say. "In that case," Val said, "everything ought to be all right, Mother. If Teddy can't do anything without Jamie, then you should be okay until a transfer back to Dock is made."

"I hope so," Marguerite said. "I just don't know. Teddy is certainly an underhanded schemer."

Pot calls kettle black, Valerie thought. Did it never occur to her mother that if those two would scheme with her, they might very well scheme *against* her?

"I don't know how I can help you," Valerie said, "but if there's anything I can do, say the word."

"I was hoping that you might be able to talk to Teddy, and tell him I've changed my mind," she said. "Tell him it's because your father would be terribly disappointed to know that I'd transferred control to someone other than Dock. I certainly don't want Teddy to think that I'm suspicious of him. It might offend him. I want this done in a very civilized way."

The way you planned my wedding, Valerie couldn't help thinking. "Well," she said, "I don't think there's a chance that I'll get to talk to Teddy before you do, but if he calls I'll broach the subject."

"That would be awfully helpful, Val, dear," she said. "I've already talked to Dock Wainwright, by the way, and told him that I want the money transferred back to his firm. So he said he would get the paperwork ready at his office, and he's waiting to hear from Teddy. He's already left word with Teddy's secretary."

"Okay," Valerie said. "Is there anything else?"

"No," Marguerite said, then she added, "but it wouldn't hurt if you'd be nice to Teddy, only until this is over, I mean, so that it works out smoothly."

Valerie wanted to scream, but instead she said, "Of course, Mother. I'll be nice to Teddy. For your sake."

"It's for your own as well," Marguerite pointed out. "After all, Val, dear, you are my sole heir."

"I'll do my best," Valerie said. "Now, I'd better get off the phone because I've got a very busy day."

"Yes," Marguerite said. "I won't keep you. Good-bye, then."

"Bye, Mother," Valerie said and hung up the telephone.

She put her head in her hands and massaged her forehead as if to wipe away the worries that her mother's telephone call had brought on. *Life is never simple,* she told herself, *but can't there be days with little reprieves?* She lifted her head again and looked down at Elvis, spread out in his bed beneath the desk.

"Elvis," she said. "We need a vacation. Just the two of us." Elvis wagged his tail in response. "Wait. Not so fast. On second thought," she said, "make that the three of us. You, me, and Wyn.

Oh, scratch that! What am I thinking? Make that . . . what? The eight of us. You, me, Wyn, the four wolfhounds, and Mina, the cat. How does that sound, Elvis? A vacation for eight. Maybe on some nice quiet, sunny island with no telephones or faxes, no pagers or cell phones, no E-mail, no TV. Just us animals."

She leaned down and gave him a few strokes, then straightened back up. "I like the idea, Elvis," she said. "I like it a lot, and I think you will, too."

Wyn paced in the library, the dogs watching him idly, the cat perched in regal solitude on a high-backed baroque chair. He had already called Dexter Willingham IV, his lawyer in Palm Beach, and had a long discussion with him about finalizing the divorce.

Willingham had been relieved because, although he could have billed for many more hours if the case had been dragged out, he was utterly sick and tired of Arielle Conrad and her screaming tantrums. She had even approached him at a grand charity function, pointing her finger and shouting obscenities at him in front of dozens of white-tied and ball-gowned grandees in one of Palm Beach's finest ballrooms. He had spoken to Myron Goldman, Arielle's lawyer, a number of times about the situation, but Goldman seemed incapable of controlling his client.

The whole process could be virtually over by the end of the week if all went well. Neither Wyn nor Willingham anticipated any problem in instantly resolving the case. However, the telephone hadn't rung in the last hour, and Wyn was beginning to get nervous.

What if Arielle had changed her mind about something, and decided to throw some final wrench into the process? She might hold out for more when she discovered that he was ready to settle.

Santo walked into the room on virtually silent feet, and Wyn caught sight of him out of the corner of his eye. "Where've you been, Santo?" he asked. "I haven't seen you all morning."

"I overslept," Santo said honestly. "I know that if you need me, all you have to do is call the cottage, so I guess my usual mental alarm clock just didn't go off this morning. I'm sort of under the weather."

"You have the flu or something?" Wyn asked.

"No," Santo replied. "Just . . . like a little cold or something."

"I happened to notice that you've been out late a lot recently," Wyn said with a smile. "You found somebody up here that's hot to trot?"

Santo averted his eyes, then turned his gaze to Wyn. "Aw, not really," he said. "Just been working out a lot. Gone to a couple of bars with some of the guys from the gym. You know, just shooting the shit."

The telephone rang, and Santo hurriedly picked up the receiver. "Stonelair," he said.

He listened for a moment. "Please hold," he said. He turned to Wyn. "It's Dexter Willingham for you," he said.

"I'll take it," Wyn replied, sighing with relief. He took the receiver from Santo. "Hey, Dex," he said. "What's going on? I was beginning to get a little worried."

"I've spoken to Myron Goldman," Willingham said, "and he foresees no difficulty bringing this to a very quick close. The only problem at this point is that he can't seem to locate Arielle."

"What do you mean, he can't locate Arielle?" Wyn asked.

"Exactly what I said," Willingham answered. "She's not at home. In fact, no one picks up at all. He said he'd made some phone calls, but so far he's had no luck. He'll get back to me as soon as he's spoken with her."

"Aw, shit," Wyn said in exasperation. "This could take forever, knowing Arielle."

"Or it could take an hour, Wyn," the lawyer replied reasonably. "She could simply be at the hairdresser or out shopping. Who knows? We'll probably find her in very short order."

"I hope so," Wyn said, "because I want to get this over with."

"I understand, Wyn," Willingham said, "and I'm glad you've reached that decision. However, our hands are tied until we've located Arielle."

"I realize that," Wyn said with a sigh. "I think I'll make some calls myself, Dex, and you let me know the minute you hear anything."

"Will do," the lawyer said. He chuckled then. "Don't worry about it, Wyn, if she's in Palm Beach, we'll find her in the next hour or so. You know how small this town really is."

"That's for sure," Wyn replied. "Okay, Dex. I'll talk to you later."

Wyn hung up the receiver and stared off toward the pool for a few moments, wondering where he should call first to try to locate Arielle.

"Trouble?" Santo asked, looking over at his boss.

Wyn turned to him. "They can't find Arielle, and we need to get hold of her right away. Wouldn't you know it? I decided to go ahead and get this divorce business over with, and what happens? Arielle suddenly does a disappearing act."

Santo stared at Wyn, his mind thrown into a maelstrom of conflicting thoughts. *Should I tell him that I know where Arielle is? No,* he immediately decided, *because then Wyn would wonder how I know, and I certainly don't want Wyn to know that I've met with her behind his back.* And what about Arielle's little plot? He'd have to get hold of her as soon as possible to let her know what was going on. That would put a stop to it. Or would it? He really didn't know.

"What's wrong with you?" Wyn asked. "This is what you've wanted me to do, and now that I've done it, you don't have anything to say?"

"Sorry," Santo said, clearing his throat. "I was just wondering where she might be. This is good news, though. I think it's the smartest thing you've done in a long time."

Wyn nodded. "Well," he said, "I guess you could say that Val, you know, the vet, had something to do with it." He smiled, almost sheepishly.

"What do you mean?" Santo asked, trying to act as if he didn't have any idea that there might be a budding relationship between his boss and the veterinarian.

"Oh, come on, Santo," Wyn replied. "You know I've been seeing her."

Santo nodded. "Yeah, I knew that, but I just thought it was, like, real casual."

Wyn looked at him with a serious expression. "It's more than that, Santo," he said. "Much more."

"Well," Santo said, "I guess congratulations are in order, huh?"

"Maybe," Wyn said. "Anyway, I'm going to get on the telephone and see if I can help dig up Arielle. If you think of anything, let me know."

"I will," Santo said. "I'm going down to the stable, check on things there, but I'll give a call if anything comes to mind."

"See you later," Wyn said.

Santo turned and left the room, trying not to hurry, heading down to the stable where he would try to get hold of Arielle in privacy.

Wyn watched him leave. *What's going on with him?* he wondered. *He hasn't been acting like himself lately.*

Chapter Twenty-Six

Tiffani jerked and missed a key on the computer's keyboard. *Damn!* she thought. *The creepy bastard's done it again. Scared the life out of me. Except this time, I'm already nearly jumping out of my skin.* She quickly planted a big smile on her fuchsia-painted lips and turned around, thrusting her large breasts out and giving her long, curly hair a big swing, a habit she'd developed, certain that men found it irresistible.

"Hi, Santo," she said, forcing cheer into her voice. "How are you?" She was chewing gum and popped it.

Santo returned her smile with the mere semblance of one and that was an effort. "Okay, Tiff," he replied. "You doing all right?"

"Yeah," she said. "I've got tons of typing to do. A lot of checks to get ready for signing and stuff." She paused for a moment, considering her next move. "Are you going to be working in here today?"

Santo shook his head. "That's why I came by," he said. "I've got a lot of stuff to do, too, and I wondered if you could hold the fort down today."

"Sure!" she said gaily, almost shuddering with relief. *How good can my luck get?* she thought. "I'd be glad to. I'm way behind on paperwork, so I'll be right here except to maybe run out and get a sandwich or something later on."

"That's cool," he said. "Oh, yeah, if Mr. Conrad calls down

here for me, tell him I'll call him right back. Okay? Then you give me a buzz at my cottage. I'm going to be working over there."

"Yeah, I'll do it for sure," she said, thinking that he was acting pretty odd. The creepy giant never left his post, and while she was working at the stable that usually seemed to be his post. Maybe the boss had him doing something else? Maybe he and the boss had a fight?

Oh, well, who cares, she decided. *He'll be out of the way, and that's the best news I've had all day. I'll just have to watch out for old man Reinhardt, but that shouldn't be much trouble. He's always in a world of his own. Never even speaks to me, just nods. I'll be able to help Teddy out, and nobody will ever know the difference. Except Teddy.* My *Teddy.*

"See you later," Santo said, then went back out the door.

"Yeah, sure," Tiffani said. "See you." When she was certain that he was gone, she picked up the telephone receiver and dialed a number.

In the privacy of his cottage, Santo quickly punched in the number on his cell phone. Once. Twice. Three times. Four. *Nada. Fuck.* He was about to press the end button when she answered.

"Hello?"

"It's Santo," he said. "Maybe it's time we had a little talk."

"I was hoping you would see it my way," Arielle said.

"I'm not sure I do," Santo replied, "but I want to discuss it. Something's come up."

"What do you mean?" she asked.

"Wyn's going to settle," Santo said. "He's already contacted your lawyers about it, but they haven't been able to reach you."

"I guess his little girlfriend brought on this sudden change of heart," Arielle said.

"Yeah."

"So now that he's found somebody he wants," she went on, "he's finally willing to get rid of me."

"You could say that."

"Listen, Santo," she said, "could you get away from there now? I want to talk to you in private."

"What about Lolo?"

"He's over at the polo grounds. He might be back soon so we'd have to meet someplace."

"You mean you don't want him involved?" Santo asked.

"No way," Arielle said. "He can't handle it. I'm very disappointed in him. I thought he was more of a man." She paused, then added, "Like you."

"What've you got in mind?" Santo enjoyed her obvious flirting.

"We'll talk about it when I see you," she replied. "Can you get away?"

"Sure."

"I know a place between Saratoga Springs and Albany," she said. "We'd have privacy there. Nobody in the world we know would see either one of us."

Santo listened as she gave him the name and address of a motel. "I can be there in less than an hour," he said.

"Good," Arielle said. "I knew I could count on your help, Santo."

"I don't know," he said, "but I'm willing to discuss it."

"See you in an hour," she said and hung up.

Santo depressed the end button on his cell phone and flipped it shut. He felt life stir in his groin and smiled as he headed out to the garage.

Valerie had just finished examining George and Jesse, two Labrador retrievers, and giving them Lyme disease vaccinations. She was filling in their charts and sipping coffee when the telephone jangled.

"Yes?" she said, still focused on a chart.

"Val," Tami said teasingly, "guess who's holding on line four?"

"I don't have any idea," Valerie replied. "Is it friend or foe?"

"Oh, it's definitely friend," Tami said conspiratorially. "In fact, I would say it's probably a whole lot more than that."

Tami hung up, and Valerie pressed the line four button. "What can I do for you, Mr. Conrad?" she asked.

"Ask not what you can do for me, Doc," Wyn retorted, "but what I can do for you."

"The possibilities are infinite, I'm sure," she said with a laugh, "but did you have something specific in mind?"

"Indeed, I did," he replied. "I want to wine and dine you again tonight at my humble abode, then see what happens from there. If you're not already bored with my company, that is."

"I'm certainly not bored with your company, Mr. Conrad," she replied, "but why don't you come over to *my* humble abode for a change and let me show off my culinary skills?"

"Because I have something special in mind," he said, "and I think we ought to do it here at Stonelair. Besides, I'd like to cook for you since I know you'll be tired after a long day at the office."

"Why, thank you, Mr. Conrad," she replied.

"How about eight?" he asked.

"I think I can fit that into my schedule," she said.

"I'll see you then."

"Okay, bye." She hung up the phone and squeezed herself with her arms. "This is what they call dreamy, Elvis," she said, looking down at him. "I hope you've felt it at least once in your life. Dreamy, dreamy—"

The telephone jangled again, and she reached over and picked it up. "Yes?"

"Val," Tami said in an alarmed voice, "it's Colette on line two, and she's absolutely hysterical. It's something about Hayden, that African pygmy hedgehog of hers."

"I'll get it," Valerie said. She immediately pressed the line two button. "Colette, what's going on?" she asked.

"V-V-Val, darling," Colette managed to say, "someone's m-m-murdered Hayden!"

"Give me ten minutes to get there, Colette," Valerie replied.

"You're a darling," Colette said.

Valerie pushed the button for Daphne's line. "Daphne," she said, when she'd picked up, "I have an emergency that make take about an hour. Could you cover for me?"

"What's the emergency?" Daphne asked.

"Colette Richards's African pygmy hedgehog," Valerie replied.

"Oh, no," Daphne said. "Of course I'll cover for you. I hope it's nothing serious."

"I'm not really certain," Valerie said noncommitally. "I'll leave the charts with Tami."

"Sure, Val," Daphne said. "Let me know what happens."

Valerie hung up, gathered up her charts and carryall, put Elvis on his leash, and rushed out to reception to leave the patient charts with Tami.

Santo knocked on the motel room door, and it was opened at once by Arielle.

"Come on in," she said, swinging the door wide.

Santo stepped into the room and noticed that she was dressed in a filmy blouse that left little to the imagination and a micromini skirt that barely covered her silk bikini panties. Bottles of vodka and tonic sat open on a bedside table, along with two glasses. One of them wore Arielle's plum lipstick.

She saw him looking at the bottles. "Want to wet your whistle?" she asked.

"I better not," Santo replied. "I don't have much time. I've got to get back to Stonelair."

"Oh, come on, Santo," she cajoled, running a fingertip down his chest, "as big a man as you are, one itsy-bitsy drink won't do you any harm. Besides, I hate to drink alone."

Santo shrugged. "Okay," he said, "just one."

Arielle padded over to the bedside table on bare feet and poured a generous portion of vodka into a glass and added a splash of tonic. She handed it to him, then picked up her own.

"Cheers," she said, tapping her glass against his.

Santo nodded and took a sip of the drink.

"Let's get comfortable," she said, spreading out on the bed and patting the cover next to her.

"We need to talk," Santo said, eyeing her hungrily.

"So we'll talk," she said. "Here." She patted the bed a second time.

Santo shrugged his massive shoulders again and strode over to the bed and sat down facing her on the spot she'd indicated.

She looked into his eyes and ran a fingertip down his chest once more. "Tell me, Santo," she said softly, "what's on your mind?"

"It's like I told you on the telephone," he said, "Wyn's decided to settle, so you can drop all your plans to get rid of him. But . . ."

His voice trailed off into silence, and he took another swallow of vodka and tonic.

"But," Arielle said, "we both know that I'm worth more with him dead. Isn't that right?"

Santo nodded slowly.

"If I accept a settlement," she went on, running a hand up and down his powerful biceps, "I'd be getting a fraction of his worth. But if he suddenly dies and a settlement hasn't been arrived at, I'm still legally his wife . . . And if he marries again, he might change his will, leaving you out in the cold." She lifted her micromini skirt and smoothed out an imaginary wrinkle in her black silk panties.

Santo watched her with unabashed lust in his eyes. She'd always flirted with him, but they'd never actually made it. Things were different now, though. They weren't under Wyn's watchful eyes, and besides, she and Wyn were going to be divorced or . . . Wyn was going to be dead.

"We would have to move fast," Arielle said, unbuttoning her sheer blouse down to the waist. "Before the lawyers track me down and offer me a deal."

Santo nodded, but his eyes were riveted to the perfect breasts that were revealed right in front of him, within his touch.

"I know you could pull it off, Santo," she said seductively. "And I would go there with you to help if need be." She took a sip of her drink. "Just think, we could go off together."

"That would certainly look suspicious," he said.

"I mean eventually," Arielle said. "After it's all over, and I've got his money."

"What about Lolo?" he asked, his hand beginning to rub her naked thigh.

"Lolo," she said nastily. "What a joke. He's not half the man you are, Santo. He doesn't deserve a woman like me. Especially with all the money I'm going to have. And don't worry, he'd be terrified to talk. Even if he knew anything."

She reached up and ran a finger down his thick neck and back up to his lips, rubbing them, then trying to penetrate them.

Santo caught her wrist in his hand. "We need to work this out. Plan on exactly what we'll do—tonight," he said.

"And we will," she said. "But let's have some fun first, why don't we?"

Santo loosened his grip on her wrist. "You were always a little crazy, Arielle," he said.

"So were you," she said, reaching between his muscular thighs and stroking the erection that was visibly pressing against his pants.

"I'm in a real hurry," Santo said. He set his drink down and took hers out of her hand and placed it next to his. He stared into her eyes for a mere instant before his massive torso was on top of her.

"Yeah," he whispered, "we'll work out the details later."

Chapter Twenty-Seven

Colette sat at the kitchen table, a soggy linen handkerchief wadded in her wrinkled hand. Her eyes were red-rimmed and swollen from the fitful tears that still came.

Valerie was leaning back against the center island, looking over at her with a deeply saddened heart. Colette looked her age today, she thought, and her normally optimistic and extravagant demeanor was subdued. Valerie cleared her voice. "Colette, I know it's difficult to make decisions now, and I don't want to seem insensitive and crass. But I have to know what you want to do with him."

Colette looked up at her. "Oh, darling," she said, "you could never be insensitive or crass. I . . . I think I'll bury him in the garden and put a little marker there. That way we can visit him. What do you think?"

"I think that's a very good idea," Valerie replied. "I'll help you do it."

"No, Val," Colette replied. "You don't have to do that. I'm quite capable. I'll find a little box and wrap him up and put him in it, then do it myself."

"You're sure?" Valerie asked. "I don't mind at all, you know. I loved Hayden, too."

"I know, darling," she said, "but I think maybe I'd better do this alone. Just me and Hayden, maybe Puff Puppy if he'll behave himself." She heaved a melancholy sigh. "I'll wait until after the police have been here and gone. I should've called them a long time ago, but I simply couldn't face having them here. I appreciate your doing it, Val."

"I'm glad you let me call them," Valerie said. "This is getting to be really scary, especially when you think that somebody actually came into your house to do it."

Colette shivered anew. "Oh, the very thought," she cried. "I feel so . . . violated, Val darling, I can't begin to tell you."

"Well, I think that this was clearly a premeditated act," Valerie said. "But I don't think that whoever did it was after you."

Colette looked at her again. "You don't think so, really? It's just like with Eddie, isn't it? The same person, I would venture. Whoever murdered poor Noah knew exactly when and where and how. The same with Hayden." Her voice broke, and she paused a moment before continuing. "It's awful to think that someone would take out their hate on innocent animals, no matter who or what has angered them."

Valerie strode over and put an arm on Colette's shoulder, patting her tenderly. "I have a feeling, Colette," she said, "that you and Eddie may not be the targets at all."

Colette looked up at her, her watery blue eyes questioning. "Then who, Val?" she asked.

Valerie went around and sat down at the table opposite her. "It sounds crazy, I guess," she said, "but Hayden and Noah were my patients, and you and Eddie are my friends. Neither you nor Eddie can think of anybody that might have a grudge against you." She paused and looked Colette in the eye. "But I know of at least one person who has one against me."

Colette's eyes widened in alarm, and her hand flew to her breast. "Oh, Val, darling," she cried. "You can't think . . . but . . ."

Valerie nodded.

"Oh, it's too dreadful," Colette said. "Teddy surely couldn't do anything this repugnant."

"I don't really know what he's capable of," Valerie responded, "but I'm seriously thinking about it. I don't know who else both has a grudge against me and knows who my patients and friends are."

"Will you tell the police?" Colette asked.

"I don't honestly know," Valerie said. She sighed wearily. "I certainly don't want to, but we have to get to the bottom of this, Colette. If Teddy didn't have anything to do with these crimes, then he shouldn't have any problem proving it. At the same time, of course, I hate to put him through police questioning if he's innocent. Imagine how that'll make him feel."

"It's so hard to know what to do," Colette said. "I wonder what's keeping the police anyway?"

"They shouldn't be much longer," Valerie said.

Valerie's cell phone rang and startled them both.

"I guess I'm a little jumpy," Colette said.

"It's no wonder," Valerie replied, slipping the cell phone off her belt and flipping it open. "I'll just be a minute," she apologized.

Valerie pushed the talk button. "Valerie Rochelle," she said. As she listened, she slowly turned away so that Colette couldn't see her face. She didn't want her friend to catch the increasingly worried expression there.

"Doesn't sound good," she finally said, trying desperately to control her reaction to Wyn's news. She didn't want to disturb Colette unnecessarily. Colette had received enough terrible news today.

"Hold on for a minute, Wyn," she said. "I'm over at my friend Colette's, and I need to speak to her for just a moment." She pressed the hold button.

"Colette," she said, "there's an emergency out at Stonelair. Something's wrong with a horse. Will you be all right if I leave you alone until the police get here?"

"Of course, Val," Colette said. "You must go tend to the horse. There's not a thing more you can do for Hayden. Or me."

Valerie pressed the hold button again. "Wyn," she said, "I'll come right out there."

She pushed the end button, then snapped the phone shut and slipped it back on her belt. "I'm sorry, Colette," she said. "Are you sure you can handle the police?"

"Of course I can," Colette responded. "I may be old, but I'm not a fool."

"I didn't mean to imply that you were," Valerie said.

"I know you didn't, darling," Colette said. "I'm just a bit touchy, I suppose. Forgive me." She paused a moment, then went on. "And Val, I don't think I'll say anything to the police about Teddy. What do you think? Perhaps I should just tell them that you have some ideas that they should discuss with you. Is that all right?"

"I think that's perfect, Colette," she replied. "I hate to leave you now, but I'd better run."

"I'll be fine," Colette said. "Now run along. You've got work to do. Oh, and why not leave Elvis here with me? He and Puff Puppy can keep each other company. They get along so beautifully."

"You're sure?" Valerie asked.

"Certainly," Colette said.

They brushed cheeks, and Valerie shouldered her bag. She leaned down and gave Elvis a pat. "See you later, Elvis," she said. Then she rushed out to her Jeep.

Chapter Twenty-Eight

Lydia looked up from her desk when Teddy walked into the office. "Thank God, you're here," she exclaimed. "The telephone's been ringing off the hook, and let me tell you, boss, there are some people who want to talk to you real bad. And pronto isn't fast enough. Catch my drift?"

"Hello to you, too, Lydia," he said with a smirk on his face. He went over to his desk and sat down in his chair, then began rifling nervously through paperwork stacked there.

She turned to face him, hair aflame with fresh carrot-red dye, eyes flashing brightly with purple shadow and black liner. "Listen, Teddy," she said earnestly, "I'm dead serious. The shit's starting to hit the fan. Or I should say *fans*, to be more precise. I don't know exactly what's going on, but I've got a damn good idea, boss. And I'm telling you, you'd better get your ass in gear and start making some mighty sweet phone calls. They're going to be asking for your pretty blond head on a nice big platter."

"You think I don't know that, Lydia," he said angrily. "I don't need you telling me what to do. I've got enough on my mind as it is."

"Humpf!" she went on, "I've had to listen to old Dock Wainwright all day long. Marguerite de la Rochelle and her nasty-mouthed cousin, Jamie de Biron, want their money back. Plus a half dozen other clients. And I mean they want it *now*. No wonder you're like a damn cat on a hot tin roof. I am, too."

Teddy looked at her furiously.

"I'm telling you, Teddy," she exclaimed, shaking a tangerine fingernail at him. "You're in trouble this time. The brokers are climbing out of the woodwork, calling by the bushel load. Wanting *their* money. Something to do with your margins, little buddy. Like maybe something to do with all that trading you did on credit and now they want their money. All that money you've gone and lost!"

"Shut up, Lydia," he cried. "I get the message, loud and clear."

She stared at him for a minute before replying. "All right," she said angrily, "but I can't take this much longer, Teddy. Seriously. I don't like being part of a sinking ship. And that's what this is. It's the fucking Titanic, and I think I'm going to have to get in one of the lifeboats."

"Then do whatever the fuck you want," he shouted. "I don't fucking need you."

"That's all you've got to say?" she cried, rising imperiously to her feet. "I've devoted myself to you for the last six years, Teddy de Mornay. Always going to bat for you, lying for you, cheating for you, and sometimes cleaning up your damn messes so nobody'd know the real you. And that's all you have to say?"

"Just get out, if you're going," he snapped nastily.

Lydia stomped one leopard-patterned stiletto heel on the floor with rage, then turned and got her pocketbook out of a desk drawer. She paused dramatically at the door and glared at Teddy.

He returned her look. "Get out, Lydia," he spat. "Go get that hot young stud you're so crazy about and get him to fuck your brains out. I'm sick of trailer trash around here anyway."

She looked momentarily stunned. "I may live in a trailer, *Mr.* de Mornay," she said between gritted teeth, "but you're the trash." She turned and left, slamming the door behind her with a resounding bang.

Teddy snatched up his message slips and stared at them for a moment. He swiveled in his desk chair wih agitation, then started to lift the telephone receiver.

It rang before he could pick it up, and he waited for the machine to click in so he could screen the call. When his message was finally over, he heard Tiffani and immediately answered.

"Hey, babe," he said.

"Teddy, we've got to talk."

"We're talking, aren't we?" he said with frustration.

"No, I mean in person, Teddy," she replied. "It's really important."

"Come on, Tiff," he said huffily. "I'm very busy right now, and
besides, we have a big date late tonight. Remember? A really special date. A special little party, just the two of us."

"I know, Teddy," she said seriously, "but I need to talk to you
right away. In person. I-I can't discuss it over the phone."

"Goddamn. Can't it wait till tonight?" he groused. "I'm really
tied up here."

"Teddy," she said in exasperation, "I have to talk to you *now.*
At my place."

She sounded as if she might burst into tears. *What the hell now?*
he wondered. Everything was beginning to go sour. But the game
wasn't over yet, and he had to protect his little investment in Tiff.

"Shit, Tiff," he said, "I've got to do some really important stuff
here. Make some calls and all."

"You'll understand once we talk."

He sighed. "Fuck it. I'll be over in a few minutes."

He replaced the receiver in its cradle and sighed again. "Shit,"
he said aloud. "I knew it was time to unload her." He got up to
leave, then sat back down. *One more call to make,* he thought. *Do
a little potential damage control.* He picked up the receiver and
dialed the number.

She answered on the third ring. "Hello?"

"Marguerite," he said. "It's Teddy."

He thought he heard a sharp intake of breath before she
replied. "Well, hello, Teddy. How are you?"

"I'm fine," he replied. "I thought I might stop by later and take
you out for drinks and dinner. I'd like to talk to you."

There was a long pause, then Marguerite said, "I think that
would be lovely, Teddy, but why not have drinks and dinner
here. It would be so much nicer than a restaurant, don't you
think?"

"Great," he said. "I have some errands to run. What if I come
on over when I'm finished?"

"Perfect," she said. "It'll be such a pleasure to see you, Teddy."

He hung up the receiver, then headed out to the Jaguar.

That takes care of one bitch, he thought. *Now to go take care of another one. Tiffani. What's wrong with her anyway?* he wondered. *Just when I'm about to get her out of my hair once and for all, she has a problem. Another problem. Just what I need. Oh, well,* he consoled himself as he fired up the Jaguar's engine, *I'll be through with the bimbo tonight. Yeah, late tonight after I'm finished with her, I'll tell her good-bye forever. Then evict her from the cottage.*

Valerie stomped on the brakes at the gates to Stonelair and reached out and pushed the intercom button in one swift movement.

"Val?" It was Wyn's voice, not Santo Ducci's.

"Yes," she replied.

"Down at the stable," his disembodied voice said.

The gates immediately started opening, and she inched the car forward until she could finally race between them and on down the lane that led to the stable. She pulled into the parking area, braked with a screech, and cut off the engine.

She jumped out of the Jeep and grabbed her gear. She could already hear noise coming from the stables. The horses, whatever might be the matter, sounded very disturbed. She saw Wyn coming toward her. His face was still partially bandaged, but his body language did enough to convey his worry.

"Hey," he called to her, "slow down. I don't want you to kill yourself."

"I'm okay," she said, approaching him now. "I've never had an accident."

"And I don't want you to start now," he said. He kissed her lips and put an arm around her shoulders.

She was thrilled by his touch and couldn't ignore it, despite the fact that she was intent on getting to the stable and the horses. She smiled up at him. "I'm glad to see you even if the circumstances aren't the best."

"Likewise, Doc," he replied. "Why don't you let me carry that bag for you?"

"No, it's okay," she said. "I'm used to it, Wyn."

"Okay," he said.

"Is Santo with the horses?" she asked.

"He is now," Wyn replied.

"Uh-oh," she said. "Do I detect a note of anger in your voice?"

"Well, a little," he admitted. "I was up in the library and thought I heard noise from the stables. I called down there, and nobody picked up. Nobody! The Reinhardts had gone into town to do some shopping, that I knew. The girl who works part-time here had just left, I guess, because it was quitting time for her, but Santo should've been down there and he wasn't."

They reached the door to the office in the stable complex and went in.

"Anyhow," Wyn continued, "I called his cottage over and over. He wasn't there. Finally, he picked up and came running down here and saw that all hell had broken lose. That's when I called your office. That girl Tami gave me your cell phone number."

They went through the tack room and on into the stables, and Valerie was shocked by the state of panic among the horses. She turned to Wyn. "Does one of them seem to be more affected by whatever it is than the rest?" she asked.

"They're all spooked, some of them more than others," he said. "But they're all acting so crazy it's hard for me to tell. I guess I overreacted a little when I saw what was happening."

Santo appeared from the other end of the stable, walking toward them. Even from a distance, Valerie could see that he looked very worried.

He nodded to her as he drew up to them.

"Hi, Santo," she said.

"Hi," he replied, then looked away, shamefaced.

Valerie went to the first stall, set down her carryall and medical kit, then approached the barred door. The horse, Clever Cookie, was highly agitated, rearing and snorting and twitching, his eyes enormous with fear. It was almost as if there were a fire in the stable, she thought.

"There hasn't been any smoke they could smell?" she asked.

"No," Wyn said. "None at all."

"Any loud or strange noises?"

"Nope," Wyn said, shaking his head. "I've been here, and I would've heard it, too."

Valerie looked back into the stall. "Hey, Clever Cookie," she cooed through the opening. "Hey, buddy, what's troubling you?" She reached one of her hands past the bars to let the horse smell it, but Clever Cookie didn't even make an effort to approach her. He was totally spooked by something. She noticed the electrical conduit running through the stall.

She turned back around. "Wyn," she asked, "does the electrical conduit run through all the stalls?"

He nodded. "Yes," he said, "why?"

"Is it possible," she said, feeling that she was grasping at straws, "that there's a short or something running through that line, and the horses could've been shocked?"

"I don't think so, Val," Wyn replied. "The lights are on those lines, and there's nothing wrong with them." He turned to Santo. "Just to be sure, Santo, why don't you throw the circuit breakers for this building?"

Santo nodded and set off toward the office, where the circuit breakers were.

"I guess we can give it a few minutes and see if there's any change in their behavior," Wyn said.

"It's a long shot," she said, "but this is really strange. I've never seen anything like it, except where there's smoke."

"Me either," Wyn said.

"I'm going to walk past all the stalls," Valerie said, "and try to spot the horse that's the least spooked."

She began going from stall to stall, Wyn following along with her, looking into each one, watching each horse for a minute.

Suddenly the lights went out, and they both flinched. They stopped in their tracks but recovered quickly.

"That was pretty crazy, knowing that it was coming," Valerie said.

"This whole situation is pretty crazy," he said.

There was sufficient daylight coming in from outside, so they continued walking down the length of the stalls, looking in on each horse. When they arrived at Demon's stall, they both noticed that the immense stallion was definitely agitated, but he seemed relatively calm compared to most of the other horses. Wyn began talking to him quietly and reached in, trying to stroke his neck. Demon seemed to want the attention, but he was reluctant.

Wyn turned to Valerie. "Do you think the lights have been off long enough?" he asked. "Should they've calmed down in this length of time if it had to do with a shock or something?"

Valerie looked at him and shrugged. "I don't know," she said, "but I would think so. It's been several minutes, and you're here with them. They know you and trust you, so I would think that if that were the problem they would've calmed down by now. But there hasn't been any change, has there?"

"No," he said. "I'll go tell Santo to turn the power back on. Be right back." He dashed off in the direction of the office.

Valerie went back to Clever Cookie's stall to retrieve her carryall and medical bag, then walked back down to Demon. She would begin her work with him.

Wyn and Santo returned from the office, hurrying to where she stood.

"What're you doing?" Wyn asked.

"I'm going to need you and Santo to help me tether Demon to the stall," Valerie said. "I've got to get blood from one of the horses for toxicology. Quite frankly, I don't know what else to do. Demon seems to be the least disturbed, so I think he's our best bet."

Wyn and Santo both approached the stall. Wyn opened the door slowly, and he and Santo eased themselves inside. In a flash, Wyn caught Demon's bridle, and before the horse managed to rear away, Santo clipped on a rein and snapped it to a ring in the stall wall.

They backed away as the big horse tried to rear. "Demon," Wyn whispered. "It's okay, boy. It's okay." He stroked Demon several times, trying to calm him. Santo left the stall, stepping outside and watching.

Valerie had retrieved a syringe from her medical bag and slipped into the stall with Wyn.

"You sure you want to do this, Val?" Wyn asked quietly without turning around. He continued stroking Demon.

"I have to get some blood," she said, "and I've done it many a time. I'll just stay clear of his hindquarters." She sidled up next to Wyn and began her rhythmic cooing to calm the agitated horse. She reached up and began stroking Demon's neck, locating the jugular vein. She concentrated on stroking him there, then, when he seemed somewhat distracted by their strokes and whispers, she quickly plunged the syringe into the vein and began drawing blood.

Demon reacted instantly, shifting his feet and trying to rear, but she managed to get enough blood for toxicology, then gingerly backed out of the stall.

Wyn joined her after a moment. "You're a brave woman, Doc," he said.

"It's my job," she said, taking the needle off the syringe and leaning down to put it in the special container in her medical bag. She straightened back up. "I'm going to call the clinic to come pick this up for immediate testing," she said. "I think it would be best if I stayed here for a while and watched them. See if I can get any inkling of what's going on."

She slipped the cell phone off her belt, flipped it open, and dialed. "Tami, it's Val. I need somebody over at Stonelair right away. I've got a blood sample that needs a toxicology screen ASAP, and I mean ASAP."

She listened a minute, then said, "Oh, great. I'd forgotten that you know where this place is. Tell Daphne I want you to pick it up. Somebody will be waiting with the blood at the front gate. Got that?"

She listened for a moment longer, then pressed the end button, snapped the phone shut, and replaced it on her belt. "Santo, do you mind waiting up at the gate with this for me? It'll probably take Tami about fifteen or twenty minutes to get here, so you don't have to leave quite yet." She held up the vial of blood.

"Sure," he said, nodding. He took it from her.

"I want to take a look at the others," she said, and started slowly walking down the length of the stalls again, first one side, then the other. Every single one of the horses was still in some state of panic.

"It's just like you said," she remarked, turning to Wyn. "Some of them are more acutely affected than others, but they're all spooked. I've never seen anything quite like it." She looked thoughtful for a moment. "Was anybody in here with them this afternoon?" she asked.

"Not as far as I know," Wyn replied. He turned and looked over at Santo, who stood near Layla's stall, seemingly distracted.

"Santo," he said, "do you know if anybody was in here with the horses this afternoon?"

Santo shrugged. "Tiff was here at work," he said. "I saw her in the office around lunchtime, I guess. I told her I wasn't feeling so hot and was going to go take a few Tylenol and go spread out. She said she had a lot of paperwork to do and would call me if anything came up. Said she might go get a sandwich or something."

"So you weren't here all afternoon?" Wyn asked.

"No," Santo said. "I told you, I—"

"It's okay, Santo," Wyn said. "You can't help it if you were sick." He sighed. "So she was the only person around, right?"

Santo nodded. "Yes. The Reinhardts had gone into town, so she was alone."

"After they pick up the blood at the gate, why don't you go give her a call, Santo?" Wyn said. "See if she knows anything."

"Okay," he said. "I guess I'd better get up to the gate now." Santo turned and walked toward the door to the tack room.

When he had left, Wyn turned to Valerie. "I don't know what's wrong with him, but he sure isn't acting like himself."

"How do you mean?" she asked.

"I can't put my finger on it," he replied.

"It's probably nothing. Circumstances being what they are, you're probably reading too much into his behavior."

"Maybe you're right, Doc," he said. "You're a very sensible woman."

They continued checking on the horses, and Valerie remained perplexed by their behavior. She'd never felt quite so defeated. Nothing in her training had prepared her for anything like this. She hated to let Wyn down, and she felt almost sick at the prospect of not being able to help the horses.

Wyn took her hand and squeezed it. It was as if, she thought as she turned to look at him, he could sense her feelings.

"It'll be okay, Doc," he said, smiling.

"I hope so," she replied, a worried look on her face.

They walked on, arriving at the last stall, pausing to look in on the horse there, then turned and started back up the way they'd come. Suddenly, Valerie stopped dead in her tracks and jerked on Wyn's hand.

"Look!" she said in a near whisper.

"What?" he asked, turning to face her.

"Oh, my God, Wyn!" she exclaimed, leaning down to the floor to pick up a small object just outside one of the stalls.

Valerie held a gel capsule between two fingers. It was just like medication would come in, and inside she discovered a fine white powder.

"Can you think of a pill that any of the horses might be taking that looks like this?" she asked Wyn.

He shook his head. "No," he said. "I'd have to check with Santo, but I can't think of a thing." He looked at it closely. "Isn't it a lot smaller than most horse pills?" he asked.

"Exactly," she said. "And I can't think of anything that we'd use that resembles this. Let me run up to the gate and give this to Santo to give Tami. We can run it through toxicology, too. I bet it'll be the same thing that shows up in Demon's blood."

"I'll go with you," he said.

"You can wait here," she replied.

He shook his head. "No, I want to keep you in my sight."

Chapter Twenty-Nine

Teddy sat down on Tiffani's big bed, where she was spread out, her eyes teary, her expression troubled. Her long curly hair, the product of much untalented cutting, dyeing, bleaching, and styling—what color *is* it? he wondered—was fanned out around her head.

He took one of her hands in his and held it, looking down at the thin gold and silver junk rings she wore on every finger. The fuchsia polish on her fake nails was chipped, and the gold-tone and silver-tone bangle bracelets at her wrists were bent and scratched from wear.

Every time he'd made a move on her, she'd shaken her head from side to side and whined. "Not yet, Teddy," she'd say. "Not yet. We have to talk."

"So let's talk, babe," he'd said, but so far she'd hardly said a word.

He was quickly losing his patience with her. *Shit,* he thought, *this is ridiculous.* He'd already snorted a few lines of coke. It was time to get busy. He had to get her to start talking.

"I'm worried about you," he said. "Won't you tell me what's wrong?"

"Well," she began slowly, finally responding to his apparent concern, "there's something we need to talk about."

"Okay," he said, sliding an arm around her shoulder.

"Well," she said, looking down into her lap, then back up at him, "you told me that those pills you gave me wouldn't hurt anybody. Those pills you told me to give the horses."

Teddy was silent for a moment, wondering what further absurdity she would present him with now. "That's right," he said. "They wouldn't hurt anybody."

"Well," she said, "I was having second thoughts. That's why I asked you to come over. And then Santo called me at home, saying the whole place was in an uproar." She paused. "They're analyzing blood and one of the pills I dropped."

Teddy stared at her openmouthed. "You dropped a pill?" he said.

She nodded. "Yeah, but it wouldn't matter, Teddy," she replied, "because they're analyzing the blood anyway. Santo said there are millions of dollars in horses there, and they're calling in the police. He said I was in big trouble because I was the only person there."

"That's bullshit," Teddy snapped. "They can't prove you did a thing."

"I know that," she said. "I can tell them that I went out to get a sandwich for lunch, which I did, and anybody could have come in and done it." She looked at Teddy, a hard glint in her eyes. "Or . . . I could tell them that you gave me the pills to give to the horses because you wanted to get even with your vet friend for going out with Mr. Conrad."

Teddy looked over at her and saw that look in her eyes, and he knew that she was telling the truth. *She would do it,* he thought. *The bitch would implicate me just so she wouldn't go down alone, even after all I've done for her.*

Then he had a sudden inspiration. *Nobody's ever seen us together,* he thought. *Nobody has any idea that we even know each other. Unless . . .*

"Tiff," he said calmly, "you didn't tell anybody else about the stable business, did you?"

She shook her head. "No, Teddy," she replied. "Do you think I'm crazy?"

He smiled. "Smart girl."

"But some of my girlfriends know I've been hanging out with you. I've told them all about you and me."

The smile faded from his face, and he looked crestfallen. *Is she lying?* he wondered. But then he realized that of course she wasn't lying. She'd probably been bragging to her friends all summer. Telling them about how she was screwing her rich landlord, Teddy de Mornay. Getting a rent reduction *and* free dope.

How the fuck do I clean up this mess? he asked himself. He made a decision. He'd tell her not to worry, that he'd fix everything and come back later as planned. *After my meeting with Marguerite,* he thought, *I'll come over, ready to party. Maybe bring a little something extra special, make sure greedy Tiff gets her share and then some. She was my tenant,* he'd tell the cops, *but I have no idea why she'd poison any horses. Pretty girl, too. Damn shame about her overdosing like that . . .*

It was going on seven o'clock, and Val and Wyn had agreed that they'd have dinner later, after their long vigil at the stables. The horses had largely calmed down, but a few were still spooked. Their agitation, of course, only served to disquiet those that had calmed down. It might be hours yet, depending on what they had in their systems, before they were all back to normal.

Val had called the police to report what had happened, and they had paid a brief call, looking around the stables and questioning both Val and Wyn. She had told them about Noah's almost certain poisoning, Hayden's death, and assured them she would let them know as soon as she had a report on the blood work and capsule. She'd reluctantly told them that the only person she knew who had a grudge against her was Teddy de Mornay.

Santo had given them Tiffani's name and address, and they were supposed to question her as well as Teddy. Finally, after the police had left, Val had agreed to go home and change and check on Elvis, then come back for dinner. Santo and the Reinhardts would be at Stonelair tonight, Wyn had told her, so if there was any problem, there would be help at least.

She'd finished taking a quick bath, made up her face, brushed her hair, and was rummaging through her closet, exasperated because she couldn't figure out *what to wear*. She stood back and looked at her closet, considering the possibilities that presented themselves and cursing herself for not taking the time to do more clothes shopping when she was in New York City.

Wyn had told her that tonight was going to be a special dinner, so she wanted to look special.

She began pushing hangers apart, quickly scanning what hung on them, then moving on. Then an old djellaba that she'd picked up on a trip to Tangier years ago jumped out at her. She'd forgotten all about it. She pulled it out of the closet and held it up.

Perfect, she thought with a smile. *And Wyn will get a kick out of it. Wait till I tell him about bargaining for it in the Medina.* Ankle length, it was made of a white gauzy fabric that was embroidered with real gold thread around the neck, on the long sleeves, the hem, and down the bodice. It unbuttoned practically to the waist with little frog closures of gold.

She slipped it on over her head, then buttoned the bottom three or four buttons, and turned in front of the mirror. *Really perfect,* she thought, delighting in the rediscovery of the Moroccan garment. *It's summery and sexy and exotic and dressy, but casual, too.*

Now, if she could find the little gold sandals that she'd worn with it, she'd be all set. She delved back into the closet, searching the floor, under piles of shoes of all kinds, and *voilà.* There they were, needing a dusting off, but none the worse for wear.

She took them into the kitchen and wiped them with a damp paper towel, then dried them with another one. She tried them on, and they still fit. *Well,* she thought, *at least something's working out right today.*

She looked at the clock on the kitchen wall. Just time enough, if she hurried. She checked to make sure Elvis had enough water and food, then grabbed her carryall and keys. She checked the back door to make certain it was locked, then headed for the front, Elvis following along behind her.

At the door, she leaned down and petted Elvis. "I'll be late, old boy," she said, "so you can have a nice nap." She looked into his eyes. "And I promise that you'll meet the new man in my life and all of his animals, too, very soon." She hugged him, then got up and left, making sure she'd locked the door behind her.

She fired up the Jeep and pulled out of her driveway, wondering what Wyn was up to. *What's so special about tonight?* she wondered. *Was he having someone else over?* Probably not, because he didn't see anyone else, at least not that she knew of. But he'd told her to dress up more than usual. *Why?* She couldn't think of a thing. *Was it just a matter of the food?* Maybe.

She sped down the road, eager to get to Stonelair. Excited to find out what Wyn would think was special.

Darkness had fallen, and the odd couple in the big car was speeding down the road, headed toward Stonelair. At the wheel was Santo, in Stonelair's Range Rover. When they arrived, should anybody be about, which was highly unlikely, they would think nothing of seeing him driving in alone. His passenger would simply slide to the floor until the car was safely parked in the garage at his cottage.

He'd hardly ever used the garage, usually walking over from the parking area at the stables, but tonight he'd even brought the remote for the garage door. *Open sesame,* he thought. *Then close and conceal.*

Sitting next to him in the front was Arielle. She was chain-smoking cigarillos, occasionally taking a sip from a little silver flask in her pocketbook. She had come dressed in her extraordinarily sexy way, perhaps adding a little extra pizzaz on Santo's account. The snakeskin micromini, the sheer blouse unbuttoned to the waist, thus exposing her perfect breasts, the stilettos. The effect of her outfit was not lost on him. It was as provocative now as it had been earlier in the day. He knew that Arielle was a shark, of course, but she was the sexiest shark he'd ever come across. Maybe they really would be a great team.

"We're just about there," he told her.

"So now I do my disappearing act, right?" Arielle said.

He nodded. "Slide all the way down onto the floor and keep your head down. We don't want the video cams to pick you up."

Arielle took a quick swig of vodka from her flask, then slid to the floor of the Range Rover. She tucked her head down but managed to take a couple of drags off her cigarillo before handing it to Santo to put out.

"It'll only be for a few minutes," he said, reaching over and stroking the top of her head. "Just don't get up until I give the clear."

"Don't worry," she said. "I'm fine."

The road leading to the estate appeared ahead, and Santo flipped the turn signal and began to brake. He made the turn, and the gates to Stonelair loomed in front of him. He pulled over to the security post and punched in the code. The video cams were like evil eyes tonight, but he didn't care. They couldn't pick up Arielle.

The gates opened, and he drove swiftly past them. "We're in," he said to Arielle, "but don't get up yet. Not until we're in my garage."

Arielle shifted on the floor. "Not soon enough," she complained. "This is really cramping my style."

"I'll work all the knots out later," he said.

"I bet you will," she replied, "and I can hardly wait."

Chapter Thirty

Teddy sped along the country road in his silver Jaguar, the cocaine still racing through his bloodstream. He didn't dread his talk with Marguerite. Not now. He was on a high and felt like he could conquer the world. *What's a little chat with Marguerite?* he thought. *Nothing. Nada. Zilch.* He'd always been able to sweet-talk her, hadn't he?

Tonight would be no different. He and Marguerite were two of a kind. She'd always been crazy about him, so determined for him to be her son-in-law. *Maybe,* he thought, *maybe I'll be a whole lot more to her than that. After all, she's still a damn good-looking woman, and I'm just her kind of man.*

Yeah, he thought, turning onto the road that led up to her house, *I bet I can sweet-talk her straight into bed and right out of trouble.*

Marguerite sat at the head of the magnificently laid dinner table, with Jamie at the foot and Teddy to her right. The food was simple, but beautifully served and delicious. There was a fresh salad of mixed greens, poached salmon with a dill and lemon sauce, tiny new potatoes, and haricots vert. Teddy, however, had picked at his food, moving it around his plate, as if by doing so it would disappear, and he would seem to have eaten.

The coke had suppressed his appetite, and the surprising presence of Jamie had done nothing to stimulate it.

"I'm so glad you came by, Teddy dear," Marguerite said. "We do need to talk."

Teddy nodded.

Jamie looked over at Teddy. "We've asked that our money be returned to Dockering Wainwright, you know."

"Yes, I know," Teddy said, "and that's why I wanted to talk to Marguerite. I really think you're jumping the gun. Both of you. If only you'll give me a chance to—"

"You've had your chance," Jamie said.

"Yes, indeed," Marguerite added. She pointed a bejeweled finger at Teddy. "I want to know what's happened to my money."

"Marguerite, I can explain if—" Teddy began.

"You do that, Teddy," Jamie snapped. "Explain what's happened to Marguerite's money. And mine. And make it quick."

Teddy had forsaken any pretense of eating and put down his fork and knife. He sat in his chair uneasily, crashing from the cocaine high, his stomach churning, sweat beading his face and neck, his world crumbling down around him. He thought he might be sick.

"Tell us, Teddy," Jamie insisted. "Tell us this minute. If you can explain, then explain away. We're waiting."

Teddy feigned a smile, sickly though it was, and tried to rally. His world as he knew it depended on convincing these people that they would not only get their money back but make more. Greed was the key, he knew. "As you know, there have been some market fluctuations recently," he began, "especially in the high-tech sector—"

"Yes, yes," Jamie said angrily. "Every idiot who watches CNBC knows that."

"Well, because of these fluctuations," Teddy said, deciding to give them a grain of truth, hoping that would appease them, "I've had to move money from one account to another. You understand, just to cover temporary losses. And—"

"Where is our money!" Jamie thundered.

"Yes," Marguerite chimed in, "quit this ridiculous prevaricating, Teddy. Tell us what we want to know."

Teddy glared at them both, angry now. He wasn't accustomed to being yelled at. Not by anyone. "I don't have to sit here and take this," he said between gritted teeth. "Who do you think you are—"

There was the rustle of movement behind him, and Teddy saw Marguerite and Jamie look in that direction. He turned, following their eyes, and saw Dockering Wainwright standing directly in back of him with policemen at his side.

"Teddy," Dock said, "I'm sorry to do this, but you might as well leave with these gentlemen peacefully. Save yourself any embarrassment in front of Marguerite and Jamie."

"What the hell are you talking about, Dock?"

"I think you know the answer to that," Dock said. "We've had a long chat with Lydia Parsons, your secretary. Former secretary, excuse me. These gentlemen are here to arrest you."

"Arrest me?" Teddy shouted. "You're crazy. For what?" He jumped to his feet, china, silver, and crystal clattering as he knocked against the table. He started toward the door.

The policemen moved in quickly, each taking an arm and restraining him before he could leave the room. Teddy struggled in their grasp, but it was useless. The coke high that had made him feel omnipotent was gone, and in its place was a staggering powerlessness.

"You'll be charged with misappropriation of funds, young man," Dock said, "and I'm sorry to say you'll be charged with securities fraud and God alone knows what else." He cleared his throat, then said, "If you gentlemen don't mind, would you read him his rights outside so that Mrs. de la Rochelle doesn't have to witness such a scene?"

The police cuffed Teddy and began walking him out of the room. "You'll pay for this, Dock," Teddy said. "You too, Marguerite. All of you will pay."

When they were gone, Dock turned to Marguerite. "I'm happy to say that I think we've managed to save most if not all of your money, my dear." He looked at Jamie. "Yours, too, Jamie. Teddy didn't have it long enough to do any real damage."

Marguerite rose and strode over to the old man. She took one of his hands in hers. "Thank you, Dock," she said, "and forgive me for deserting you. I was very foolish."

"I think your daughter has pretty good instincts, Marguerite," he said. "You might do well to listen to her in the future."

They sat in a small conservatory surrounded by a veritable forest. Huge potted palms interspersed with ferns of several different kinds, orchids, many of which were in colorful bloom, gardenia bushes, camellias, lemon and orange trees—the variety and beauty was endless, Valerie thought. As if their perfume wasn't enough, a bitter orange incense burned in hidden corners, infusing the room with a heady and exotic aroma that she found irresistible.

Some of the glass in the conservatory windows was actually cut Bohemian crystal in blues and reds and whites, and overhead was a crystal chandelier lit with thirty-six burning tapers. The light was subdued but dazzled nevertheless, reflecting off the windows, the chandelier, and the table's Venetian glassware, silver, and exquisite china.

The marble floors were covered with a multitude of Turkish kilims, some running over others. Even the table had been draped with a richly colored kilim that looked unbelievably beautiful.

Tonight is special, all right, she told herself. She didn't think she'd ever eaten in such magnificent surroundings, and the combination of the opulent with the earthy only made its appeal seem that much more luxurious and exotic.

"I don't believe it," Wyn had said when he greeted her at the door. "You're wearing a djellaba. It's perfect for tonight. Perfect!"

"Are you just saying that?" she'd asked. "Or trying to make me feel better about my crazy wardrobe?"

"No, Val," he'd said, "I really mean it. You'll see why."

And now, of course, she did. He'd planned a sort of Arabian Nights dinner in the conservatory, which felt almost like eating in a luxurious pasha's garden. The rugs and the incense and the flowers and plants and the food itself had made the evening a feast for all the senses. They'd had a lamb dish and couscous and unidentifiable tiny fried fish, and delicious sweet cakes of all kinds, many saturated with honey and nuts.

Wyn had gone to fetch some brandy, because they'd decided to have a drink in here before going to the library. The room was hard to leave, its beauty so enticing. They would wait until the candles had burned a little lower, then move on to the library, where Val was certain further delights of a different nature awaited her.

Wyn stepped into the conservatory, the brandies in hand. He looked so extraordinary, she thought, dressed in a wildly colored silk smoking jacket. It was made of several different stripes of silk, individually sewn together, with velvet lapels and cuffs. He'd laughed about it and told her that his mother had bought it for him in Paris years ago. But she could tell that he loved it.

He handed her a brandy, then sat down at the table next to her. "Cheers," he said.

"Cheers," Val said, and they clinked glasses, then took sips of the fiery liquid.

"Now," Wyn said, "there's just one more little thing to make this evening special, and I think the time has come."

She looked into his eyes. "I think the evening has already been so special that I don't know if I could stand anything else."

"Somehow, I think you'll be able to appreciate this one more thing." He slipped his hand into the pocket of his jacket and pulled out a box.

Valerie's eyes grew wide. She couldn't help but be reminded of the night only a short time ago when Teddy had given her the ring, but she didn't want thoughts of that night to intrude, to ruin the exquisite pleasure—and love—that she had found with Wyn.

He took one of her hands and placed the box in it. "This is for you," he said. "I hope you like it."

She looked down at the box, then opened it without hesitation. She drew in her breath, stunned by the ring that sat winking up at her.

"Oh, Wyn," she said, "I've never seen anything so beautiful in my life! I mean it. It's the most beautiful ring I've ever seen."

She took it out of the box without being told to and slipped it on her finger. It fit perfectly.

Wyn was grinning from ear to ear, watching her every expression, listening to her every word, enjoying the sight of her taking it out of the box and putting it on.

She leaned over and placed her hands on his shoulders, then kissed him on the lips. "Thank you, Wyn," she said. "I love you."

"I love you, too," he said tenderly.

They kissed a moment longer, then he drew back. "Let me see it on you," he said.

She held the ring up proudly, twisting her finger this way and that. "It matches my eyes perfectly."

"That's what I hoped," he said, "and believe me, it took a lot of calling around and sending pictures back and forth before I found what I hoped would be just the right diamond for you."

"Diamond?" she said. "You mean it's not an emerald?"

He shook his head. "No, it's a green diamond."

"I didn't even know there was such a thing," she said in wonder, looking at the stone anew.

"Well, Doc," he said, "stick with me and you might learn a thing or two." He looked into her eyes, and she held his gaze. He leaned down and kissed her lips, his arms encircling her in their warmth.

Valerie almost sighed aloud with happiness. The feel of his lips on hers and those powerful arms drawing her to him sent a quiver of excitement up her spine. *I could stay like this forever,* she thought as she returned his kisses. *In his arms, against his warm body, feeling so completely loved by the man I love.*

Wyn drew back. "Come with me," he said softly, gently leading her toward a velvet upholstered chaise nestled among the conservatory's profuse greenery. There, surrounded by the intoxicating perfume of exotic blooms, he eased her down onto the chaise, then removed his smoking jacket and lay beside her. He took her into his arms again, drawing her next to him, his hands stroking her lovingly, his lips seeking out hers once more.

Valerie reveled in the feel of his hard and determined maleness against her own soft and yielding flesh, and his distinct and tantalizing masculine odor aroused her more than the scent of a thousand flowers. As his lips lingered on hers, she began to stroke him slowly and tenderly, wanting their exquisite togetherness to last forever.

His lips moved to her neck, where he kissed her reverently

before trailing down to the barely exposed cleavage between her breasts. As he inhaled her sweet femininity, Valerie felt her heart swell with pleasure and passion and love for this man whose every touch increased her desire for him.

Wyn lifted his head and looked into her eyes. "Let's undress," he said.

She nodded, a smile of anticipation hovering on her lips.

He stood and held out a hand to her. She took it and let him pull her to her feet. Within mere moments he had taken off her clothes and laid them across a chair, then she removed his and placed them atop her own. They stood before one another, their eyes taking delight in one another's magnificent nakedness.

Wyn began brushing his fingertips across her shoulders, down her arms, then in circles around her creamy breasts. Valerie gasped and drew nearer to him, almost as if she needed to support herself against him, but in reality unable to bear their separation any longer. She stroked his powerful shoulders and chest, then brought her hands down onto his buttocks, savoring their hard roundness. She felt Wyn's hot breath on her neck and his maleness assert itself against her.

He took her hand and eased her back down onto the chaise, positioning himself over her, poised as if to enter her. But he waited, his eyes lingering on hers before his tongue swept over her breasts and flicked at her nipples, arousing each one in turn. Valerie reached for his throbbing manhood, her fingertips brushing lightly down it and then encircling it with her hand. Wyn gasped, then lowered himself atop her body, pressing his hungry lips to hers once again, urgent now despite his wish to hold off.

Valerie wrapped her arms around him as he entered her, slowly, tenderly, relishing her enveloping warmth and the sweetness of her juices. Her desire for him almost overwhelmed her as she felt his manhood inside her, filling her up. She began to move against him, her body craving glorious release. But Wyn continued to move gently, restraining himself, drawing out their mutual pleasure for as long as possible.

Valerie tried to check her own urgency, concentrating on the ecstasy of each moment, trying not to rush the inevitable. But with his deep, slow thrusts, her body suddenly began to convulse with climax after climax, engulfing her in a pleasure and happiness such as she'd never known, and, crying out, she clasped him to her with all her might.

Wyn's passion for her was instantly heightened by her powerful contractions, and he drew back, hesitated a moment, then in a final mighty plunge found release. His entire body spasmed atop her as he let out a joyful groan.

He collapsed onto her, panting as she did, but peppering her face with kisses, his hands all over her at once. "I . . . love . . . you, Val," he said breathlessly. "I love you . . . so much."

"And . . . and I love you," she replied, holding him tightly.

They lay silent for a while, letting their breathing return to normal before Wyn finally eased off of her and lay at her side, an arm draped around her shoulders.

"Did I tell you that I love you?" he asked, squeezing her shoulders.

"Yes," she said. "But you can say it as often as you like . . . if I can."

"You're permitted," he said, nibbling on her ear. "And encouraged."

"I love you, Wyn."

"Ah, Doc," he whispered, kissing her gently, "I can't believe how lucky I am."

He hugged her, then drew back and looked into her eyes. "Think we ought to repair to the library, as they say?"

"I think we'd better do it quickly or we'll never get there."

"You're right," he said and laughed.

They rose to their feet, then Wyn reached for the long candle snuffer and slowly began extinguishing all the candles before they dressed and left the magnificence of the conservatory.

Valerie looked around the room, wanting to remember its every detail before it was completely darkened. *This has been the most special night of my life,* she thought. *And it happened here, in this wonderful, magical room, a moment in time I'll never forget.*

* * *

"The Reinhardts didn't notice anything," Santo said. "Their lights are out, so they're in bed. They always go to bed really early."

"I remember," Arielle said. "The screwballs are almost never up after the sun goes down."

They sat on the couch in his cottage, drinks on the coffee table in front of them.

"So nobody will know we've come in?" Arielle asked.

Santo nodded. "It's highly unlikely that Wyn and the vet would've noticed, and even so, it would just be me, driving down to my cottage."

"What's this business about the video cameras you were telling me about?" Arielle asked.

"It's very simple," Santo said. "The cameras saw me leave earlier to pick you up. They saw me come back in alone because you were hidden. They're going to see me leave alone again because you'll be hiding, after Wyn's dead. Then they'll see me come back in alone later. I can make it look like I was gone during the time of the murder by replacing the videotape that shows me coming back the first time and leaving the second time. I'd have to fiddle with the timers, make the tape look continuous, because the time is printed on them. I could wipe out everything but my trip to pick you up and make out like I'd spent the night away. I've got a girl lined up who'll let me spend the night, and she could be a witness that I was there all night."

He paused and took a sip of his drink. "There are several options, depending on how I want to play it."

"It's sounds complicated to me," Arielle said. "You'd have to be here to fix the timers and change the videotapes."

He nodded. "Yeah," he agreed. "That's why I'm leaning toward ripping the damn cams out when we leave. We'll just take them with us and get rid of them. Then tomorrow I cruise in after being out on a hot date all night. Shocked as shit by what's happened while I was gone."

"I like it," Arielle said. "It's not as complicated." She took a long drag on a cigarillo and blew a streamer of smoke toward the ceiling. Then she turned and looked at Santo. "And how are you going to do it?"

"I'll show you," he said. He got to his feet and went back into the bedroom, then reappeared with a dirty-looking white towel in his hand. He sat down next to her and pulled the towel back to reveal a gun, dark and oily and menacing.

"This is a Smith & Wesson Mark 22," he said, "With a silencer. It's called a Hush Puppy."

"A Hush Puppy," Arielle said mirthfully. She reached for it, but Santo grabbed her hand.

"It's loaded," he said, "and we don't want any mistakes."

"Don't you trust me?" she asked.

"Yes," he said, "but accidents happen."

Arielle looked miffed and took a swallow of her drink, then set the glass down. "When's this going to happen?" she asked.

"Every time she's out here," he said, "they end up in the library. Wyn virtually lives in that room, and it has several sets of French doors. So I'll wait until a little later, when I think they've had time to finish dinner and get to the library. Then I'll mosey up there and wait outside for the right moment. Too bad he told his doctors about stopping the injections. That would have been much easier. This way, there are two of them to worry about."

"I want to watch," Arielle said.

"We discussed that at the motel," he said. "You're here in case I get hurt. You can get us out of here. I've got to be able to get the videocams, but you'd have to drive."

"Santo," she cried, "what if you get hit and knocked out or something? What then? I won't be able to move you, and you won't be able to get the cameras."

"We've been through all that, Arielle," he said. "It isn't going to happen. They'll be like sitting ducks in there, and I'll be outside. I'm an expert shot. Plus, the timing's perfect. It will look like whoever poisoned the horses did them in. It's a win-win situation."

She still looked worried.

"If anything happened to me, which is extremely doubtful," he went on, "you get in the Range Rover and drive like hell out of here. Cover your head with a towel or something going through the gates, then get Lolo to help you ditch the car."

She smashed the cigarillo out in an ashtray. "I would still like to watch," she said. "Watch Wyn and his new girlfriend go down."

"You've got to be here," he said emphatically. "Ready to leave.

It's really important." He put a massive arm around her shoulders and pulled her to him. "Come on, Arielle," he said, "you're getting what you always wanted. All of Wyn's money. And me."

She kissed him hard on the lips. "You're right, Santo," she said. "It'll work out perfectly, and I'll get everything I want."

Wyn and Valerie walked to the library arm in arm and were greeted, as usual, by the Irish wolfhounds, who leapt up from their various positions and bounded over for licks and pets.

Valerie began her routine of petting and stroking and cooing to the dogs, trying to divide her attention among them equally, only making certain tonight that their large tongues laved her new diamond in the process.

"See that?" she said, looking up at Wyn. "They know this is a new ring, and they have to put their special good luck licks on it."

He looked at her with an affectionate grin. "You think of everything, don't you?"

"I try to," she said.

"I'm going to put on some music," Wyn said. "Any requests?"

"No," she said, "I'll let you choose."

The dogs settled down, and Valerie wandered about the room, looking at the books, paintings, and bronzes, picking up bibelots, examining them, then putting them back down again. She noticed several leather boxes on a bookshelf, their tops propped open to display the fantastically embellished guns nestled in specially fitted satin-covered niches. She took one out and looked at it closely. It was decorated with elaborately carved gold, silver, and bronze. She'd never seen anything like it, except in pictures in some of her father's old auction catalogs.

"Watch it," Wyn said from across the room, where he was rifling through CDs that were stacked next to the CD player. "Some of those are loaded," he said.

"They're really beautiful."

"They were my father's," he said. "Some of them are Purdy's, Holland and Holland, different makers. You wouldn't believe what they go for nowadays."

"Have you ever used them?" she asked, placing the gun back in its niche.

"Sure," he said. "Growing up, Dad would take me out to shoot. It was target practice, though. He didn't get into hunting at all, and neither did I."

"I bet you were a good marksman," she said.

"Not as good as Dad was," he said, "but pretty fair." He put a CD in the player and pressed the play button.

Suddenly the room was flooded with melodious instrumental chords. "Whoa!" he said. "That's a little loud." He adjusted the sound, then picked up his brandy snifter and went over to a wall switch, where he turned off the big chandeliers, leaving only the painting lights, a desk lamp, and a couple of table lamps burning. He sat down on one of the big Chesterfield couches, watching her.

"What is it?" she asked. "The music, I mean." She picked up another of the elaborately carved guns and looked at it closely.

"Spanish Renaissance music," he replied. "From the fifteen hundreds. I like to listen to it in this room sometimes."

"It's very . . . haunting," she said. "Beautiful." She replaced the gun in its case, then went to the couch and sat down beside him. She held her hand up in front of them, looking at it with a smile of satisfaction on her face. "Like this," she said. "Beautiful." She leaned over and kissed him.

Wyn set his brandy snifter down and embraced her, and they began to kiss in earnest, their lips and tongues exploring, their hands traveling the terrain of one another's bodies. In moments that seemed somehow outside of time or place, they became lost in each other, suspended within a paradise that was of their own making and for them alone. They reached a point of breathlessness, as if from a fever brought on by their desire.

Valerie drew back reluctantly and looked into his eyes. "I-I'll be right back," she said, almost in a whisper. "I want to freshen up."

"Hurry," he said. "I'll be waiting."

She rose and leaned down, kissing the top of his head. Then she padded across the needlepoint rug and through a passageway between bookshelves, on her way to the nearest bathroom, anxious to return to his waiting arms.

The lone figure, dressed in black, had watched Valerie and Wyn through the conservatory's big glass windows, cursing the

Bohemian glass inserts that were difficult to see through. Watched, fascinated, as Wyn gave her a ring, and she slipped it on. Watched as they went at it like horny teenagers. Then moved with them as they inevitably migrated to the big library, watching through binoculars from beyond the terrace as she wandered about the room and he messed with the CDs. Watched as she fiddled with antique guns. Watched in disgust as they made out on the couch.

Then watched as Valerie got to her feet and left the library.

Now! It's time!

Bending down and scurrying across the terrace practically on all fours, the black-clad figure rushed through the open French doors and stood up.

Then:

Pop!

Pop!

Pop!

Pop!

All four dogs slumped, the powerful tranquilizer darts immediately knocking them out.

Wyn, standing at the CD player, thought he heard a strange cracking sound above the music. He turned around and stared in horror at the black-clad figure.

"Daphne—?" he began.

Phump! The Heckler & Koch P9S made a muffled explosive sound, barely detectable above the music, thanks to the pistol's Qualatech silencer.

He jerked back, his eyes enormous, then down he went, blood spraying from his head.

Valerie came down the hallway and entered the room just as Wyn fell. From between the bookcases, she looked across the huge room, and her mouth opened in terror. But she clamped it shut before any sound could come out, then dropped down to a crouch and scuttled to the bookcase where the gun cases were. She pulled out the first one her shaking hand could find, then stood up, ready to fire.

Running up to the terrace, he saw someone standing in front of the open French doors. He grinned. *A piece of cake,* he thought. *First her, then him.*

As he fired he heard the gunshots. His Smith & Wesson Mark 22 had a silencer. *What the hell?* He didn't know, but he saw the body drop. *Got the vet. Now I've got to get him.* He stepped forward to look for Conrad, but didn't see him. *Where is he?* Then he saw Wyn's body sprawled on the floor. *What's going on?* But he didn't have time to figure it out. *Those gunshots—got to get out of here.*

Valerie stood with the heavily ornamented pistol in her hand, quivering from head to toe. The shots she'd fired had made her ears ring. Even from this distance, she could see that Wyn was dead. His body lay inert, sprawled on the floor in front of the big walnut cabinet that housed the CD player. His eyes were wide open, and there was no sign of life in him.

She walked over to the other body. The person she was certain she'd murdered. She looked down.

My God. Daphne Collins.

Why? she asked herself, staring at the body. *We were friends, weren't we?*

She looked around then, almost in an otherworldly daze.

Blood.

It was everywhere.

Valerie stood over the body—Daphne's body, she reminded herself—looking down at it with utter dispassion. Daphne's eyes, usually so bright with curiosity, were now stone-cold. Dead, they looked. Her lips, normally ready with a smile, were drawn into a thin, colorless, and unfamiliar line. Her blond hair hung about her face in Medusa-like snakes, the tendrils matted and dirty.

After an eternal minute, Valerie stepped closer, then knelt beside the body, noticing the blood that stained the dark needlepoint rug. A Jell-O-like pool of it had fanned out in a small kidney shape on the oak floor where the head rested. Its taint suddenly assailed her nostrils with its unmistakable metallic odor. But she was accustomed to it and didn't recoil or tremble or feel the urge to faint or vomit. Her composure remained intact.

Reaching out a hand, she took one of Daphne's blood-smeared hands in her own. She held it there for two full minutes, feeling for a pulse. She didn't detect one, but then she hadn't expected to.

She'd seen death countless times in her thirty years and knew that what she was doing was unnecessary. But she kept feeling for a pulse, nonetheless, concentrating all of her efforts on the procedure, as if by feeling hard enough she could produce the heartbeat she was certain she wouldn't hear. After a few more moments she gently replaced the hand on the rug and got to her feet.

There was no doubt that Daphne was dead.

Dead, she thought without emotion. She had gone completely numb and felt like a zombie operating on remote control. The stone-cold expression on her face didn't change with this awful knowledge. There was no quiver of fear or horror or sadness about her lips. No tears of remorse or grief sprang to her eyes. Anybody happening upon the macabre tableau would think her an ice maiden, seeing her features thus composed.

She walked over to the *bureau plat* and reached down and picked up the receiver, then dialed the number with a steady hand. When a voice answered at the other end, she replied in a cool, even voice.

"This is Dr. Valerie Rochelle," she said. "I just murdered someone."

Chapter Thirty-One

Santo ran quickly to his cottage and hurried in. Arielle jumped up from the couch where she was sitting, her eyes huge with fright.

"What *happened?*" she gasped. "I heard shots!"

"I'm not really sure," Santo replied. "Something went wrong."

"Oh, *Jesus!*" Arielle exclaimed. "Hadn't we better get out of here?"

"We're going to haul ass," Santo said. "We've got to beat the cops." He withdrew the Hush Puppy from his waistband and studied it closely.

"What about the Reinhardts?" she asked.

"Their lights are still out," Santo said. "I don't think they heard anything." He looked back down at the gun, then shoved it back in his waistband. "There's nothing wrong with this silencer as far as I can tell," he said, still baffled by the turn of events.

"If the silencer works," Arielle asked, "then who fired the shots?"

"I don't know," Santo said. "I didn't see anything much except her taking a hit." He wasn't going to tell Arielle that he'd seen Wyn sprawled on the floor in a pool of blood, but that he hadn't shot him. He'd explain that later.

"It had to be the silencer—" Arielle began.

"Come on," he said. "We're haven't got time to stand around here talking. We're getting out of here. You were supposed to have the car ready."

Arielle grabbed her flask off the coffee table, then rushed into the kitchen and looked at the liquor bottles on the counter, finally selecting a bottle of Stoli.

"Hurry," Santo growled. He was already past her, through the laundry room, and going into the garage.

Arielle rushed after him, vodka bottle in hand.

Santo fired up the big Range Rover, then opened the garage door using the remote. He backed out into the drive, turned onto the road that led to the stables and on out to the gates.

We're out of here, he thought, *on our way to freedom.*

Shit! The video cameras. Almost forgot them. I'll just dismount them when we get to the gate, and take them with us. Then show up tomorrow morning, like I planned.

He gave the Range Rover gas, anxious to get to the gates and out of this place.

Valerie stood looking over toward Wyn's body. Her icy façade, a defensive response to the horrible reality she'd witnessed and been a part of, began to crack. She'd been on automatic pilot, hardly aware of what she'd been doing. Fixated on Daphne, Wyn's death had barely registered.

Now she began to shake uncontrollably, and bile rose up in her throat. She thought she was going to throw up and started for the bathroom. She stopped suddenly near the bookcases when she heard a loud moan. *From over near the CD player,* she thought, *I'm sure of it.* A chill went up her spine, but she turned around and looked back into the big room.

Her heart began to race. She rushed to the spot where she had seen Wyn's body and stopped in her tracks. For a moment she thought she would faint. His body wasn't there. She saw the blood on the rug leading toward his desk, and then she saw him, crawling with all his might toward the telephone.

"Wyn!" she cried, running to him. She reached him and got down onto her knees, tears already streaming from her eyes, flowing down her cheeks in rivulets. Her body shook with both relief and joy.

He moaned again, louder this time, and moved his head, trying to look up at her. "Hey, Doc," he breathed. "Got shot."

"I know you did," she cried, still shaking all over. "I know you did."

"Doc," he said, "open . . . open that drawer." With a crooked finger, he indicated a small drawer in the *bureau plat*.

Valerie opened it immediately. "What, Wyn?" she asked. "What is it?"

"See . . . see that row of buttons?"

"Yes," she said, "I see it."

"Push the one marked 'Front Gates,' " he said. "Push it hard."

Valerie did as she was told, depressing the button with all her might, then she turned back to him.

He started to say something else but only a groan escaped his lips.

"Shhh," she said. "I've already called the police. They should be here any minute with an ambulance. I thought you were dead, Wyn. You looked dead, and there was so much blood."

His eyes were still open, and there was a hint of a grin on his lips. "It's . . . it's nothing, Doc,"

Valerie didn't know whether to believe him or not, but she could plainly see the track of the bullet along the side of his head. It looked like a scalp wound, only she didn't want to take any chances.

"Wyn," she said, "lie perfectly still." Maybe she could do something for him. Maybe she could stop the flow of blood, for he was still bleeding. It was all over the rug. "Just stay right where you are. I'll be right back."

"Don't leave me, Doc," he said.

"I'll be right back," she said. "I'm just getting some scissors off your desk."

Her eyes scanned the top of the desk until she saw scissors in a malachite cup. Grabbing them, she ran back over to him and started cutting the gauzy hem of her djellaba away.

"The dogs," he muttered.

"They must've been shot with tranquilizer darts," she said. "I'll take the darts out, but they won't come around for a while yet. They should be just fine."

"Good," he gasped.

The Range Rover pulled to a stop at the front gates, and Santo pushed on the remote to open them. When they didn't at first open, he pushed on the remote again. Still they didn't move.

What now? he wondered.

He opened the car door and jumped out, holding the remote pointed directly at the gates. Still they didn't budge. *What's going on?*

He ran toward the gates, constantly pressing the remote to no avail. When he reached them, he grabbed hold of them, one iron bar in each of his hands, pulling with all his might. Nothing. They didn't budge an inch. "Jesus!" he swore aloud.

"What's the matter?" Arielle cried from the car.

"The remote won't open the gates," Santo called back to her.

"What do you mean it won't open them?" she cried.

"Just what I said, you stupid bitch," Santo yelled.

He ran back to the Range Rover and got in the driver's seat. "Listen," he said, "hold on tight. We're going to have to ram the car through the gates. I don't know any other way to open them."

Santo backed up the Range Rover, aimed directly toward the point at which the two gates connected, then stomped on the gas. The car launched into the gates at breakneck speed, and there was an earsplitting grind of metal against metal that practically drowned out Arielle's scream.

The gates didn't give.

"Shut the fuck up, Arielle," Santo roared. He backed the car up again, farther back up the lane this time, then stomped on the gas again.

The big car roared forward and hit the gates at about thirty miles an hour. The shattering sound of the impact was even louder than before.

Santo, his seat belt firmly secured, was fine, but Arielle was thrown first backward, then forward, and almost went into the windshield. Santo started to back up a third time. At that moment, he heard the screeching sirens of police cars and ambulances, and saw their flashing red and blue lights as they raced down the road. From overhead, the sound of a helicopter's churning rotors was deafening, and its powerful search floodlights swept the entire scene, rendering the night surreal. The police cars and ambulances appeared on the opposite side of the gates, which suddenly began to part.

Santo flung the car door open and started to run, but before he got twenty feet he was tackled by two policemen who manhandled his wrists behind his back and slapped cuffs on him.

Two other policemen rushed to Arielle's side of the Range Rover and jerked open the door. She began screaming and crying all at once, blindly kicking and flinging her arms at them, but she was pulled out of the car and cuffed before she could inflict any bodily harm.

"You're both coming into the station," a big officer grunted as he strolled up, taking in the scene. "Get 'em out of here."

The library had become crowded with policemen and EMS personnel. Wyn was on a stretcher now, and they were about to carry him out to the ambulance.

"Thank God," Valerie said. She turned to the policeman standing next to her. Cawley, his name tag said. "I've got to go with him, Officer Cawley," she said frantically. "I've got to."

"You placed the call, right?" he said.

"Yes," she replied.

The officer retrieved the Purdy pistol that Valerie had used to shoot Daphne. "Is this it?" he asked, showing her the weapon.

Wyn lifted his head from the stretcher.

"You couldn't have killed her with that, Val," Wyn said. "It's loaded with blanks. Nearly all of them are." He looked toward Cawley and winced in pain. "Check it out, officer," he said. "You'll find blanks in that gun and nearly all the others."

Cawley looked down at it, then back up at her. "Let her go to the hospital," he said.

Chapter Thirty-Two

Wyn and Valerie dismounted and led their horses into the stable yard, where Helmut Reinhardt took the reins from them. He would put the horses in their stalls. Then, hand in hand, they started up the stone path that led to the house. Winter was around the corner, and it was already cold and gray. They could see smoke rising skyward from the library's great chimney.

Their faces and ears were red from the cold wind, but they were oblivious to any discomfort. Under their riding jackets, they both wore heavy sweaters, and in any case, they were too happy to allow the weather to interfere with their time together.

When they reached the library, they greeted the Irish wolfhounds and Elvis, who had become a steadfast friend and member of the pack within two days. They shrugged out of their jackets and took off their gloves, but left their boots on for the time being. They would wait until they had warmed up to change into something more comfortable.

Wyn went to the drinks table and poured them both a snifter of brandy. He turned to her and handed her one, then lifted his. "Cheers, Mrs. Conrad," he said.

"Cheers, Mr. Conrad," she replied. They had married two weeks before in the conservatory at Stonelair. Valerie and Wyn had invited Marguerite, who had been impressed by the splendors of Stonelair and had determined that Wyn might be worthy of a de la Rochelle, although she had disapproved of the presence of all the animals at the wedding.

They clinked glasses, then sat down on one of the big Chesterfield couches. "That was a wonderful ride," Wyn said.

"Yes, it was," she agreed. "How does your head feel? Any aches? Pains?"

"It's okay," he said. "Funny, now that it's quit bothering me, I forget about it." He looked over at her. "It was a close call, wasn't it?"

"Very close," Valerie said.

"I knew there was a reason I stopped seeing Daphne Collins," he said seriously. "She was pretty and smart and desirable. I guess we went out together for a few months, around the time I met Arielle, but I began to think that Daphne was irrationally possessive. Maybe even a little obsessed with me."

"She was obsessed all right," Valerie said.

"Yes, but I had no idea she'd actually moved up here after I bought Stonelair," Wyn said. "And to think, once she found out about us, how she started killing your patients to get back at you. It's so crazy how our affair meant so little to me but everything to her."

Valerie patted his shoulder. "It's not your fault, Wyn," she said. "You were simply the object of her obsession. You didn't have any control over that."

"I know," he said, "and that's what Colette keeps telling me."

"Colette?" Valerie said. "Have you talked to her?"

"I forgot to tell you that she called today," he said. "She's really excited."

"What did she have to say?"

"Let me see," he said. "There was a lot."

They both laughed. Colette had taken to Wyn like a fish to water, and the feeling seemed to be mutual. Right now she was looking after Val's cottage, until she decided whether to sell it.

"She's got a new African pygmy hedgehog," he said. "Named it Spike."

"Oh, that's wonderful," Valerie said. "It means she's getting over Hayden's death, a little bit anyway."

"Eddie and Jonathan gave it to her for a present," Wyn said. "Isn't that great?"

"It is," Val agreed. "And just like them."

"It gave me an idea, but I wanted to ask you about it first."

"What?" she asked.

"I thought it might be nice if we give Eddie and Jonathan a husky pup to replace Noah," he said. "What do you think?"

"I think it's terrific, Wyn," she said, "but first let me feel them out about it, without letting on. You know, to see if they're ready."

"That's a good idea," he said. "They may not be, and I'd hate to put them in the position of feeling like they had to take it."

Valerie looked at him and felt her heart absolutely surge with love. *How could I be so lucky?* she asked herself for the thousandth time. *To have such a wonderful, loving, and thoughtful man to love me?*

"Colette was excited about you setting up your own practice, too," Wyn said, "and told me to congratulate you. The bad news—or I guess sad news—from Colette," he went on, "is that they've indicted Tiffani Grant for poisoning the horses and for possession of an illegal drug. The amphetamine she used. Really nasty highly concentrated stuff. I've forgotten the specific charges, but I'm sure Colette will fill you in."

He gave her a sidelong glance. He knew that she'd been devastated to learn that Teddy had been seeing Tiffani. She'd wanted to believe that Teddy loved her in some way or other, but she now believed that he'd always used her and never really loved her at all. She'd begun to question her own judgment, and Wyn had done everything in his power to help her overcome her feelings of inadequacy and self-doubt.

"What do you think will happen to her?" Valerie asked.

Wyn shook his head. "It's a hard call," he replied. "Claims she didn't know what it was. I think a lot of it depends on the jury, what they believe. She may get off pretty light, considering."

Valerie didn't respond immediately, but sat thoughtfully looking off into space. "And Teddy?" she finally asked. "Any news there yet?"

"He's been indicted on a number of charges, but the investigation continues, Colette said. Misappropriating clients' money, breaking all kinds of SEC rules. Jesus. A lot of stuff. Apparently that secretary of his—"

"Lydia?" Valerie asked.

"Yes, I think that was her name," he replied. "Anyway, she's a material witness and word is she's a good one. It's lucky she stepped forward when she did, or all of your mother's money, and your cousin's, might have gone up in smoke."

"I'm glad they didn't lose anything," Valerie said.

"The big losers in this whole mess were Teddy and Tiffani and Santo and Arielle," he said. "Santo would've gotten a nice retirement package from me, but instead he's going to be pumping iron in a prison gym for killing Daphne. Ditto Arielle. She'd have gotten a huge financial settlement, instead of jail time if she hadn't gotten so greedy."

"You're right," she said. "I can only feel pity for them."

He looked over at her and took one of her hands in his. "Val," he said, "I've got to say that I've never respected or loved anybody in my life like you."

She laughed. "Why are you saying that now?"

"Because you just reminded me of it," he said. "Wishing your mother well even though she's been so unkind to you. Inviting her to the wedding like you did. A lot of people, most people probably, would've turned their backs on her."

"I couldn't do that," she said.

"No," he said, "I know you couldn't." He hugged her to him then. "What say we get out of this riding gear now, and go upstairs for a little romp in the hay?"

"Are you up to that, Mr. Conrad?" she asked.

"You bet I am, Mrs. Conrad," he replied.

"It seems," she said, looking up into his dark eyes, "you know me awfully well."

"And I love what I know," he said, leaning down to kiss her.